THE FAERIE WARS CHRONICLES

THE FAERIE WARS CHRONICLES

FAERIE LORD

BOOK FOUR

HERBIE BRENNAN

BLOOMSBURY

Published by Bloomsbury U.S.A. Children's Books
175 Fifth Avenue, New York, NY 10010
Distributed to the trade by Holtzbrinck Publishers

Library of Congress Cataloging-in-Publication Data
Brennan, Herbie.
Faerie Lord / by Herbie Brennan.—1st U.S. ed.
p. cm.
"Book four in the Faerie Wars Chronicles."
Summary: When a terrible plague takes over the faerie realm and causes its inhabitants to
age unnaturally quickly, Henry and Blue must find a cure in order to save the realm.
ISBN-13: 978-1-59990-120-6 • ISBN-10: 1-59990-120-X
[1. Fairies—Fiction. 2. Aging—Fiction. 3. Supernatural—Fiction.] I. Title.
PZ7.B75153Fa 2007   [Fic]—dc22   2006102610

First U.S. Edition 2007
Typeset by Westchester Book Composition
Printed in the U.S.A. by Quebecor World Fairfield
1 3 5 7 9 10 8 6 4 2

All papers used by Bloomsbury U.S.A. are natural, recyclable products
made from wood grown in well-managed forests. The manufacturing processes
conform to the environmental regulations of the country of origin.

For Nigel and Clarissa, with much love

Lovers, to bed; 'tis almost fairy time.

A Midsummer Night's Dream

Prologue

'Why don't I stay here?' Henry echoed. He knew he was plunging into one of his wretched waffles where he repeated what people said and cranked up his village idiot expression, but he didn't seem to be able to do anything about it.

'Yes,' Blue said firmly. 'Why don't you?'

They were walking in the gardens of the Purple Palace and Blue looked absolutely gorgeous. Night stocks had begun to release their scent and there was torchlight reflected on the river. If there was ever a perfect setting for a romantic moment, this was it and he knew, beyond doubt, he was about to blow it. 'Why don't I?' he asked.

'Oh, Henry, I wish you wouldn't do that,' Blue said mildly. She reached out and took his hand, so that they were walking together by the water's edge. 'You don't want to go home, I don't want you to go home, Pyrgus doesn't want you to go home, so why not stay?'

'Pyrgus doesn't want me to go home?' Henry said, surprised, then realised how stupid that sounded and managed to say something more stupid still: 'My mother would kill me.' He looked at Blue in the vain hope of her understanding and added, 'If I didn't come home.'

Blue ignored it. 'What are you going to do if you go home?'

Henry thought about it, then said vaguely, 'Exams and things.' It was anything but vague inside his head. He would do his exams and if he passed, which he probably would, he was set on a course that would take him on eventually to university, although not one of the good ones, not Oxbridge or anything like that. But whatever university he ended up in, he'd plod through to a mediocre degree, then become a teacher, because that's what his mother wanted. She was a teacher. Actually she was the headmistress of a girls' school. She kept telling him teaching was great because of the extended holidays, as if the measure of a good job was how long you could stay away from it.

'You don't *like* being at home,' Blue said, 'now your dad's gone. You don't like your mother ...'

'No, but I love her,' Henry said gloomily. That was the trouble. To say he didn't like his mother was an understatement. He couldn't stand her. But that didn't stop him loving her. He wondered if feeling guilty was a normal state of life.

'She makes you do things you don't want to do,' Blue said as if he hadn't spoken. 'And she keeps doing things you don't want *her* to do.' She turned to look at him.

Like moving in Anaïs, he thought.

'Like moving in Anaïs,' Blue said soberly. She turned away and they continued their walk. 'You're not *happy* in the Analogue World any more. I know you're not. Every time you go home, you look more miserable when you come back. And there's nothing for you to *do* there – nothing important. Just, you know ... *stuff,* like school and exams. You don't have a position, like you do here. Nobody respects you.'

Hold on a minute, Henry thought: this was getting painful. Except it happened to be true. Or nearly true. Charlie respected him. In fact he half suspected Charlie fancied him. But that was about it. Life at home *was* pretty miserable.

'Whereas if you stayed here,' Blue went on relentlessly, 'you'd have important work. You're already a hero –'

That was nonsense. If anything he was a villain because of what he'd tried to do to Blue, even though he hadn't been himself when he did it, and after more people got to know about it ...

'– because of rescuing Pyrgus from Hael when he was Crown Prince, and if you don't like your quarters at the Palace, I can make them give you something better and –'

'No, no it's nothing like that,' Henry put in hurriedly. 'I *love* my quarters at the Palace.' They were about a billion times better than his room at home and he didn't have his mother knocking on his door. He had *servants* for cripe's sake!

Blue stopped, and since she still had hold of his hand, Henry stopped too. The sound of the water was overlaid by distant street noise from the city: the rumble of carts, the occasional call from a merchant. The city came alive at night in ways it never did during the day.

Blue said quietly, 'I'm Queen of Hael now, not just Queen of Faerie. I need somebody to help me with that – you know, help me run things. Pyrgus is useless – all he wants to do is get into trouble and save animals – and Comma's too young.' She looked at him, then looked away.

It took a moment for Henry to figure what was going on here, but then it hit him like an avalanche. He blinked. 'Wait ... wait, you're not asking me to take charge of Hell, are you?'

Blue still wasn't looking at him, but she shook her head. 'No, Henry,' she said. 'I'm asking you to marry me.'

One

Two years later …

'What's going on?' Henry asked at once.

Hodge was staring out through the bars of the cat-carrier, an expression of fury on his face. Aisling was nursing a bleeding hand, an expression of outrage on hers.

'Your cat bit me!' she exclaimed. 'Vicious brute should be put down.'

'I told you to leave him alone,' Henry said. He looked directly at his mother. 'Why is he in the carrier?'

'Henry, he bit your sister. Scratched her too. Luckily just on the hand. If he'd gone for her face, he could have scarred her. She could have lost an eye.'

'I told her not to tease him,' Henry said. 'Why is he in the carrier?'

'I *didn't* tease him!' Aisling shouted.

Henry rounded on her. 'You're always bloody teasing him! Ever since I brought him home. Picking him up and poking him and taking away his food. It's no wonder he bit you. He's an independent tomcat, not some sort of stuffed toy. He just wants to be left alone.'

'I don't think we need that sort of language,' his mother said stiffly. She stared at Henry for a moment, then went on. 'The point is that he attacked your sister and drew blood. There's a risk of tetanus or cat-scratch fever. We can't just ignore something like that. You know I was against his coming to live here in the first place.'

Henry looked his mother directly in the eyes. 'Why is he in the carrier?' he asked for the third time.

She looked away, to one side. 'Oh, we're not going to have him put down, if that's what you're thinking. Anaïs has gone to get the car. We're taking him to the vet to be neutered.'

For a moment Henry simply stood there, stunned. Then he said, 'You're getting him neutered because he scratched Aisling? As a *punishment?*'

'No, of course not,' his mother said impatiently. 'It's just that he'll be more placid when he's neutered. Less likely to attack people.' She sniffed. 'And a lot cleaner.'

'Mum, he's never attacked anybody in his life except Aisling and that was only because she teases him. She teases him *all the time*. And what's this about cleaner?'

'Tomcats spray,' his mother said. 'They mark their territory. I don't think even you want that sort of smell about the house.'

'He doesn't spray *in* the house,' Henry said. 'He's *never* sprayed in the house. He may spray a bit in the garden, but that's a different thing.'

'It's not something they can help,' his mother said reasonably. 'It's territorial, just as I said, and it's only a matter of time before he starts to do it in the house. We've all decided it's better to do something about it before he actually starts.'

'Not *all*,' Henry said at once. '*We* didn't *all* decide anything. You and Aisling and, I suppose, Anaïs decided. *I* didn't decide anything. I wasn't even consulted – and he's *my* cat!' Technically, he was Mr Fogarty's cat, but Mr Fogarty hadn't seen him in two years so he might as well be Henry's cat.

'Try to keep your voice down, Henry,' his mother told him. She waited a moment, as if he needed time to control himself, then went on in her most reasonable tone. 'We thought it would be a great deal easier on you if we simply went ahead. I know how much you love that old cat and that way you wouldn't have to worry about the effect of anaesthetic or the operation going wrong. I actually thought you'd gone out.'

This was the way it had always been. His mother kept insisting every nasty little thing she ever did was *for his own good*. And it was worse since Anaïs moved in. Anaïs herself was all right – Henry quite liked her and she'd even sided with him about bringing Hodge home – but when it came to the things Henry's mother really cared about, like that stupid little scratch on Aisling's hand, she always seemed to get Anaïs on her side. Like now. Anaïs had gone to bring the car to take Hodge to the vet. Not because he sprayed in the house or would ever spray in the house, but because he bit Aisling in self-defence and Henry's mother wanted to teach him a lesson.

It was the sort of thing Henry had had to put up with since he was a little boy. And with Dad long gone he was in an all-female household and it was steadily getting worse. But he wasn't a little boy any more and he wasn't going to put up with it.

Henry walked over to the carrier. 'Not this time, Mum,' he said and flicked the catch.

Hodge burst out of his cage like a rocket.

Two

'You did *what?*' Charlie exclaimed, grinning delightedly.

'I let him out,' Henry said. 'There was a kitchen window open and we haven't seen him since. I think he knew what they were going to do to him.'

They were sitting side by side on a park bench. The sole of Charlie's left trainer was starting to come away and she was fiddling with it ineffectively. Henry thought she looked very nice in a cuddly sort of way now she'd started to put on a bit of weight. She left the shoe alone suddenly and asked, 'Why didn't you want him fixed?'

'I'm not having Hodge fixed,' Henry said. 'Apart from anything else, he's not really my cat.'

'No,' Charlie said. 'He's Mr Fogarty's cat. You still haven't heard from him?'

'Mr Fogarty? No. No, I haven't.'

Charlie said casually, 'It's been eighteen months.'

Actually it had been more than two years, but Henry had to be careful. The story was that Mr Fogarty had gone to see his daughter in New Zealand, leaving Henry to look after his house and his cat ... a story that was getting thinner every month. Charlie hadn't brought it up before, but Henry's mother went on endlessly about the arrangement. It was only the regular cheques that stopped her pushing it too far. They were simply signed 'A. Fogarty' and she assumed the A stood for 'Alan.'

'You know what old people are like.' Henry shrugged vaguely.

Charlie stared out across the ornamental lake, watching two swans glide gracefully towards the shore. 'I was just wondering what you were going to do next year, when you go to uni.'

'Who says I'm going to uni?' Henry asked. 'I mightn't make the grades.'

'Oh, you'll make the grades all right,' Charlie said. 'And then you'll be off. Where are you going to apply – Oxford? Cambridge?'

'No chance,' Henry said. 'I'm not that bright.'

This time Charlie shrugged. 'Doesn't matter. Wherever you pick it'll mean moving away – there's nothing locally. And if you move away, you won't be looking after Mr Fogarty's house or saving Hodge from a fate worse than death or seeing me or anything.'

Henry picked up the real worry at once. 'Oh, I'll be seeing you all right. I can come home at weekends.'

'Not every weekend.'

'No, maybe not. But, you know ... some.'

'Some?'

'Yes,' Henry said. 'Some.'

'Did you know swans mate for life?' Charlie asked suddenly.

'I think I read it somewhere.'

'If one dies, the other one won't mate again,' she said as if he hadn't spoken. 'Not ever.' She turned her head to look at him and licked her lips lightly. 'Henry, I think we should stop.'

'Stop what?' Henry asked stupidly.

'Going out together,' Charlie said.

For once Henry had the house to himself when he got home. He found some yoghurt in the fridge, took it up to his room and sat down to write a letter.

Dear Mrs Barenbohm, he wrote, then paused.

It was getting complicated already. Angela Fogarty, Mr Fogarty's daughter, had married an American industrialist called Clarence Barenbohm, then emigrated to New Zealand with a great deal of his money after the divorce. She insisted on using the Barenbohm name for everything except financial transactions, which she conducted under her maiden name.

Henry's pen lurched into action again and wrote, *I write to tell you that I do my A Levels this year and next year I hope to go to university. I don't know where it will be (the university)*

He paused again. He wasn't even sure he *would* be going to university. Despite what he'd said to Charlie, he thought he'd probably get the grades all right, but when he tried to discuss his future with his mother, she got evasive, which was a bad sign. Part of him suspected there might be money worries, but she wouldn't come clean and tell him. Anaïs claimed she didn't know.

He shrugged. It didn't matter. Even if he never went to uni, he wasn't hanging around here when he left school.

but there are no suitable educational establishments locally, he went on. *This means that soon I will be unable to look after your father's house and cat (Hodge), as I have done in the past, for very much longer.*

I appreciate the money you sent – He crossed out

sent and inserted *have been sending,* then stared at the page wondering if he should write it all out again. After a moment he decided it wasn't a school essay and went on, *but I very much regret I will be unable to keep on with our arrangement as it has been to date. I am writing to tell you this now while there is still time for you to make other arrangements or otherwise sell the house* (Angela thought her father was dead and the house hers under the terms of his will; only Henry knew differently) *or whatever it is you would want to do. Please write back to me marking the envelope 'Personal' and let me know what you decide to do and if I can help you further in any way apart from continuing our present arrangement beyond the New Year.*

He signed the letter *Henry Atherton,* then immediately wrote a PS:

PS Some children broke a downstairs window, but I had it repaired with money from the Contingency Fund. He knew he should leave it at that, but somehow could not stop his hand writing: *PPS I might be able to continue to look after Hodge (the cat) even after I stop looking after the house or even after I go to university. I wouldn't want him put down or anything.*

He sat staring at the words for a long time. Best not to mention the current little problem with Hodge or the fact that Henry had no idea where he was at the moment. Hodge was bound to come back – he was too old and fat and lazy to make his own way in the world any more. The trick would be to make sure Henry's mother never got her hands on him.

... *even after I go to university.* How on earth would he look after a tomcat while he was attending university? But he'd think of something. He owed that much to Mr Fogarty. And to Hodge. His hands were trembling slightly as he folded the letter.

Since there was *still* nobody downstairs, he stole a stamp and an airmail sticker from his mother's desk, then pulled his coat back on again; the sooner he posted this off the better. When he opened the front door, Hodge was waiting for him on the doorstep.

'Ah, there you are,' said Henry.

Against Hodge's furious protests, Henry bundled him into the cat-carrier. 'It's for your own good,' he hissed, sucking one thumb where the brute had drawn blood. 'You *really* don't want to hang around here.' It was going to be a pain racing off to Mr Fogarty's house to feed Hodge in the middle of exams, but he couldn't see any alternative. He knew his mother.

As he waited for the bus, Henry thought about Charlie and what she'd said about not going out together any more. He was surprised how little upset he felt. He'd been close friends with Charlie ever since they were little kids, but the romantic interest had started less than a year ago and to be absolutely honest, Charlie had been keener about that than he was.

The bus journey was a nightmare. Hodge wailed all the way and several passengers took to staring at Henry as if he was committing murder. But he settled once they left the bus, and by the time Henry was carrying him along Mr Fogarty's cul-de-sac he was looking around through the mesh of the carrier as if he recognised the place.

Mr Fogarty's house, the last one on the street, was looking distinctly the worse for wear despite Henry's best efforts. Most of the trouble dated back to the days of

Mr Fogarty's own occupancy – he'd pasted brown paper on the bottom panes of the downstairs windows to stop people looking in, seldom bothered with minor repairs and had a habit of leaving half-eaten hamburgers to rot down the side of his sofa. Now it was unoccupied, the process of decay was visibly accelerating. Even if Henry hadn't been planning to leave, it would make sense to sell the place before it fell down.

He carried the caged Hodge to the front door and let himself in – he had his own set of keys. Then he walked through to the kitchen, set the carrier on the floor and unlatched the side. Hodge stretched, looked around suspiciously, then walked out slowly.

'Do you want your Whiskas now or would you prefer to go out the back and kill everything that moves?' Henry asked him conversationally. Hodge walked to the back door and sat down facing it. He waited patiently. 'So it's the killing fields, is it?' Henry said. He walked over, shot the bolt, then unlocked the back door.

Two strangers were standing on the lawn outside.

Henry frowned. He wasn't anything like as paranoid as Mr Fogarty, but the back garden *was* private property and he couldn't see any reason for these two to be poking around.

The man was in his mid-thirties, stockily built with a shock of red hair that was turning prematurely grey. He had on a sharp green suit and suede shoes. The girl seemed a lot younger. She might have been his daughter, except she was dressed in a blouse, skirt and coat that looked as if they'd come from Oxfam.

'Can I help you?' Henry asked coolly.

It was like one of those scenes from a movie where everything goes into slow motion and movement seems to leave trails. The man turned (slowly) towards him. 'Henry ...?' he said.

The girl turned towards him just as slowly. 'Henry!' she exclaimed. He watched the smile begin to spread like a pouring of honey, illuminating her face, transforming her into a radiant beauty.

They stared at him expectantly. Henry felt a curious emptiness in the pit of his stomach. He stared back at them blankly. Now he could see her face, he knew the girl, of course. 'Nymph?' he whispered.

'Henry!' the man said again. He began to grin and the grin told Henry at once who he was, although it was impossible.

Henry felt his jaw begin to drop and stared and stared until eventually he said what he had to say, what he knew to be true even though it wasn't true, couldn't possibly be true.

'Pyrgus?' Henry said.

Three

'You're *old!*' Henry blurted. It was stupid, but he couldn't think of anything else to say. They were sitting round the table in Mr Fogarty's kitchen. Hodge had jumped onto Nymph's lap and was curled purring while he had his ears tickled. Close up, Pyrgus still looked in his thirties, maybe even *late* thirties. Henry found himself wondering if this was some sort of spell thing, set up as a disguise.

'I wouldn't put it quite like that,' Pyrgus said. 'But I know what you mean.'

'What are you doing here?' Henry asked. What he really wanted to ask was why they were wearing ordinary clothes, Pyrgus in particular: his suit could have come from Marks and Sparks. Henry had never seen them wearing gear like that before. Clothes in the Realm were generally a bit mediaeval looking and Forest Faeries like Nymph wore Grecian-style tunics, nearly always in green. 'Why are you dressed in –' he pulled the word out of two-year-old depths '– Analogue clothes?'

'I have to live here,' Pyrgus said, as if that answered everything. He caught Henry's expression and grinned again, a little sheepishly this time. 'Nymph came with me because we got married.'

For a long beat Henry gaped in stunned amazement;

then he exploded, '*Married?*' He looked at Nymph, who smiled a little. 'The two of you are *married?*'

She nodded. 'Yes. Very shortly after you last saw us actually.'

'You can't be married,' Henry said. 'Not really.' But he was grinning all over his face. He liked Nymph and she was perfect for Pyrgus. The way Pyrgus looked had to be a spell thing. He glanced at Nymph. 'Don't you miss the forest?'

'There are forests in this world,' Nymph said calmly. 'A wife must be at her husband's side.'

Charlie mightn't go along with that one, Henry thought. She'd taken to feminism in a big way over the last six months and kept talking about independence and equality and the way women were oppressed by traditional values. Which Henry sort of agreed with really, although to be honest it wasn't on his mind much of the time. 'Is the age business ... like, some sort of magic thing?' he asked, returning to an earlier thought.

The smile on Pyrgus's face disappeared as if he'd thrown a switch. 'It's an illness, Henry,' he said softly. 'That's why we're here.'

four

Chalkhill was dressed in a shocking-pink silk knicker-bocker suit with fashionably clashing electric-blue suede knee boots and a sweet little lime-green slithskin apron. Brimstone stared at him in distaste. 'Were you followed?' he asked.

'No, of course not,' Chalkhill said. 'I took precautions.' He smiled broadly. The spell coatings on his teeth flashed and sparked and played a cheery tune. 'Isn't this *fun*? The old team back together again. Really, Silas, I'm so excited I could *dance*.'

'Have you brought the money?' Brimstone asked drily.

'In my knickers,' Chalkhill said. He caught Brimstone's blank look and added, 'In case somebody tried to steal it.'

They were waiting together on the doorstep of a lonely, tree-shrouded mansion set in the outer reaches of the Cretch. There was a legend that it had once belonged to the Master Vampire Krantas, and whether or not this was really true, it certainly looked the part. Gothic towers and spires reached for the sky like spindly fingers. From somewhere deep inside, a bell was tolling hollowly.

'I thought you'd given up that nonsense,' Brimstone muttered.

'What nonsense?'

'The camp act,' Brimstone said. 'It may have served some purpose when you were spying for Lord Hairstreak, but everybody knows it's just a performance now.'

Chalkhill sighed. 'Perhaps, but the performance has become a part of me.' He glanced philosophically into the middle distance. 'It may be that life itself is a great actor seeking parts to play. It may be –'

'Just don't try it on with the Brotherhood,' Brimstone told him.

They could hear slow footsteps in the depths of the building, and after what seemed like an eternity, the heavy oakwood door swung open. A hollow-eyed Faerie of the Night in evening dress stared down on them. 'Ah, Brimstone,' he said. The eyes swung to regard Chalkhill with an ill-concealed expression of disgust. 'And this must be the Candidate.'

Brimstone nodded shortly. He felt no urge to explain. Everybody knew Chalkhill's only real function was to provide money. Lots of money, warm from the knickers.

'Walk this way.'

They followed the creature through a maze of winding corridors until they emerged into an enormous stone-flagged kitchen. The forbidden smell of Analogue World coffee wafted from a cauldron on the stove. Brimstone wondered briefly if it was to be used as an hallucinogenic.

Their hollow-eyed guide looked around him, frowning. 'Wrong turn,' he muttered. He swung on his heel. 'This way,' he said firmly.

They approached, and passed, a sweeping staircase. 'D'Urville!' a voice hissed angrily.

D'Urville stopped and looked up. 'Ah, there you are, sir,' he said.

Brimstone recognised the Faerie of the Night at the head of the stairs as Weiskei, the Brotherhood Sentinel, a beaky little pain-in-the-ass with a habit of sticking his nose in where it wasn't wanted. He was wearing a red robe with his official lamen on the breast and carrying a ridiculous ceremonial sword. He stared at Chalkhill with even more distaste than D'Urville had. 'I take it this is the Candidate?'

Brimstone nodded.

'Why is he dressed like a circus clown?'

Chalkhill started to say something, but Brimstone signalled him to silence. 'Where do we get ready?' he asked shortly.

Weiskei glanced at him. 'You're Sponsor, are you not, Brother ... Brother ... ah, Brother ...?'

'Brimstone,' Brimstone said, frowning with irritation. What was the matter with the man? They'd only known each other for a quarter of a century; not well, admittedly, but well enough. Unless Weiskei was trying for a put-down, the little tort-feasor.

'Brimstone,' Weiskei echoed and there was a momentary blankness in his eyes that was disturbing. But he rallied quickly. 'Follow me.'

They followed him to the antechamber of the Lodge Room, a stuffy pigeonhole of a place with heavy black curtains blocking any daylight from its windows. The only illumination came from the stub of a candle stuck onto a skull on a side table. It was supposed to remind the Candidate of his own mortality, but Chalkhill didn't seem impressed.

Weiskei pompously took up guard position with his

back against the Lodge Room door and his ceremonial sword upraised. Brimstone swung his demonologist's shawl over his shoulders. 'Take off your shoes and socks,' he instructed Chalkhill. Then, as an afterthought, 'And that idiotic apron.' As a petulant expression began to crawl across Chalkhill's fleshy face, he added patiently, 'It's symbolism, Jasper. Supposed to show humility.'

'Oh, very well!' Chalkhill exclaimed.

The man had painted his toenails! Was there no end to his theatrics? Brimstone looked away tiredly. There was nothing he could do. There was nothing anybody could do. The Brotherhood was desperate for Chalkhill's money.

They settled down to wait. The candle had started to gutter precariously before the Lodge Room door finally opened.

A loin-clothed creature with a jackal's head peered out.

'Good grief!' Chalkhill exclaimed.

'Hoodwink the Candidate, Brother Sentinel,' the creature instructed, his voice muffled by the mask.

'At once, Brother Praemonstrator!' Weiskei exclaimed, snapping to attention. He produced a hoodwink from the folds of his robe and pulled it over Chalkhill's head. Brimstone knelt quickly and rolled Chalkhill's left trouser leg up to his knee. Chalkhill giggled.

The man was utterly impossible. But obscenely rich, Brimstone kept reminding himself. And the Brotherhood had never needed his money more than it did today.

Not if they wanted to regain their former glory.

five

The battlefield looked exactly the way it did the day the Civil War ended. Evidence of violence was everywhere. Spell-driven explosives had gouged vast craters out of solid rock. Grasslands were withered and burned. The few surviving trees stood barren and bare. There were mangled, bleeding bodies everywhere, most motionless, some mewling softly in their pain, a few still trying desperately to crawl away on limbless stumps.

The illusion was perfect. You could smell the blood and the unmistakable stench of military magic. Blue picked her way carefully through the debris, her face impassive. The memorial was here by her order. It was her penance.

Although she knew the bodies were phantoms, she only knew it with her head. Her gut clenched in pity and horror – the horror she herself had brought about. She talked to no one about it, not even Madame Cardui, but she knew beyond a doubt that had she made different decisions when she first became Queen, the brave soldiers immortalised in this gory spectacle would never have died. The Realm would never have rent itself in two. Faerie would not have fought faerie. The guilt of it drove her back. For one full day in every month, Blue forced herself to walk and look and smell and remember.

Her guards were two squat demons. The vicious little brutes scampered from rock to rock several yards away, but she knew from experience their stubby wings could carry them to her side within a second if danger threatened. She only ever came here accompanied by the demons. She claimed the choice was political: she was Queen of Hael now, after all. But the real reason was that she could not bring herself to parade her guilt in front of her regular faerie guard. Even penance had its limits.

One of the pseudo-corpses was an officer she knew by sight, a former Captain in the Palace Guard. He would have been a Major now, if things had been different, maybe even a Colonel. Instead he was dead, his real body buried in the military plot on Imperial Island. One small tragedy within the greater tragedy, yet it was this memory that forced a tear from Blue's eye. She wondered, not for the first time, whether the Realm would have been a better place had she followed her brother's example and refused the throne when it was offered her.

The thought of Pyrgus brought her attention back to the here and now and the crisis that might yet become a greater threat to the Realm even than the Civil War. Was there anything more she should be doing? She ran through the checklist in her head and decided there was not. What else could she do? What else could *anyone* do? Some things were beyond control, even for a Queen. But at least Pyrgus had a chance now, since she'd insisted he live in the Analogue World. He mightn't like her decision, but he'd had to admit it made sense. And mercifully, events back here were moving slowly. While that continued, there was hope.

She wished Henry were with her.

Even now, so long after it happened, Blue felt herself flush at the memory. How stupid she'd been! Admittedly she was just a child then, scarcely more than fifteen, but even so she should have known better. Men never liked to feel pursued and boys were even worse. She'd been mad to ask Henry to marry her. Anyone with half a brain could have told her what he would do. In fact Madame Cynthia *had* told her what he would do, but Blue had typically ignored the advice. She sighed. Where was Henry now? Still at home in the Analogue World, of course, but did he have a steady girlfriend? Was there someone in his life who took his hand and smoothed back his hair and made him feel a little better about himself?

It was stupid, but she felt a rush of sadness that even overwhelmed her guilt about the Civil War.

The demons were by her side. Blue jerked away on reflex – she could never get used to the speed with which the creatures moved ... or her basic revulsion to the breed. But they meant her no harm, of course. Their red eyes were staring outwards, their bodies in defensive posture. These were her subjects now, whether she liked it or not, and they would protect her without a single thought for their own lives.

Blue followed the direction of their gaze to find out what had triggered the alert. The gruesome battlefield stretched out dismally in all directions, but there was a figure silhouetted on a distant hillock, and the fact that it was upright meant it was no illusion. The demons were watching it intently, chittering softly to each other in those curious lobster-claw clicks they used in places where telepathy was blocked.

'At ease,' Blue said softly. It made little difference. Both her guardians were aquiver, watching the approaching figure like cats focused on a bird. She had a horror that one day they would disembowel an innocent, perhaps some poor subject who pressed forward to present a petition. So far it hadn't happened: demonic discipline was extraordinary. But she still worried.

The figure was a messenger. She could tell by the curious loping gait as it approached. As it came closer, it resolved itself into a trance-runner, prominently identified by the insignia of his Guild. The man's eyes were fixed on a point high in the sky, while his right hand clutched an ornate ceremonial dagger that he plunged up and down as if it were a staff. Somehow he managed to avoid all obstacles.

'Stand down,' Blue ordered firmly. The dagger, if nothing else, might have triggered an attack, but the demons would not move now unless she was directly threatened.

Although the runner could not possibly have seen her, he swerved to stop a few discreet yards away. Light alone knew how far he had come, but he was not even breathing heavily. His eyes gradually lowered and regained their spirit; then he sank to his knees. 'Majesty,' he said, extending his dagger, hilt first.

Blue took the weapon. The gesture was symbolic of the fact that the Guildsman meant her no harm, but it was more than that. Deftly she unscrewed the top of the dagger and shook a scrap of parchment out of the hollow hilt. There was a moment as the embedded security spells sensed her essence; then the parchment expanded into a standard Palace message scroll.

As Blue began to read, her eyes widened in sudden alarm.

Six

Since coffee had a psychedelic affect on faeries, Henry brewed them all a pot of tea. Nymph stared into her mug with suspicion, but Pyrgus had had it before and drank his in great draughts as he explained.

'The Faeries of the Night organise their own health services and I'm afraid there still isn't much communication between theirs and ours. Not that I think it would have made much difference. I can't see why our people would have spotted anything amiss either. The very first case, the first one we know about anyway, was a kid called Jalindra and everybody thought she'd just caught the horse-sniffles. All Cretch kids get horse-sniffles sooner or later and the early symptoms are similar.'

Mr Fogarty, while he was still in residence, had amassed a peculiar assortment of mugs. The one Henry had given to Pyrgus featured a flock of poultry listening intently to one of their number who was singing. The title of the picture, running underneath the rim, was *The Bantam of the Opera*. He watched as Pyrgus set it to one side and went on seriously. 'Jalindra was four years old when she caught the bug. A year later she was a middle-aged woman. Six months after that she was dead.' He stared down at the table top and added, 'From old age.'

'We have that here,' Henry said. 'Premature aging. It's called ...' He searched his memory for the name and surprised himself by finding it. '... Werner's Syndrome. There was something about it on telly a couple of weeks ago. It's a gene thing apparently. The youngsters never grow very much and they go grey and wrinkled while they're still children and they get old people's diseases like heart attacks and cataracts and they all die young.' He set his own mug to one side. It had a fish motif below the words *Cod Moves in Mysterious Ways*.

But Pyrgus was shaking his head. 'Not the same thing. This one has been spreading through the population. Not just Faeries of the Night, either. Faeries of the Light as well.'

'Like Pyrgus,' Nymph put in.

Henry became aware of a tightening in the pit of his stomach, as if he'd suddenly begun to feel afraid. Which he had. He didn't want Pyrgus to have some ghastly disease that reduced his lifespan to eighteen months. He glanced at his friend and realised suddenly he now looked far more like his father, the old Purple Emperor, than he did like the boy Henry had known. It was creepy as well as scary. Henry said hesitantly, 'But you're not ...? I mean, they've found a cure, haven't they? You're not, like –' he gave a sudden, very false laugh '– going to die or anything?'

'No, he's not,' said Nymph firmly.

Henry looked at her. He didn't like the fact she was the one who'd answered him. But before he could say anything else, Pyrgus was talking again. 'Let me tell you the whole thing, Henry,' he said easily. 'It's a bit tricky and I want you to understand.'

Understand what? Henry thought. But he only said soberly, 'Go on.'

Pyrgus said, 'This isn't a disease like anything we've ever seen in the Realm before. It isn't in the medical records, and there's nothing like it in our history. It started in the Cretch with poor Jalindra and moved outwards. It was a very slow spread at first. The healers thought it was a rare condition and didn't pay much attention. Actually –' He stopped suddenly and licked his lips.

'What?' Henry asked.

A look of embarrassment crept over Pyrgus's face. 'To be honest, in the early days nearly everybody thought it was a Faerie of the Night disease – only Faeries of the Night could get it. Because that's the way it looked.' He shifted in his chair. 'There's still a lot of prejudice against Faeries of the Night. Blue's doing all she can, but you can't really make up laws about that. It all comes down to the way people *think*. And you can't really blame them for being prejudiced against Faeries of the Night after all the stuff Hairstreak did.'

'No,' Henry agreed. He was a bit prejudiced against Faeries of the Night himself.

'Anyway,' Pyrgus said on a whistling out-breath, 'by the time we *did* start to take it seriously, by the time Faeries of the Light started to get sick, it had spread too widely for us to tackle the problem by isolation. So the healing wizards had to study it properly and what they found out was weird.'

'*Really* weird,' Nymph said with emphasis.

Pyrgus leaned forward. 'The thing is, Henry, this disease doesn't just make you *look* old, or mess up your body so you go wrinkled and grey. The healers are calling it TF – temporal fever. It actually interferes with time. You start to live your life faster than you should.'

Henry blinked. 'I don't think I followed that.'

Pyrgus sat back in his chair again. 'No, it's not all

that easy. Look, imagine you caught it from me –' He noticed Henry's expression and added quickly, 'Which you can't; I'll explain why in a minute. But imagine you had it now. Every so often, you'd come down with bouts of fever. Then you'd sink into a coma. We'd put you to bed and wait for you to come out of it and if it lasted for more than a day or so, we'd watch you getting older. That's what happens from the *outside*. But *inside* – what *you* experience – it's completely different. You don't know you're lying in a bed at all. Once the coma starts, everything around you suddenly speeds up. You find yourself thinking and doing things at breakneck speed. If you'd planned to go away on holiday tomorrow, that's what you'd do. And you'd race around doing holiday stuff, but instead of it all taking weeks, it would all be over in a few seconds. You see?'

'Yes …' Henry said uncertainly. 'Actually, no.'

'You start living your life very fast. Then after a while it stops and you're jerked back to the present and you're in bed recovering and you start living again at the normal rate. Except you've aged by whatever number of years you've already lived. The fever has burned up your future.'

After a moment, Henry said, 'So you come back *remembering* the future? You know what's going to happen to you?'

Pyrgus chewed his lip. 'Yes and no. It's all a bit of a blur – even while it's going on. But the thing is, the future you remember is burned up. You won't live it, because you already have. Are you following?'

Henry blinked and said nothing. After a moment Pyrgus said, 'What can happen, if you're lucky, is you might pick out a detail or two about other people's futures or what's going on generally. But only where it touches your own *personal* future and you'd be surprised how little that is. I mean a big war in the Realm could pass you right by if you didn't happen to be in it. Most people don't remember enough to be useful.' An odd expression crossed his face. 'Most people ...'

They sat looking at each other. After another moment, Henry said, 'And this is what you're going through?'

'Was,' Pyrgus said. '*Was* going through. The effect stops when you're in the Analogue World. That's why I said you couldn't catch it from me. The disease goes dormant here. You don't have the symptoms and you can't pass it on.'

'So that's why the two of you are in my world?' Henry said.

'Yes,' Nymph said. 'Blue's idea was that we wait it out until somebody finds a cure.'

Henry grinned. 'And that's why you came to see me?'

But Pyrgus didn't grin back. He shook his head. 'We came to see you because Mr Fogarty is dying.'

Seven

The fear was back and this time it was much worse than it had been when he was worried about Pyrgus. 'He can't be!' Henry said. But he knew Mr Fogarty could very well be. He might look tough as old boots, but he had to be nearly ninety. The reality was a lot of old people fell off their perches long before that. Not that reality would stop Henry going into denial. 'He can't be,' Henry repeated. 'What about his treatments?' Mr Fogarty was getting rejuvenation spells from Palace wizards in the Faerie Realm. They were supposed to rebuild the vital organs. At the time they started, Henry frankly hadn't noticed much change in Mr Fogarty's appearance, but Madame Cardui had once remarked the treatments made him 'frisky.'

Pyrgus ignored the question. 'He's caught the disease, Henry. He's got TF.'

'You said humans couldn't get it!' Henry snapped accusingly. He pushed his chair away from the table and began to walk nervously around the kitchen, his eyes suddenly moist.

'I said the disease goes dormant in the Analogue World: it doesn't seem to exist here,' Pyrgus told him patiently. 'That's not the same thing.'

'You see,' Nymph said gently, 'TF uses up your future.

Young people have a lot of future to use up. But Mr Fogarty hasn't. At his age it can't be more than a few years, even with rejuvenation treatments. It's what Pyrgus told you, Henry – bouts of fever, except the fever burns up time. When you're young, you can afford several bouts. When you're eighty-seven, like Mr Fogarty ...'

'How many has he had?' Henry demanded.

'Just two,' Nymph said. 'But they've left him very old and very weak. He can't get out of bed.'

'But he could recover,' Henry said desperately. 'I mean, he's basically very strong and with spells and things ...'

'Another bout will kill him,' Pyrgus said bluntly. 'Even without one I don't know how long he can last.'

Henry stared at them. He hadn't laid eyes on Mr Fogarty for the past two years, but somehow that didn't matter. Just as it didn't matter that Mr Fogarty was difficult and cranky and paranoid and awkward. He loved the old man and it was only at this moment he realised just how much. 'Then you must get him here!' he said suddenly.

Pyrgus, the older, mature, greying Pyrgus, stared at Henry almost sorrowfully.

'Come on,' Henry said eagerly. 'It's obvious. You bring him back home, back to the Analogue World. Then he won't have any more bouts. He can do what you're doing and just wait here for a cure.' Some of his eagerness died down. It *was* obvious – too obvious. They must have thought of it already.

'He won't come,' Nymph said.

'Then make him!' Henry shouted. 'What's wrong with you? Just send him back!'

'Have you ever tried to make Mr Fogarty do anything he didn't want to do?' Pyrgus asked.

Henry jerked his chair out and sat down again. He leaned across the table. 'Wait a minute. *Why* won't he come back? He's still got his house here. He's still got his cat. I can look after him.' *And bog university*, he thought.

'We don't know,' Pyrgus said. 'It's not somewhere to live, that's for sure. Even if he didn't want to come back here –' he glanced around the gloomy kitchen '– he could stay with Nymph and me. Or we could buy him a mansion if he wanted. Gold goes a long way in your world, Henry. But he won't come and we don't know what's going on inside his head.'

'Have you tried to find out?' Henry demanded.

For the first time, Pyrgus showed signs of losing patience. 'Of course we've tried!' he snapped. 'Don't you think I *care* about Mr Fogarty? If it hadn't been for him, I'd have been dead years ago.'

'Pyrgus delayed leaving the Realm himself to try to persuade Mr Fogarty to come too,' Nymph said. 'It cost Pyrgus another five years of his future.'

Henry seemed to collapse in on himself. 'I'm sorry. I'm sorry, Pyrgus – that didn't come out the way I meant it to. Of course you've all done your best.'

'*We* have,' Pyrgus said. 'The thing is, he might pay more attention to *you*.'

He never has in the past, Henry thought. Aloud he said, 'You want me to go back to the Realm?'

Pyrgus nodded. 'Yes. I can't go with you – once I get back to my world the disease reactivates. But Nymph will make sure you get there safely.' He looked at Henry expectantly.

And there it was, all laid out in front of him. Return to the Realm. It was something he'd thought about – dreamed about – for the past two years. But how could he go back? How could he face Blue? He could feel the hideous embarrassment rising in him even now and prayed his face had not gone crimson. He wondered if Pyrgus knew that Blue had wanted to marry him. He wondered how Blue felt about that today. He wondered how he'd been such an idiot, such a *coward*, to run away. He couldn't go back, not if it meant seeing Blue again; and it *had* to mean seeing Blue again. There was *no way* he could go back.

'The other thing is,' Pyrgus was saying, 'he wants to talk to you.'

'Mr Fogarty,' Nymph said, as if Pyrgus's words needed clarification. 'He's been asking for you.'

'Has he?' Henry asked foolishly. It tumbled through his mind that Mr Fogarty might want to sort out legal stuff. His will, or what to do with the house or whatever. Except he'd already done all that; and besides, there was absolutely no need for Mr Fogarty to die now, not when he could just come back and wait for a cure the way Pyrgus was doing. Surely even Mr Fogarty couldn't be batty enough not to realise that?

'There may not be a lot of time,' Pyrgus said soberly. 'Is it possible for you to go straightaway?'

Of course it wasn't possible to go straightaway. He had school and exams and his mother and the business with Charlie, such as it was, and besides, there was absolutely no way he could ever face Blue again, not after what had happened.

Henry squeezed his eyes closed. 'Yes,' he said.

Eight

She could see the splash of blue on the Palace steps even before she landed the flyer. Chief Wizard Surgeon Healer Danaus was waiting for her in his full regalia, which meant the message was true – although she'd never doubted that for an instant – and suggested the situation might even have grown worse.

Blue slid from the craft and ran across the lawn. Her demon guards took wing to keep up with her. Danaus hurried down the steps to greet her. He was a big man, shaven-headed and overweight, but he managed to move nimbly with speed, so that they met by the rose bower. Danaus bowed deeply, a little out of breath. As he straightened, he glared at her flanking demons with distaste. They stared back at him impassively, their red eyes unblinking.

'Is he ...?' Blue asked anxiously.

'Another bout of temporal fever, Majesty,' Danaus said. He was one of the old school who had been trained never to look a royal in the eye, so his gaze was trained on a spot beyond her right ear. It gave him a curiously shifty look, but Blue would have trusted his judgement anywhere, particularly in matters of medicine.

'But he's not ...?' she asked again, softly.

Danaus shook his head. 'He still lives, Majesty. But I fear ...'

'Not long?'

'No, Majesty.'

'Is he in pain?'

'No, Majesty.'

'Can you do anything for him?'

'We have introduced support elementals into his blood. They have raised his energy levels slightly. He continues to refuse stasis. Apart from pain control, there is nothing else we can do. I fear a cure for the condition eludes us. And even if one were discovered tomorrow –' He hesitated.

'You think it might be too late?'

'Yes, Majesty.'

'I want to see him,' Blue said.

A pained expression crawled across Danaus's fleshy features. 'Majesty, his condition has deteriorated considerably since his second bout of temporal fever. I fear the sight of him might prove distressing to Your Majesty ...'

'I'm sure you're right, Chief Wizard Surgeon Healer,' Blue said shortly, 'but I still want to see him.' Before he could protest further, she swept past him to hurry up the steps of the Palace.

As they followed in her wake, one of her guardian demons, perhaps sensing her dislike of the man's pomposity, turned round to bite him in the bottom.

There were flowers in the sickroom, but the place smelled of old age and decay. Mr Fogarty was sitting up in bed, propped by a mountain of pillows. Madame Cardui was seated in a chair beside him, holding his hand, but apparently asleep. Despite the Surgeon Healer's warning, Blue was shocked by his appearance. He'd always been a thin man, but now he was cadaverous. His skin stretched parchment-thin across his skull, his lips were drawn back over discoloured teeth and his eyes looked huge, yet sunken. She could count no fewer than seven glass containers of healing elementals on the shelf above his head. The creatures swam down translucent tubes to enter his body at the top of his spine. She suspected they were the only things keeping him alive.

All the same, his voice sounded strong as he shook Madame Cardui's hand and said, 'Wake up, darling – Queen Blue's here.'

Madame Cardui's eyes jerked open. After a moment of obvious disorientation, she scrambled to her feet. 'Oh, forgive me, my deeah – I must have nodded off.' She gestured to the chair she'd just vacated. 'Please sit down, Your Majesty.' Some of the spirit returned to her eyes and she added, 'Perhaps *you* can talk some sense into this old fool.'

'Do sit, Madame Cynthia,' Blue said. Although her spymaster hadn't contracted the temporal fever, she was looking almost as old as the Gatekeeper. She must be worried out of her mind about losing him. To Mr Fogarty, Blue said, 'How are you, Gatekeeper?'

'Remarkably well, considering I'm dying.' Mr Fogarty's voice sounded like dry leaves.

'Blue, deeah, tell him he *must* go back to the Analogue World. Order him, if you have to.'

Mr Fogarty turned his head to look fondly at Madame Cardui. 'You know she won't, Cynthia. And if she did, you know I wouldn't go. What's she going to do then? Throw a sick old man through a portal?'

Madame Cardui glared at him. 'Your last bout of fever nearly killed you. Your *first* bout of fever nearly killed you, come to that. You know you won't survive another. Alan, we care about you. Nobody wants you dead. The minute you translate, it puts the disease on hold. Our healers are working hard to find a cure and when they do, you can come back.'

'I know all the arguments, Cynthia,' Fogarty said in a tone that dismissed them utterly.

Blue said, 'She's right, Gatekeeper. You know that too. What I can't understand is why you won't listen to her.'

'I can't tell you that.' He stared into the middle distance, his face like granite.

'Can you tell me *why* you can't tell me?'

Fogarty glanced at her sideways and the smallest hint of a grin twitched at his lips. 'You never give up, do you? Few more years' experience and you'll make a memorable Queen. They'll sing about your exploits in the next millennium.' He shook his head. 'No, I can't tell you why I can't tell you. It's important I stay here. Out of stasis, before you bring that up again. And believe me, I know the dangers. I know how ill I am, I know how close to death I am and, yes, Cynthia, I know another fever bout will kill me. And before you say it again, I do know another bout could hit me in the next five minutes.'

'Then why –?' Madame Cardui began.

'None of that matters,' Mr Fogarty cut her off. 'I won't be going home to the Analogue World and that's an end to it.'

Blue said, 'Is there any way we can make you more comfortable, Gatekeeper?'

Fogarty said, 'Get Henry here. I'm running out of time.'

Nine

'Can you see anything?' Brimstone asked.

'Nothing,' Chalkhill confirmed. 'Not so much as a chink.'

'Put your wrists behind your back.'

'What are you going to do?' Chalkhill asked at once.

'Bind them!' intoned the Praemonstrator. Outside the Brotherhood his name was Avis and he made a living hiring out ouklos, but the jackal mask gave him a certain gravitas.

'Oooh!' Chalkhill exclaimed and crossed his wrists behind his back at once.

Avis tied them expertly with a soft piece of silken rope. 'Let the Initiation commence!' he commanded.

Brimstone took Chalkhill by the elbow and began to lead him towards the Lodge Room door. As they reached it and stopped, Chalkhill leaned over to whisper, 'Silas, he hasn't tied me very tightly. I could get free if I wanted to.'

'It's symbolic!' Brimstone hissed back impatiently. 'I told you that before. It's *all* symbolic. Death and resurrection. If it wasn't symbolic, we'd have to kill you.'

'Wouldn't want that,' said Chalkhill cheerfully. 'What happens now?'

'What happens now is you shut up and let me get on

with it,' Brimstone told him. But he relented enough to add, 'I introduce you to the assembled Brothers and propose you for membership. You're not allowed to see them until you've been accepted. That's why you're hoodwinked and Avis is wearing the mask.'

'That's not Callophrys Avis, is it?' Chalkhill asked. 'The one with the funny wife?'

At his own initiation, Brimstone swore an oath never to reveal the name of another Brother on pain of having his tongue removed, his eyes gouged out, his breast ripped open and his heart stopped by a magical current that tapped the fundamental power of the universe. 'That's him,' he said.

From behind them, Weiskei said, 'Are you two ready?'

'Yes,' Brimstone told him shortly.

'Knock thrice on the door, Brother Sponsor,' Callophrys Avis instructed. 'In your own time.'

'Here we go,' Brimstone whispered to Chalkhill. 'I want you to do what you're told, keep your mouth shut unless you're spoken to and, above all, don't camp it up.'

'Of course,' Chalkhill whispered back in the shocked tones of one wrongly accused. 'I'll be good.'

Brimstone reached out and knocked thrice on the heavy oakwood door. The sound reverberated hollowly.

It was peculiar working blind. After an expectant second, Chalkhill heard the door open, and a waft of heady incense assailed his nostrils, overlaid by the distinctive scent of magic. Darkness knew what sort of spells were operating in the Lodge Room, although he expected he'd find out soon enough.

A strange voice asked sonorously, 'Who knocks?'

'One who stands without ...' Brimstone whispered in Chalkhill's ear.

Chalkhill frowned under his hoodwink. 'Stands without what?' he asked softly.

'Just repeat the words!' hissed Brimstone. '*One who stands without ...*'

'One who stands without,' said Chalkhill loudly. It occurred to him he couldn't be looking his best with a bag over his head, but there was nothing he could do about that now.

'*And seeks entrance within,*' Brimstone prompted.

'And seeks entrance within,' Chalkhill echoed, wondering how an exchange as banal as this could form part of the ceremonial of the most feared Brotherhood of the Realm. Or what used to be the most feared. Whether his new friends could reclaim that position remained to be seen.

'Child of Earth, arise and enter the Path of Darkness,' said the strange voice. There was another firm knock; then the voice called, 'Very Honoured Hierophant, is it your pleasure that the Candidate be admitted?'

A new voice, distorted yet hauntingly familiar, said loudly, 'It is. Admit Jasper Chalkhill in due form. Fratre Stolistes and Dadouchos, assist the Praemonstrator in the reception.'

There was a shuffling of feet; then the voice of Praemonstrator Avis sounded no more than a yard or two in front of him, still muffled by the jackal mask. 'Child of Earth, unpurified and unconsecrated thou canst not enter our sacred hall!'

Then consecrate me, Chalkhill thought, *and let's be getting on with it.*

Two new voices chirped up then. The first said

slowly, 'Child of Earth, I purify thee with water.' Something hit him in the face through the hoodwink and after a moment he felt the cloth go damp.

The second voice said in a grating singsong, 'Child of Earth, I consecrate thee with fire.' There was a whooshing sound and he felt the heat of a torch around his upper body.

'It is done, Honoured Hierophant,' the two voices intoned in unison.

'Conduct the Candidate to the foot of the altar,' ordered the Hierophant.

Chalkhill felt Brimstone take his arm and urge him on. He tried to make a brave front of it, but it was almost impossible to stride forward with any sort of swagger when you couldn't see where you were going. What would happen if he tripped over the incense burner? Or walked smack into a pillar?

Brimstone jerked him to a halt at what he assumed to be the foot of the altar. Certainly the voice of the Hierophant was closer now as he asked, 'Child of Earth, why dost thou request admission into this Order?'

Chalkhill realised his imagination was beginning to run riot. He could visualise the Lodge Room vividly, a sweeping hypostyle hall in polished marble with golden inlays. The Brothers were robed and stately, highly powerful magi every one. Then it occurred to him this was exactly the reason for the hoodwink. Successful initiation was largely to do with the Candidate's state of mind. You could impress him with an actual marble hall, but it was cheaper to let his imagination do the work. But Brimstone was whispering in his ear again.

'*My soul is wandering the Realm searching for the Darkness of Occult Knowledge,*' Brimstone prompted.

'*And I believe that in this Order, the knowledge of that Darkness may be obtained.*'

'My soul is wandering the Realm searching for the Darkness of Occult Knowledge and I believe that in this Order, the knowledge of that Darkness may be obtained,' Chalkhill repeated dutifully.

'Well spoken, Wanderer!' the Hierophant exclaimed heartily. 'Remove the hoodwink!'

Chalkhill blinked a little as the hood came off. His eyes took a moment to adjust to the light. Then the marble hall of his imagination disappeared to make way for the reality of a smallish, square, carpeted room with incense burning on a cubical altar and only two pillars in the place, one black, the other silver. Chalkhill stared in horror.

Between them, seated on an obsidian throne, was Lord Hairstreak.

Ten

It occurred to Chalkhill he needed a loo. It was years since he'd worked for Hairstreak, but the little shit was capable of holding a grudge for a lifetime. The painful ingenuity of his revenge was legendary.

Hairstreak must have read something of his inner turmoil from his face, for his lip curled slightly and he said, 'Not expecting to see me, Jasper?'

Chalkhill opened his mouth, then closed it again, like a fish. He made a second attempt with no greater success, then finally squeaked, 'No.' Since it never helped to be rude to a turd of Hairstreak's stature, he managed to swallow hard and add, 'Your Lordship.' What was the man doing here anyway? He'd never, ever shown the slightest interest in the Black Arts, yet here he was now, not just a member of the magical Brotherhood, but apparently leading it. The implications hardly bore thinking about.

'Well,' said Hairstreak easily, 'I'm glad to hear my Brothers have been holding to their oaths.' His eyes pierced Chalkhill like stilettos. 'Will you be faithful to your oath, Jasper?'

'Me? Yes. Certainly. Definitely. You know me, Your Lordship. Soul of discretion. Tact. Obedience. Faithful? Definitely. And loyal. Yes, indeed. To the Brotherhood. If they'll have me. And you, sir. Personally. Definitely. My word. My oath. Whatever you want, Lord Hair – Lord Hair – Lord Hair –' His mouth went into an endless loop and he couldn't seem to finish what he was saying.

Hairstreak sighed impatiently. 'Yes, yes, I get the message, Jasper. No trouble from you, now or hereafter. That about it, would you say?'

'Definitely!' Chalkhill confirmed. He wondered if he dared risk putting out a contract on Hairstreak. The Guild of Assassins was very reliable and everybody knew Hairstreak had fallen on hard times since the Civil War. His security might not be what it used to be.

Hairstreak smiled chillingly. 'Excellent,' he said. He glanced towards a black-robed minion on his right. 'Bring in the coffin!'

'Coffin?' Chalkhill squeaked. It was already on its way, carried by six pallbearers, rather well made in oak with polished brass handles and, worryingly, brown bloodstains splattered all across its surface. The pallbearers set it down directly in front of the altar.

'Get in,' Hairstreak ordered with obvious relish.

The door would have been spell-bound by now, so any hope of making a run for it was out the window ... except there wasn't any window. He was doomed and there was no loo in the coffin. Chalkhill realised his thoughts were running riot, making no sense even to him, but it was so difficult to rein them back. 'You should have warned me!' he hissed furiously at Brimstone.

'About what?' Brimstone hissed back. He seemed completely unperturbed by Hairstreak, but then Brimstone had always been like that: skinny, ugly, wrinkled, hard as nails and tough as boots. There were stories that he'd won a fight with Beleth before Queen Blue killed the demon king. Which meant a great deal more then than it did now Hael was under Realm control.

Chalkhill said, 'About Hairstreak. About having to be murdered.'

'It's symbolic. I told you,' Brimstone said impatiently. 'Now stop making a fuss and get into your coffin.' He hesitated. 'Better give me the money now.'

'No way!' Chalkhill snapped. He had a feeling that the money might be the only thing keeping him alive.

'If you two have *quite* finished ...' Hairstreak glared.

Since there was nothing else to do, Chalkhill jerked his elbow out of Brimstone's grasp and climbed into the coffin, a wary eye on Hairstreak as he did so. There was a curious sound from the assembled Brothers, somewhere between a sigh of gratification and a crocodile hiss.

'Lie down,' Hairstreak ordered. 'Cross your arms over your chest.'

Like a corpse, Chalkhill thought. The trouble was, he'd been accustomed to obeying Hairstreak's orders without question and somehow he couldn't break the habit now. He lay down and crossed his arms over his chest. The coffin was quite comfortably padded, but it definitely smelled of old, sour blood. He kept thinking *sacrificial lamb.* He kept thinking *death, destruction, slaughter.*

The pallbearers closed the coffin lid.

Chalkhill nearly lost it then. The experience was quite different from the hoodwink, which had let in lots of light around the edges. Now the darkness was total; almost tangible. His breathing grew laboured as the air inside the coffin thickened. He felt hot. Was this the start of a cremation? He started to sweat profusely. Sombre music sounded in his ears, the result of some stupid spell cone, by the smell. Now he kept thinking, *decay, corruption, putrefaction.* He wondered if it would do any good to burst into tears.

The coffin lid opened again, letting in light and some blessed air. Avis was leaning over him, still wearing that stupid mask and loincloth. He had a dagger in one hand. *This is it!* Chalkhill said, but all that came out was a whimper.

'You're supposed to stand up now,' Avery prompted, his voice muffled by the mask.

Chalkhill leaped from the coffin and fell into a weird fighting stance, legs bent, one hand outstretched, palm flat, in a chopping motion. Avis ignored him and placed the tip of the dagger lightly against his chest. 'Do you solemnly swear and attest you will truly, faithfully, honestly and diligently uphold the principles of this Unholy Order, preserve its secrets on pain of having your tongue removed, your eyes gouged out, your breast ripped open and your heart stopped by a magical current that taps the fundamental power of the universe?' Avis muttered speedily. 'Do you further agree, attest, swear and undertake to endow this sacred Brotherhood with all your worldly goods, hitherto and hereafter accumulated, limited only to the amount previously agreed with your Sponsor, so help you Darkness?'

Chalkhill looked at him.

'Say *I do,*' Brimstone prompted.

'I do,' Chalkhill said.

There was a scattering of applause among the congregated Brothers. Hairstreak said formally, 'Welcome to our Order.' Then he added in a bored voice, 'Do you have any questions, Frater Chalkhill?'

'When do I get to talk to God?' asked Chalkhill promptly.

Eleven

The city was a lot different from the last time Henry had been here. The milling crowds of Cheapside had disappeared, leaving the streets eerily quiet. Highgrove was no better. Even the bustling commerce on the Loman Bridge had dwindled to a trickle. Although it was a warm enough day, Henry noticed Nymph kept the windows of the carriage tightly closed and was struck by a sudden frightening suspicion. 'They're not all dead, are they?' he blurted.

Nymph looked at him in surprise. 'Who?'

Henry's head was filled with something he'd been reading for his History exams – an account of the Black Death in Europe. The disease had spread like wildfire in the 14th Century, killing one-third of the population of the Continent. A traveller at the time left vivid descriptions of empty city streets and the stench of death. 'The people,' Henry said.

Nymph continued to stare at him for a moment, then suddenly relaxed and shook her head. 'No. No, the death rate isn't very high yet. But people are frightened, so they don't go out much any more.' She glanced out the window of the carriage and added inconsequentially, 'It hasn't reached the forest yet.'

'How –?' Henry hesitated. He didn't want to sound

like a wuss, but he badly wanted to know. 'How ... contagious is it? I mean, how easy is it to get?'

'Well, we're not even sure how it spreads, but you don't want to take stupid chances,' Nymph said matter-of-factly, which didn't tell him anything. He was wondering how he could pursue the topic further when Nymph asked a question of her own: 'What happened between you and Blue, Henry?'

It drove the thoughts of disease from his head. *What happened between you and Blue, Henry?* He knew somebody was bound to ask him that eventually and Nymph had always been direct. He felt his brain falling back into its familiar defensive manoeuvres – *Me and Blue? You think there was something between me and Blue?* – then decided, with a massive effort, that it was time to break old patterns. He'd never survive the next few hours – meeting Blue again, which he was bound to do – if he didn't get a grip on himself. Besides, he liked Nymph and had always found her easy to talk to. She didn't tease you and she didn't play games and she didn't have an agenda. He took a deep breath, stared out the window again and said, 'I blew it.'

After a moment, Nymph asked gently, 'How?'

Henry turned back to look at her. 'You won't tell this to anybody, will you? I mean, I wouldn't want – I mean, it might embarrass –' Nymph said nothing, just looked at him soberly. Henry said, 'No, of course you won't.' He returned to staring through the window. 'It's old history now, anyway: I don't suppose anybody really cares.' He sighed. 'Blue asked me to marry her.'

'Really?' Nymph sounded surprised.

'Oh, yes,' Henry said. 'I don't know what got into her. It was after that business with Beleth, of course, and the kidnap and everything and I suppose she was very upset and –'

'What got into her was that she loved you,' Nymph said quietly.

It shut Henry up completely. The carriage, a surface transport, rumbled over the great wooden bridge. He could see the broad sweep of the river winding lazily between the dockside warehouses on one bank and the ancient, overhanging residences of Highgrove on the other. After a while he said, 'I couldn't. I just couldn't.'

'Why not?'

Why not? There had been so many reasons and he wasn't sure Nymph would understand a single one of them. She was a very uncomplicated girl. She'd fallen for Pyrgus and married him. Simple. At least that's what he assumed had happened. What did he know? He said, 'She was too young, for one thing.'

'In the Realm some girls get married at thirteen,' Nymph said. 'It's even younger in the forest – I could have got married at twelve if I wanted to. Blue was older than that two years ago.'

'Yes, I think she was fifteen. Maybe just sixteen, I'm not sure. But that's *here.* In my world you don't get married that young. You just *don't!*' Actually there were some countries where you did, but he pushed the thought aside.

'Was age the only reason?' Nymph asked without a hint of judgement in her voice.

For just the barest moment, Henry thought he was going to cry. It would be terrible if he cried in front of Nymph, hideously embarrassing. Then the moment passed and a dam broke and he said with brutal honesty. 'I was afraid.'

Nymph waited.

Henry said, 'I just panicked. You've lived in the Realm all your life; you don't know what it's like for me. None of you do. I feel really out of place here. I'm not a hero or a prince or somebody that Blue deserves. I'm just a schoolboy. I have this awful mother and my father's lovely, but he's weak and everybody expects me to, you know, just do normal things. Like exams and becoming a teacher. If I married Blue I'd be a consort or a king or something and I'd have to rule the Realm with her, or help her out at least. I don't know how to do that. I hardly even know how things *work* here. I could never make the changes.'

'Mr Fogarty did,' Nymph said.

Mr Fogarty was dying, Henry thought. The carriage rolled to a stop. It had reached the ferry that would take them to Imperial Island.

Twelve

Imperial Island looked the same as ever, but Henry's heart began to pound the moment the ferry docked. He was very much afraid. He was afraid of meeting Blue, afraid of what she would say and what he should say. He was afraid of how Mr Fogarty might look now he'd lost most of what little future he had left. But, oddly, he wasn't afraid that he'd fail to get Mr Fogarty to come back to the real world. He knew, in the depths of his being, Mr Fogarty wasn't going to die yet. Henry could handle the old man. He'd always been able to handle the old man even in his most stubborn moods. Henry would get him to come home and the fever would stop and he could come back to the Realm when the wizards found a cure.

The guards at the ferry dock were all wearing surgical masks, but several had them pulled down around their necks so nobody seemed too worried about infection. Nymph was treated with huge deference, Henry noticed, and wondered why; then he realised she was married to the former Emperor. Pyrgus may have lasted only seconds in the job, but he was still a Prince of the Realm, which meant Nymph was probably a city princess now, as well as a forest princess in her own right. Henry himself was treated politely, but he had the strong feeling nobody actually remembered him. Which was fine – he'd never felt comfortable as Iron Prominent, Knight of the Grey Dagger, largely because he never thought he deserved it.

'Shall we walk from here?' Nymph said, cutting in on his thoughts. 'Or would you like me to order a carriage?'

'Walk,' Henry said shortly. 'It's only a little way.' And it would give him time to get his thoughts in order, figure out what he was going to say to Blue. Or to Mr Fogarty, which was really far more important.

But moments later he was sorry for his decision. The path they took was the same one he had walked that night with Blue. The memories, already fresh in his mind, flooded over him in vivid detail. His discomfort must have shown on his face, for Nymph asked, 'Are you all right, Henry?' When he nodded, she added kindly, 'It's okay, you know. Everybody understands.'

He had the idea in his mind that Blue would be waiting on the steps of the Purple Palace, maybe even flanked by guards who would arrest him for ... for ... for insulting the Queen or something. But that was stupid and he knew it and he wasn't really surprised to find no one waiting on the steps at all. Nymph led him in through a side door; they walked familiar corridors; then suddenly he was in the doorway of Mr Fogarty's sickroom. 'I'll leave you alone,' Nymph whispered, but he hardly heard her.

Mr Fogarty looked awful. To be honest, he looked dead. He was laid out on a bed, eyes closed, with skin the sort of grey colour that wouldn't have been out of place on a corpse. There was no sign at all of breathing, but there were tubes running into his body from a shelf above the bed, which gave Henry a little hope. If he was dead, somebody would surely have taken them out. Unless he had died within the last few minutes. There was no one else in the room.

'Mr Fogarty,' Henry whispered in something close to panic.

Mr Fogarty opened his eyes at once. He looked at Henry for a moment without moving his head, then said sourly, 'You've cut it fine.'

Henry sat on the edge of the bed, taking care not to sit on Mr Fogarty's legs, which hardly showed up at all under the covers and were so stick-thin they would have broken like twigs under the impact of Henry's bottom. There were little … *things* … swimming up and down the tubes that penetrated Mr Fogarty's spine. They were repulsive and Henry could hardly take his eyes off them. It felt as if he'd stumbled into some sort of horror movie.

On top of which, the conversation was not going well.

'But *why* won't you come back with me?' he asked for the third or fourth time, aware his voice sounded whiney and shrill and even a little desperate, yet not able to control it at all, because he *felt* whiney and shrill and more than a little desperate. 'Your old house is great –' which was a lic, but it was certainly no worse than Mr Fogarty had left it '– but I've talked to Pyrgus and we can get you somewhere else if you want and you'll be very comfortable until the wizards find a cure –'

'The wizards won't find a cure,' said Mr Fogarty bluntly.

'Yes, of course they will!' Henry said with conviction,

except it came out sounding patronising, the way people sounded when they talked to somebody very old and a bit deaf and gaga. It was dangerous to patronise Mr Fogarty. He licked his lips. 'They have magic and stuff.'

'Magic!' Mr Fogarty snorted. To Henry's surprise he pushed himself up in the bed and all of a sudden the old fire was back. He glared at Henry. 'Those clowns know nothing about magic. You ever see a caterpillar?'

Henry blinked. 'Caterpillar?'

'Little hairy wormy thing with legs,' Fogarty growled.

'Yes, I know what a caterpillar is,' Henry said, miffed. 'What's that got to do –?'

'First couple of weeks of its life, month at most, your caterpillar trolls about eating plants,' Mr Fogarty said as if he hadn't spoken. 'It gets maybe thirty thousand times bigger than it was the day it was born. Well developed little animal. It's got eyes and taste buds and antennae it uses to smell. Great jaws. Uses its front legs to hold on to food. Inside it's got intestines and all sorts of useful organs.'

'Mr Fogarty, what –?'

'Shut up, Henry. Then one day, the caterpillar – which has never done anything but eat, remember – starts to spin silk. This thing that's spent its life avoiding birds and wasps, spent its life *surviving,* Henry, it spins silk and wraps it round itself like a mummy until it can't breathe any more. It commits suicide.'

'That's –'

'Can't put it any other way, can you? Caterpillar kills itself. Then, inside this silk cocoon it's spun, hanging from some leaf or branch or wherever, the caterpillar rots. Rots right down into liquid. Not a thing left of it. Jaws gone, all six eyes gone, intestines gone. Everything. Henry, *there is nothing left of that caterpillar!*'

Maybe it was something to do with the disease, or maybe it was just old age, but Mr Fogarty was definitely losing it. Another bout of fever would burn up the rest of his future for sure. Five minutes after it hit him he'd be dead. His only hope – his *only* hope – was to come home to the Analogue World and he was lying there delivering a nature lecture. 'Mr Fog –' Henry attempted to cut in.

'So it hangs there, this bag of liquid,' Mr Fogarty said excitedly. 'Until next thing you know, the sac suddenly turns transparent, then splits and out comes –'

'A butterfly,' Henry said. 'Mr Fogarty, we really don't have time for –'

'A *butterfly!*' exclaimed Mr Fogarty. 'A thing with wings and heart and blood and nervous system and ovaries or testicles and even a special organ that lets it keep its balance when it's flying. What comes out is about as different from the caterpillar as you could get. *And nobody on the planet has the least idea how the caterpillar does it!*' He pushed himself forward until his face was only inches away from Henry's own. 'Now *that's* magic!'

Henry opened his mouth and shut it again. Mr Fogarty collapsed back on the bed. 'You have to find the magic,' he said softly. 'You're the caterpillar, Henry. You're the only one can do it.'

Thirteen

'How,' hissed Black Hairstreak furiously, 'did he find out?'

Brimstone glared back. 'Not from me.'

'Then who?' Hairstreak demanded.

'How should I know?' Brimstone asked him crossly. He felt nervous around Hairstreak, but not *that* nervous. His Lordship had fallen on hard times since the Civil War. The country estates were gone and they were meeting in miserable little city lodgings. Hairstreak needed the Brotherhood far more than the Brotherhood needed him. And the Brotherhood needed Brimstone. He was the only one who could revive their lost fortunes.

But Hairstreak was not about to back down either. 'You're his Sponsor,' he said shortly.

'A formality,' snapped Brimstone. Then, to turn the screw, added, 'Undertaken at *your* request.'

It had the desired effect. Hairstreak backed down a little – you could see it in his eyes. Brimstone looked pointedly around the room, a small gesture designed to keep Hairstreak in his place. The lodgings weren't even in a fashionable part of town. In the old days they'd been an artisan dwelling, tarted up at the turn of the century by a merchant who wanted somewhere to stash his mistresses. Now they were just seedy. As was Hairstreak himself, if the truth be told. The velvet suit had seen better days and his boots were worn and scuffed.

All the same, it never did to underestimate the man. He might be in disgrace, but he was still a Lord, with a Lord's connections. And he was still head of the Brotherhood, a fact Brimstone had to live with. To take some of the tension out of the situation, he said, 'I'm not sure he *has* found out anything really.'

'He asked when he could speak to God,' Hairstreak reminded him. 'I'd say that was a pretty good indication he *has* found out something ... really!'

'There's been talk,' Brimstone said. 'You know there's been talk. That's what got him interested in the first place. It's all rumours, tittle-tattle, nothing specific, nothing important.' He fixed Hairstreak with a gimlet eye. 'He's just parroting something he picked up in a tavern. Testing us out. If he hadn't heard the rumours, he would never have joined the Brotherhood.'

Hairstreak stood up suddenly and jerked open a cupboard hidden in the panelling of the wall. 'Want a drink? There's gin, simbala or Analogue coffee.' When Brimstone shook his head, he poured himself a shot and strode back to his chair. 'Did you get the money?'

Brimstone shook his head a second time. His lip curled slightly of its own accord.

'Why not?' Hairstreak demanded.

'I have no plans to root around in Chalkhill's knickers,' Brimstone said coldly. He caught Hairstreak's blank expression and added, 'He keeps it in his knickers. At least that's what he told me.'

'He keeps it *where?*'

'Oh come on!' Brimstone said impatiently. 'You know

Jasper just as well as I do – you employed him long enough. The man's a pervert.'

'Yes, but he's a rich pervert,' Hairstreak muttered sourly. 'He is *going* to pay?'

'Yes, of course. I've arranged a bank draft.' It would be made out to Brimstone, but he felt no urge to mention that. He was the one who would be spending the money after all.

'When?'

'When did I arrange it?'

'When will it be paid?'

'Seventy-two-hour clearance,' Brimstone said. 'Best you can do with a sum that size.'

'Three days …' Hairstreak mused thoughtfully.

Brimstone frowned. 'Something wrong with that?'

'I was just thinking about the *rumours* Chalkhill's heard. About talking to God. He's not going to be satisfied until he's found out what's behind them.'

'I don't suppose he is,' Brimstone agreed. Chalkhill was nothing if not curious. Besides which, he was parting with an obscene amount of money. Nobody in his right mind would do that just to join a clapped-out Lodge of sorcerers who couldn't even raise a demon any more. It was an open secret that Chalkhill realised there was something afoot. He might live without knowing details *before* he was a member of the Brotherhood, but once he parted with his gold, he'd want to have the truth.

'Do you trust him?' Hairstreak asked.

It was a good question and one Brimstone hadn't considered. His whole attention had been on reeling Chalkhill in, not worrying about the consequences. 'Do *you?*'

'Not much,' Hairstreak said. 'He was a good enough spy, but he puts his own interests first. When I employed him, he was too frightened of me to set a foot out of line – and besides, I had the manpower then to keep an eye on him. I'm not sure that's the case any more.'

'He looked frightened enough when he saw you in the Lodge Room.' Brimstone shrugged.

Hairstreak gave an inward, wicked smile. 'Not the way he used to be. Not the way he *should* be. Not to the very depths of his *soul.*' His eyes swung round to lock on Brimstone and the smile became more chill. 'A lot of people make that mistake these days. They think because I backed the wrong horse in the Civil War, I'm no longer a force to be reckoned with.'

'Do they?' Brimstone asked drily.

Hairstreak tossed back his drink and set down the glass. 'When the money comes through, I want you to kill him.'

Brimstone stared. Jasper and he went back a long, long time. They'd been on *adventures* together. They'd set up a business together – Chalkhill and Brimstone's Miracle Glue factory had been the foundation of Brimstone's own fortunes at one time and the company would never have been established without Chalkhill's help. Chalkhill, for all his irritating ways, had been a loyal support to Brimstone for more years than he cared to remember. Kill Chalkhill?

'Yes, okay,' said Brimstone.

fourteen

'What's he mean by that?' Nymph asked. She'd materialised in the corridor the minute Henry came out of the sickroom. Now they were seated together in an antechamber, drinking something that tasted like tamarind juice.

'I don't know,' Henry admitted. 'To be honest, I think he's a bit –' He wanted to say Alzheimer's, but didn't think Nymph would know the term, so he circled his finger at the side of his forehead instead. But even while he was making the gesture, he wasn't all that sure. Mr Fogarty's talk about caterpillars sounded cuckoo, but what he said afterwards seemed sensible enough.

'But he's definitely going to come back with you?' Nymph pressed. 'Back to the Analogue World?'

'Oh yes,' Henry said, aware he still sounded surprised. The minute he'd repeated the suggestion, Mr Fogarty agreed like a lamb. Nymph had set arrangements in motion and now they were both going over the conversation in detail while they waited for things to happen. The trouble was the conversation didn't make a lot of sense. What made even less sense was why Mr Fogarty had insisted on seeing Henry in the first place. If he'd decided to come home and wait for a cure, he certainly didn't need Henry to hold his hand. It would have been easier and a whole lot safer for him to use a portal when he first became ill. And if he'd still wanted to see Henry for whatever reason, all it would have taken then was a phone call.

'What else did he say?' Nymph asked. 'After the butterfly business and the bit about finding the magic?'

'Not much,' Henry told her. 'He said I was the only one who could do it and I said he had to come back to the Analogue World before he had another bout of fever because another bout of fever would probably kill him and he said yes, all right. So I thought I'd better get it organised before he changed his mind.' He grinned at her, a bit pleased with himself.

Nymph grinned back. 'We knew you could do it, Henry. Pyrgus said you could, and I knew you could as well. Everything's going to be all right now.'

'Yes,' Henry agreed. 'Everything's going to be all right.'

Fifteen

Henry stared. It was the first time he'd seen the Palace portal and he was mightily impressed. The equipment was in a temple, for one thing. He was looking up at a raging blue fire that flared between twin pillars before an altar. The technicians who serviced it were dressed as priests. Henry vaguely remembered Pyrgus telling him the whole concept of moving between worlds had once been a religious experience in the Realm. It still was, by the look of things.

'I normally use just a little portable translator,' Henry said to Chief Portal Engineer Peacock, who'd escorted them to the temple. The devices, ironically, had been Mr Fogarty's invention.

Peacock sniffed dismissively. 'They're a bit of a fashion accessory these days,' he said in a tone that left no doubt about what he thought of *that* nonsense. 'Never trusted them myself.' His face took on a different expression altogether as he followed Henry's eyes to the blue flame and added proudly, '*This* has been going for centuries.' He laid a hand fondly on the obsidian casing of the controls.

'What do we do?' Henry asked. 'Just walk into the fire?' He was fairly sure that was what they were supposed to do, although he didn't fancy the thought now he was actually looking at it.

'One at a time,' Peacock said. 'You first, since you know the Analogue World. Then Gatekeeper Fogarty when he gets here. And then Princess Nymph. That way, you can make sure he's all right as he comes through, sir, and the Princess will be bringing up the rear. I understand Prince Pyrgus will be waiting too. It all takes just a second or so.'

And it would all happen in a minute, Henry thought with painfully mixed feelings. He'd been dreading meeting up with Blue on this trip and now he was going home again without so much as a glimpse of her. Relief mingled with regret and even a surge of resentment. Even though he didn't want to meet her, he didn't want her to ignore him either. Actually being ignored was the worst thing of all. 'I wonder what's keeping Mr Fogarty?' he said to no one in particular.

'They may have to carry him,' Nymph said. 'He's terribly frail.'

'Should have come home earlier,' Henry said without much sympathy because he was feeling sorry for himself over Blue. As a distraction, he turned back to Chief Portal Engineer Peacock. 'Could you explain to me how it works?' he asked.

A huge smile crossed Peacock's face. 'Well, sir, I –' He stopped. There was an immediate change of atmosphere in the temple and a sudden silence. Peacock was looking at something over Henry's shoulder. Henry turned.

Blue was standing in the doorway. There was a tall, slim, very handsome young man by her side.

Henry couldn't take his eyes off her. She was ... she was ... He took a deep breath. Blue had grown a little, unless it was his imagination, perhaps lost a few pounds. And she'd let her hair grow. It was no longer the short, boyish cut he remembered. Now it cascaded to her shoulders. *She was utterly, totally gorgeous!*

He wondered who the man was with her.

She walked differently as well. Not affected, but confident, very upright, sort of … regal. As she moved into the room, the priests bowed deeply to her, like a wave. Henry watched her, mouth open, as she approached, wondering if he should bow too, but unwilling to stop looking at her. He had never seen anything so beautiful in his life.

She'd seen him, but she wasn't smiling.

'Hello, Blue,' said Henry, his heart pounding.

'Oh, Henry, I'm so sorry!' Blue said, and threw her arms around his neck.

Sixteen

She smelled of musk and jasmine and for a moment he was lost to everything but the scent of her skin and the scent of her hair. His heart was thumping so wildly now he was certain she must hear it. He wanted to hold her and kiss her on the mouth. He wanted to –

She was crying! He could feel her tears on his cheek and suddenly the world came rushing in and he relaxed his arms and stepped away. He raised his head and was looking into the eyes of the handsome young man, who looked back at him without expression.

Henry's mind began to function again. *So sorry?* So sorry about what? What had Blue got to be sorry about? He was the one who ...

Still looking into the eyes of the young man, Henry suddenly knew, beyond doubt, that this was Blue's new love. *Oh Henry, I'm so sorry.* So sorry I took you at your word. So sorry I didn't wait. So sorry I found somebody else. *So sorry we're to be married?*

'Blue ...' Henry croaked, then stopped. What was he going to say? You should never have listened when I turned you down?

'I know you came as soon as you could,' Blue said.

The young man, his eyes still on Henry's, said inconsequentially, 'You don't know who I am, do you?'

Henry said, 'No.' His voice was small.

The young man gave a brief, bleak smile. 'Comma,' he said shortly.

'Comma,' Henry echoed. *Comma?* Blue's peculiar, sneaky, chubby little brother? 'Comma?' It couldn't be Comma. Nobody could change that much, even in two years. But now the name had been spoken Henry realised the young man had Comma's eyes and the turn of Comma's jaw. It was incredible.

Comma nodded. His face was sober. He had a well-modulated voice and an air of sophistication Henry couldn't match. 'I'm sorry we meet again in such dreadful circumstances,' he said.

But really Henry couldn't take his eyes off Blue. Why had he ever let her go? What was there in his life now that came even close to ...? He gazed at her adoringly, vaguely aware he must look like a puppy, and felt a rising excitement that came out of nowhere. *Maybe it isn't too late!*

Blue said, 'What will you do now?'

Henry stared at her, not really knowing what she was talking about, not really caring. He allowed himself to smile a little. 'What?' he asked.

Then he watched it happen in a sort of ghastly slow motion. Blue's tears dried and a look of horror crawled across her face. Her eyes grew wide. 'No one's told you!' she said. She glanced around with growing anger. But the faces that looked back were just as puzzled as Henry's own. 'No one's told you,' she said again, not angrily this time, but quietly, with shock. She looked him in the eye, her face a wooden mask.

'Henry, Mr Fogarty is dead,' she said.

Seventeen

'My guess is they plan to kill you once the money is paid over,' Madame Cardui said calmly.

They were in a standard Security Chamber, a purposeful confusion of hanging drapes and full-length mirrors that reflected her cloaked and hooded figure scores of times. Chalkhill shivered. He had a feeling she might be right, but that didn't mean he wanted to face up to it. 'I'm sure my old partner will protect me,' he said without much conviction. *And if he doesn't, you will, you old hag,* he thought. *You're the one who got me into this.*

Madame Cardui snorted. 'Silas Brimstone? He would sell his own mother for sixpence. No, I'm afraid your only hope is to expose the Brotherhood before they move against you.'

The trouble with a Security Chamber was you never knew where to look. Which was the whole point, of course. All the reflections duplicated the person you were talking to and the curtains deflected their voice so you couldn't even follow the sound. It means assassins didn't quite know what to attack, but it was hael trying to carry out a sensible conversation. He selected a reflection of Madame Cardui at random and wailed at it, 'But that only gives me to the end of the week!'

'Can't you ask your bank to slow the transfer?'

'I've already done that,' Chalkhill told her. 'Standard clearance is seventy-two hours. They've pushed it back to six days – a working week. But they won't go any further. They say more delay would ruin their reputation.'

'Such a shame,' said Madame Cardui.

The deep hood meant he couldn't see her face, but he sensed she was smiling and felt a sudden chill. She'd sounded so plausible when she first approached him and frankly her proposition had appealed hugely. But there'd been no talk of killing then and especially no talk of killing *him*. He began to suspect the old witch had a hidden agenda. All the same, he felt compelled to venture, 'Can't *you* do anything?'

'My deeah, I would if I could – you know that. But I can't. My hands are tied. We're all supposed to be *friends* with those ghastly Faeries of the Night these days.'

Chalkhill was a ghastly Faerie of the Night himself, but he let it go. For better or worse, Madame Cardui was his paymaster now. However tricky she proved, she couldn't be more dangerous than Hairstreak and he'd survived for years as Hairstreak's spy. Besides, he knew that whatever she said, she wasn't likely to let him be murdered while he remained a valuable asset. At the moment, he was the only asset she had. No one else had managed to infiltrate the Brotherhood.

He decided the talk of death was just meant to put pressure on him, hurry him up a little, as if he hadn't enough motivation already. Darkness knew Hairstreak had played the same game often enough. To move things along – perhaps even take control of the situation – he asked, 'Any new intelligence?'

A hundred hooded heads shook negatively. 'Only confirmation of what we already know. The Brotherhood is up to something.' There was just the barest hesitation before she asked, 'Did *you* find out anything else, Mr Chalkhill?'

For a moment he debated keeping it to himself, then decided against it. This early in the game he needed to ingratiate himself with Madame Cardui, reassure her he was loyal. Besides, what he *had* learned was little enough and of doubtful importance. 'Hairstreak looked taken aback when I asked to speak to God,' he said.

'Ah,' said Madame Cardui, as if he'd told her something interesting. 'How did he respond?'

'Brushed it off as a joke. "I'm the only God you'll find round here" or some such. But I'm sure I rattled him.'

'And your analysis?'

Chalkhill opened his mouth and closed it again. Hairstreak had never asked for his analysis of anything in the old days. Madame Cardui was obviously a very different sort of spymaster. His eyes flickered from one reflection to another. The fact was he didn't *have* much of an analysis. Everything he'd done so far had been prompted by greed and gut instinct. Plus some loose tavern talk. He doubted the Painted Lady would be impressed by *that*. 'Well, it's obviously a code-name ...'

'Yes, of course,' Madame Cardui cut in impatiently. 'But what does it stand for? A person? Some important ally? Another country, perhaps? Or does it simply stand for whatever it is they're scheming about – the name of their current *project?*'

How am I supposed to know, you stupid old sow? Chalkhill thought. Aloud he said, 'I don't think that's important. I –'

'It most certainly is, Mr Chalkhill,' Madame Cardui cut in again. 'In my experience, people are often foolish enough to choose code-names that hint at exactly the thing they're trying to conceal. For example, if 'God' refers to a person, we might infer someone in authority, someone with power. Whereas if 'God' is the code-name for a project, we may be forgiven for assuming it was a grandiose project, something far-reaching and all-consuming.' Her voice took on a steely edge. 'Like a plot to overthrow the legitimate ruler of the Realm.'

Chalkhill jumped as if stung. He'd been thinking much the same thing himself, which was why he was so interested in what Brimstone was up to. By playing both ends against the middle, he hoped to ensure himself a high position in the new order if the Brotherhood plot succeeded, or ingratiate himself with the old order if it failed. The trouble was he didn't *know* what Brimstone was up to. He didn't even know where Brimstone *lived,* although he hoped to remedy that soon. 'Oh, I'm sure it's nothing like that, Madame Cardui,' he said smarmily. Because whether it was or whether it wasn't, it was better if *he* found out first. Cardui was too suspicious for her own good. He didn't want her poking into things on her own account, oh no.

'Why not?' Cardui asked sharply. 'Lord Hairstreak has tried that sort of thing before. Have you not heard the Analogue expression about a leopard and its spots?'

Chalkhill wasn't big on Analogue expressions, but caught her drift easily enough. 'Ah yes, Painted Lady, but that was Lord Hairstreak acting on his own account, acting *politically,* you might say. What we are dealing with now is the Brotherhood, which is, I suppose you might call it, a *religious* organisation, of which

Lord Hairstreak just happens to be temporary head. Times have changed, as you mentioned yourself just a moment ago, and one may well act as a brake on the other.' He realised he was making no sense at all, even as he said it, but hoped it might muddy the waters enough to divert her paranoia.

It didn't work. 'You would call the Brotherhood a *religious* organisation?' Madame Cardui asked incredulously.

'Wouldn't you?' asked Chalkhill innocently.

'Not entirely,' Madame Cardui told him. 'I think of it more as –' She stopped as something flashed orange in the mirrors.

Chalkhill drew back with instinctive loathing. Every mirror now showed a dwarf crouched at the Painted Lady's ear. Chalkhill recognised it immediately, of course – that hideous creature Kitterick, with the toxic teeth. He shivered.

Madame Cardui stood up abruptly. 'I am required elsewhere,' she said without preliminary. 'Report to me directly when you have more information, Mr Chalkhill.' Then she was gone.

With a whisper of hidden machinery, the mirrors changed position, leaving Chalkhill to stare woodenly at his own reflections.

Eighteen

Brimstone still wore his demonologist's shawl when weather permitted. The horned symbol kept people at a distance – that or his body odour – even though the demons were tamed now. It suggested, he often thought philosophically, that once people were conditioned to a particular response, most of them were too lazy to rid themselves of it when it was no longer necessary.

He was wearing the shawl now. It permitted him to move unmolested through one of the roughest districts of the docks, a favourite ploy when he wanted to avoid being followed. The ruffians might leave *him* alone, but anyone who tried to follow risked their gold, their limbs and possibly their life. Not that there were many ruffians about at the moment. They seemed to be just as nervous of the plague as everybody else. All the same, he didn't *think* he was being followed.

In fact he was sure of it. Brimstone stepped to the river's edge and flagged down a passing water-taxi. The driver pulled in warily. 'Where to, Guv?'

'Mount Pleasant,' Brimstone told him loudly, which was nowhere near where he wanted to go, but he could change the destination once he was aboard. Meanwhile, anyone who *might* be listening would be sent off in the wrong direction. Couldn't be too careful, even with the streets half empty. He made to step on the boat.

'Got your cert?' asked the driver.

Brimstone glared at him. 'Cert?'

'Your chitty, Guv. Signed by a healer. Certifying you're disease-free.'

For a minute Brimstone didn't believe it. He ratcheted the glare up a notch. 'What are you talking about, you cretin?'

'Can't get on a public vehicle without your cert,' the cabbie explained patiently. 'New regulation. Proposed by the Mayor, passed by the Queen, God bless her.'

'When did this happen?' Brimstone asked, appalled. Every time he turned around, that royal trollop enacted something else that took away your freedom. No bear-baiting, no cock fights, no duels. You weren't even allowed to poison someone in a vendetta any more. Now it was freedom of movement.

'Hour ago,' the driver told him.

'An *hour* ago?' Brimstone repeated. 'With no public announcement?'

The driver shook his head. 'Oh, there's been a public announcement all right, Guv. They posted a notice on the door of the cathedral.'

'And how,' asked Brimstone sarcastically, 'do they expect somebody to arrange for a healer's certificate *if he's a Faerie of the Night who isn't allowed into the Lighter cathedral?*'

'Dreadful, ain't it?' agreed the cabbie sympathetically. 'All the same, sir, that's the law. I don't make it, but I can't break it, as the saying goes. I'm only following orders. I just work here. I'm not paid to think.'

'Double fare?' Brimstone suggested.

'Hop in, Guv.'

Brimstone climbed into the boat. It was nice to know some things hadn't changed.

He settled himself into the rear of the cab and pulled across the tattered sunshade. Not that there was any sun, but it protected him from prying eyes. The cabbie struck a spell cone, which spluttered for a moment, then flared into life. 'Mount Pleasant, was it, Guv? The posh end, I suppose?'

'Whitewell,' Brimstone told him shortly. 'The one past Cripple's Gate.'

'Could have sworn you said Mount Pleasant,' the cabbie muttered. 'I must be getting senile.'

Brimstone closed his eyes as the boat began to gather momentum. Queen Blue's latest law was disturbing as well as inconvenient. Any imbecile could see it would be wildly unpopular, especially with those who didn't have Brimstone's access to funds for bribes. The Queen was answerable to nobody, but the Mayor was running for re-election next year. The fact he'd proposed it showed how bad the time plague had become.

If he wasn't careful, it would be completely out of control before he could exploit it properly.

Brimstone opened his eyes and leaned forward. 'There's an extra seven groats for you if you ignore the speed limit,' he told the cabbie.

Nineteen

Henry breathed a sigh of relief. It was a mistake. (It was a really *stupid* mistake, made by a really stupid nurse.) He looked across the room to where Mr Fogarty lay asleep on the bed, looking just the way he had when Henry left him. Somebody had taken that horrid tube out of his back, which probably meant he didn't need it any more, which was more good news.

'He's just sleeping,' Henry told Blue.

'Henry ...' Blue said.

'No, really,' Henry told her. 'He always sleeps like that. On his back. I mean, he was sleeping like that when I left him. It's just that you can't see his breathing. Lots of people would make the same mistake: he breathes very shallowly when he's sleeping.'

'Henry ...' Blue said again.

'No, really,' Henry repeated with a little smile. 'Look, I'll show you.' He strode across the room. 'Mr Fogarty,' he said brightly. 'Wake up, Mr Fogarty.' The old boy would be cross about losing his beauty sleep, but at least that was better than this nonsense about his being dead. It had everybody running around like headless chickens.

Mr Fogarty did not move.

'Henry ...' Blue said.

Henry reached down and shook Mr Fogarty's shoulder. The old man's head rolled loosely to one side and his eyes remained closed. Blue appeared beside Henry and gripped his arm. 'He's dead, Henry,' she said gently.

Henry turned to look at her, his eyes desolate. 'He can't be dead. I was talking to him just a few minutes ago.' He turned back and seized Mr Fogarty's wrist, feeling for a pulse. There was none.

Blue said, 'I think we should leave him now, Henry. The priests will look after him from here.'

Henry stared at her. 'Priests?'

'They cast a spell to open his mouth.'

'Why would they want to do that?'

'To release his soul.' Blue tugged his arm. 'Come on, Henry. We should leave them to do their work.'

Although he hadn't seen them enter, the room was filled with wizards in their ceremonial robes. Some had Trinian servants carrying rosaries, thuribles and other religious equipment.

'He's not from your world,' Henry said. He couldn't think straight, but somehow it felt wrong that Mr Fogarty should have his mouth opened by a spell. Surely he should be in a proper coffin, ready to be buried in a proper grave? It occurred to Henry he didn't know Mr Fogarty's religion, or if he even had one. But people who were dead should go to the nearest Church of England, where the vicar would conduct a service and say nice things about them –

He was a bank robber, but everybody loved him, said an imaginary vicar inside Henry's head.

– and then when everybody had paid their respects, they were carried to the churchyard and …

Henry discovered there were tears streaming down

his face even though he didn't feel all that sad. He didn't feel anything really, except perhaps numb.

'He wanted our funeral rites,' Blue said. 'We discussed it days ago.'

That was before I came, Henry thought inconsequentially. *That was before I even knew.*

The room was swimming behind a veil of tears, so he allowed Blue to lead him out into the corridor and down the Palace stairs.

Twenty

It was like his very first visit to the Realm when he'd ended up in the Palace kitchens, fussed over by matronly women. Now Blue brought him here again and sat him at a scrubbed pine table amidst the bustle and the cooking smells. Someone plump in an apron brought them steaming mugs of what turned out to be tea – a kind thought because tea was expensive in the Realm, but they all knew where he came from and wanted to make him feel at home.

Henry stared down into the amber liquid – they didn't know about adding milk here – and watched ripples spread across its surface as a teardrop struck it. For some reason he couldn't stop crying, even though it was unmanly and embarrassing.

Blue sat on the bench beside him, so close that her thigh touched his. She curled her hands around her own mug as if to warm them. She had very long, slender fingers. He loved her fingers. She seemed more feminine than he remembered, probably because of the dress. He loved her dress.

'What are you going to do?' Blue asked softly.

Henry looked at a point somewhere beyond her shoulder. He should write and tell Mr Fogarty's daughter that Mr Fogarty was dead, except Mr Fogarty's daughter already *believed* Mr Fogarty was dead because Henry had lied to her on Mr Fogarty's instructions. So he couldn't write to her now. But he would have to go back and tell Hodge. Hodge would want to know.

Henry's body began shaking uncontrollably and he felt Blue's arm around his shoulders. 'Hush,' she said into his ear. 'It's all right, Henry. It's all right.'

But it wasn't all right. Everything had changed. Everything had ... stopped.

'I think I'd better go home,' Henry said.

'Will you stay for his funeral?'

He turned his head slightly and focused on her face. After a moment he said, 'Yes. Yes, I should stay for the funeral, shouldn't I?'

'He would have liked that.'

They stared into their mugs together, but neither of them drank.

'It will be a proper funeral,' Blue said. 'A State funeral, with full honours. He was our Gatekeeper.'

It didn't make any difference. Mr Fogarty had always been impatient with ceremony, but he was dead now so it wouldn't matter to him what they did. But to please Blue, Henry said, 'That's good. That's very good.'

'I'll have your old room made up,' Blue said.

Pyrgus didn't know. He would have to go back and tell Pyrgus. 'I have to go back and tell Pyrgus,' he said.

'It's all right,' Blue said. 'We've sent Nymph already.'

That was the right thing to do. Nymph was Pyrgus's wife now. He wondered if Pyrgus would come back for the funeral and risk another bout of time fever. 'When will it be?'

'The funeral? In three days.'

The same as funerals at home, he thought.

'Henry?' Blue said. 'After the funeral … Will you go home straightaway?'

Everything had changed, but nothing had changed. He didn't want to go home. He was miserable at home, had been for the past two years. He didn't want to live with his mother any more, didn't want to go to university and then teach in some mouldy old school until he died. But somehow he had to. There simply wasn't any choice. He looked at Blue and nodded. 'Yes, I think that would be best. I'll go home straightaway.'

'I'm afraid that won't be possible, deeah,' said a familiar voice behind him.

Twenty-One

The house was a small Tudor mansion surrounded by trees and set in its own grounds. The estate agent claimed it had once belonged to Queen Elizabeth the First, although she'd never actually stayed there. (Pyrgus looked her up after he bought the place and discovered she was quite a famous Analogue World monarch.) It was private, comfortable, a little gloomy and equipped with an astonishing number of vanity mirrors. He kept catching sight of himself unawares and thinking he was looking at his father. It was a weird feeling.

He tore his attention away with an effort. 'So it's happened?' he said.

Nymph nodded. 'Yes.'

He'd noticed a difference in her since the fever aged him. It was a subtle thing, but definitely there. She was more sober when they were together. She seldom teased him any more. It was almost as if she was treating him ... with deference. He knew where it was coming from, of course. When she looked at him, she saw exactly what he saw in the mirror – a middle-aged man. That couldn't be easy for her, however much she loved him. The time plague had to be stopped soon and not just for the sake of the Realm. If they couldn't call a halt to it, their marriage was at risk.

'Henry was there?' he asked.

Nymph nodded again. 'Yes.'

'In the room?'

'Yes,' Nymph said soberly. 'Henry didn't realise Mr Fogarty was dead – he thought he'd just fallen asleep.'

'Which explains why he never told anybody.'

'And why he was so shocked when Blue told *him*,' Nymph agreed.

'He was preparing to take Mr Fogarty home?'

'Waiting beside the Palace portal, exactly the way it was prophesied,' Nymph said.

'But *he* thought he was taking back a *living* Gate-keeper!' Pyrgus exclaimed with budding understanding. 'Not just the body, as we assumed.'

'Exactly,' Nymph said.

The window of their living-room looked out across a sweeping lawn bordered in the distance by a line of trees. A peacock strode across the grass, bobbing its head. Peacocks were magnificent birds, found only in the Analogue World now they'd become extinct in the Faerie Realm. This one had come with the house, the property of the previous owner who was too soft-hearted to move it from its old home. At dusk it gave eerie calls. Pyrgus thought it might be looking for its wife, who'd died just before the house changed hands.

'Blue still doesn't know?' he asked.

'No.'

'Do you think she suspects?' Pyrgus knew his sister very well. The slightest suspicion and she'd be on it like a terrier.

'I doubt it,' Nymph said. 'I don't see how she can. Now that Mr Fogarty is dead, you and I and Madame Cardui are the only ones who know.'

'Blue's smart,' Pyrgus said. 'We should never underestimate her.' All the same, he was reassured. He watched the peacock wander off, then asked, 'Is Henry very upset?'

'Terribly,' Nymph said. 'I felt so sorry for him. I desperately wanted to tell him.'

Pyrgus glanced round at her. 'But you didn't?'

'Of course not.'

'Good,' Pyrgus said.

After a moment Nymph stood up and walked across to join him at the window. 'Were you watching the peacock?'

'Yes.' Pyrgus nodded. 'I think he misses his mate.'

Nymph said, 'Are you going back to the Realm?'

Pyrgus said, a little bleakly, 'Yes.'

'You don't have to, you know.'

'Yes, I do,' Pyrgus told her.

Nymph licked her lips. 'It's dangerous. It's very dangerous.'

'I know.'

'For everybody.'

'I know.'

'I'll go with you,' Nymph said.

'Yes,' said Pyrgus.

Twenty-two

It was peculiar: they kept off the streets, but congregated in the taverns, as if a stomach full of ale would protect them from the fever. The man sitting opposite Chalkhill had a lot of stomach and a lot of ale. His breath smelled like a brewery.

'Are you sure it was him?' Chalkhill asked.

'Skinny little runt, looks a thousand years old, wears a demonologist's shawl? Sounds like the description you put about, Mr Chalkhill.'

It was a very rough area and a very rough tavern. Chalkhill was aware his expensive clothing made him stand out like a jester at a funeral. But nobody took your money seriously unless you looked the part. Besides which, he was armed to the teeth.

'So where did he go?' he asked his informant.

The big man stared at him silently.

'Oh, all right,' Chalkhill exclaimed. Since he'd gone back to his camp act, he sighed explosively and added, 'Whatever happened to trust, I wonder?' He produced a small bag of coin and tossed it on the table. Conversations at the neighbouring tables stopped at once.

The big man's big hand swallowed up the bag and the conversations started up again. 'Mount Pleasant,' he said.

Chalkhill frowned. 'Mount Pleasant?' It was among

the wealthiest districts of the city, not one of Brimstone's old haunts at all.

'That's what he said,' the big man confirmed, with an expression that suggested he wasn't going to give back the coins.

Well, perhaps Silas had come up in the world. Or perhaps Hairstreak was funding him. His Turdship may have fallen on hard times, but Hairstreak wouldn't be Hairstreak if he didn't have a little something stashed away. Or perhaps the Brotherhood had taken up a collection. Or perhaps Brimstone was just visiting a rich relative.

What did it matter? If Brimstone was headed for Mount Pleasant, that's where Chalkhill had to go. The old hag had made it clear she wanted results and she wasn't noted for her patience. Not that he was inclined to hang about himself.

Chalkhill felt more exposed on the waterfront than he had in the tavern and stood nervously while three water-taxis sailed right past ignoring his shouts and waves. But the fourth mercifully pulled in.

'Mount Pleasant,' he exclaimed grandly as he stepped aboard.

'Double fare without your chitty,' the driver told him conversationally.

Chalkhill had no idea what he was talking about, but he was well used to rip-offs. He drew a stimulus from his concealed armoury and pointed it at the man's head.

'Perhaps on second thoughts ...' the cabbie said. He took a spell cone from his bag and cracked it. 'You sure you want Mount Pleasant, Guv?'

Chalkhill put the stimulus away. 'Of course I'm sure. Do I look like a ... like a ... like an unsure person?'

'Not even slightly, sir,' the cabbie said. 'It's just that I had an old boy an hour or so ago told me Mount Pleasant and when he got in, he didn't want to go there at all.'

Chalkhill blinked. 'How old?' he asked.

'How old what, sir? The old boy? Very old, sir. Mind you, he looked like a retired demonologist to me – still wore the shawl. That sort of thing ages you, I always say.'

'Where did he really want to go to?' Chalkhill asked.

'Whitewell. Remember it clearly 'cause it didn't sound at all like Mount Pleasant.'

'Which Whitewell?' There were two in the city, one north, the other to the west.

'The one past Cripple's Gate. Now, sir –' The cabbie actually managed a fake smile. 'It's Mount Pleasant for you, sir. Nothing *unsure* about that, eh?'

'Take me to Whitewell,' Chalkhill growled. 'The one past Cripple's Gate.'

twenty-three

There was a moment of confusion, then Henry opened his eyes to darkness. He couldn't remember where he was, or how he got here. He couldn't even remember where he'd been. There was something about coming to the Faerie Realm with Nymph, then ... then ...

No, it was gone. He knew he'd been doing *something* in the Realm, but for the life of him he couldn't remember what. Every time he tried, it was as if his mind went soggy and a white fog swirled across his memory.

The darkness was absolute.

He was on his knees, on a hard floor. He shouldn't be on his knees (which hurt quite a lot now he thought of them). Surely he should be standing up? Surely he was standing up – or maybe sitting down, but certainly not on his *knees* – before he ... before he ...? Where the hell *was* he?

You didn't often get darkness like this. In the dead of night there was always starlight or moonlight or reflections from street lights. Even in a curtained room, some light filtered through. But there was no light here at all. He thought he might be underground.

There was a dry smell of decay.

Still on his knees, Henry began to feel afraid. 'Hello ...?' he whispered.

He felt the floor with one hand. It was hard, like rock, flat with a sandstone texture. It was cool, but not exactly cold, and dusty. The dust rose to catch in his throat and make him cough. For some reason he tried to suppress the cough, keep it as quiet as possible. So the cough turned into a little cough, hardly more than a clearing of the throat. He shouldn't have said *Hello,* not even in whisper, not when he didn't know where he was or who might be close by. He was in the Realm now and the Realm was different from his own world. The Realm was a lot more dangerous.

Henry climbed cautiously to his feet, very much aware of the thumping of his heart. He swallowed hard to get rid of the dust. Without moving from the spot, he reached out cautiously in front of him. His hands touched ... nothing. He reached behind him with the same result.

The air was quite stuffy, as if he was in an enclosed space. He stretched out one foot. The floor in front of him seemed solid enough, but he really didn't fancy walking forward in the darkness. He might be near the edge of a cliff or a pit or a crevasse.

What he needed – badly – was light.

He was still wearing his own clothes, the ones he'd been wearing when Pyrgus and Nymph turned up at Mr Fogarty's house. (Pyrgus had looked old, Henry remembered, but couldn't remember why.) Henry began to fish in his trouser pocket. Almost at once, with a surge of delighted relief, he found a Bic lighter.

And promptly dropped it on the floor.

He heard the little disposable strike the ground and skitter. Henry dropped to his knees again. It didn't sound as if the lighter had dropped into a pit, but he was taking no chances. Besides which, his only chance of finding it again was to sweep the floor carefully with his hands. Which he did, disturbing more dust. He crawled forward slowly, on his knees, sweeping carefully, cautiously, a little at a time.

Something moved and he snatched his hand away, then froze. After a moment the renewed thumping of his heart died down a little. Whatever moved was really small, probably just a cockroach. Henry didn't much like cockroaches, but at least they didn't do you any harm. Unless, of course, it wasn't a cockroach, but something poisonous, like a scorpion or a – But he forced himself to put a rein on his imagination. The lighter was his only hope. He couldn't stop looking for it now.

He leaned forward and resumed the sweeping movement with his hands.

His left hand struck something hard. He felt along cautiously and came to the conclusion it might be a wall, but couldn't make up his mind whether it was a natural structure or man-made. He might be in a cave. (How had he *got* here?) But he might equally well be in some sort of enclosed chamber.

Something rustled drily a little way in front and to his right.

Henry froze again, holding his breath. Every sound was magnified in darkness, he reminded himself. It might be no more than a mouse. But somehow, he didn't think it was a mouse. *He needed light!*

He found the Bic!

He couldn't believe it, but his right hand, the one furthest from the wall, closed around it so tightly he half wondered that the plastic didn't crack. He scrambled to his feet at once and flicked the wheel. A tiny flame flared, then died at once. The damn lighter had run out of fuel! He remembered now – he'd meant to buy a new one.

There was something white and naked crouching no more than ten feet away from him.

Henry's mind began to work at lightning speed. Of course there was really nothing there. It was purely his imagination working overtime. That's what imagination did when you were in the dark. And if there *was* something near him, it wasn't living. It was some sort of statue, maybe a gargoyle, something ugly like that because what he'd seen – what he'd *thought* he'd seen – was too ugly to be real. So it was nothing, nothing to worry about. Just a statue or a gargoyle or nothing at all, a lump of rock.

While his mind was working, his thumb took on a life of its own and flicked the little wheel again and again. There was no more gas in the lighter, but it sparked bravely: sparked and sparked and it was so dark that even that small light, the light from the sparks, was enough to let him see the *thing* that hurled itself towards him.

twenty-four

As soon as Chalkhill set eyes on the place, he knew he'd struck gold. Brimstone usually favoured pokey, unobtrusive lodgings, but the Whitewell house was very different: a large, old waterfront property with the overhanging balconies that were fashionable five hundred years ago. It looked dilapidated to the casual eye, but Chalkhill's eye was far from casual. He could almost *smell* the spell coatings, cunningly disguised but lavishly applied, that turned the place into a fortress. That sort of security cost a fortune and Brimstone was notoriously careful with money. There had to be something of importance hidden in there.

Whitewell itself was one of those districts that had seen better days. Many of the fine old buildings had been turned into tenements. One of them, almost directly behind Brimstone's new home, overlooked both its river access and the street. The toothless old crone who lived there accepted Chalkhill's coin with alacrity, offered him services in which he had no interest, then vacated the premises with an assurance that she would not be back from the tavern before midnight.

Chalkhill pulled a chair to the grubby window, fanned away a lingering odour of flatulence, and settled down to wait.

Brimstone emerged as it was growing dark.

Chalkhill drew back a little from the window, although it was hugely unlikely that Brimstone would look up. He watched as the old man scuttled down the narrow street and disappeared around a corner. Chalkhill waited fully five minutes to see if he would return, then decided the chances were Brimstone was headed for a café or a tavern to find himself something to eat. He was as frugal with his meals as he was with his money, but all the same, it would probably be at least an hour before he came back, and it might even be two. Chalkhill waited another few moments, just to be certain, then left the tenement.

There were too many people about to allow a leisurely inspection of the front door, but fortunately a narrow archway led round to the river walk at the rear of the house and there he found no people at all. He had some small chance of being seen from the balconies of neighbouring houses, but it was well worth taking, especially as it was growing darker by the minute.

Close up, his suspicions about spell coatings proved correct. But the interesting thing was they were so subtle. Most security wizards recommended coatings should be obvious to passersby, to act as a deterrent. Heaven only knew what Brimstone's coatings were designed to do, but they were virtually invisible.

Chalkhill stood for a moment wondering if he had the nerve to test the spell. It was unlikely to be lethal force – that sort of enchantment announced itself in heaps of dead birds and rodents at the foot of the wall – but, knowing Brimstone, it was likely to be nasty. But he had to get past Brimstone's securities if he was to gain entry to the house.

He stood for a moment longer, considering. Short of lethal force, the most popular securities were *lethes* and mind-benders. Any prospective burglar hit with a *lethe* promptly forgot what he'd planned to do and wandered off. Mind-benders were less specific. Some regressed you to childhood, so you pooed in your pants, some compelled you to sing loudly until the Guard arrived, some simply knocked you unconscious and left you that way until you were discovered, tried and hanged. None of them was pleasant, but even if he was found unconscious with poo in his pants, he reckoned he could simply claim he'd come to visit an old friend and triggered the spell accidentally. Brimstone might even believe it.

Chalkhill pushed through the coating to test the catch on the nearest window.

He was halfway along the street before he realised what he was doing. The house – Brimstone's house, that he'd searched for so long – seemed drab and uninteresting. Not the sort of place you would want to rob or enter or even look at for very long. It was a nonentity of a house, a bore of a house, a –

It was a mind-bender. But what a spell. So subtle you didn't even realise you'd been bent. Nothing spectacular or embarrassing, just the absolute conviction you should leave Brimstone's house alone and get on your way. This was no standard, off-the-shelf mind-bender. This spell was clearly custom-made – and by a craftsman. Chalkhill felt a surge of excitement. You didn't spend money on a craftsman-wizard unless you were hiding something important.

He spun round, but discovered he was still in thrall. Each step towards Brimstone's home turned his mind to porridge. In less than twenty yards, he could scarcely think at all. He took a deep breath and backed off until his head began to clear.

What now? The spell would wear off eventually, of course, but by then Brimstone might be home again and the opportunity would be lost. It could be a day or more before another one arose. He had an antidote, of course – all spies carried antidotes to mind-benders – but he was loath to use it. Maybe if he approached the house from a different direction . . .

Chalkhill circled the street and approached the house from a different direction. The ploy worked well enough until the house was actually in sight, at which point it was mental porridge time again. His only other option was a river approach, a landing on the Brimstone jetty, but the chances were high that the spell was omnidirectional. Only an idiot would install partial protection and whatever else he might be, Brimstone was no idiot.

It would have to be the antidote. But where to take it? Not in the street, that was for sure. Even though the plague left most streets half empty, there was still a chance that someone might pass by. And not on the river, or even near it. The aftermath was bad enough without the risk of drowning. Eventually he settled on a dark alley. He couldn't think of anywhere better.

The alley smelt of pee and was the sort of place where you were just asking to be mugged. But fear of plague had cleared out all the derelicts, so his only companion was a scrawny tomcat, which eyed him briefly without much interest, then returned to scavenging its dustbin.

Chalkhill pulled the spy-kit from his pocket and extracted the golden vial. It was one of the new fast-acting spray spells and he pushed the nozzle against the pulse in his wrist before he had a chance to lose his nerve. The tomcat glanced round warily as the vial hissed.

'*Yeee-ahhhh!*' Chalkhill howled as the inside of his head exploded. He hurled himself against one wall of the alley, bounced violently and ricocheted into a doorway. The door held, if only just, so that his momentum took him out again and slammed him face down on the cobbles. His foot caught the dustbin. The tomcat spat at him angrily and raced away. Chalkhill climbed to his feet, aching all over with a warm flow of blood dribbling from his nose. He stood for a moment, breathing heavily.

'*Ooooowwwww!*' The second wave hit him. He spun on his axis, flailed his arms and punched in a small, leaded window.

'Bog off – I'm drunk!' a cross voice called out from inside.

Chalkhill hurled himself backwards and sent the dustbin flying. The metallic clatter was unreal. Along the alley lights began to appear in the windows. Plague or no plague, somebody was bound to come out soon. Maybe none of this was such a good idea. Maybe …

'*Waaaaaaaaaahhhhhhh!*' Wave three. 'Yabba-dabba-dabba-dabba-dabba!' Chalkhill chattered. Sparks danced before his eyes. The world spun round and round. He began to hallucinate pink snakes. Sensing his helplessness, a large rat emerged from the shadows to gnaw at his ankle. In a sudden suicidal impulse he ran head down towards the nearest wall.

Then it stopped and so did Chalkhill, mercifully having only grazed the wall. He stood, paining and panting while the hallucinations died away. He was bruised and bleeding and the rat had ripped flesh from his leg.

He just hoped it would be worth it.

Twenty-five

It was worth it! He could actually feel the spell membrane break beneath his hand, but there was no mind-bending whatsoever. In fact he was experiencing exceptional clarity and some increased energy despite the pains throughout his body. His fingers fiddled with the catch, the locks gave way, the window swung back silently and Brimstone's house lay open before him.

Chalkhill climbed through, vowing to lose a little weight. He closed the window carefully, triggered the coatings that left it opaque from the outside, then snapped a light cone.

He was in a nicely proportioned room – these old houses all had nice proportions – but one that was completely empty of furniture or fittings. Brimstone clearly wasn't making full use of the big house. Which wasn't surprising. He always lived frugally. Probably just moved himself into three or four rooms. Except that begged the question of why he needed a big house in the first place, even if it was old and probably cheap.

Chalkhill started to creep forward so he wouldn't make the floorboards creak, then remembered he was alone in the house and strode out of the room.

He was in the main hallway by the front door, which was devoid of furniture as well. There were several doors leading off it. Chalkhill opened two at random.

They led to empty, unfurnished rooms. Two more ... two more empty rooms. In minutes he'd covered the ground floor. All the rooms were empty. There was a kitchen without pots or pans or any cooking equipment whatsoever – the place smelled of dust and looked as if it hadn't been used for more than a century. Strange ...

Brimstone had to be living upstairs. Maybe he'd set himself up a bed-sit. Maybe he used spells for cooking – some men did when they didn't really care about the taste – or maybe he just ate out all the time as he seemed to be doing tonight.

Chalkhill climbed the stairs, his footsteps echoing on the bare floorboards. He reached a landing where a half-open door revealed a bathroom, but that looked as little used as the downstairs kitchen. He went up another flight to the bedroom wing. Chamber after chamber was empty, not so much as a mattress on the floor, not so much as a tattered blanket in a cupboard. The whole place was absolutely, totally deserted. What was going on here?

His light spell was beginning to dim, so he cracked another and leaned against a wall to think. This was definitely the house where the cabby claimed to have taken Brimstone. More to the point, this was the house Chalkhill had seen Brimstone leave at dusk. He *had* to be living here, yet there was no sign of human habitation whatsoever.

Which meant Chalkhill had missed something.

He went back downstairs and double-checked the rooms. All empty, like that stupid kitchen. He was double-checking the kitchen when a small sound behind him caused him to spin round, heart suddenly pumping. There was a familiar figure silhouetted in the doorway.

'What kept you?' Brimstone asked him sourly.

Twenty-Six

For the first time in her long life, Cynthia Cardui felt old. It wasn't just the stiffness in the joints or the little pains that were one's constant companion, it was the way emotions lost their power. One was calm. One was far more logical than one ever was in one's youth. But, as if in horrid compensation, life grew cold.

She stared down at the body of her lover. He had always been a thin man, thin and wiry, but since the life force left him, he looked shrunken, like a dried-out husk. So strange to see him like this and yet feel ... nothing.

The embalmers glided around her like wraiths, sober-faced women who all seemed to have slim hands with long fingers. They had inserted tubes into the major arteries of each thigh and attached them to terrible machines. One pumped out every last drop of his remaining blood, the other pumped in spell-bound *gravistat* to replace it. The gravistat liquid acted to dissolve internal organs while triggering the process of petrification.

They were removing the brain now. (For some reason brains resisted the action of the gravistat.) Since it was important to preserve the skull intact – no cuts were permitted – the embalmers inserted an iron hook and expertly drew it out through the nose.

Cynthia watched as the glistening lump of greyness dropped into a jar. Strange to think of all the prejudice and wisdom it had once contained; and all the love. By faerie custom, it was treated with little deference. She knew that when she left, it would be minced and laid out on a rock behind the palace to feed the birds.

The gravistat itself was beginning to drain out now. The embalmers were used to the smell, but Cynthia took a step backwards. In itself, the liquid was odourless, but once mixed with liquefied intestines, the stench was extreme. From somewhere behind her, a priest-wizard began a sonorous chant.

Had she and Alan done the right thing? The question was almost irrelevant. They had done the *only* thing. The tragedy was how much their actions had cost. But how bravely he had borne it. He had always been much more determined than she was, much less concerned with the personal consequences.

Such consequences …

She doubted she would ever take another lover, not at the age she'd reached now. She had no children and her profession meant she had few friends. (And was about to lose the most important of them, in all probability.) In such circumstances, she was likely to die alone. But at least Alan had not. She had been with him through the worst of his illness and poor dear Henry had been with him at the end. All exactly according to plan.

She realised suddenly someone was speaking to her and turned to find the Chief Embalmer by her side. 'I'm sorry – my mind was elsewhere.'

'The pose, Painted Lady?' the woman asked her. She wore the expression of professional sympathy that was an embalmer's stock-in-trade.

Cynthia looked at her blankly. 'What are you asking me?'

'For the memorial,' the woman prompted. 'I understood you wished to select the pose.'

Ah, the memorial! She fancied Alan himself would have found this aspect of his death quite entertaining. What pose should be selected? Should he lunge forward with an upraised sword, like so many military heroes? Should he clutch a book or a scroll to emphasise his wisdom? She could almost hear him snort derisively at any of the classic postures.

All the same, she would have to choose something. He was Gatekeeper of the Realm, after all, and there was a plinth already prepared for him in the Palace Memorial Garden of Remembrance. Her Alan would join a long line of Gatekeepers stretching back through the centuries. It was a fitting tribute to a great soul.

'Would the Painted Lady care to study some designs?' the embalmer asked politely.

Cynthia glanced down to find the woman was holding a large leather-bound volume opened at a painting of the Memorial Garden. Spell coatings presented her with detail after detail of remembrance figures of the other Gatekeepers, including, she noticed with surprise, Tithonus, the Gatekeeper who betrayed his own Emperor.

'He must be dressed in his Gatekeeper's robes,' Cynthia said uncertainly.

'Of course, Painted Lady.' The woman glanced delicately towards the bed. Cynthia followed her gaze and discovered the embalmers were doing it already.

How would Alan *want* to be remembered? She wished she had discussed it with him before he died, but there had been so many more immediate things to consider.

'There is a certain urgency, Painted Lady,' the woman told her gently. 'The gravistat ...'

Cynthia understood. Once introduced, the gravistat worked quickly. The body had to be placed in its correct position before the tissue turned to stone.

She hesitated, then all of a sudden knew what she should do. Alan had always loved tinkering with gadgets and machinery. It was how he would want to be remembered.

She took the book from the woman and closed it with a snap. 'Take his workbench from the Gatekeeper's Lodge and bring it to the Garden of Remembrance,' she instructed firmly. 'Place him beside it, leaning over. He should have a portable portal in his hand.' She stared soberly at the woman. 'Try not to make him look an idiot.'

'Of course not, Painted Lady!' the embalmer exclaimed.

With her final duty done, Madame Cardui swept from the room. Now she had to face the fury of her Queen.

Twenty-Seven

It wasn't heavy and it wasn't strong, but the thing struck Henry with such mindless fury that his face was lacerated and bleeding from a hundred cuts before he could raise a hand to defend himself. The useless lighter flew from his grasp as he struck out wildly.

The creature was about the size of a dog. It looked, in the brief flash of the sparks, like something almost human, scrawny and leprous. But a human that had fangs and claws.

It struck him again, hissing and spitting. This time it clawed his arm, ripping the sleeve of his coat and opening the flesh beneath. The pain was hideous, far worse than the scratches on his face. Henry staggered backwards and suddenly there was light.

The creature howled.

Henry clutched his injured arm. The light was blinding, but his eyes adjusted. He looked around in panic. There was a shattered stone sarcophagus beside him. There were bones strewn on the floor. He was in a ruined tomb. One wall was broken down and sunshine streamed in through it. The creature that had attacked him was crouched in a corner, cowering from the light. It had large, nocturnal eyes.

In the instant it took him to look, Henry realised he'd

torn down a hide curtain that had been blocking out the light. It was crudely sewn from animal skins and hung – could it have been hung by the thing that attacked him?

The thing clearly did not like the light. It growled and hissed from its gloomy corner, but made no move to attack him again. Now he could see properly, any resemblance he'd imagined between the creature and a human being quickly slipped away. It was humanoid in shape, but that was where any likeness stopped. It didn't look human at all. But at the same time, it didn't look like an animal either. It looked like nothing he had ever seen before. He kept thinking of a science fiction movie. The thing in that had come from Outer Space.

Dear God, but his arm was on fire.

He had to get away.

On the face of it, there was nothing to stop him. The wall was broken. The way lay open to the outside. But to reach the opening, he had to move a step or two towards the creature. And to escape, he had to climb a pile of rubble with the thing at his back.

Henry took a tentative step forward. The creature spat again and lunged at him. Despite its humanoid appearance, it reminded him of a cat. Henry backed off – which left him further from the opening than ever.

He stood quite still, trying to think despite the growing pain. If he moved forward, the thing assumed he was attacking and fought back. If he stayed where he was … Well, he couldn't stay where he was, could he? If he stayed where he was, he would bleed to death or starve to death or have the thing attack him anyway once night fell and the tomb returned to darkness.

Henry ran for the pile of rubble. The creature howled and launched itself at him again. He feinted to one side and ran past. Then the thing was clinging to his leg, biting and scratching. Henry kicked back violently and shook it off. Then he was on the rubble, scrambling upwards. The thing was in a frenzy now, screaming, howling, jumping. But it avoided the pool of light.

Henry was almost at the breach in the wall when the rubble crumbled beneath his feet, causing him to slide back down. The movement sent the creature berserk, but it still remained outside the pool of light. Without pause or thought, Henry ran back up the slope and this time he made it through the opening. He tripped as he emerged and fell heavily onto his injured arm. The jolt of pain was indescribable.

He lay for a moment, feeling fire in his arm and a second fire in his leg. Both injuries were so extreme he wondered briefly if the creature might be poisonous. Or perhaps it just carried some heavy-duty bacteria, like a komodo dragon. Either way, the injuries it inflicted hurt like hell. But the good news was the thing hadn't followed him out of the tomb.

After a while, he dragged himself to his feet and looked around. The tomb was a sandstone ruin that must have been built centuries ago.

A stony desert stretched around it as far as his eyes could see.

Twenty-Eight

'What are you doing here?' Blue demanded sharply.

'Nice to see you too,' Pyrgus told her, and grinned.

But Blue was in no mood to be charmed. She couldn't *believe* what Madame Cardui had done, let alone understand it. Henry might be in a hundred sorts of danger, might be injured, might be dead. She had no idea at all what she should do. And Pyrgus picked this very moment to turn up, against everything she'd told him to do – dammit, against everything she'd *ordered* him to do. The awful thing was he looked so much like their father. She had to keep reminding herself and reminding herself and it was so *difficult* to be firm. She gritted her teeth. 'You know you shouldn't be here!' she hissed at him fiercely. 'You know you're ill! You know it isn't safe for you to leave the Analogue World!'

He did that thing with his ear that their father used to do. 'The situation's changed, Blue,' he told her soberly.

They were in the Portal Chapel. Blue was going nowhere, but needed desperately to talk to Chief Portal Wizard Engineer Peacock, who was *not here,* could you believe it? Pyrgus had just stepped out of the blue fire, with Nymph behind him. 'Changed?' Blue said quickly. Something leaped inside her. Had somebody found a cure?

Pyrgus said, 'Henry needs me.'

Blue blinked at him. 'Henry …' She didn't know where to begin to tell him what had happened. Eventually she said, 'Henry's not here.'

'I know,' Pyrgus said.

It was too much. 'How do you know? How could you know – it's only just happened! You've only just arrived!' She looked at Nymph, who was hovering silently in the background. 'What's going on, Nymph?'

When Nymph said nothing, Blue swung back to Pyrgus. 'I can't believe how old you look. You can't risk another bout of fever.'

'I don't feel any different,' Pyrgus said annoyingly. 'I feel exactly the same inside.'

There were portal priests gathered in a small, nervous huddle a discreet distance away, pretending not to listen. 'Bring me Engineer Peacock!' Blue shouted at them. 'Find him and bring him here at once!' The group broke apart as priests scuttled in various directions. To Pyrgus, she snapped, 'I don't care *how* you feel. We've *had* this conversation and I ordered you to stay in the Analogue World and –'

'And you're Queen,' Pyrgus finished. 'I know. I know.' He put his arm around her shoulder (the way their father used to do, dammit!) 'I'm not just trying to be difficult. I have to be here for Henry.'

Blue leaned towards him. 'Henry isn't *here!*' she hissed angrily. 'Madame Cardui used a *transport* spell on him!'

'I know,' Pyrgus said infuriatingly.

Twenty-Nine

They were in the place they always used to meet as children, the little conservatory behind the throne room where their father kept his orchids. The smell of magic almost overpowered the scent of flowers: nowhere in the entire Palace was more private, more secure.

'She used a *transport*,' Blue said angrily. 'She just sent him off and she doesn't know where or how far or anything! He could be anywhere – *anywhere!* He could be on the other side of the world. He could be eaten by a haniel. She won't tell me why. I've *demanded* an explanation and she won't tell me why. She just did it, right there and then in front of me. I couldn't believe it. Why, Pyrgus? *Why?* Do you think she's getting senile?' It was a serious question. Madame Cardui was very old now. She'd always had a mind like a razor, but at her age she might be losing it. A sudden thought occurred to Blue. Perhaps the Gatekeeper's death had unhinged her.

Pyrgus said, 'What have you done with her?'

Blue stared at him, then said reluctantly, 'Put her in detention.' She couldn't believe she'd done that either. Madame Cardui was her most trusted friend and advisor, head of the Imperial Secret Service. But this was *Henry* they were talking about. Using a transport like that was nearly the equivalent of murder. How many people ever found their way back?

'I see,' Pyrgus said. He turned away from her and began fiddling with one of the orchids.

There was something about the place, or the way he looked and acted like their father, that calmed Blue down. Or at least allowed her anger to ebb a little so that she began to think more clearly. 'Pyrgus, what are you doing here?'

'I told you, Blue. I'm here for Henry.'

'I know what you told me – it didn't make sense. You know something about this business, don't you?'

'What business?'

'Stop it, Pyrgus!' Blue said sharply. 'You know why Madame Cardui transported him, don't you?'

Without turning round, Pyrgus said, 'Yes.'

'That's why you kept saying *I know*. I thought you were just trying to be irritating or sympathetic or something.'

Pyrgus nodded. 'Yes.'

Blue waited. When he said nothing more, she exploded. 'Well, what? What's happening?'

'I can't tell you,' Pyrgus said softly. He sounded genuinely regretful.

There was a knock on the door, muffled by the privacy spells. 'Oh Light!' Blue exclaimed, exasperated. She stomped to the door and threw it open. 'What? What? Didn't I say explicitly we weren't –'

Chief Wizard Engineer Peacock was standing on the doorstep. 'I'm sorry, Ma'am. They said I was to come immediately.'

Blue caught the sleeve of his robe and pulled him inside. She slammed the door. 'Is it possible to trace a transport?' she demanded. 'Not a portal – a transport spell?'

The Chief Engineer frowned. 'Well ...'

'It's the same technology, isn't it?'

Peacock looked at her uncomfortably. 'Essentially, Your Majesty. But not exactly.'

Blue glared at him. 'Well, can you? Can you find out where the spell has sent somebody? Even roughly?'

'I would need to know where the spell was applied –'

'In the kitchens,' Blue said impatiently. 'In the Palace kitchens.'

'And I would need the casing of the spell cone.'

'The burnt-out cone?' What had Madame Cardui done with the spent cone? When it happened, the little shell was the last thing on Blue's mind. Probably just dropped it. But she could order a search of the kitchens. And have Madame Cardui searched as well.

Peacock was still frowning. 'It's sometimes possible to analyse the residues. But ...'

'But?' Blue asked.

'But only sometimes, Majesty.'

'But sometimes you can and they will tell you where the spell sent the person?'

'Sometimes, Majesty.'

She caught his expression and asked, 'What? What is it, Chief Engineer?'

Peacock shrugged helplessly. 'Majesty, a full analysis takes months.'

When the Chief Engineer left, Blue rounded on Pyrgus again. 'You won't tell me what's going on?'

'I didn't say that.' Pyrgus shook his head. 'I said I *can't* tell you. It's not the same thing.'

'*Why* can't you tell me?'

'I can't tell you that either.' Pyrgus seemed genuinely uncomfortable. He stopped fiddling with the flowers to come across and take her by both hands. 'Look, Blue, I would if I could – you know that. I know what Henry means to you. He means a lot to me too. I certainly wouldn't be risking another fever bout if he didn't. But I can't tell you what it's all about – not yet, at any rate. What I can tell you is that we're going to do everything we can to make sure Henry is all right.'

Blue glanced at him sharply. 'We? Who's we?'

'Well … me,' Pyrgus said. 'Or me and Nymph. Although she –' He stopped, as if he'd been about to say too much and said instead, 'Look, Blue, I can tell you this – I can *promise* you this: I'm going to go off and look for Henry. Now. I'm going to go off and look for him now, without any delay. I have …' He hesitated. He knew Blue was going to forbid it, lecture him on the dangers of staying in the Realm while he was carrying the time plague.

Blue said, 'You have an idea where he might be.' It was as much a statement as a question.

Pyrgus glanced away, glanced back. 'Yes.'

'I'm coming with you,' Blue said firmly.

thirty

The door was cunningly concealed behind a sliding panel and the trigger was a piece of peeling wallpaper. Chalkhill would never have found it on his own, never in a thousand years. He stared suspiciously at the steep stone steps leading downwards. 'After you,' he said.

'Oh, go on!' Brimstone snapped impatiently. 'What do you think – I'm going to push you? Break your neck?' He gave a dry, cackling laugh. 'You think I went to all this trouble to get you here just to *murder* you? I could have done that in the Lodge Room if I'd wanted to.'

'Went to all what trouble?' Chalkhill stepped back from the doorway. 'What trouble? What?'

'You don't think you'd have found this place if I'd really wanted to keep it quiet?' Brimstone snorted. 'I left more clues than a paperchase. I knew you'd be following me.'

'How did you know?'

Brimstone ignored him. 'But with luck, anybody following *you* would miss them.'

'Why should anybody be following me?' Chalkhill asked. He'd known Brimstone for a million years, but the creature always made him paranoid. He smelt so dreadfully of *sulphur*.

'There's more at stake here than you could possibly

suspect,' Brimstone said mysteriously. 'More people involved than Madame Cardui.'

'How did you know about Madame Cardui?' Chalkhill gasped, then bit his tongue. If Brimstone didn't *really* know, Chalkhill had just confirmed it. Amateur mistake. Naughty, naughty Chalkhill.

'Oh, all right, I'll go first,' Brimstone said impatiently. He gripped the handrail and began to negotiate the steps like an elderly crab. Light spells flared from the walls as he did so.

After a moment, Chalkhill followed. 'Is this the cellar?'

'Catacombs,' Brimstone said over one bony shoulder. 'Nearly two miles of them, packed together like a maze.'

'Catacombs?' Chalkhill echoed. 'You built catacombs?'

'Don't be stupid,' Brimstone told him. He stopped abruptly and clung to the balustrade, hissing. After a moment he went on breathlessly. 'They date back to the Great Persecution. Red priests of the Raddled Faction used to hide their corpses down here so they wouldn't be eaten. Hid themselves as well, so they wouldn't be turned into corpses. It's crude engineering, but very well concealed. The owner of the house doesn't even know the catacombs are here: I made sure of that when I rented. Not that I thought he would. I only found out about them myself through a rare old manuscript.' He started down the steps again.

A thought occurred to Chalkhill and he asked, 'Are you *living* down here, Silas?'

'You bet your life I'm living down here,' Brimstone said. 'You think I'd let something this important out of my sight for longer than I had to?'

'Something what important, Silas? What something?'

'You'll see.'

Brimstone reached the bottom of the steps and stopped again, breathing heavily. God alone knew how the old fool expected to get back up them again. 'Are you all right, Silas?' Chalkhill asked with feigned concern.

'You must have pissed off Hairstreak,' Brimstone said. 'He wants me to murder you.'

The staircase ended in an arched corridor rough-hewn out of bedrock. There were niches in the walls every few yards, housing bits of tibias and skulls. It was crude engineering, as Brimstone had said, but effective enough. Chalkhill reckoned they had to be under the river here, yet everything was bone dry. He wondered if he should run back up the steps – the chances of Silas ever catching up with him had to be close to zero. But instead, he asked curiously, 'Are you going to?'

Brimstone sniffed. 'Not likely. I can trust you more than I trust him for this little bit of business.'

'What little bit of business?' Chalkhill frowned.

'That's what I want to show you,' Brimstone said. He caught his breath at last and started down the corridor. He must have set up light spells here as well, for it lit up as he went. 'Stick close,' he called back. 'This place can be confusing if you're not used to it.'

Chalkhill hesitated for a fraction of a second, then started after him.

It was, as Brimstone said, confusing. The arched corridor turned quickly into a maze of cramped tunnels, which bulged into smallish chambers from time to time and occasionally opened out into charnel galleries. There were bones and skulls everywhere. The whole place smelled of must.

Now he'd left the stairs behind, Brimstone had regained his old sprightly self and scuttled along without apparent discomfort. 'Nearly there,' he called over his shoulder.

They reached a chamber that clearly had been modi-fied in recent years. There was a heavy metal-clad door set into the wall at one end.

Brimstone produced a massive key. 'Put on your lenses,' he instructed. He dragged a heavy pair of dark-ened goggles from his pocket and fitted them carefully around his ears.

Like Brimstone, Chalkhill was a Faerie of the Night. He produced his own dark glasses – rimmed with ormolu worked into an impressively baroque design – but hesitated. 'There's not much light down here.'

'Just do it,' Brimstone said. He inserted the key in the lock and turned it with some difficulty. Then he grabbed the handle and pulled back the massive door.

Chalkhill's jaw dropped as he stared inside the room.

Thirty-One

Blue hesitated in the doorway. Comma had been such an *odious* child, sneaky, pompous, sly. She'd loved him, of course – he was her half-brother after all – but she could never bring herself to like him. It almost seemed as if the change had occurred overnight, temperament and looks together. He lost weight, gained height and suddenly he was a good-looking young man, full of new-found courtesy, sensitivity and understanding. The odious child was Comma then. Comma now was ... Comma now was ...

Comma now was levitating gracefully close to the ceiling of the practice hall. The tight-fitting suit accentuated the sleek muscularity of his body as he swooped and soared in complex, graceful patterns. He would have a devastating affect on girls one of these days. Blue shook her head. Who was she fooling? He *already* had a devastating affect on girls. There were eight of them in the practice hall, members of the Royal Ballet, and every one was watching him with adoration.

As Blue herself watched, one of the girls took off with expert skill and soared to join him. She had long, dark hair tied in a tight bun and the sort of body that comes with years of training. Her eyes were glazed with concentration as she induced the levitation trance.

Comma reached for her and took her hand. Blue stared, enraptured, as the two floated, light as thistledown, into the dance steps of a classic *pas de deux*. They moved gently at first, then faster, but always gracefully, parting, soaring, reaching, closing for a brief embrace, then onwards, heavenwards. Blue recognised a movement from Februa's *Heliconius,* one of her personal favourites. She wondered briefly if the dancers would end it at the kiss; and when they did, she noted the envious looks on the faces of the other girls.

The dark-haired girl sank slowly back down to the ground, unable to maintain her trance, but Comma stayed easily aloft. Clearly he had a talent that would take him far. Blue stepped into the hall and at once the ballet girls ran to greet her with elaborate, elegant curtsies. Blue returned their smiles, then said softly, 'Leave us.' The girls scattered like doves, taking their exits in small, swift steps. Above her head, Comma sank gently towards her.

'Security?' Blue asked without preliminary as he landed. She noticed that despite the efforts of the levitation he had scarcely broken a sweat.

In the old days he would have made a fuss, demanded to know at once what her visit was about, accused her of interrupting his practice and Light only knew what else. As it was, the new Comma only smiled and nodded and walked lightly to close the double doors with their self-activating spells. 'Secure now, Blue,' he said. 'Is there a crisis?' He blinked and added, 'Other than the ones I know about.'

So many crises. But at least she could trust him now. In fact, she realised suddenly, she could trust him completely. Comma was still young, but he was intelligent and calm, with a surprising, if unobtrusive, grasp of Realm politics. Which was just as well, considering what she was about to ask. She gave him a warm, fond smile. 'If there is, you'll have to handle it.'

He frowned slightly but was intelligent enough to understand. 'You're leaving the Palace?'

Blue nodded. 'It's possible I might be away for quite some time.'

Comma waited, his eyes on her face.

Blue said, 'I want you as Acting Emperor while I'm away.'

Thirty-two

Pyrgus waited.

An old Realm saying, *The Purple Palace never sleeps,* drifted through his mind. It was meant as a political comment – your rulers work tirelessly on your behalf – but now he could see the literal aspect of it as well. Move from your quarters at any time of the day or night and the corridors were bustling: servants ... guards ... messengers ... He was watching them now from the shadow of an archway. Unlike the city streets, the plague made no difference to the Palace traffic. It was an almost constant stream.

But only *almost* constant. If you were patient, opportunities arose. He remembered that from childhood when he'd defied his father to slip away – usually from some punishment or other. You waited, then you seized your chance and made a dash. With a little luck, no one noticed you until it was too late. With a lot of luck, no one noticed you at all.

He should have realised Blue would want to come. But his attention had been so focused it simply never occurred to him. If it had, he'd have kept his mouth shut, of course, but too late for that now. What he had to do now was get away without her. She'd be furious when she found out, but better that than have her ruin everything.

The trouble was he felt really sorry for Blue. She loved Henry – he'd known that for years – and now Henry was in greater danger than he'd ever been in his whole life. Not knowing what was happening must be tearing her apart. Not to be allowed to help was even worse.

The corridor was suddenly empty. Without a second's hesitation, Pyrgus stepped from the archway, ran a hundred yards south, then slipped into a little-used servants' passage. He moved along it quickly, listening intently for sounds of anyone approaching. No servant would stop him, of course – he was still a Prince of the Realm and, besides, was known to have the plague – but best that he should not be seen. People talked. It would be a disaster if word of his actions reached Blue.

Halfway along the passageway, he stepped through a doorway into an empty chamber and waited, leaving the door open a crack. Blue was no fool. It would be so like her to assign one of her miserable little agents to track him if he left his quarters.

Seconds ticked by into minutes as he listened, holding his breath. After a while, he began to relax. Perhaps he'd misjudged her. Perhaps she'd learned to trust her big brother.

He was about to step back out into the passageway when he heard a sound. Pyrgus froze. He placed his eye to the crack. His field of vision was limited and the corridor was poorly lit, but after a moment a shadowy figure slipped silently past, a Trinian to judge from his height. Pyrgus grinned. Little sister still didn't trust him after all.

He waited until he was certain the agent was clear, then cautiously vacated the chamber and made off back the way he'd come. But instead of returning to the main corridor with its renewed bustle, he slipped through an archway and crossed an empty gallery that took him to a second servants' passage running parallel to the first.

He hesitated. There was someone coming. He could hear heavy breathing, dragging footsteps and a curious metallic clanking. Clearly not another agent. He risked a quick glance down the corridor. An old cleaning woman was approaching, dragging an empty bucket and a mop. Pyrgus stepped back into the shadows and she passed him without so much as a glance.

Pyrgus waited until the woman's footsteps faded, then slipped into the passageway. He wasn't entirely familiar with this part of the Palace, but quickly discovered Blue's agent had done him a favour by sending him this way. The passage led to a gloomy wooden staircase, which took him to a storeroom that opened into the basement corridors beneath the main entrance hall. It was an area Pyrgus knew well – he'd hidden down here often enough as a child.

Moving quickly now, he raced along until he found a second staircase, which took him to a disused area of the Palace kitchens. The place had a ghostly feel, but he ignored it and pushed through a heavy doorway into exactly the passageway he was looking for. It ended at a locked door leading outside. Pyrgus grinned and inserted his master key. (Some perks to having been a Crown Prince after all!) The solid old spells recognised him at once and slid back the bolts. In a moment, Pyrgus was outside, breathing the fresh, clean river air of Imperial Island.

Blue's agents could not be tracking him now, but all the same he moved cautiously. Nymph had promised to arrange for a personal flyer, fully charged and ready for take-off, to be hidden in the grove of trees beyond the Gatekeeper's Lodge. There was absolutely no chance of anyone else going there during the period of mourning that followed Mr Fogarty's death. Once Pyrgus reached it, he was free and clear.

But not free and clear yet. There was a Volunteer Guard posted along the perimeter of the Gatekeeper's property. They would not be particularly vigilant – their duties were largely ceremonial – but he couldn't risk their seeing him all the same. So he took a circuitous route through the shrubberies, crossed the little ornamental river by way of the stepping stones, then climbed a low wall and dropped into the Gatekeeper's grounds.

It occurred to him suddenly that his problems getting here were nothing beside Nymph's problems arranging for the flyer to be brought in secretly. But he was so used to trusting Nymph now, so used to her terrifying efficiency, that he felt not the slightest stirring of surprise when he caught his first glimpse of the dull sheen reflecting from the vehicle's exterior spell coatings.

He ran through the grove like a wraith, jerked open the flyer door and climbed thankfully inside.

'What kept you?' Blue asked sourly.

Thirty-Three

There was gold carpeting on the floor, velvet drapes on picture windows, a little ante-room for Kitterick. In many ways, it made her personal quarters at the Palace seem positively utilitarian. But, however luxurious, a prison was still a prison.

Madame Cardui dressed carefully. She was far too old for field work, of course, but that was of small account now that field work had become necessary. If dear Alan was right, they all must play their part. Thus she abandoned her usual flowing silks for form-fitting assassin's black, spell-treated to turn it into body armour. The effect was actually quite fetching: how gratifying to have kept one's figure. How sad that Alan wasn't here to see it.

She extinguished all lights, then walked to the window and drew back the curtains. The first glow of dawn had begun to illuminate the horizon far to the south. She stood for a moment, staring at the increasing light.

Poor Blue. Madame Cardui felt not the slightest resentment at her own incarceration. In the circumstances, what else could the child do? Another Emperor might well have ordered her death, or had her tortured until she gave an explanation. Blue had been nothing but patient, generous and thoughtful. She had even specified low security in return for Madame Cardui's pledge not to attempt an escape. A pity to repay her with another betrayal.

It was such an *odd* situation to be in. All the old certainties had been turned upside down. She was reminded irresistibly of her stage days as the diverting young assistant to the Great Myphisto. She had been a real beauty then. The audience could scarcely take their eyes off her – especially the men. And while they watched *her,* Myphisto prepared his sleights of hand. *Miracles Without Magic,* they had called the show. Not a single spell used ... and that was guaranteed.

She dragged her attention back to the present. Focus. She had to focus. There were so many imponderables in the present situation, so much to lose if they got things wrong.

She turned away from the window and flicked a bell-ring on her finger. Kitterick appeared at once. With his usual efficiency he had anticipated her next move and was himself dressed in black, doubtless spell-armoured as well, with a pointed hood that made him look like a demented pixy. He had dyed his skin black as well, which was possibly a step too far, although his natural orange would, admittedly, have been a trifle garish in the morning light.

'I assumed we would be leaving, Madam,' Kitterick told her.

'Your assumption was correct,' said Madame Cardui.

He waited, patient as ever, for his briefing. Kitterick had been in her service for more years than she cared to remember and still looked much as he had done the day she hired him. How did Trinians manage it? They never seemed to age at all – although they did have something of a reputation for dying suddenly. Would she have bartered sudden death for youthful looks and energy? Such a bargain was hardly open for her now. Not only had she lost her looks – although not her figure, one was forced to admit – but what she was about to do held its own risk of sudden death.

Madame Cardui blinked. Losing Alan had made her morbid. All she could think about was death in one form or another. Such a waste of energy and the ruination of one's concentration. She must pull herself together.

'We have no time to lose,' she told Kitterick.

'No, Madam,' Kitterick agreed.

'It is important that we leave the Palace – and indeed the city – at the earliest opportunity.'

'Yes, Madam.'

She took a deep breath. 'But it is equally important that the discovery of our escape be delayed as much as possible.'

'To give us a greater head start, Madam?'

'Precisely, Kitterick. To that end, I have instructed our captors that I shall not be requiring breakfast this morning.'

'Very self-sacrificing, Madam.'

'They will, of course, attempt to feed us lunch, but by then, if all goes well, I shall be long gone.'

Kitterick missed nothing. 'You, Madam – not *we*?'

'I, Kitterick. I expect you to remain here, confuse our captors and, if necessary, create a diversion.'

'Of course, Madam.' He looked at her fondly. 'Will you be requiring me to murder the guards, Madam?'

'Nothing so crude, Kitterick,' said Madame Cardui. Bad enough she had to break her word to the Queen without adding slaughter to her sins. She sighed. 'You'll find a doppelgänger in my mattress.'

This time Kitterick's look was one of open admiration. He went to the mattress, extruded a talon to slit it open, then fumbled inside until he drew out a desiccated package about the size of a building brick. 'I presume this is she, Madam?'

Madam Cardui nodded. 'It's freeze-dried, so we only need add water.'

'After you have gone, Madam?'

'No, I think we should activate it now – just to be sure. You can use the decanter on the bedside table.'

'Of course, Madam.' Kitterick set the brick on top of the counterpane and poured the contents of the decanter over it. There was a slight sizzling sound as the package began to enlarge.

Kitterick moved back sharply when the arms and legs appeared, floppy at first, then uncurling and expanding into three dimensions. After a moment, it was possible to discern a body threshing and writhing. A moment more and a living, breathing replica of Madame Cardui was lying on the bed. Madame Cardui stared down at it. The thing had cost a fortune, but she had to admit the investment had been worth every penny. The resemblance was uncanny, right down to that unfortunate mole on the buttock.

'How would you prefer her dressed?' asked Kitterick, not at all phased by the creature's nudity.

'A simple nightgown will suffice,' said Madame Cardui. 'Then tuck her into bed. When the servants arrive with lunch, tell them I am indisposed – unwell. You might even hint at the possibility of plague.'

'Queen Blue is likely to order a medical examination,' Kitterick said.

'The doppelgänger can withstand that, so long as they don't expect it to speak. All internal organs and systems are faithfully duplicated. With luck, they will assume its silence is due to the illness. They will discover the truth in time, of course, but by then I will be long gone. I shall leave now. Divert them as long as you can, then go to my city quarters. *You* are not a prisoner, of course, so there will be no difficulty. But I shall expect you to be discreet, make sure you are not followed and so forth.'

'Of course,' Kitterick murmured. 'Will you be hiding in your city quarters?'

'Oh, no – I have several urgent things to do: best you know nothing of them. But I shall return eventually, I hope. In the meantime, I rely on you to keep them clean and look after Lanceline.' Madame Cardui returned to the window and threw it open. 'Au revoir, Kitterick.'

'Au revoir, Madam,' Kitterick replied.

She drew a reel of wire from the pocket of her armour and expertly attached one end of it to the windowsill. She clipped the other to her belt and jumped from the window to abseil down the outside wall like a spider on a silken thread.

Kitterick watched until she was safely on the ground, then detached the wire and closed the window.

Thirty-four

There was a savage sun beating down and no shade except leeward of the crumbling tomb. It was so very, very ... hot. But Henry needed to get away from the tomb. He didn't think the thing would follow him into the sunlight, but he couldn't be sure. Besides, the sun would not stay up forever. When night fell the creature might emerge.

Which way to go?

Henry looked around in something close to panic. The desert was featureless – a rock here, a flat slab there, a sea of spreading, shimmering sand but no landmark other than the ruin. In a landscape like this, one direction was as good as any other.

All the same, he hesitated. He was beginning to pour sweat. It stung his eyes and soaked his underarms. He would need water soon and he had no water at all. How long could you survive in a desert without water? Days? Hours? He thought maybe days, if you were lucky, but he was fairly sure it wasn't more than a week. So if he walked the wrong way, went deeper into the desert instead of out of it, he could be walking to his death.

Which way to go?

Henry shivered. His arm and leg were burning up now and the shivering made him wonder if he was starting a fever.

There was a sound from the tomb, a rodent rustling. The creature was moving about inside. He didn't think it would venture out into the sunlight, but the noise unnerved him so much that he moved despite his pain, stumbling away from the ruin. With no landmarks, no pointers, nothing to guide him, one direction really was as good as any other.

He made a decision. He would walk until he was out of sight of the tomb. That way, if the creature did come out, it wouldn't find him. When he was out of sight, he would sit down and examine his wounds and try to think. Take stock of his position. That sounded like the proper thing to do.

There was a great deal of rock close to the ruin and a section, half-exposed, of what looked like man-made pavement. But all of it gave way to featureless sand, flat at first, then drifting into dunes. It was hell to walk on. It sucked at his feet and drained the little energy he had left in his legs. He had to rest even before he lost sight of the tomb. He squatted on the sand, looking back nervously. The ruin shimmered through a heat haze, as if it were under water. After a while, he climbed painfully back to his feet and started off. He felt better when he lost sight of the tomb completely.

But now there were no landmarks at all.

Henry sat down again. The wound on his arm had stopped bleeding and closed over, but it was rimmed with a greenish thread and pulsed pain in time with his heartbeat. But the pain wasn't too bad and so far, luckily, there didn't seem to be much swelling.

The wound on his leg was another matter. His trousers were torn and soaked with matted blood so that the material stuck to the flesh. He gritted his teeth and tried to peel it away, but the skin seemed to be coming too and the pain was almost unbelievable. Eventually, in desperation, he unbuckled his belt and eased the trousers down to get sight of the wound.

He wished he hadn't. The wound on his arm was a claw slash. The wound on his leg seemed like the result of a bite. Even in so short a time, it had swollen dramatically, stretching and discolouring the skin while the site of the bite itself oozed a foul-smelling, yellow pus. That one was going to need medical attention, and soon. He poked the skin cautiously and was rewarded by a wave of agony so extreme that he almost threw up.

Henry pulled his trousers up again and buckled the belt. There was nothing he could do about his injuries yet, so the only thing to do was ignore them and concentrate on ...

On survival.

How did you stay alive in a desert?

Henry squeezed his eyes shut and tried to remember anything he'd read or seen on TV about survival. What would the S.A.S. do in a situation like this? Strangely, information started to trickle through from foggy corners of his memory. Find shelter from the sun ... preserve your energy ... travel only at night ... drink your own urine if you can't find water ...

He opened his eyes again. The desert stretched endlessly in all directions, barren and bare. Not a tree, not a rock, no shelter of any sort. How did you find shelter when there was no shelter to be found? But the business about travelling by night was a good idea. It would be cooler at night. He could get further with less energy and he'd sweat less so he'd need less water.

But he'd still need some. Without water he would die in days.

He began to think about drinking his own pee. The idea sounded gross, but he could probably live with that. The problem was ... the problem was ...

The problem was *how?*

He couldn't pee in a bottle and drink from that because he didn't have a bottle. He couldn't pee in a hollow on a rock, because there were no rocks any more. He couldn't pee on the ground: the hot sand would soak up the precious fluid in a second. So how ...?

Henry bent forward in the sitting position and considered angles. It was a fairly batty thought, but he might just be able to do it. Although only if he managed a strong jet – a trickle wouldn't hack it. He straightened up and decided to shelve the problem for the moment. He wasn't *that* thirsty yet.

So what did he do now? Rest until nightfall, then move off again? It had to be the sensible thing, but something kept telling him not to do it. Nightfall was still hours away. The sun was hotter than anything he'd ever experienced. If he sat here without shelter he'd be a baked husk by dark. And God knew how bad the wound in his leg might be by then. Maybe it was best to move on now, while he still had some energy left, trust to luck that he was going in the right direction, trust to luck that he'd find help before it was too late.

Trust to luck he wouldn't die.

With a massive effort, he pushed himself to his feet.

Thirty-five

Lord Hairstreak looked around his seedy office and wondered where his life had gone.

The rot had set in after the brief Civil War. Too many bad decisions, too many gambles. But most of all, the collapse of the market. Demon servants were a thing of the past since his niece became Queen of Hael. Hard to believe anybody could be so stupid as to free the slaves, but Blue had done it. Lost herself an almost unimaginable source of income at the stroke of a pen. More to the point, lost Hairstreak his percentage.

He closed his eyes briefly. Such a sweet, sweet deal while Beleth was alive. Five per cent of earnings from every demon placed in servitude. *Five per cent!* He'd never lacked for money then and never thought he ever would. Even when Blue killed Beleth it didn't occur to him things might be different. He'd simply assumed the old arrangement would continue with a new name on the contract. The worst he expected was that she'd try to cut back a little on his percentage. But only a little. Blue needed Hairstreak as much as Beleth ever had if the market was to continue: he was leader of the FON after all and only FON used demon servants. He never thought, not for an instant, that Blue would stop the trade altogether. Even now her decision made no sense to him. If he'd lost millions when his five per cent disappeared, imagine how much Blue herself had lost. As Queen of Hael she would have harvested every penny of the remaining ninety-five per cent.

But pointless to dwell on the past. What was done was done and nothing he could do would change it. The trick was to replace his former source of income. And now, thanks to that old goat Brimstone, it looked as if it just might be possible.

The only problem was he didn't trust Brimstone.

Hairstreak opened his eyes again. The cloud dancer was pretending to sit on the chair, but had miscalculated slightly and seemed to be hovering an inch or two above it. Not that it mattered since the dancer wasn't truly there at all. Its home was a wholly different dimension. But now the strain on the fabric of reality was making Hairstreak nauseous and he decided to conclude the business as quickly as possible.

'Can you do it?' he asked. The question was, of course, rhetorical. Cloud dancers could track down anybody anywhere. And their unique access to the faerie brain made them more efficient at extracting information than a torture chamber. Brimstone's secrets wouldn't stand a chance against this thing.

'For the standard fee,' the cloud dancer told him. The voice was as bizarre as everything else about the creature. It reverberated through the air and through your mind, but not quite synchronised so everything produced a weird mental echo.

'Yes, yes,' Hairstreak said impatiently. Of course for the standard fee. Everybody knew about cloud dancers and their standard fees. It was the one aspect of this transaction he had not been looking forward to. But at least the thing wouldn't ask for money. Money was in short supply.

'I can do it,' the cloud dancer confirmed.

And that seemed to be that. After a moment, Hairstreak said, 'Well, get on with it.'

'The fee is payable in advance,' the cloud dancer said.

There was silence in the little room. The thing remained not quite sitting on the chair, gazing patiently at Hairstreak.

'Oh, very well!' snapped Hairstreak. He rolled up the left sleeve of his jerkin.

The cloud dancer floated towards him, curling itself sensuously into a foetal ball.

Thirty-Six

'What is it?' Chalkhill gasped.

'You know what it is,' Brimstone told him shortly.

That was true enough. Although he'd never seen one before – or imagined he ever would – there was no possibility of a mistake. Chalkhill swallowed painfully. 'How did you get it?'

'That's none of your business,' Brimstone said. He walked through the doorway.

The chamber was lined with lead and the floor sparkled with inlaid quartz. Bowls of rotting offal had been set at the cardinal points. All the same Chalkhill hesitated. 'Is it safe?' he called in after Brimstone.

The man is an idiot, Brimstone thought. *But a necessary idiot.* 'Safe as houses,' he called back. Which was hopefully the truth, otherwise they were both dead and half the country with them.

Chalkhill approached cautiously, sidling through the doorway like a crab. Not once did he take his eyes off the cage. 'Are you sure?'

'The bars are reinforced titanium,' Brimstone said. 'Nothing could break through them.'

'But what about ... you know ... its powers?'

'The lead should take care of any of that nonsense,' Brimstone said. 'Besides, it's crippled.'

'I thought it looked a bit funny,' Chalkhill said. He seemed to be getting his nerve back, for he took a step closer to the cage. 'What are you going to do with it?'

'Get it out of here, for one thing,' Brimstone said. 'It's only a matter of time before Hairstreak comes after me.' He glanced at Challkhill, who was poking his umbrella through the bars. 'Don't do that.'

'I thought you and Hairstreak were buddies? Brothers of the Brotherhood and all that?'

Brimstone snorted. 'His Lordship only joined the Brotherhood to set up a new power base. What does Hairstreak care about the arcane knowledge? Six months after his initiation he was running the show. That's what a title does for you.'

Chalkhill's nervousness was evaporating quickly. He walked round the cage, examining it from different angles. 'Where are you going to take it? Somewhere else in the city?'

Brimstone shook his head. 'The city's not safe. I'm not sure anywhere in the Realm is safe. I'm going to move it out of the country.'

Chalkhill was sinking back into his familiar camp act, for he opened his eyes wide, pursed his lips and said, 'Wooooo!' Then he smiled. 'That's going to be a very dangerous undertaking. I mean, it would be tricky even if Hairstreak wasn't after you, but if he is ... well, woooo ... I can't *think* how you'll manage it.'

'By getting you to help me,' Brimstone said. It wiped the smile off Chalkhill's face.

Thirty-Seven

'You can't come with me,' Pyrgus hissed. 'You can't! You can't!'

'Where are you going?' Blue hissed back fiercely.

'I can't tell you,' Pyrgus wailed.

'*Why* can't you tell me?' Blue demanded.

'Because it mightn't work out right if I do,' said Pyrgus desperately.

Blue was on it like a mosquito. She stared at Pyrgus soberly. '*What* mightn't work out right?' she asked. Then, before he could answer, she said, 'Look, Pyrgus, don't you think it's time you told me what's going on? I don't care if you don't want to. I don't care if you think you shouldn't for some stupid reason. Because let me tell you this: if you don't tell me now – tell me everything – about Henry and where he is and why Madame Cardui did what she did and what you're up to and how it is that I'm the only one who doesn't know what's going on –' She drew in a shuddering breath. 'If you don't tell me all of it, right now, Pyrgus, you aren't going anywhere!'

She was only his little sister. 'Like you're going to stop me!' he snapped back. The minute he spoke, he realised it was a mistake.

Blue smiled. 'Oh, I can stop you all right,' she said

sweetly. 'You always forget you made me Queen because you were too *chicken* to be Emperor –'

'I wasn't too –' Pyrgus shouted, outraged.

But Blue was in full swing. 'And as Queen,' she said firmly, 'I can call the guards and have you put in jail. Or I can trigger the Palace securities so any flyer that takes off is blown out of the sky.'

'That won't do you any good,' Pyrgus told her furiously. 'I can take off before the guards get here and the Palace securities won't blow *this* flyer out of the sky because you'll be on board –' he made a sarcastic mimic of a high-pitched voice '– and you're *Queen*.'

Blue tilted her head upwards and continued calmly. 'But the real reason I can stop you, the *real* reason this flyer will not take off until you tell me ... is *this!*' She opened one slim hand. An obsidian disc the size of a seven-groat piece was nestling in her palm. It writhed and sparkled with spell charges.

Pyrgus's jaw dropped. 'That's the flyer's power-pack! How did you get it out?'

Blue glared at him fiercely. 'I came here with a wrench!'

'Give it here!' Pyrgus shouted.

Blue's jaw jutted. 'No!' she shouted back.

He hurled himself at her and they wrestled on the floor. He tried to pin her down, but couldn't. Despite his greater strength, it was like trying to hold an eel. Then she got a hand free and tickled him so he had to hug her arms to make her stop. And after that they rolled about a little more, giggling.

'We haven't done that since we were children,' Blue said as he relaxed his grip.

'No, we haven't,' Pyrgus said a little breathlessly. He smiled down at her.

'It was like wrestling with Daddy,' Blue said. 'You look just like him now.'

For some reason, it sobered them both and they climbed back to their feet. Blue said, 'I'm worried about your time fever thing.'

'I know,' Pyrgus said. He dusted himself down. 'It's not fair. I know it's not fair. Look, I'll tell you as much as I can – as much as I know. If I do that, will you give me back the power-pack?'

'Yes,' Blue said.

'And will you let me get on with things without interfering anymore?'

'It depends what you tell me,' Blue said in the sort of tone that promised nothing.

'All right,' Pyrgus said. 'That's fair enough. When you know what's going on, you'll know how important it is that we do things my way.'

Then he told her.

Thirty-Eight

'Mr Fogarty saw the future,' Pyrgus said.

Blue looked at him blankly.

'Well, *remembered* it,' Pyrgus corrected himself.

Frowning, Blue said slowly, 'Are we talking about his fever?'

Pyrgus nodded enthusiastically. 'Yes. Yes, that's exactly what we're talking about.' Now he'd decided to tell her – at least tell her some of it – he was feeling an enormous sense of relief. He'd never liked the idea of cutting Blue out of their plans, not least because of the trouble he'd be in when she found out. Besides, she might have some sensible ideas. Light knew they were going to need all the help they could get, even with everything Mr Fogarty told them.

'You can't remember the future, can you?' Blue asked.

'No, I –'

'And you've had the fever.'

'Yes, but –'

'Then how come the Gatekeeper could?'

'If you'd let me get a word in edgeways, I'd tell you,' Pyrgus said crossly. He wondered what life would have been like if he'd had a brother. Then he remembered he *did* have a brother, or a half-brother at least, but that was Comma, who didn't count. He realised Blue was standing silent for once and went on. 'It's different for humans. With me – with us – with faeries – it's just a blur mostly and even then only snatches of your own future. But Mr Fogarty could see other stuff, things that would happen elsewhere in the Realm. Like a prophet. And when he came out of the fever, he remembered.'

There was a long silence in the cabin of the flyer. Then Blue said, 'Oh.'

'What he remembered was Henry finding a cure for the disease.'

'Henry?'

Pyrgus nodded. 'Yes.'

'Finding a cure?'

Pyrgus nodded harder. 'Yes. Yes!'

Blue still looked bewildered. 'Well ... that's good, isn't it?'

'Sort of,' Pyrgus said. 'The trouble is, Mr Fogarty also remembered Henry *not* finding a cure.'

'This is silly,' Blue said sharply. 'You're making it all up so I –'

'No, I'm not – I swear.' Pyrgus came across quickly and sat down beside her on the flyer bench. 'During the first bout of fever he had the first memory – Henry finding a cure. Then he had a second bout very quickly after and this time he came back with a different memory. Henry *didn't* find a cure and the disease spread and it killed thousands, Blue – *hundreds of thousands*. It just about wiped out the Realm.'

'But –'

'He didn't tell anybody but Madame Cardui and she thought the illness was giving him hallucinations: what he saw wasn't the future at all. But Mr Fogarty thought the future wasn't set yet and what he saw were two different *possibilities*. In one possible future, Henry saved the Realm, in the other one he didn't.'

'Why didn't Mr Fogarty –?' Blue began, then stopped, as the answer to her own question occurred to her.

Pyrgus said, 'Mr Fogarty thought that if he risked a few more bouts of fever, he might remember enough details to make sure we reached the right future. That's why he wouldn't go back to the Analogue World. He knew that would stop the fever attacks and the rest of us might drift into the future where the Realm was wiped out.'

Blue was staring at him intently. 'You mean he sacrificed himself to save the Realm?'

'I don't think he meant to,' Pyrgus said. 'He probably thought he could survive more fever bouts than he did. But – yes. Yes, he did sacrifice himself for the Realm.'

There was a tiny clock built into the dashboard of the flyer. Blue suddenly realised she could hear it ticking. She licked her lips. 'Did he ...?'

'Remember enough to make sure a cure is found? Sort of ...' Pyrgus said. 'Yes and no.'

'Yes and no – *what?*' Blue asked irritably. 'Are we in the future that has the cure or aren't we?'

'It depends.'

Blue closed her eyes the way their mother used to do when she was exasperated beyond measure. 'On what?' she asked quietly.

'On whether we do it right,' Pyrgus said. 'Mr Fogarty couldn't see everything all at once. He got a detail here, a detail there. He didn't find out how to bring about the future with the cure, but he did notice certain things happened in the good future that didn't happen in the other one. So he had the idea that if we all did the things he'd seen us do in the good future, then that might help bring it about, even if what we were doing had nothing to do with the cure or Henry or anything obvious.'

'That's why Madam Cynthia used the transport,' Blue said in an instant of revelation.

'Yes,' Pyrgus said. 'We didn't know how that would make a difference, or even if it definitely *would* make a difference, but Mr Fogarty saw it happen in the good future, so we thought it best for her to do it.'

'Even though it put Henry's life at risk,' Blue said flatly.

'Blue, we had to –'

'I know, I know,' Blue cut in quickly. 'I'm not blaming you. It's just –' She shrugged. 'You know.'

'Yes, I know,' Pyrgus said kindly. 'There was an awful lot of discussion. We all love Henry too, you know.'

'Yes,' Blue said. She stared at him thoughtfully, her face set. 'So Madam Cynthia transported him because that's what Mr Fogarty remembered?'

'Yes.'

'And you're going after him because that's what Mr Fogarty remembered?'

'Yes.'

'So while everybody's racing round doing what Mr Fogarty remembered, what am I supposed to be doing?'

Pyrgus licked his lips warily. 'Actually, Mr Fogarty couldn't remember you doing anything. I mean, he didn't say you were just sitting there doing nothing, he didn't think *that*. But as I said, he couldn't remember everything, otherwise we'd all be certain what was going on. And I expect you were doing a whole lot, I mean really *contributing,* but he just didn't remember that. For some reason . . .' He trailed off lamely.

Blue opened her mouth to say something, but Pyrgus suddenly got a second wind and said, 'We talked for ages, all of us, about whether to tell you. I mean, that was really, really important, you being Queen and everything. But eventually we decided it would be better if you didn't know.' He saw her expression and his enthusiasm disappeared again. 'In case you did something you ... shouldn't ... do ...'

Blue flipped the obsidian disc into his hand. 'Start the flyer,' she said crossly.

Thirty-Nine

Henry thought he might be dreaming. His eyes were open, but what he was seeing wasn't making any sense. The face staring down at him was blue, for cripe's sake. Blue skin, blue hair, blue eyes. Behind the blue face was a blue-white sky, bleached by the relentless sun.

Henry closed his eyes and discovered there was water on his lips. It was a marvellous discovery, a truly marvellous, cheer-you-up discovery. He smiled and was still smiling as he sank into the dreamless darkness.

He woke with a start. He was still lying on the sand, but he seemed a little better. Much of the pain had gone from his arm, although his leg ached through that scary numbness. But the main thing was he felt stronger *in himself*, as if he'd had an energy shot. And it was night, which meant it was cooler. In fact it was so cool he shivered. He moved his head and discovered someone had lit a fire.

His energy shot ran out abruptly. (Just moving his head seemed to have done it.) He lay there, breathing heavily and staring out towards the flames.

He was lying propped against a massive boulder, which wasn't where he fell. That meant somebody had moved him or moved the boulder and he didn't think the boulder was so likely. Somebody moved him, then lit a fire, but left him a little way from the fire, underneath the boulder.

Henry groaned. He wasn't sure if the groan reached his lips.

In the firelight he could see he was in a large natural hollow, protected on three sides by rocks. There was no sign of vegetation, nothing to explain where the firewood came from.

A silhouetted figure passed between him and the fire.

'Nnnnyyyhhh,' said Henry.

The figure returned to his field of vision as it trotted towards him. Henry blinked and the figure resolved itself into a naked boy. His skin looked jet black in the firelight.

'Are you awake?' the boy asked anxiously. He squatted by Henry's side.

Who are you? Henry thought, then discovered his mouth wasn't working properly as he asked, 'Oooo or ooo?'

But the boy understood him somehow. 'Lorquinianus – Lorquin. Tribe Luchti.' He held a bulging little leather pouch under Henry's nose. 'Do not talk and for Charaxes' sake do not move. Just drink.' He placed the pouch to Henry's lips.

Henry was expecting water, but the liquid was tart and slightly viscous. It cooled his mouth like menthol, then trickled in a cold stream down his throat. It had to be a stimulant, and a powerful one at that, for he felt his strength beginning to return at once. His breathing eased and his eyes began to focus properly. Lorquin, the boy, looked hardly more than twelve years old, small for his age and very lightly built. There was no way this youngster could have carried Henry on his own.

Despite the warning not to talk, Henry made a massive effort and said, 'Hello, Lorquin. I'm Henry.' Then he drank a little more of the liquid. Lorquin smelled funny, not exactly unpleasant, but a body odour that was ... smoky.

'Are you too hot?' Lorquin asked.

Henry started to shake his head, thought better of it and simply said, 'No.'

'Too cold?'

'A little.' He smiled at the boy. Regardless of who had actually moved him, he felt grateful to this youngster.

'I'll find something to cover you,' Lorquin said. 'I don't want to move you closer to the fire. I don't want to move you anywhere more than I can help.'

'Thank you,' Henry whispered. Even though he was feeling better, he didn't much want to be moved yet either.

'The best thing,' said Lorquin soberly, sounding more grown-up than he looked, 'would be for you to get more sleep. Sleep through the night, if you can; just lie still and rest if you can't. You have to gather up your strength – you'll need it.'

'Why?' Henry asked.

'I have to amputate your leg tomorrow,' Lorquin said.

forty

Henry came to again feeling worried, without being able to remember exactly why. It was morning now. The fire was a small pile of glowing embers and the air had a dawn chill, but the sun was already dominating a cloudless sky with the promise of another brutal day to come.

He was still lying underneath his boulder and somebody had covered him with a very light, leathery membrane, like the wing of a giant bat. *Lorquin.* It was the boy Lorquin who'd saved him. He struggled to sit up.

Lorquin was squatting just a few yards away from him, watching him intently with large, round eyes. Henry blinked. The boy wasn't black at all, but blue – skin, hair, eyes – just like the creature Henry had seen in his dream. Except it wasn't a dream and it wasn't a creature. That must have been Lorquin too. He wasn't quite naked either: he carried a small pouch on one hip, tied round his waist with a leather thong.

'Are you all right?' Lorquin asked. 'I didn't think you would survive the night.'

Henry placed his back against the boulder. 'I'm fine,' he said automatically, then caught himself and added, 'I'm okay. Bit shaky, weak. But I'm okay, I think. Who brought me here?'

'I did,' Lorquin said.

In daylight, the boy seemed smaller and skinnier than ever. 'How?' Henry asked.

'Carried you,' said Lorquin. He had a wary look about him. His eyes kept flicking away from Henry to check his environment.

Okaaay, Henry thought. Maybe the kid was boasting, maybe he was stronger than he looked. Didn't really matter. At least Henry was here – wherever *here* was – and not dead.

'How is your leg?' Lorquin asked.

The memory flooded back at once. *I have to amputate your leg tomorrow.* Or had he just dreamed that? Cautiously he said, 'It's sore.'

'And numb?'

'Yes. Numb,' Henry confirmed.

'Vaettir got you?' When Henry didn't answer straightaway, Lorquin added, 'Looked like a vaettir bite.'

'Don't know,' Henry said. 'Got it from a thing in a tomb.'

'Pale and thin and fast? Nasty teeth?'

'That's it.'

Lorquin nodded. 'Vaettir all right. They're not exactly poisonous, but when they bite you, the wound mostly won't heal. It gets infected and stays infected and 'ventually kills you. Better have another look. Take your trousers down.'

Henry hesitated, then realised modesty hardly came into it when you were dealing with a boy who ran around naked. He unfastened his belt as Lorquin rose to his feet and trotted over with a curiously loping gait. As Henry carefully pushed the trousers downwards, he realised he might be in bigger trouble than he thought. The leg looked horrible. The swelling had extended well above the knee and into his thigh. The whole thing was hideously discoloured.

Lorquin bent over it and sniffed. 'Wound smells bad,' he said conversationally. 'Think I was right.'

After a moment Henry said, 'About what?' He had a nasty feeling he knew the answer.

Lorquin straightened up. 'Bad enough if it stays in the leg. If the infection travels into the rest of you, it shuts down your innards. When it shuts down your heart, that kills you. Of course by then you don't really care.' He looked at Henry. 'If it spreads. Only sure cure is to take the leg off.'

'I'm not having my leg off,' Henry said.

'You don't have to do it yourself,' Lorquin said. 'I can do it for you – I have a very sharp knife. I have a saw thing for the bone.'

'I'm not having my leg off!' Henry said again.

'I work really fast.'

'What age are you?' Henry asked.

Lorquin blinked at him. 'Ten. 'Leven. I dunno. What's that got to do with anything?'

Henry wasn't sure, except that it was hard to take a little kid seriously. And Lorquin was a really *weird* little kid. Henry wanted to ask him why he was blue, whether that was his natural colour or some sort of dye. Henry wanted to ask him what he was doing out in the desert all on his own without his mum and dad. Henry wanted to ask him if he really *had* carried Henry, how he knew about vaettirs, why he wasn't wearing any clothes, how …

Lorquin was the most self-assured youngster Henry had ever seen – far more confident than Henry had been at age ten or eleven. And the way he stood there, all blue and naked in the sand: he looked like he *belonged* in the desert. Which he probably did. He must do. Anybody who could wander about naked in the desert without dying had to live here. And if he lived here, he had to know things. Actually it was obvious he *did* know things. He knew about vaettirs and lighting fires when there was nothing to burn and finding bat stuff to cover people who got cold. Maybe he knew about bite wounds as well.

Henry's leg twinged with such sudden violence that he gasped.

'You okay?' Lorquin asked at once.

When his heartbeat settled down a bit, Henry said, 'You say cutting off the leg is the only sure cure. Is there any other cure that isn't so sure?'

Lorquin looked thoughtful. 'I once saw a clever man lance the infection. That works sometimes. Only when the wound isn't as far gone as yours, though.'

'Let's try it,' Henry said.

Lorquin produced a piece of knapped flint from his pouch. It looked for all the world like a prehistoric arrowhead from a museum exhibit and it took Henry a moment to realise this was his knife. He swallowed. 'What happens?'

'You cut at the heart of the wound and it lets the badness out. Sometimes you have to squeeze the leg.'

'I'll do it,' Henry said quickly. He licked his lips. 'Heat the knife in the fire.' Heating the knife would sterilise it.

Lorquin stared at him as if he'd gone mad. 'Fire will crack the knife,' he said.

It probably would. What the hell, Henry thought, he had so many malevolent bacteria in his leg already, a few more wouldn't make any difference. 'Give it here,' he said, holding out his hand.

'Don't put my knife in the fire.'

'No, I won't,' Henry promised. He took the flint and noticed with a flicker of relief the knapped edge really was razor sharp. 'How do you know the heart of the wound? Where the teeth marks are?'

Lorquin shook his head. 'Look for a place where the swelling has gone green with a black dot in the middle of it.' He pointed. 'There – see?'

The skin around the area was stretched taut and hurt like hell when he pressed it with his finger. 'This it?'

'Yes. Cut deep.'

Henry licked his lips again. He took a firm grip on the flint. The kid was probably right. It was like lancing a boil. It hurt a bit at the time; then the pus oozed out and all the pain and swelling were relieved. Well, maybe it hurt a *lot* at the time. Didn't matter. It had to be worth it. He stared at the stretched skin and thought about the pain when he'd poked it with his finger. Poked it gently. With a *blunt* finger. He couldn't begin to imagine what it would be like to cut it with a stone knife.

'And wide.'

'Pardon?' Henry said.

'Cut deep and wide. *All* the badness must come out.'

'You do it,' Henry said and handed back the knife.

Lorquin slashed once across the taut skin, passing directly over the black spot in the middle. Then he cut again swiftly at right angles. A splattering of blood and pus stained his blue skin. More blood and a greenish ooze flowed copiously down Henry's leg. Lorquin dropped the knife, reached across and squeezed the leg firmly with both hands. 'Ahhhh!' Henry screamed. The pain was indescribable. For a moment he thought he was going to faint. Then he thought he was going to die. Then it ebbed.

Lorquin leaned forward to look. 'Might not have to lose your leg, after all,' he said.

forty-One

'I thought we were going to Haleklind,' said Chalkhill.

Brimstone shook his head. 'No.'

'New Altran?'

'No.'

'The Feltwell Crescent?'

'Hairstreak has cousins in the Feltwell Crescent.'

'Where then?' Chalkhill demanded.

'Buthner,' Brimstone told him shortly.

Chalkhill blinked. 'That godsforsaken wilderness? The Faeries' Graveyard?'

'Yes.'

'There's nothing there,' Chalkhill wailed. 'The country's run by savages and half the population are nomads. They *eat* people in Buthner.'

'That's an urban myth,' said Brimstone.

'How can it be an urban myth when there aren't any towns?' When Brimstone failed to answer, Chalkhill pressed, 'Why a haelhole like Buthner?'

'Can you think of anywhere better to hide something?'

He had a point. Chalkhill stared through the window of the coach, wishing it was an ouklo. Although they were only just approaching the southern border of Altran, the weather outside looked oppressively hot. Heaven only knew what it would be like when they reached Buthner.

And why didn't they have any guards? They were going to need someone to protect them from the savages.

The coach hit a pothole and jarred Chalkhill's spine. 'Why couldn't we have flown?' he demanded. 'An ouklo would have been ten times as fast and a million times more comfortable.'

'Hairstreak may be watching the airports.'

'He doesn't have the manpower for that any more! The little creep has hardly any money. Except mine now,' Chalkhill added sourly.

'Oh, you can stop payment on the draft,' Brimstone said, as if suddenly remembering something unimportant.

'Are you serious?'

'Perfectly. I don't need the Brotherhood any more. You can stop payment at the border – there'll be banking facilities.'

The old cretin was infuriating. Why hadn't he mentioned this before? It might be too late now, although Chalkhill would bend heaven and earth to make sure no gold was actually transferred. Because he was angry at Brimstone he said, 'If you'd told me that sooner, I could have used the cash to hire a private flyer. Quite untraceable.'

'It won't fly,' Brimstone said. He had a small purse on his lap and was fiddling inside it.

'What won't fly?'

Brimstone nodded back towards the trailer that was transporting their captive.

'Of course it will fly!' Chalkhill exclaimed. 'It's a full-grown –'

'Quiet!' Brimstone hissed urgently. 'If the coachman finds out what we're carrying, we're finished. These carriages have very thin roofs.'

'All right, I won't mention what it is,' Chalkhill said. 'But you know what I mean.'

'Of course I know what you mean,' Brimstone said crossly. He dropped his voice another notch. 'It will fly under its own power, but it panics if you try to put it into anything spell-driven. Darkness knows I tried. That's how it got injured.'

'How ironical,' Chalkhill said. It was hard to get his head around. But then there were a lot of things about this little escapade that were hard to get his head around. 'All the same –' he began.

Brimstone waved him to silence. 'We're coming up to Customs. This is the tricky bit. So keep your mouth shut and let me do the talking.'

'Gladly,' Chalkhill said. 'It's your head.' Except it wasn't. If Customs found out what they had in the trailer, it would be both of them for the chop, however much he pleaded innocence and ignorance.

The border was marked by a flimsy rustic fence that looked as if it wouldn't stop a migrating slith, but its spell coatings were guaranteed to halt anything short of a full-scale invasion. The Customs Houses, build in the reign of Scolitandes the Weedy, were on a monumental scale, with vast warehousing to hold confiscated goods. The times were less troubled now, the formalities far more relaxed, but the Customs Officers were watchful and anybody found trying to smuggle contraband usually disappeared for a very long time. If he wasn't hanged.

Chalkhill shuddered as Brimstone climbed down from the coach.

The officer was covered in braid and as self-important as a pigeon. He ignored both Brimstone and the driver while he strutted round the coach and stared up at the covered trailer behind it.

'What's this then?' he asked.

'Crated nants for export,' Brimstone said. He produced documents in triplicate and handed them across. 'You'll find the papers are in order.'

'Maybe I will and maybe I won't,' the officer told him. He studied the papers carefully.

'Clement weather for the time of year,' said Brimstone conversationally. Coaches leaving the country passed through the archway up ahead and into a short tunnel. When they emerged, they were on foreign soil.

The officer ignored him. After a while he glanced up towards the trailer. 'Those things live?'

'Not much good dead,' Brimstone said.

'Let's see then.'

'They're crated,' Brimstone said.

'I know they're crated. Let's see them.'

'That'll mean opening the crate,' Brimstone said. 'It's very well sealed.'

'Better get on with it then.'

Brimstone sighed and nodded to the coach driver, who climbed down and pulled the tarpaulin off his trailer. Chalkhill began to climb out as well, preparatory to making a run for it. 'Get back in the coach,' said Brimstone conversationally. Chalkhill recognised the undertone of menace and backed off at once.

'See?' said Brimstone as the huge crate came into view.

'I see,' said the official. 'Now I want to see *in*.'

Brimstone nodded again at the driver, who produced a crowbar from his toolkit and began to prise off one side of the wooden crate. After a moment, the siding fell away to reveal the cage inside. The heavy titanium bars were reinforced with fine wire mesh. Beyond it crawled the nants, several hundred thousand of them, their stubby wings beating furiously. Brimstone waited. The Customs Officer bent forward to peer closely through the mesh. As he did so, the nants set up their familiar, grating, high-pitched whine. The man drew back at once.

'Would you like to go inside, Officer?' Brimstone asked innocently. 'There's a double door to keep them from escaping.'

'No, thank you,' said the officer stiffly. He glanced at the papers again, then nodded to the coachman. 'Crate them up again. You're free to go on.'

'Thank you, Officer,' said Brimstone unctuously.

The coachman pushed the wooden side back onto the crate and secured it roughly before drawing the tarpaulin over it again. In the darkness, the nants began to settle and their high-pitched whine died down. The Customs Officer stepped aside and waved them onwards with large, sweeping motions of his arm, as if he was suddenly anxious to get rid of them. The coachman climbed back into his seat. Brimstone made to join Chalkhill inside the carriage.

From somewhere deep inside the covered crate, a voice called, *'Help!'*

The scene froze for an instant; then the Customs Officer slowly turned his head towards the trailer.

'Just my little joke,' said Brimstone quickly. 'I'm a ventriloquist.'

'I don't think so,' said the Customs Officer. 'Get it opened up again.'

forty-two

'Go!' screamed Brimstone at the coachman.

The man whipped the horses at once and the coach sprang forward, hurling Chalkhill backwards to fall heavily on a none-too-well-padded seat. '*Squeak!*' he gasped.

'Guard!' shouted the Customs Officer. 'Halt that coach!'

Armed men began to pour in a steady stream from the Customs Houses. Brimstone leaned out of the coach window and tossed a multi-coloured ball towards them. As it struck the ground, it began to belch a rolling, rainbow smoke.

'Look out!' called one of the men. 'It's a screamer!'

On cue, the ball emitted a blood-curdling shriek. Chalkhill clapped his hands over his ears. The running guards split into two streams like a river striking a stone. The screamer bounced between them, gathered speed and hurtled towards the open door of the Customs House building. As the smoke rolled over the men, they too began to howl. Several of them broke ranks, dropped their weapons and ran off in sudden panic.

Brimstone struggled to close the window of the coach as it hurtled towards the archway. Behind him, the jolting motion disturbed the nants again and they set up a discordant wail that echoed the screamer.

The screamer itself clicked loudly and metamorphosed into a score or more of smaller, multi-coloured spheres, which bounced, scattered and finally flew with unerring aim towards the windows of the Customs House.

'Evacuate!' someone shouted.

Each of the smaller spheres was shrieking now, filling the air with a manic howling that scrambled thought and chilled the blood. The horses leaped forward as if stung, then thundered through the archway en route for the tunnel. Brimstone had the window closed now so that the noise outside was muted to a bearable level. All the same, Chalkhill could hear the sound of shattered glass as spheres crashed through windows.

All went black as the coach plunged into the tunnel. From behind came the *clump-clump* of regular explosions. Then the coach emerged into the sunlight. Chalkhill dragged himself to his feet and opened the window again. He leaned out and craned to see behind. The massive structures of the Customs Houses were collapsing one after another in a pall of rising dust and smoke. The shriek of the screamer was replaced by a wailing siren. Flames leaped towards the sky as billows of black smoke rolled across the ground. Men were running everywhere, their faces grey with panic.

The coach picked up speed as it drew away from the scene of destruction.

'That went well,' Brimstone remarked.

Chalkhill said nothing. All he could think of was that he hadn't managed to stop payment on his bank draft.

forty-three

'Where are we going?' Blue asked as the flyer soared above the treetops.

'I don't know,' Pyrgus said. He was seated at the controls, wrestling with the unfamiliar instrumentation rather than using spell-driven voice commands like any sensible pilot. She wondered why he always liked to do things the hard way.

'What do you mean, you don't know?' Blue demanded. 'You're supposed to be flying this thing.'

Pyrgus sighed. 'I mean I don't know where we're going *ultimately*. I don't know where we're going to try to find *Henry*.' He risked a glance away from the instrument panel so he could glare at her briefly. 'I told you that.'

'I know you told me that, but you've been telling lots of lies lately. How am I supposed to spot the rare occasion when you're moved to tell the truth?'

The flyer started to lose height and Pyrgus returned hurriedly to his controls. 'Well, I *really* don't know where Henry is,' he muttered sourly.

He wanted to be left alone because there was something he still wasn't telling her – Blue recognised the signs from childhood. 'If we're not going to find Henry,' she said firmly, 'where *are* we going? Or did you just decide to take a little pleasure jaunt in the middle of the night?'

'There's no need for sarcasm,' Pyrgus told her firmly. 'It's not ladylike and it's not regal and it doesn't suit you.'

'Just answer the question, Pyrgus.'

Pyrgus lowered his head. 'Going to mut mam dwee,' he muttered.

'What?'

Pyrgus punched a console button fiercely. 'Going to meet Madame Cardui,' he said. 'She knows where Henry is.'

'Madame Cardui's in jail.' Blue frowned. 'At least she's under house arrest in the Palace. By my orders.'

'She's escaped,' Pyrgus said.

Blue stared at the back of his head. 'How do you know?'

'She told me that's what she was going to do. I expect she's done it by now.'

'She told *me* she wasn't!' Blue exclaimed, open-mouthed. 'She *promised* me she wouldn't even *try* to escape.'

'She lied,' said Pyrgus shortly. He threw a switch that put the flyer on autopilot and turned to look at her. 'Blue, you mustn't be cross. Not with her, not with me, not with any of us. We're all trying to do the right thing, because if we get this wrong, the Realm's at stake. And so are some of us personally, come to that. If we're in the wrong future, Madame Cardui catches time fever and dies. So do Comma and Nymph. I've already got it and I don't recover.' His voiced dropped. 'You get it too, Blue.'

'Mr Fogarty saw all this?'

'In bits and pieces, yes. But it all comes from us getting into the wrong future. All of it.'

'I get the fever and die?' Blue said.

Pyrgus shook his head. 'Mr Fogarty didn't see that. Didn't see your actual death. But you turn into an old woman, all weak and feeble and crabby with arthritis and you're trying to rule a Realm where everybody's dying and it spreads to animals and it just gets worse and worse.' He looked at her earnestly. 'Blue, we couldn't let that happen – we just couldn't. Maybe we were wrong not to tell you everything, but Mr Fogarty just didn't *see* where you came in, so we thought it better not to take the risk.'

After a long moment, Blue said, 'I understand.' Her eyes flared briefly. 'I think you were all wrong what you did, but I understand.' She came across and put a hand on Pyrgus's shoulder. 'All right, now where are we meeting Madame Cardui?'

Pyrgus hesitated for just the barest second, then said, 'Myphisto Manor.'

'Oh dear,' Blue said.

forty-four

At the height of his popularity, Madame Cardui's late husband, the Great Myphisto, accumulated enough gold to build himself a country retreat in the most fashionable sector of Wildmoor Broads, tantalisingly close to the Nikure Barrens. True to his nature, he used no spells in its construction, yet the place was not at all what it seemed.

On the face of things, it appeared to be a small, charming manor house set in wooded grounds beside a running stream. But the woods were a stage set, a combination of cunningly painted forest backdrop fronted by stands of artificial trees. The brook, for all its babble, contained not a single drop of water. It was a mechanical contrivance constructed from shreds of metallic paper.

Nor did the whimsy stop there. Myphisto's visitors reported that the imposing entrance door was painted on a blank wall. Should you look through any of the picture windows, you would see rooms that did not, in fact, exist. The ghost that haunted the manor's long gallery was created by a calculating placement of sheet glass and mirrors. Certain guest chairs in the banquet hall wailed horribly when sat upon. There was a revolving staircase that led the unwary to a different floor each time it was used. There was a great bird, a masterpiece of papier mâché, that swooped down from the rafters on hidden wires. The music room had a clockwork orchestra. There was a booth in the hallway containing the top half of a turbaned automaton that played chess.

From the air, the gardens were cunningly laid out to represent the grinning face of a circus clown, with clumps of dahlias as its eyes. 'Are you going to land in the grounds?' Blue asked a little anxiously.

'Are you out of your mind?' asked Pyrgus. 'We're going to have a hard enough time just walking through them.'

He brought the flyer down (with surprising skill) to one side of a laneway flanking the estate. They followed the wall until they reached the entrance gates.

'Careful,' Blue warned.

'I'll have to try it,' Pyrgus told her. 'His tricks cycle through a random sequence. Sometimes what you see is what you get.' He pushed the gates, which sprang open at once.

'Well, go on,' Blue urged.

Pyrgus stepped through the gates and vanished. The gates themselves slammed shut. Blue waited. After a while, Pyrgus approached on the laneway, looking perplexed. 'What happened?' Blue asked.

'I'm not sure,' Pyrgus frowned. 'I think I was grabbed by mechanical arms and there may have been a trapdoor of some sort. It all happened very fast. How did it look to you?'

'Like an invisibility spell, but without the shimmer.'

'Well,' said Pyrgus with no great enthusiasm, 'the good news is I came out through a door in the wall we can use to get back in. I examined it carefully and it doesn't seem to be gimmicked.'

He was right about the door, but when they entered the grounds they couldn't find the house. At first they wandered through an artificial forest with paths that changed and changed again each time they retraced their steps. Then, when they solved the maze eventually, they emerged into an open space where the perspectives were all wrong. They could see the house all right, but it kept receding as they walked towards it. It took them almost fifteen minutes to realise they were actually walking towards a series of reflections. Even then, they might have wandered confused for another hour had not a uniformed butler emerged from the undergrowth and offered to show them the way.

'Do you think I should tip him?' Pyrgus asked Blue quietly.

Blue gave him a withering look. 'Don't be silly – he's a machine. The Great Myphisto had dozens of them made.'

They found Madame Cardui poring over an enormous map scroll spread out across a dining table. She half turned as they entered. 'Pyrgus deeah, just in –' She stopped. 'Ah.' There was a long pause; then she said, 'Your Majesty.'

'Never mind my majesty, Madam Cynthia,' Blue said. 'I had your word you wouldn't try to escape.'

'Indeed you did, deeah, and I would break it again if I thought it would help the Realm.' She looked across at Pyrgus. 'Why did you bring your sister?'

'Didn't have much option,' Pyrgus muttered.

Madame Cardui turned back to Blue. 'My deeah, you have my apology, for what it's worth. Can I assume Pyrgus has explained why we failed to involve you?'

Blue nodded, a little grimly. 'He explained. I'm not sure I accept it.' *Or quite understand it, for that matter,* but she decided not to complicate things.

'Well, it *is* complex,' Madame Cardui said sympathetically. 'And perhaps we were wrong in what we did. Poor Alan didn't see you in the future we are striving to bring about, but that doesn't necessarily mean you aren't there. In fact I'm sure you are. Nonetheless, we took what we thought to be the safest course. But it may not have been the correct course, or, indeed, the only course. In any case, we will soon know.'

Something in her voice alerted Blue at once. 'Why do you say that, Madame Cardui?'

'Alan saw this meeting, here in this room. It took place between Pyrgus and myself. You were not present. Now you are. The future has already been altered.'

'Oh,' Blue said. She glanced at Pyrgus, who was ostentatiously studying a mechanical canary in a golden cage, then looked back at Madame Cardui. 'For the worse?' she asked.

Madame Cardui said seriously, 'That depends on why you did not show up in Alan's visions.' She smiled bleakly 'In any case, we shall soon find out.' She turned back to the map. 'Since you are here and the future has been changed, I see no reason to continue blocking your involvement. Frankly, I felt uncomfortable with what we were doing, but as I say, we believed it to be the safest course. I hope you will forgive us.'

'Yes, of course,' Blue said in a voice that gave away little. Then she stepped forward and her old assertiveness surfaced abruptly. 'Even if the future really *has* changed, that doesn't mean we have to forget about Mr Fogarty's visions. Some of them may still be helpful.'

'That had occurred to me,' said Madame Cardui quietly.

'Pyrgus says he doesn't know where Henry is now,' Blue said, 'but you do – is that right?'

Madame Cardui nodded. 'Yes. Alan told me.' She pointed to a segment of the map.

Blue leaned forward. 'Buthner?'

'I'm afraid so.'

'So you and Pyrgus planned to go to Buthner?'

'Yes.'

'With how many men?'

'As an entourage? None.'

'How did you expect to survive?' Blue asked without irony or edge. 'Buthner is one of the most dangerous regions in the world.'

Madame Cardui shrugged. 'I was simply following Alan's visions. In the successful future he foresaw, we went alone.'

'So you think we should still go alone? Without support or guards?'

'Yes.' Madame Cardui turned towards her. 'Do you have a problem with that?'

'No,' Blue said without hesitation. 'Not if it gets Henry – not if it helps save the Realm. Do we fly or go overland?'

Madame Cardui said, 'We can't fly directly into Buthner. The natives have no understanding of modern spell technology. They think flyers are giant birds that have swallowed the people inside them. Any passenger who disembarks is believed to be cursed and killed on sight. The typical Buthneri is a simple, primitive creature I'm afraid, and very, very vicious. However, the Realm has friendly relations with the Government of

Hass-Verbim, which borders on Buthner to the north. We can fly there, then cross the border on foot.'

'Do you know exactly where Henry is?' Blue asked.

Madame Cardui shook her head. 'No. We shall have to search for him.'

Blue said, 'What is it, Madame Cynthia? What are you not telling me?'

Madame Cardui smiled. 'How well you know me, deeah. Yes, there is something. At least there *might* be something. In the two futures that Alan foresaw – both the good and the bad – Henry was in Buthner. But your appearance here means we have now entered a third possible future, different from both the others.' She sighed. 'I'm afraid in *this* future there is no guarantee at all that Henry will be in Buthner.'

'Or even still alive,' Pyrgus put in helpfully.

forty-five

Henry's leg still wouldn't support his weight and it hurt worse than at any time since the vaettir bit him. But it was a clean pain and the swelling was way down and what came out when Lorquin squeezed the wound was good red blood, not the yellow-green slime that had oozed earlier.

Lorquin had built him a crude shelter using branches of deadwood – where had he found them? – and the batwing thing that had covered Henry when he was cold in the night. Lorquin had also given him water, a little more of the tart juice and fed him something white and bloated that Henry didn't care to examine too closely. It tasted of roast garlic and satisfied his hunger remarkably well.

'Lorquin …?'

'Yes, En Ri?'

'Your … ah … colour. Is it natural?'

Lorquin looked at him blankly.

'The blue colour,' Henry said, half wishing he hadn't started this. 'Is it, like, your own skin colour, or do you use, you know, dye and stuff?'

'I am Luchti.' Lorquin shrugged, as if that explained something.

'Luchti's your tribe – right?'

'My people,' Lorquin said.

'Where are they?' Henry asked.

Lorquin made a vague gesture towards the distant horizon. He looked impatient with the whole conversation. Or possibly just puzzled.

Henry licked his lips. 'How is it you're alone in the desert? You *are* alone, aren't you?'

Lorquin nodded. 'Yes.'

'Why is that?' Henry asked. 'I mean, why aren't you with your people?'

'I seek the draugr,' Lorquin said. To Henry's surprise he smiled suddenly and broadly. 'I find you.'

Henry wondered what a draugr was, but thought he might come back to that in a minute. He had a shrewd suspicion what might be going on here. 'You're about to become a man, aren't you?'

Lorquin stuck his narrow chest out proudly. 'Yes.'

Bingo, Henry thought. He'd read about this sort of thing somewhere, or possibly watched a documentary on television. Lots of primitive tribes had puberty rites for young boys. They marked the transition from childhood to manhood. You were turned loose to fend for yourself in the bush or the jungle or the desert, and if you survived the ordeal, you became a man. Sometimes it got really heavy. Young Masai or Zulu or somebody had to go and kill a lion before they were allowed back in the tribe. He hoped Lorquin's *draugr* wasn't something like that, but there was a chance it might be. He opened his mouth to ask, but Lorquin beat him to it.

'Finding you was a good omen, En Ri,' Lorquin said.

'Why's that?' Henry asked.

'When the Companion stands, we know the vaettir lives,' Lorquin said incomprehensibly.

For some reason it stopped Henry dead. 'Lorquin,' he said. 'The draugr thing is something you have to find in order to become a man? Like a treasure? Some rare plant? Something your tribe values very highly?' Even as he asked, he knew what the answer would be, but he really, really didn't want the situation to unfold the way he thought it was going to.

Lorquin grinned at him. 'The draugr is something we have to kill, En Ri.'

The word *we* flashed neon lights. 'We?' Henry echoed. 'You mean you and me?'

'You are the Companion spoken of in the Holy Sagas,' Lorquin said benignly.

'Actually I'm not –'

'And as Companion you will help me find the draugr, just as the songs say.'

'Lorquin, I don't know anything about your songs. Or draugrs. I don't know what they are. I don't know where I am. I don't know how I got here. I don't know how to get out of this desert. I don't even know what country I'm in. I can't –'

But Lorquin wasn't listening. He had that faraway look on his face evangelists get when they're trying to convert you. 'As Companion it is fated that you will help me *kill* the draugr.'

Even though he saw it coming, the words chilled Henry. He'd been telling nothing but the truth when he said he didn't know where he was or how he got here and now, with an awful inevitability, he was being drawn into something dangerous, probably something *hideously* dangerous if his past visits to the Faerie Realm were anything to go by. The trouble was, he owed Lorquin his life. He couldn't let the kid nurse him back to health, then just walk away and leave him to whatever dreadful task his tribe had decided would turn him into a man.

Henry took a deep breath. 'This draugr ...' he said cautiously. 'That's not another name for a vaettir, by any chance?'

'Oh no,' Lorquin said. 'The vaettir only guides us to the draugr. The draugr is the vaettir's father.'

forty-six

Chalkhill was complaining again. About the dust, about the heat, about the discomfort, about *everything*. Brimstone was beginning to wonder why he'd bothered to bring him. Then he glanced at the native bearers patiently carrying the crate and remembered. Chalkhill was the one with the gold. Chalkhill had always been the one with the gold.

But that would change soon. Oh yes, indeed.

'My feet are sore,' Chalkhill complained. 'You said we'd have got there by now.'

'We're close,' Brimstone told him.

'I hope this is going to be worth it.'

'Oh, it'll be worth it all right. You have no idea how much worth it it's going to be.'

The terrain actually wasn't too bad, despite Chalkhill's complaints. When they crossed the border there was a little greenery, some shrub and several open roads – beaten earth roads, to be sure, but maintained. And there were porters hanging round the Border Post. The trouble was there were no carriages, no horses, no pack animals and the use of spells was strictly forbidden by an exceptionally backward, superstitious Government. Brimstone tried to persuade their original coachman to take them further, but the man refused to cross the border even for an offer of double pay.

Since then, the broad road had become a track, the weather had grown hotter and the surroundings had become a little desolate, but nothing to justify Chalkhill's incessant moaning. The porters were carrying the crate and their supplies. The only thing Chalkhill was carrying was a mechanical click-gun, a primitive device compared with the spell-driven weapons at home, but what could you do? The penalty for smuggling magic was slow dismemberment and he hadn't been prepared to take the risk.

'What's this place called?' Chalkhill asked belligerently.

'What place?'

'The place we're going – what's it called?'

'Koob ban Eretz Evets,' Brimstone said. 'Roughly translates as *The Mountains of Madness*.'

Chalkhill frowned. 'Madness?' he asked. 'Mountains?'

'Yes.' Brimstone wished Chalkhill would stop talking. It was hot and he was tired as well (tired, but uncomplaining) and most of all he didn't want the natives listening in to his business. They pretended they didn't understand Faerie Standard, but Brimstone knew differently.

'Then we're not close,' Chalkhill snarled. 'If we were close, we would see them. You can see mountains for miles.'

Brimstone sighed inwardly. 'Not these ones,' he said. 'They're screened.'

For a moment he thought Chalkhill might be satisfied, but no. 'Magic screened?' Chalkhill frowned. 'I thought you said there was no magic in –?'

'There isn't,' Brimstone said quickly. It didn't do to talk too much about magic in front of the porters. The natives had a reputation for killing anybody they suspected of sorcery. He'd told Chalkhill that (and made him switch off his stupid spell-sparkle teeth), but the man never listened. 'It's an optical illusion. Like a mirage in reverse.' It was one of the reasons he'd chosen Koob ban Eretz Evets for this little jaunt. The mountains were hael to find without a current map. The mirage effect changed with the seasons, then changed again due to some random factor nobody quite understood. If you mapped them immediately after a change, you had a six-week window before your map became obsolete. The map Brimstone was following had only days left, but by then they would be there. He planned to leave a personalised tracer to help with the return visit and to hael with what the locals thought about magic.

To his irritation, the illusion intrigued Chalkhill. 'How do you reverse a mirage?'

'It's not really a mirage,' Brimstone said shortly. 'A mirage is just a reflection of something a long way away: it isn't real. The Mountains of Madness are real enough, but there's something in the atmosphere that reflects different territory on top of them.'

Frowning, Chalkhill said, 'So you think you're look-ing at a field or a lake when you're actually looking at the mountains?'

'Something like that. More likely desert. Most of Buthner is a wasteland.'

'Why madness? Why are they called the Mountains of Madness?'

'How should I know?' Brimstone snapped. 'Maybe the illusion drives the locals mad. How would you like to live where mountains keep appearing and disap-pearing?'

'When does it stop?'

'When does what stop?'

'The illusion. Or do you find out you've reached the mountains when you walk into them?'

It was entirely possible, Brimstone thought, that he would murder Chalkhill after all. The man was a haemorrhoid and always had been. He never stopped talking, he never stopped complaining and he was a total liability on a trip like this. His money had admittedly been useful, but once they reached the mountains, Brimstone planned to pay off the porters. Wouldn't do to have them see where he hid his treasure. He and Chalkhill could haul it into place between them, but once he'd set up the protections, he had no more need of Chalkhill. Or his money, heh-heh-heh. He'd have more money than he could ever spend for the rest of his life. And more power. It would be a pleasure to enjoy it without Chalkhill in his face.

'What?' Chalkhill asked.

Brimstone looked at him blankly. 'What what?'

'You're thinking,' Chalkhill said. 'That usually means trouble.'

Brimstone smiled at him. 'No, not at all. Thinking? Perish the thought! I was just pondering how intelligent your questions were. About the hidden mountains. Intelligent. Very. But you won't have to walk into them. Bump your nose? Good grief no. You'll see them soon. One minute not there, next minute they've appeared. Just like m –' He stopped himself in time. 'Just like a perfectly natural, completely understandable optical illusion caused by the unique layering of the air in this wonderful country. So keep a look-out, Jasper, because –' He stopped. Chalkhill's mouth was hanging open and his eyes were bulging in their sockets. Brimstone turned his head.

Behind him, the Mountains of Madness rose up in all their sudden splendour.

Forty-Seven

Brimstone was going to try to kill him, Chalkhill thought. The double bluff was typical. Hairstreak wants Brimstone to kill Chalkhill. Brimstone tells Chalkhill this, as if butter wouldn't melt in his mouth, to show he has no intention of killing Chalkhill. Then Brimstone kills Chalkhill anyway. Probably once they had this damn cage hidden.

Well, two could play at that game. Once they had this damn cage hidden, Chalkhill would move first. With Brimstone out of the way and the location of the cage in Chalkhill's head, Chalkhill could go home and negotiate any deal he pleased. He could have anything he wanted with this knowledge: more wealth, fame, power, whatever. And more importantly, he could enjoy it all without Brimstone in his face.

It would be easy to kill Brimstone. The old fool wouldn't be expecting it and Chalkhill was the one with the click-gun. But not quite yet. Although the porters were dismissed, the cage still had to be put in place and that was a two-man job.

'How much further do we have to push this?' he asked breathlessly. His legs ached, his arms ached, his shoulders ached and he was positively pouring sweat in a hideously disgusting smelly manner.

'As far as we need to,' Brimstone said irritatingly. He was one of those skinny old men who never seemed to sweat at all. Not that it made much difference to his smell. Even now, with the good old days of demon servants a receding memory, he still had the whiff of sulphur about him.

'Yes, but how far is that, Silas?' Chalkhill asked. Before they got their marching orders, the porters had lugged the crate high into the foothills. Once they'd gone, Brimstone had discarded the packing and released the nants to lighten things up a bit. With everything stripped away, the cage itself was a lot lighter, but even so, getting it as far as the cave mouth had been a struggle and now they were manhandling it along a warren of tunnels that ran deep into the mountain itself. Brimstone had clearly been here before, for he seemed to know exactly where he was going.

'Not far,' Brimstone said in exactly the same tone he'd used when he told Chalkhill the mountains were close. Then, rather surprisingly, he nodded towards the cage and added, 'Feeds on light.'

Chalkhill stared through the bars. 'Seriously?'

Brimstone paused to lean against the cage and nod his head. 'Photosynthesis. Nearest thing to a leaf – who'd have thought it? But then you can't really imagine one taking a dump, can you? Anyway, we have to hide it away so deeply it won't be found, but it must have a light source otherwise it starves to death. No good to us dead, eh? But I have just the place. Come on, you've caught your breath now: a bit more effort and we're there.'

It took more than a bit more effort, but when they finally did get *there*, Chalkhill had to admit Brimstone had chosen an amazing location. It was a vast cavern deep in the heart of the mountain, guarded by a complicated maze of tunnels. Crystal formations clung to every wall and hung down in stalactites like chandeliers. But the stroke of natural genius lay high above in the vaulted ceiling. A crevice in the bedrock of the mountain let in a beam of sunshine that shone into the cavern like a searchlight and reflected back from ten thousand crystal facets.

'Shouldn't go hungry,' Chalkhill remarked.

'Let's get it underneath the beam,' Brimstone said. 'That way we'll be sure.'

Together they manhandled the cage across the cavern floor and into the beam. It looked like a display piece or a particularly elaborate stage set. Chalkhill stepped back and reached surreptitiously for his click-gun. Then hesitated. If he killed Brimstone now, he might have problems finding his way out of the mountain. He *thought* he knew the route through the winding tunnels, but frankly he wasn't sure. It was difficult enough pushing a heavy cage without trying to remember exactly where you were going. Best to wait until they were out in the open again. Unless Brimstone tried to kill *him*, of course, in which case he'd use the click-gun and take his chances.

'There now,' Brimstone was saying. 'Isn't that a pretty sight?' He stepped back and briskly brushed the dust off his hands. 'Now we'd better set up the Guardian.'

Chalkhill blinked. 'Guardian?' Brimstone hadn't said anything about a Guardian.

'Don't think we can leave a thing like this unguarded, do you?' Brimstone snapped. 'We'll put a Guardian in the outer cavern.' He frowned suddenly. 'Or do you think it would be better wandering the tunnels? We want something that keeps people out as well as keeping *that* –' he jerked his head in the direction of the cage '– in.'

Chalkhill stared at him. 'Just a minute, Silas – you did say Guardian?'

'Yes, yes. What do you think I said?'

'A *magical* Guardian?'

'Of course a magical Guard –' Brimstone broke off and a slow smile spread across his face. 'You don't *really* think I'd come on a job like this without my spells, do you?'

'But they dismember you in this country if you bring in spells!' Chalkhill wailed. It had never occurred to him Brimstone might risk it. But the old scrote obviously had. Which meant that he, Chalkhill, was standing here armed with only a click-gun, while Brimstone could well be stuffed to the gills with magical armaments.

'Only if they catch you.' Brimstone grinned. 'Right, I'm going to need your help again.' He started to walk back towards the outer cavern.

Chalkhill stood for a moment, open-mouthed, then hurried after him. 'What sort of Guardian are you going to set up?' he burbled. 'You can't use a demon since they made Blue Queen of Hael. A captive spirit will find a way to break free eventually. I don't think a thought form is going to hold what we have in here. I can't imagine –'

Brimstone stopped and looked him soberly in the eye. 'I was thinking of the Jormungand,' he said.

'My gods,' squeaked Chalkhill, 'not the Jormungand!'

forty-Eight

Compared to the crystalline cave with its sunlight beam, the outer cavern was gloomy, but not entirely dark since quite a lot of light shone through. Water filtered through as well, a rare commodity in this parched country, leaving the cavern dripping and dank. In many ways a perfect home for the Jormungand.

Chalkhill was still whingeing, of course. *Are you sure about this, Silas? Do you realise how dangerous this is, Silas? Couldn't you try something less adventurous, Silas?* Adventurous! The man wouldn't recognise an adventure if it bit him in the backside. There was no two ways about it, Chalkhill had long outlived his usefulness. Realistically, his mother should have thrown him away at birth. Except that there was one small use for him now. The raising of the Jormungand required a sentient sacrifice.

Brimstone pasted on his most reassuring smile. 'It really is a very simple operation, Jasper,' he said kindly. 'But if it makes you feel any better, you can be gone before the Jormungand actually gets here.' *Gone.* That was a good one. Chalkhill would be gone all right. 'I just need your help with the initial preparations.' He jacked his smile up a notch, then jacked it down again at once. Overdo the smiles and Chalkhill was bound to get suspicious. With good reason, of course.

'What sort of help?' asked Chalkhill suspiciously.

'Oh, just setting things up,' Brimstone told him vaguely. 'I'll do the actual work.'

Chalkhill licked his lips. 'I thought the Jormungand came from Hael. I mean, won't that be the same as using demons now? I mean, won't Queen Blue's new position ...?' He swallowed and trailed off, looking at Brimstone imploringly.

It was worth being patient. A little patience would reassure the idiot, make him much more tractable when the time came. 'Not exactly *from* Hael, Jasper,' Brimstone said patiently. 'Although many highly intelligent people have made that mistake. Actually, the Jormungand comes *through* Hael, but its natural home is Midgard, another level of reality altogether.' The *nether regions* of Midgard, but no sense worrying the poor soul with that little piece of information. 'So you see, Queen Blue has no jurisdiction in the matter whatsoever.'

'But won't her demons interfere?'

'Why would they? It's none of their business and the creature passes through their world very quickly.' It was a half-truth, of course and a slippery one. Since the Jormungand was a water creature and Hael a fire region Blue's newly liberated demons would experience considerable disruption as the thing passed through. But there was nothing they could do about it except send a diplomatic protest that would end up in Midgard anyway. Meanwhile – Brimstone risked another innocent smile – Chalkhill would be reassured.

Chalkhill wasn't reassured. 'Won't it disrupt the Realm?'

'The Hael Realm or the Faerie Realm?' Brimstone asked blandly.

'The Faerie Realm,' Chalkhill said. 'Who cares about the Hael Realm?' He plucked at Brimstone's sleeve. 'Look here, Silas, I really think this is getting much too dangerous, even to protect something like –' He nodded towards the entrance of the inner, crystal cavern. 'I'm sure I read somewhere that the reason nobody calls the Jormungand any more is because it has such a disruptive influence.'

It would be pleasant to kill him now and stop this endless prattle, but that would hardly be a sacrifice. Brimstone made a monumental effort. 'Only at a *local* level,' he said smoothly. 'Usually just an earthquake or two, rivers drying up, the occasional hurricane ... that sort of thing. In a godsforsaken country like this, who's going to notice? Or give a toss?'

'Will we be able to get away? Before the earthquakes and the hurricanes?'

'Oh, it's not immediate!' Brimstone exclaimed. 'The effect builds up over a period of several days – something to do with the strain on the fabric of reality.' He smiled thinly. 'You'll be a distant memory, Jasper, long before anything unpleasant happens.'

To his relief, Chalkhill seemed reassured, for he said, 'All right, Silas, what do you want me to do?'

The preparations took three quarters of an hour. When they were finished, the gloomy cavern was furnished with a temporary altar set with unlit spell cones at each corner, a circle of free-standing black-light candles and a series of tortuous glyphs painted freehand on the floor by Brimstone.

'Is that it?' Chalkhill asked. 'Is that all you need to call up the Jormungand?'

'Actually this calls up Bartzabel, the Jormungand's keeper. But if you keep him sweet, he'll lead in the

Jormungand. The whole thing's not as easy as it looks. It needs a lot of concentration.' And blood, Brimstone thought, but pointless upsetting the sacrifice. 'Now, I want you to stand over there in the north and *don't move unless I tell you.* That's very important. If you wander about it can disturb the energies with unforeseen consequences.'

'Yes, all right,' Chalkhill said and walked to the northern wall of the cavern. 'Here okay?'

'Perfect,' Brimstone said. 'Now stand still and shut up while I perform the orison.'

Most of it was in a language Chalkhill didn't understand, but at the climax of the orison, things got a little clearer. 'Thou House of Idleness wherein I shall set up the Throne of Justice,' Brimstone intoned. 'Thou cold body that I shall fashion into a living flame. Thou dull ox that I shall turn into the Bull of Earth. Bartzabel! Bartzabel! Bartzabel!'

As usual, it was the name that did it. There was a shimmering in the air before the altar as something small and compact began to manifest. Chalkhill leaned forward for a better view. He'd seen several of Brimstone's demon evocations in the good old days, but this seemed to be something of a different order.

'I unbind thee from thy chains,' called Brimstone loudly. 'Come forth and manifest! Come now, in fair and pleasing form, from thy palace of seraphic stars! Come, be my slave, thou spirit Bartzabel!'

Chalkhill wasn't sure what he was expecting – something creepy with horns, no doubt – but what he got was a chicken. He stared in utter astonishment as the bird materialised a few feet from the ground, dropped to the floor of the cavern, then strutted towards Brimstone.

'Cluck!' said the chicken fiercely.

Forty-Nine

In the old days, Brimstone would have wrung its neck. 'In fair and pleasing form!' he snapped, using the formula he learned in demonology school. 'Preferably your proper shape.'

The chicken transformed at once into a motleyed clown who cartwheeled the remaining distance and whispered, grinning, into Brimstone's ear, 'You sure you really want to do this, Silas?'

Brimstone jerked back. 'You're not Bartzabel!' he hissed.

'Is that Bartzabel?' asked Chalkhill from his station in the north.

'I'm not Bartzabel!' the clown roared delightedly and threw himself into a bewildering series of cartwheels that ended with him sitting on the makeshift altar. He spread his hands in the manner of an entertainer searching for applause and said, 'Ta-rah!'

'Don't move!' Brimstone called urgently to Chalkhill. He had a horrid suspicion he knew who this buffoon was, and if he was right, it was trouble.

'No, don't move,' echoed the clown. He made a small gesture with his left hand and Chalkhill froze into immobility.

'I can't move!' Chalkhill gasped. He seemed to have difficulty even breathing.

The clown jumped down from the altar, ran like a ballet dancer towards Brimstone and stroked his face affectionately with both hands. 'Sooo sweet of you to let me out.' He grinned.

Brimstone scowled. His suspicion was crystallising into certainty. 'How did I do that?' he asked.

'I booby-trapped the Bartzabel ritual!' the clown told him. 'What a jape, eh? What a joke!' He pushed his face forward so his nose was no more than an inch from Brimstone's own. 'On you!'

'Who ... is ... this idiot?' Chalkhill asked with considerable difficulty, and bravely, Brimstone thought, considering his captive circumstances.

'This is Loki, the Trickster,' Brimstone said sourly. He glared into the clown's eyes, as if daring it to contradict him.

But the creature drew back, smiling. 'You know me! How flattering! I've always so much wanted to be famous.'

'What's ... he ... doing ... here?' This from Chalkhill again, who seemed determined to interfere with everything that was none of his business.

'He's the Jormungand's father,' Brimstone told him shortly.

The shock of the news must have eased the paralysis around Chalkhill's chest, for he managed to say clearly, 'He's *what?*'

'His mother was rather large,' Loki said across one shoulder. 'And odd.' But his attention was clearly elsewhere. He began to walk round Brimstone in a tight, slow circle. The broad smile slowly faded as he leaned forward to murmur in Brimstone's ear. 'I ask you again, Silas: do you want to do this? Do you really want to call my son?'

'Yes,' said Brimstone stiffly.

'Just a minute,' Chalkhill put in. 'He may have a point. Do we really, really, *really* want –?'

'Shut up, Jasper,' Brimstone said. 'I've been threatened by scarier things than this.'

'So you have!' exclaimed Loki delightedly. 'And so you will again! But what makes you think I'm threatening you? I simply want to make sure your mind is made up –' the smile vanished abruptly '– and that you know the price!'

'I know the price,' snarled Brimstone. With an effort he stopped himself glancing towards Chalkhill.

'What's the price?' asked Chalkhill anxiously.

Fortunately Loki ignored him. Even more fortunately he dropped his voice even further to whisper mischievously in Brimstone's ear. 'The blood price, Silas – now or later!'

'I know the price,' Brimstone repeated stolidly.

Loki took a step back, his face benign. 'I'll go and get him, shall I? My dear, sweet Jormungand? He's with Angrboda, I believe. She spoils him rotten, but then mothers do, don't they?' He began to walk backwards, grinning at Brimstone. 'You're absolutely, positively, sure ...?' he asked lightly.

'Yes!' Brimstone snapped.

'Just checking,' Loki said, and vanished.

The cavern suddenly felt empty and very, very silent.

'What was all that about?' asked Chalkhill after a moment.

'Nothing,' Brimstone told him.

'Silas ...?'

'What? What is it now?'

'I still can't move.'

Good, Brimstone thought. That will make the sacrifice a whole lot easier. Good old Loki. Aloud he said, 'It'll wear off in a minute.' He was wondering if there was anything else he needed to do. Call the Jormungand directly, for example. Or start making the wild promises one used to intrigue these creatures. Or –

There was a *straining* in the dank atmosphere of the cavern.

'What's happening?' Chalkhill asked at once.

Brimstone caught sight of a curious shimmering above the altar and took a cautious step backwards. The Jormungand was big. And indiscriminating. No sense in being too close when it materialised.

The shimmering began to take a solid shape. The air was abruptly filled with the scent of the sea, a pungent overlay of fish, salt and rotting weed. From the direction of the cage inside the inner cavern an unearthly wailing began. Closer to hand a curious crackling whispered above their heads.

'I don't like this,' Chalkhill said.

The Jormungand serpent was beginning to form. Brimstone could see it clearly now, coil upon glistening coil. The creature was far larger than anything he had ever called from Hael. It was the perfect guardian for his treasure. But best show it who was boss at the earliest opportunity. 'Get a move on!' Brimstone called.

The serpent snapped into existence with an audible *pop*. It slammed down on the altar, smashing it completely. The huge head with its dragon teeth swung round, eyes glowing, in search of its sacrifice.

'Over there!' Brimstone shouted excitedly, pointing at Chalkhill.

But Chalkhill was no longer in the north. Fear had

snapped his paralysis and he was racing towards the exit tunnels as fast as his chubby legs would carry him. The serpent lunged after him, but missed, jaws closing with a vicious snap. Chalkhill plunged into the tunnel. The beast was far too big to follow. It swung round to glare at Brimstone.

'Oh, no you don't!' said Brimstone firmly. 'I'm the one who called you.' He thought quickly. 'Tell you what: you can have the next person who enters this cavern. Slow death, fast death, it's entirely up to you. What do you say to that, then?'

'Aaaaaarrr!' roared the Midgard Serpent.

fifty

The Arcond of Hass-Verbim, an old friend of Blue's father, insisted on a banquet and sat beaming as course after exotic course was delivered to the table by a herd of liveried stumpies. Blue worked hard to curb her impatience. She desperately wanted to move on, to cross into Buthner, to find Henry and bring him back safely. But the diplomatic niceties had to be observed, and besides, even if they were in Buthner this very second, she had no idea where to look for Henry, let alone find him.

Pyrgus was feeling impatient as well. He had that distant look he got sometimes, was taking very little part in the conversation and only picking at his food. Madame Cardui was doing rather better. She was seated on the Arcond's left and, rather to Blue's relief, was claiming most of his attention.

'Dreadful place,' the Arcond was saying in response to her question about Buthner. 'I can't imagine why you want to go there. Most of it, quite frankly, is wilderness. Desert, really. Hideously hot. There are a few shanty towns round the edges, no central government at all – just local warlords who control their own regions and fight among one another. And the people ... oh, my dear, the people!'

'Dreadful too?' asked Madame Cardui with a half smile.

The Arcond relaxed back in his chair. 'Oh, I shouldn't be too hard on them. They're just trying to survive, after all. You'll find porters at almost all of the border crossings. They'll pilfer anything they can from your luggage, but most of them won't try to kill you. You need to keep out of the shanty towns unless you have an armed guard, and a substantial one at that. I notice ...' He trailed off diplomatically.

'No entourage,' Madame Cardui confirmed. 'No guards, no servants. We are travelling, shall we say, incognito.'

'How intriguing,' said the Arcond. He glanced at Blue, then back again. 'Well, doubtless you have your reasons. But if you plan to visit the townships, I would strongly suggest you permit me to provide you with an escort.'

'I'm not sure we will be,' Madame Cardui told him. 'What can you tell me about the desert?'

Blue pricked up her ears at once. So far, both Pyrgus and Madame Cynthia had insisted they had no idea where to look for Henry. She could trust Pyrgus to tell her the truth – he was the worst liar in the world – but Madame Cardui's life was devoted to secrets. She hid things almost by instinct. If she was interested in the Buthner desert, there was probably a reason.

'Not a great deal,' the Arcond was saying. 'It takes up four-fifths of the country's land surface. Several million square miles of ... nothing really. Sand. A few water holes – one would hardly call them oases. The odd monastery. Scorpions. A scattering of undeads – barrow wights, that sort of thing. The nomads call them vaettirs.'

'Ah, so there *are* nomads?' Madame Cardui asked.

'Apparently,' the Arcond said. 'God alone knows how they manage to survive. Extremely primitive from what I hear. All sorts of stories about them. Cannibalism. Head hunting. Blood drinking. You wouldn't really know what to believe. There's something in their diet that turns them blue, skin and hair. All the information I have suggests the nomad tribes are even more dangerous than the townships, but they avoid normal people when they can, so the chances of you meeting them are slim, even if you go into the desert. You're not planning to go into the desert, are you?'

'Unlikely,' said Madame Cardui blandly.

'I'll tell you something really interesting about Buthner,' the Arcond said suddenly. 'At one time – this is very many years ago: prehistory, I suppose you'd say – at one time, it housed what was probably the most advanced civilisation on the planet. We have an archaeological body here, the Verbim Institute –' He smiled. 'I'm Honorary Chairman and I contribute to the funding. The Institute has conducted several digs in the safer areas of Buthner and the evidence is quite extraordinary. It seems that Buthner – and parts of Hass-Verbim, of course; they weren't separate countries in those days – was the heart of an extensive empire.' He half turned his head. 'Much like your Empire is now, Blue.'

'Really?' Blue said politely.

It was clearly one of the Arcond's enthusiasms, for he leaned forward to say, 'Oh, yes. Very technically advanced on the evidence we have. Magical technology. I know some scholars don't accept this, but I really do believe they may well have been more advanced than we are today.'

'I thought there was a ban on the use of magic in Buthner,' Madam Cardui put in. 'Or is that just some local warlord?'

'Oh no,' said the Arcond. 'You're quite right, Cynthia. There is a huge distrust of magic in Buthner – much more even than there is in my own country. In some areas you risk immediate execution if you're found in possession of so much as a spell cone.' He hesitated. 'You're not planning to take anything magical across the border, are you?'

'No,' said Madame Cardui without a moment's hesitation.

The Arcond looked relieved. 'Ah good.' He smiled. 'We wouldn't want a diplomatic incident.'

'Or an execution,' Blue murmured quietly.

The Arcond obviously didn't hear her, for he relaunched his monologue at once. 'I have a theory – a *personal* theory, although it is borne out by the archaeological evidence – I have a theory that it was *magic* that caused the downfall of the old Buthner Empire and the dislike of magic today is a race memory dating back all the way to that event.'

'*Really?*' said Madame Cardui, injecting far more of a note of interest than Blue had managed earlier.

Blue said quietly, 'Are you all right, Pyrgus?'

'Oh, indeed,' said the Arcond. 'You see, there's no reason for the desert. No geological reason. The desert is where the ruins are, where the main cities used to be, so clearly it wasn't a desert then. And there wasn't a general change in climate, otherwise Hass-Verbim would be a desert now as well. So how did a thriving, prosperous, urbanised community suddenly turn into a desert? It *was* sudden, you know. Our digs show that conclusively. What I –'

'Pyrgus!' Blue exclaimed in sudden alarm.

'– believe is that some powerful magical operation,

perhaps unimaginably more powerful than anything we might manage today, got out of hand. It may have been military, or something in the nature –'

'What's wrong, Blue deeah?' Madame Cardui asked.

Blue was staring in horror at Pyrgus, seated almost opposite her across the table. His head was twisted to a peculiar angle that threw the sinews of his neck into sharp relief. His eyes were rolled back so that only the whites were showing and his whole body trembled like a leaf in a gale.

Madame Cardui stood up so quickly that her chair toppled backwards. 'He's in another bout of fever!' she exclaimed.

fifty-One

'Quarantine!' Blue fumed. 'He has no right!'

'He has every right,' Madame Cardui told her. 'You'd do exactly the same thing in his position. We're lucky he didn't include us in the order.'

'He wouldn't dare!'

'I would,' Madame Cardui said casually, 'in his position. The temporal plague isn't something to take lightly.'

'But it doesn't seem to be contagious! The quarantine is nonsense.'

Madame Cardui shrugged. 'He doesn't know that. Neither do we, for sure.'

They were sitting together in an antechamber of the hospital wing in the Arcond's Palace. Through the window they could see Pyrgus, his bed encased in an isolation pod, locked in his feverish coma.

'But how do we go on?' Blue demanded. 'How do we follow our plan?' She was less focused than she sounded. Part of her desperately wanted to press ahead and try to rescue Henry, but another part of her, equally strong, wanted to look after Pyrgus. Staring at him now through the transparent coating of his pod, she was aware of an irrational dread that he would die like Mr Fogarty. As it was, he seemed to be growing older in the bed, although she knew that had to be an effect of her worried imagination.

'I'm afraid our plan is already in ruins, my deeah,' Madame Cardui said kindly. 'From the moment Pyrgus fell ill again. With or without the quarantine, he can't possibly travel. The future we are living now has deviated so much from what Alan foresaw that we must consider our original plans obsolete.'

Blue stared at her. 'Are you saying we can no longer rescue Henry? Or stop the plague?' she added as an afterthought.

'I'm not saying that for a moment. But the situation has become much more difficult and we need to revise our approach.'

'In what way?'

Madame Cardui sighed. 'I wish I knew, deeah. The thing is, Alan foresaw a future in which Pyrgus and I travelled to Buthner and effected Henry's rescue. That plan was modified when you joined us, deeah, but it still seemed largely viable. But clearly Pyrgus can no longer travel to Buthner. In fact, it seems to me that he needs to be translated to the Analogue World again as quickly as possible, otherwise we could have a real emergency on our hands. They don't have the technology for that in Hass-Verbim. You know how suspicious of spells they are here – we're lucky they have medical magic like isolation pods. So we need to get him back to the Realm with the minimum delay.'

'Will the Arcond permit it?' Blue asked anxiously.

'The Arcond will be only too delighted to see the backs of us,' Madame Cardui said. 'The plague hasn't reached Hass-Verbim yet, so the sooner he gets rid of us the better. We can transport Pyrgus, pod and all. I think you'll find the Arcond will cooperate in every way possible.'

Still staring at her brother through the window, Blue said softly, 'This will mean abandoning Henry ...'

'Perhaps not,' said Madame Cardui.

Blue looked at her.

Madame Cardui said, 'We can no longer follow our original plan, except in so far as we must assume Henry is still in Buthner. I would propose one of us returns with Pyrgus to the Realm, the other proceeds alone to Buthner.'

'I'll go to Buthner,' Blue said quickly.

To her surprise, Madame Cardui voiced no objection. 'I think you must, deeah. I'm much too old to be wandering in a desert, whereas I can be perfectly effective in having Pyrgus translated to the Analogue World. I believe it must be you who goes on and I believe you must go alone, although it pains me to expose you to the risk. But if you travel with guards, it will cut you off from contact with the natives, and I cannot imagine how you might find Henry without native cooperation. And a great deal of luck.' She gave a bleak smile. 'You must travel in disguise, of course – an attractive young woman alone is asking for trouble – but I expect you'll enjoy that.'

Despite her worries, Blue smiled back. 'I expect I will.' In the days before she became Queen, she was notorious for disguising herself as a boy and visiting places she shouldn't. The smile faded. 'Madame Cynthia,' she said soberly, 'can you advise me where to start?'

'In the desert, dahling,' Madame Cardui told her promptly. 'It's the only part of Alan's vision I believe to be still reliable. I appreciate the desert covers eighty per cent of Buthner, as our friend the Arcond mentioned, but I'm afraid it's our only chance. I believe our best hope, our *only* hope now, will be for you to make contact with the desert nomads and persuade them to help you.'

'That's the blood-drinking, head-hunting, cannibal nomads?' Blue asked flatly.

Madame Cardui smiled thinly. 'I'm hoping those reports may be exaggerated, deeah,' she said.

Fifty-Two

'Is that the tomb?' Lorquin asked.

The sun was low on the horizon so that the ruin cast a long, distorted shadow on the sand. But it was definitely the tomb. How Lorquin had found it on the basis of Henry's vague description was a mystery bordering on a miracle.

'Yes,' Henry said tightly. He was frankly afraid. He could walk now, though his leg still pained him considerably, and his arm seemed to have healed very well, but the thought of facing the vaettir again filled him with dread. He was vaguely aware of another root to his fear. It was obvious he could not survive in the desert without Lorquin. The boy had not only rescued him and saved his leg, but it was Lorquin who found food for them in this wilderness. It was Lorquin who produced water. It was Lorquin who knew his way about although there was not a single landmark obvious to Henry. If Lorquin disappeared now, Henry imagined he might live for a day or two if he was lucky, after which he would face a particularly unpleasant death. And while Lorquin showed no signs whatsoever of abandoning him, it was a nerve-wracking feeling to be so utterly dependant on a child. Henry hesitated. 'What do we do now?'

'We wait,' Lorquin said.

After a moment Henry asked, 'What are we waiting for?'

'For the sun to go down. The vaettir will come out when it's dark.'

It was exactly what Henry had suspected when he crawled away from his first encounter. The vaettir was a creature of the night. 'What do we do then?'

'We follow it,' Lorquin said. 'With small luck it will lead us to the draugr.'

This was what Henry didn't really want to think about. His memory of the vaettir was terrifying. He couldn't begin to imagine what a draugr might be like. 'Look here, Lorquin,' he ventured uneasily, 'about this draugr ...'

Lorquin said firmly, 'We must lie down, En Ri, and bury ourselves in the sand.'

It stopped Henry short. 'What? Why?'

'So that the vaettir does not smell us as it leaves the tomb. It will emerge into the half-light and that is when it is most careful. If it knows we are here, it will attack and we must kill it and then it will not lead us to the draugr.'

'What happens if *it* kills *us?*'

Lorquin looked at him blankly. 'It still will not lead us to the draugr,' he said.

It was another world, really. Lorquin didn't even think the way he did. Adjusting to the Faerie Realm was hard enough sometimes, but adjusting to a blue boy who somehow survived in the desert was just about impossible. Lorquin was already lying face down, carefully pulling sand over himself with sweeping movements of his arms. In a moment, only part of his head was visible, his eyes watchful. After a moment, Henry lay down beside him and did the same. They lay together, side by side, staring at the deepening silhouette of the tomb.

'Look here, Lorquin,' Henry said again, returning to his earlier concern. 'I may not be much good to you if – when – when we catch up with this draugr thing. I mean, where I come from, we don't go in for fighting ... creatures much or rites of passage or that sort of thing.'

'Then how did you become a man, En Ri, when your body grew hair and you ceased to have an interest in the matters of childhood?'

'I started listening to pop music,' Henry said. *And thinking about girls a lot,* his mind added irreverently. Somehow it sounded silly when compared with going out to kill a lion or a draugr. He hesitated, staring at the dying sun. 'Anyway,' he hurried on, 'the point is, I'm not experienced in any of this draugr stuff, which means I'm not much of a Companion, so it may be better if you just forget about ... well, about the whole thing, and go back to your people and maybe, if you were feeling really nice about it, you could get somebody to show me the way out of the desert.' *And I could go home,* he thought, although he wasn't quite sure where he meant by *home* or how to get there even if he escaped the desert.

'But how then would I become a man?' Lorquin asked. His eyes, peering out above the sand like a crocodile in water, were wide with bewilderment.

'Isn't there some other way?' Henry asked desperately. He racked his mind for everything he'd ever read about primitive communities. 'A vision quest or something?' Something safe. Something that didn't involve killing ... killing ... 'What exactly is a draugr anyway?' he asked.

But Lorquin's wide eyes were no longer looking in his direction. 'We must be silent now, En Ri,' he whispered.

Henry followed his gaze and discovered the pale thing Lorquin called a vaettir had emerged from its tomb.

fifty-three

It wasn't that Lorquin travelled particularly fast, it was just that he never slowed down. Henry, with his bad leg and reluctant attitude, was hard put to keep up. There was no way he wanted to follow the vaettir, no way he wanted to find out what a draugr was, but he knew all too well that if he lost sight of Little Boy Blue, his chances of survival were zero. It was a mortifying admission.

The vaettir was slightly smaller than Henry remembered it, but no less frightening. It moved with an easy grace and, like Lorquin, never slowed. Insofar as he could judge, it was heading into the deep desert. Although, as Lorquin predicted, it had been the soul of caution when it first emerged from its tomb, they were downwind of it now and it travelled without looking back. All the same, Lorquin made sure to keep a respectable distance behind, something that suited Henry very nicely.

The sun set and in its afterglow, stars began to appear. Soon they were travelling in deepening darkness and still Lorquin did not slow. He seemed to have better night vision than Henry and Henry struggled to keep up. Ahead of them, the vaettir was a moving blob, but thanks to the white colouring it did not disappear altogether.

They had been moving steadily for close on an hour,

as near as Henry could judge, when he noticed a flicker of light on the horizon. Fifteen minutes later it resolved itself into the flame of a large campfire. Lorquin dropped back and placed a warning hand on Henry's arm. 'The vaettir has done its job,' he whispered. 'But now we must be careful.'

'I thought we *were* being careful,' Henry hissed. He had a horrible feeling his situation was about to go from bad to worse.

Lorquin said, 'Now we separate, En Ri, you and I.'

'No, I don't think that's a good idea,' said Henry quickly.

But Lorquin ignored him. 'You go that way –' He pointed. 'Circle so you come to their meeting place from the north.'

'Meeting place?'

'Conceal yourself well or they may try to eat your flesh –'

'They?' Somehow Henry felt Lorquin didn't just mean the vaettir they'd been following and the mysterious draugr.

'You must wait until I am ready, En Ri, my Companion,' Lorquin said, 'Listen for the sound of the night-went.' He made a soft cooing sound deep in his throat that carried eerily across the night air. 'This will be my signal.'

'Signal?' Henry echoed in rising panic. He knew, he just *knew*, what was coming had to be straight out of a nightmare.

'On my signal,' Lorquin went on calmly, 'you must show yourself –'

Henry stopped. Show himself to whatever was congregating around the campfire? It was a horror beyond contemplation. Why should he show himself? Why should he even go any nearer to the campfire?

'Wave and shout if need be to attract their attention, although they will probably know you are there since you will be upwind of them in the north.'

Henry closed his eyes. 'Why,' he asked carefully, 'would I want to attract their attention?' His mouth was so dry he could scarcely speak, nothing at all to do with the desert heat.

'So they can chase you,' Lorquin told him cheerfully.

'They being ...?'

'The vaettirs, En Ri,' said Lorquin patiently.

That was *vaettirs* plural, Henry noted, although he couldn't pretend it came as a surprise. 'Why should I want the vaettirs to chase me?'

'So I may kill the draugr,' Lorquin explained happily. 'They guard the draugr, but if they chase you ...' He trailed off, smiling.

'Suppose they catch me!' Henry protested, heart thumping.

Lorquin shook his head. 'They never catch the Companion in our songs.' He waited, looking at Henry expectantly.

And there it was, Henry thought: his future all laid out in front of him. What in God's creation had led him here? He should be at home now, worrying about his exams, not lost in a desert with a small blue lunatic who wanted him to lure away a bunch of really scary creatures so he could somehow kill another scary creature that Henry didn't even know about.

It was as mad as it gets, but something deep inside Henry knew he was going to do exactly what Lorquin had just asked him. He was more frightened than he had ever been in his life, but he was still going to do it. Not because he was heroic. Not because he was brave. But because he couldn't think of a single way not to.

'En Ri?' Lorquin said.

'Yes, Lorquin?'

'The dangerous time is when they smell you. So circle around downwind of them as long as possible. When you hear my signal, cut quickly northwards upwind; then make sure they see you and run quickly. But you know all this already.'

'Yes,' Henry said. Especially the bit about running quickly.

'En Ri?'

'Yes, Lorquin?'

'Thank you, my Companion. For helping me become a man.'

fifty-four

For some reason he started to feel better when he left Lorquin and began his cautious approach to the vaettir gathering. The anticipation was gone and with it the worst of his fear. He was committed now, so he didn't have to worry about chickening out. He was doing something, which was always better than talking about doing something. Now he only had to concentrate.

What he was doing wasn't easy. Starlight allowed him to see, but not very far. The wilderness was mostly sand, but broken from time to time by protruding rocks. There was a dim outline up ahead that might even be a rocky outcrop. His leg still ached and the sand clung to his feet, making walking difficult. So did the protruding rocks, which barked his shins several times and tripped him up. Worse still, the north wind was erratic, sometimes dying down, sometimes threatening to change direction. He stumbled forward in constant anxiety that his scent might travel ahead of him.

The thing that looked like a rocky outcrop turned out to be the remnant rim of an ancient crater and he climbed onto it gratefully, glad to be away from the sucking sand. Moments later, he topped the rise and felt his stomach descend to his boots.

Below him was a nightmare scene. The crater formed

a natural amphitheatre. What he'd taken earlier to be a single campfire now turned out to be several, casting a dull red glow that illuminated the area all too clearly. The ground was a seething mass of vaettirs, crawling in absolute silence around a creature that could have come straight out of Stephen King's head. It was as pale as the vaettirs themselves, but easily larger than ten of them put together, a monstrous maggot with mandibles, antennae and claws. It pulsed visibly as it lay like a beached whale in the centre of the amphitheatre.

Henry stared blankly, trying to remember if he had ever seen anything so repulsive in his life. He prayed this wasn't – simply couldn't be – Lorquin's draugr, but somehow knew it was. At first, the vaettirs seemed to be milling round it aimlessly; then he noticed patterns of behaviour. Some of them carried handfuls of a soft, waxy substance that they pushed into the draugr's mouth. The giant creature made no attempt to attack them, but chewed like a contented cow.

Other of the vaettirs seemed to be cleaning the draugr's huge nocturnal eyes. They brought bladders of some liquid, probably water, and poured them onto what looked exactly like sea sponges, which they used to wipe down the great orbs at irregular intervals.

Henry watched the feeding and the cleaning for some time before he noticed that a small group of vaettirs, whose skins seemed to have taken on a pinkish hue, were clustered at the rear of the draugr, gently massaging its abdomen. Moments later the body convulsed suddenly and a glistening sac discharged from under the creature's tapering tail. The vaettirs swooped on it at once and carried it away triumphantly. The draugr had laid an egg.

The whole process was both repulsive and fascinating, like a nature documentary about insects on TV. In fact, now he thought about it, Henry suddenly realised he was watching something like the workings of an anthill. The draugr was the vaettirs' queen!

He was jerked out of his reverie by the cooing of a nightwent.

Henry went cold. When he'd agreed to this mad mission he'd imagined himself chased by a handful of vaettirs, which was scary enough. But what was down there was more than a handful. There had to be fifty or a hundred vaettirs, at least. Lorquin couldn't possibly expect him to call that lot down on his own head. And *nobody* could expect him to survive if he did.

The cooing came again.

They wouldn't all chase him anyway. That was a *colony* down there. Even if he jumped up and down and waved, they wouldn't all chase him. Some would be sent out to investigate, like soldier ants. The rest would continue to service their queen. Which wouldn't be any good to Lorquin at all. Not that the boy would ever kill a thing the size of the draugr anyway, but if he tried, his chances of getting away alive were absolutely zero with dozens of vaettirs around. So it made more sense for Henry *not* to move upwind and let some vaettirs chase him. What he *needed* to do was give young Lorquin a stern talking-to, like an elder brother, and show him how stupid this whole escapade was. And if it really *was* tribal policy to send children out to kill monsters surrounded by monsters, then he'd jolly well have to go back with Lorquin to his tribe and show *them* how stupid ...

The cooing came a third time and now the nightwent was sounding distinctly impatient.

The trouble was, he didn't know where Lorquin might be hiding now. The bird sound floated on the air as bird sounds do, without the least indication of where it came from. And if he didn't give the kid the big-brother talking-to, he was just the sort of plucky youngster who might take it into his head to attack the entire colony. Henry almost groaned aloud. If he diverted *some* of the vaettirs, it would make things a *little* better for Lorquin, even though the whole thing was still a suicide mission. But if he didn't do anything at all, maybe Lorquin *wouldn't* attack the draugr, in which case they were both safe and could creep away quietly and he could give Lorquin the talk.

Henry heard the cooing again. This time it definitely came from somewhere below him. Lorquin was moving towards the vaettirs! Henry actually did groan aloud now, but the sound made little difference. Lorquin had left him no choice. As usual.

Henry climbed to his feet and made a stumbling run upwind. Below him, he could see heads jerk up as the vaettirs caught his scent. Some might chase him, some might not. Either way, he'd probably be caught. It didn't matter now. Like much else in his life, the whole thing was a mess.

'Hey you!' Henry screamed down at the milling vaettirs. 'Come and get me!'

fifty-five

It occurred to Blue eventually that she might have made a bad mistake. Despite the southward-pointing carriage she had the uncomfortable feeling that she might as well be lost. The device was a small, one-person self-propelled chariot with an adjustable canopy for shade. In deference to the way the citizens of Buthner felt about magic, its motive power was clockwork: fifteen minutes hard work with the crank handle each morning and it would trundle along happily for the rest of the day: not fast, but with a steady pace that ate up miles. But its most impressive aspect was the life-size figure at the back. By means of ingenious gearing Blue couldn't even begin to understand, its outstretched arm always pointed southwards, as a guide to the way home.

With crumbling slabs of compressed food and a vast supply of dehydrated water tablets, she could survive in the desert for months, but it remained a problem nonetheless. The wilderness was, quite simply, immense, far larger than she'd ever imagined for all the Arcond's talk of it taking up four-fifths of the country's land surface. Worse still, it was absolutely featureless. She'd been travelling for almost three days now and every single moment of the journey was the same as every other. Around her stretched the plain of sand, a waterless ocean that reached the horizon in every direction, a mind-numbing expanse of eternal dunes. If the Arcond was right about his ancient ruins, she had spotted none of them. Worse, there was not the slightest sign of nomads.

What if she never found them? What of Henry then?

So far she had been travelling directly north, deep into the heart of the desert. But that had been an arbitrary decision. Madame Cynthia could tell her no more than she had already done. Mr Fogarty was dead: no new visions would be forthcoming, nor any half-forgotten details of his old ones. She was alone, without guidance, *and nothing was working out!*

The thought was tinged with guilt, something that had been growing in her for days. Perhaps Pyrgus and Madame Cardui had been right all along. Perhaps if she hadn't interfered, they would have rescued Henry by now and saved the Realm from the plague. Perhaps the future she'd propelled them into held no hope of happy endings. Perhaps she should have *minded her own business!*

On impulse, she pulled the carriage round so that it was no longer heading due north, but northwest. One direction was as good as any other and so long as the figure pointed, she would be able to find her way out of the desert eventually.

The impulse made no difference. For close on half an hour, she travelled through the endless sands. Blue jerked the carriage round again, more sharply this time. It was a random movement, but a glance at her pointing figure showed she was now travelling due west, towards the setting sun. Travelling west through an unbroken sea of sand.

She thought of stopping to eat something, although she was far from hungry. Madame Cardui had warned her she must eat and, more importantly, drink at regular intervals to ensure she maintained her strength. The trouble was, her compressed food tasted musty and her dehydrated water tablets, while they maintained the fluid balance of her body, did almost nothing for the dry mouth and constant thirst. She decided to eat when the sun finally set, then perhaps press on just a little further before it grew fully dark. She pushed the handle of the carriage listlessly, then caught sight of something on the eastern horizon.

Blue halted the carriage at once. She'd already discovered that mind and eyes played tricks on this cursed wilderness, especially at this time of day when the light was just beginning to fade. All the same, there was something out there and she was fairly sure it wasn't just another dune. She rummaged in her equipment until she found a glass. (What wouldn't she have given for a decently spell-driven travelling eye!) The heat haze and the low angle of the sun wouldn't permit any real resolution, even with optical help, but what she was looking at might have been a low building of some sort, or possibly some temporary structure. Was this one of the ruins the Arcond had talked about? Or could it be a pavilion erected by the nomads? For the first time, she realised she knew almost nothing about these mysterious nomads: how they lived, how they travelled … nothing. Did they have tents and pack animals?

Questions were useless. The only thing she knew was that they avoided contact. But if this really *was* one of their structures, perhaps she could reach them before they spotted her and ran away. Then, a mischievous voice murmured in her head, she would find out the truth about the cannibalism business.

Blue gently manoeuvred the carriage around, then started it off, slowly, in the direction of the thing on the horizon. She was very aware of the need for caution. If these really were the nomads, she couldn't just come storming in – she'd have to gain their trust. She had gifts – Madame Cardui had seen to that – but she was aware that gifts alone would never be enough. She was seriously considering abandoning the carriage before she got too close and making the rest of her way on foot. With luck and care, she might even be able to observe the nomads for a little while before committing herself to contact. The more she learned about them the better.

She had scarcely driven for more than ten minutes when a brutal sense of disappointment swept over her. The shape on the horizon, which had looked so like an artificial structure even when examined through the glass, suddenly resolved itself as a well-worn peak, part of a low mountain chain, hardly more than high hills, really, but beyond doubt natural formations.

For a moment she considered swinging away and heading back into the deep desert – her carriage was fine for relatively flat terrain, but there was no way it could tackle a mountain – then something else caught her eye, nestling in the foothills. This time she was close enough for the glass to show it as a series of squat stone buildings.

Once again Blue stopped the carriage. With her eye to the glass, she examined the structures carefully. This was ancient architecture for sure, but no ruin. Someone lived here, or at least had lived here until recent times. But not the nomads. These were permanent structures, built to last by settled people.

What to do? Madame Cardui had said their best hope was for Blue to make contact with the nomads, but that hadn't happened so far, and she'd no idea how to make it happen. But if people did live here in the shadow of the mountains, they might have some idea where the nomads could be found, perhaps even advise on how best to approach them.

Blue set the carriage going, aware of the lengthening shadows. Even if no one lived here any more, it would still be a place to stay. Since coming to the desert, she'd slept in the carriage, sheltered from the night wind by the canopy. Each night she'd listened to the sounds of creatures moving after dark – there seemed to be far more life in the desert at night than there ever was during the day. Nothing had attacked her, nothing had even seriously disturbed her, but the sounds made her nervous and vulnerable. She would welcome a solid stone-built wall around her.

But as she drew closer, it became obvious the place *was* inhabited. Distant figures moved unhurriedly outside and she could see a small strip of cultivated land close to the buildings: someone must have set up an irrigation system to reclaim it from the desert.

Closer still, the figures resolved themselves into green-robed, tonsured individuals, all, without exception, male. She was approaching a monastic community. It occurred to her then that she might not be entirely welcome. There were all-male monasteries in her own country, where the mere glimpse of a woman sent the monks running for cover. But by the time the thought struck her, it was too late. Her clockwork carriage was rolling over an area of stony ground that gave way to a crudely paved road. One of the green-robed figures, a thin, almost wasted, monk whose skin had turned to leather in the desert sun, broke away from his companions to walk towards her.

'You are welcome, young man,' he told her gravely. Blue blinked, then remembered she was travelling in disguise.

Fifty-Six

The ground beneath Henry's feet was rough as he ran; he couldn't see more than a yard or two ahead. In normal circumstances, he would never have tried to run in a situation like this. In normal circumstances if he *had* tried he'd have stumbled. But he was encouraged by the howling behind him – and by the speed at which the white shapes were gaining. Henry ran *fast*.

The faster he ran, the clearer his mind became. He knew he was about to die. There was no way he could outrun the vaettirs, no way he could survive so many of them when they finally caught up. But, oddly, the realisation caused no fear. In fact, the dread he'd felt earlier had been replaced by calm. He found himself thinking about his mother and Charlie and school and his exams. He found himself thinking of Blue and what a mess he'd made of their relationship. He found himself wondering how he'd gone through so much of his life not knowing what he really wanted, let alone how to get it. It seemed he'd been pushed around by his mother for years and pushed around by circumstances when he wasn't being pushed around by his mother. He'd spent so much time trying to do the right thing, but mostly what he thought of as the right thing was just the thing that other people wanted him to do. He'd never liked upsetting people, so usually he just went along. He wished Mr Fogarty were still alive. Mr Fogarty had somehow managed to do the right thing without giving a toss about how much that upset other people. Mr Fogarty *robbed banks* for cripe's sake, when he thought it was the right thing to do.

Now he was about to die, Henry suspected he might have wasted his entire life.

Except maybe he wasn't about to die after all. He wasn't quite sure, but the pursuing vaettirs seemed to be dropping back a little. Maybe they were like cheetahs – very fast in short bursts, but not much stamina. If he could just keep up his pace he might outrun them.

With his new-found clarity, he realised this made sense. Lorquin might be weird, but he was a decent kid. He'd hardly ask Henry – his *Companion* – to commit virtual suicide just so he could become a man. There might be risk – people who lived in the desert were used to that – but it probably wasn't much of a risk, however dangerous it looked. After all, it was Lorquin who had to prove himself a man. For Henry there was probably hardly any risk at all. All he had to do was keep up a steady pace and wait for the vaettirs to get tired and ...

The earth convulsed.

Henry lost his stride, then his footing, then his balance. He hurled forward and struck the ground, hard. He was on a mix of rock and desert that hurt his injured leg and filled his mouth with sand, but he hardly noticed either. The ground itself was shaking underneath him and his head resonated to a low, subsonic rumble that was somehow more terrifying than the horde of vaettirs racing after him.

For a moment he remained bewildered, then realised

he'd been caught up in an earthquake. He clung to the ground as if in danger of falling and felt it convulse again. He'd never been in an earthquake before, never even known anybody who had, but he remembered reading somewhere that they never lasted very long ... fifteen seconds, thirty seconds, something like that. He also thought he'd read that earthquakes weren't too dangerous if you were outside. It was falling buildings that killed you. All he had to do was lie here and wait. Everything was going to be fine.

Then a vaettir landed on his back, howling.

Henry twisted to try to throw it off when another one arrived, then another and another. He jerked sideways in sudden panic, but the vaettirs were pinning him. He could smell their musty stench, feel their breath on his face and neck. For some reason they hadn't started to bite or scratch him yet, but it was only a matter of time. More and more kept arriving, more and more fell on top of him. There was no possibility of escape. In a moment they'd begin to tear him limb from limb. Meanwhile it was as much as he could do to catch his breath.

There was a high, blood-chilling scream from somewhere behind him. The weight on his body eased at once; then suddenly he could breathe again. He felt something else roll off him and turned painfully. To his astonishment, the vaettirs were gone, every one. He pushed slowly to his feet. The ground had stopped shaking. The earthquake was over. He was alone in the desert. Distantly he could hear the soft pad-pad of vaettir footsteps, but they were receding, fading into nothing as he listened. Nothing was making sense any more, but he was still alive.

Then he realised it was too good to be true. He'd no idea what had panicked the vaettirs, but there was one of them returning now. He could hear its running steps quite clearly and now he could see a shape looming out of the darkness. Something inside Henry snapped and he felt a rising fury. His hands curled into fists. He'd survived a single vaettir attack before. This time he was ready for the brute.

'En Ri!' hissed the vaettir.

Henry blinked. 'Lorquin! Is that you?'

'We did it!' Lorquin called excitedly. He was beside Henry now, grinning.

'The draugr is dead?' Henry frowned. He didn't believe it.

'I killed him!' Lorquin said.

Her, Henry thought. The draugr was the vaettir queen. But he stopped himself correcting the boy.

'You were great, En Ri,' Lorquin told him. 'They will sing of you as a wonderful Companion. You lured away the vaettirs more skilfully than any Companion in the history of the world.'

It was probably an exaggeration, but all Henry could think of saying was, 'The vaettirs are gone.' Which was true, but he still had no idea why.

'They must return when the draugr screams,' Lorquin said. 'It is always so.' He grinned at Henry again. 'I made him scream big, didn't I?'

'Yes, you did,' Henry said. For the first time he noticed Lorquin was carrying a stone dagger. The blade showed a dark stain. The kid must have used it to kill the draugr. And he thought *Henry* would be sung about!

'Now I am a man!' exclaimed Lorquin proudly. 'The gods celebrated my victory – did you feel the earth move?' He seized Henry's hand and squeezed it in a curious gesture of affection. Then he sobered. 'We must go now, En Ri. The vaettirs will create a new draugr, but sometimes they wish to seek us out and take revenge.'

'Where are we going?' Henry asked.

'To join my people,' Lorquin told him happily.

fifty-Seven

The Abbot was a large, muscular man with a shaven head and drooping moustache. He looked more like a bandit leader than a monk and Blue liked him at once. But she found it difficult to tear her eyes away from his companion, a tiny, wrinkled individual in a grubby yellow robe. 'This is the Purlisa,' the Abbot said, using an archaic term that Blue vaguely remembered meant 'Treasure' or 'Precious One'.

It was clearly an honorific of some sort, so she bowed. 'I am Sluce Ragetus,' she told him, choosing one of the old aliases she used when she travelled as a man.

'We've been expecting you,' the Purlisa said, his eyes twinkling. He glanced at the Abbot. 'Haven't we, Jamides?'

The Abbot snorted.

'That's very surprising,' Blue told the Purlisa. She smiled slightly. (It was difficult not to smile at the little Treasure.) 'Until just a very short while ago I'd no idea I was coming here myself.'

'Strange are the workings of Fate,' the Purlisa remarked cheerfully. 'Isn't that right, Jamides?'

Abbot Jamides snorted again. To Blue he said, 'The Precious One forecast the coming of a hero who would rid us of a particular problem we face. I believed the omens were against it. Now he wants to crow.'

'Ah, we can all make mistakes, Jamides.' The twinkling eyes closed in a long, slow blink as the cheery grin widened. 'Although some of us make more than others.'

The last thing she needed was to be drawn into the problems of the monastery. 'I'm hardly a hero,' Blue said quietly. They were in the Abbot's personal quarters, a sparsely furnished cell that overlooked a patch of garden. She'd been offered food and drink, but it had yet to appear.

'Sometimes people are not what they seem,' the Purlisa remarked. 'Or what they think they are.' He smiled at her. 'Perhaps you are not what you seem, Sluce Ragetus?'

There was something in his tone that rang warning bells. She forced an easy smile. 'I can assure you, Purlisa –'

But Jamides, the Abbot, interrupted her. 'I grant it was clever of you to disguise yourself as a man,' he said.

'So much less trouble in a monastery,' the Purlisa twinkled.

The Abbot looked through the window with an expression of distaste. 'Difficult for the monks when there's a woman about.' He nodded sagely, then added, 'The younger monks.'

'They have erotic thoughts,' the Purlisa explained.

The Abbot looked back at her sternly. 'All the time.'

'Distracting,' said the Purlisa. He looked at her fondly and added, 'From their religious duties.'

'Lord Abbot –' Blue began, wondering what on earth she was going to say.

But the Abbot waved her words away unspoken and his expression softened. 'You need have no worries about us, of course. As Abbot I am too disciplined for erotic thoughts and the Purlisa is too old.'

'Almost,' the Purlisa said.

The Abbot looked at him quickly and frowned.

The Purlisa blinked benignly. 'She's very pretty underneath the spells.'

'Ah,' Blue said. She had the feeling she was in serious trouble, but it was all she could do not to laugh. 'About the spells ...'

The Purlisa pursed his lips and waved a warning finger. 'Forbidden here in Buthner. Absolutely, positively illegal. Hideously strict penalties: some might even say barbaric. And nowhere is magic more blasphemous than in a monastery.' He smiled cheerfully again. 'Still, I expect you didn't know.'

The Abbot looked at her fondly. 'And you *have* saved us so much trouble with the younger monks ...'

'I imagine we could overlook it,' said the Purlisa.

'I imagine we could overlook it,' echoed the Abbot.

They both beamed at her.

'How did you know?' Blue asked. She'd taken a chance with the spells largely because Madame Cardui claimed they were espionage grade and entirely undetectable.

'The Purlisa is a mystic,' said the Abbot.

The Purlisa flickered his hands spookily. 'I see beneath appearances,' he said in a sepulchral voice. He smiled, then sobered. 'For example, I see there is a worry in your heart.'

Blue stared at him. The desire to laugh had suddenly disappeared.

'I expect it's a lost love,' said the Abbot. 'With women it's always a lost love.'

'It *is* a lost love,' the Treasure said crossly. 'And there's no need to mock just because you're too *disciplined* –' he lowered his voice and mumbled '– or too ugly –' the voice raised again '– to have a lost love of your own.' He turned to Blue and said kindly, 'It is a lost love, isn't it?'

This little old man was incredible. Blue said, 'Yes, it is.'

'It is interlinked. It is interwoven. It is part of the tapestry of life.'

'Everything is part of the tapestry of life,' the Abbot grumbled. 'That doesn't solve our problem.'

'It is part of the part of life's tapestry that *involves* our problem,' said the Purlisa impatiently. He glared briefly at the Abbot, then turned back to Blue and smiled. 'What's your birth name? I expect it's something more melodious than Sluce Ragetus.'

For a moment Blue considered making up another name, then decided she simply couldn't lie to the Precious One. 'Blue,' she said. 'It's Holly Blue.'

The Purlisa looked at the Abbot. 'Why is that name familiar?' he asked.

'It's the same name as the Realm's Queen Empress, you old fool,' the Abbot told him. To Blue he said, 'You're not related, by any chance?'

To her surprise, Blue felt herself blush.

The Abbot blinked. 'You *are* the Queen Empress?'

Blue nodded.

'You see, Jamides! A royal soul! Exactly as I predicted!'

The Abbot ignored him and frowned at Blue. 'But what are you doing in the Buthner desert?'

The Purlisa began to pace and gesture wildly. 'A royal soul!' he said again, delightedly. 'It's just *precisely* what I predicted. Admit it, Jamides – go on, admit it!' He swung round to grin at Blue. 'It's what I said, isn't it? A lost love?'

'I suppose it is,' Blue said. 'A lost love.'

'You see! You see!' He actually waved two fists in the air. 'You must tell us of your lost love,' he said. 'Then the Abbot will tell you of our problem. Then it's entirely possible that I shall tell you how one may form part of the other.' He pulled out a chair and sat down suddenly, a smug expression on his face. The Abbot promptly took a seat beside him.

'There's not much to tell,' Blue said. 'My friend Henry –'

'Your *love* Henry,' the Purlisa corrected her.

Blue hesitated, then said, 'Yes, all right. My love, Henry, has disappeared and I think he may be in the Buthner desert and I came to look for him. It's more complicated than that, but that's the main thing.'

The Abbot looked up at her sharply. 'Just a minute. Did you say *Henry*? That's a human name.'

Blue said warily, 'Yes, it is. Henry is a human boy.'

'You see?' the Purlisa exclaimed. 'Human! Didn't I say human? Now will you take my visions seriously?'

'I do take them seriously!' the Abbot hissed. 'I've always taken them seriously. But they're not always right. And you must admit your last one was so far-fetched –'

Blue suddenly realised she was the only one still standing and sat down. 'Excuse me,' she said, 'but Henry may be in danger. Can you help me find him?'

The Purlisa beamed at her. 'You help us. We'll help you!'

An acolyte appeared with a tray, which he set down before Blue, then silently withdrew.

The Purlisa pursed his lips and nodded. 'See?' he said. 'A younger monk.' He smiled triumphantly at Blue. 'You did not disturb him in the slightest.'

Fifty-Eight

They let her eat in peace (a bowl of cold soup, some wonderfully crumbly bread, a selection of home-made cheeses, sliced meat, fruit and, best of all, a jug of clear, cool water) although they watched every mouthful as if they were starving themselves. When she finished, the Abbot said, 'There is something we would like you to see.'

From the outside, the monastery was deceptive. When she'd approached, it had appeared to be a single, rambling building. Now she realised it was more like a small community, a village of several buildings, some of which appeared to be dug into the mountainside itself. The structures surrounded a hidden garden, more lush and carefully tended than the agricultural strip Blue had seen as she arrived. They passed a shallow, worn stone basin elevated to shoulder height on a pedestal. Inside it the monks had planted a miniature replica of the garden embellished with a tiny brick-built pagoda.

'The home of our last Abbot,' the Purlisa remarked when he noticed her looking at it.

'A model of his home?' Blue inquired politely.

'Oh, no, he lives there now. He has grown very small since he became immortal.'

She was still trying to work it out as they led her from

the garden through an archway into one of the structures hewn into the mountainside. The corridor they entered seemed to descend and eventually led to a flight of narrow stone steps, illuminated by flickering torches: no glowglobes here, of course, in this anti-magical country.

'This portion of the monastery was once a military fortress,' the Abbot explained. He looked mildly pained. 'I'm afraid below we will find the dungeons.'

'Nonetheless,' the Purlisa chipped in, 'we must descend. Are you psychic, Queen Holly Blue?'

'I don't think so,' Blue said hesitantly.

'Ah good,' said the Purlisa. 'Psychics often find the atmosphere disturbing. So much suffering. We blessed the cells and torture chambers, but I'm not sure it's made much difference.' He smiled suddenly. 'However, we will not be delayed long; then we can return to more cheering surroundings and discuss our plans.'

Blue noted the word *our*. It seemed she was being drawn into the monastery's problems whether she wanted it or not. But she couldn't see what else she might do. Without help, she could only go back to her aimless wandering in the desert.

'Please be careful,' the Abbot said. 'The steps are rather steep.'

Psychic or not, Blue found the tunnels horrid. They were rough-cut in the bedrock, gloomy, claustrophobic and, surprisingly, dank: in one area water streamed down the walls. But perhaps it wasn't so surprising. A monastery, as much as the ancient fortress before it, needed a reliable water source. This monastery was probably built on top of one.

The tunnel opened out suddenly into an underground

plaza, leading in turn to what had clearly once been holding cells. Their doors all stood open so Blue could see some had been converted into austere, joyless bedrooms (only a monk on penance would elect to sleep here), but others remained in their original condition, with chains and fetters hanging from their walls.

'Renovation programme,' muttered the Abbot, as much to himself as anybody else. 'Not much funds, so it will take a while.'

'We just want you to look for a moment,' said the Purlisa, without explaining at what.

'To your left,' said the Abbot and pointed.

The chamber was much larger than the miserable cells and seemed to have been used for torture. There was still some rusting equipment left in place – a metal chair with a fire drawer beneath its seat, a broken rack, a whipping post. In the centre of the room, a cage hung suspended by a chain from a hook in the ceiling. Inside it was the huddled figure of an old man, his head turned away from them.

'What are you doing to him?' Blue asked, appalled.

'Look again,' said the Purlisa quietly.

Blue looked again. The door of the cage, like that of the chamber itself, hung open.

'Why does he stay in there?' Blue whispered.

'He won't come out,' the Abbot told her quietly. 'We tried putting his food in the centre of the floor so he'd have to leave the cage, but he starved for three days rather than come out. So now we feed him there.'

Blue licked her lips. 'But he must come out for ... you know ...'

The Abbot shook his head. 'Not even for that. You can tell from the smell. Fortunately he eats very little.'

Blue's stomach was knotted. She felt such a wave of pity for the creature in the cage that tears began to well up in her eyes. Then the crouched old man turned his head. 'My gods,' Blue gasped before she could stop herself, 'it's Brimstone!'

The Purlisa reacted at once. 'You know this person?'

Blue knew him all right. Brimstone was the demonologist who'd once tried to sacrifice her brother to the demon Beleth, who'd helped the Prince of Darkness attack her Realm by way of the Analogue World. What was he doing here, on the edge of the Buthner Desert? What interest did the Abbot and his little Treasure have in him?

'What's the matter with him?' Blue whispered.

'We think a cloud dancer may have got to him,' said the Abbot.

fifty-Nine

'You located him?' Hairstreak asked the cloud dancer.

'Yes.'

'You reached him?'

'Yes.'

'Where was he?'

'Near the Mountains of Madness.'

Hairstreak frowned. He'd never heard of Mountains of Madness. 'Where's that?'

'The Kingdom of Buthner.'

Buthner? That godsforsaken hole? What did Brimstone think he was doing in Buthner? Then, like a thunderbolt, an answer occurred to him. Hiding something. Brimstone had to be hiding something. Except it couldn't be the one thing that interested Hairstreak: he'd never have managed to smuggle *that* out of the country. So it had to be something else. Unless he *wasn't* hiding something. Unless he'd gone to Buthner *for* something. Hairstreak felt his mind go into a whirl of indecision. This was why he'd hired the cloud dancer, dammit. 'What was he doing there?' he demanded.

'I don't know,' the cloud dancer said.

Hairstreak glared at it. 'You don't know?' he repeated. 'Didn't you bother to *ask* him?'

The cloud dancer said, 'Yes.'

When it became obvious the creature wasn't going to elaborate, Hairstreak said, 'And …?'

'He refused to tell me.'

'Of course he refused to tell you!' Lord Hairstreak exploded. 'What did you expect? If the old goat was prepared to tell people, I'd have asked him myself. That was the whole point of hiring you, you insubstantial cretin. So you could force it out of him. Didn't you try to force it out of him?'

The cloud dancer said, 'Yes.'

When it became obvious for the second time the creature wasn't going to elaborate, Hairstreak repeated, 'And …?'

'I think I may have overdone it.'

This was turning into a minuet. Hairstreak controlled his fury with an effort. 'Why do you think you may have overdone it?'

'Because he is now insane.'

'You sent him mad?' Hairstreak screamed. 'So he can no longer answer questions?'

The cloud dancer said, 'Yes.'

Hairstreak thumped the table with such force that the surface cracked. 'And what are you going to do about it?' he demanded.

A portion of the cloud dancer's arm disappeared as it reached into its own dimension, then reappeared with a wide-necked jug, which it placed on the table before Hairstreak. Then it pushed two fingers down its throat, retched violently and vomited a quantity of curdled blood into the jug.

It stared triumphantly at Hairstreak. 'Return your fee,' it said.

Sixty

'Where did you find him?' Blue asked. Thankfully, they'd left the former dungeons and were now sitting together in the garden, shaded from the merciless sun by an enormous spreading tree of a type she'd never seen before.

'Wandering in the desert,' the Abbot said. 'One of our monks happened on him, otherwise he would have been dead within a few hours. As it was, he was *nearly* dead.'

'And was he in that state –' even talking about Brimstone, she shied from using the word *mad* '– when you found him? I mean, was he – ?'

The Abbot nodded. 'Yes. He is very old. We thought he might die. We tended to his body – we have healers in the monastery – and he recovered. But we could do nothing for his mind.'

'Forgive me,' the Purlisa put in. He was seated beside her on the bench and she noticed his sandaled feet didn't quite reach the ground. 'But you know who he is?'

'He is one of my subjects,' Blue said. 'His name is Silas Brimstone. He is a Faerie of the Night who once ran a manufacturing business in the capital.' She hesitated, then added, 'He is not a good man.'

'That would accord with my visions,' said the Purlisa.

There was something about him that made her feel they had been friends throughout her entire life. Blue said quietly, 'I think you'd better tell me about your visions.'

'Since I was little,' the Purlisa said (and Blue somehow refrained from smiling), 'there have been times when God granted me revelations of certain matters past and present, sometimes, although not often, future. I fear what you say is correct. This Silas Brimstone is not a good man. He has raised the Midgard Serpent.'

Blue looked at him blankly. 'What's the Midgard Serpent?'

'This is where it gets hard to believe,' the Abbot muttered.

The Purlisa glanced at him crossly, then turned back to smile at Blue. 'Do you know of the Old Gods, Queen Blue?'

'Oh yes,' Blue said without elaboration. It wasn't so long ago since she'd been face to face with one of the Old Gods herself.

'Before the dawn of our history, one of them – his name was Loki – married a giant and fathered three children by her. The middle one was a sea serpent –'

The Abbot snorted derisively.

'It's a whole other reality!' the Purlisa snapped. 'I've told you that before, Jamides.'

'You've told me, but I don't believe you.'

'Please don't quarrel,' Blue said. 'I'd really like to hear this story.'

'Yes, stop quarrelling, Jamides.'

'I wasn't quarrelling.'

'Well, stop snorting then.' The Purlisa turned back to Blue. 'I don't suppose for a minute it was a natural birth. The father was very tricky and may have used magic to transform the poor little mite. But in any case the Emperor of the Old Gods got to hear about the business and decided that the birth was an abomination –'

'Well, you would, wouldn't you?' put in the Abbot.

The Purlisa ignored him. '– and threw the serpent into the great ocean that encircles Midgard.'

'Where luckily it discovered it was a *sea* serpent,' the Abbot said, casting his eyes heavenwards.

'Where it began to grow and grow until it was so large it was able to surround the whole of Midgard.'

'Excuse me,' said Blue. 'You saw all this in a vision?'

The Purlisa shook his head. 'No, no, I saw none of this in a vision. It's recorded in the Annals of the Old Gods.'

'Which some of us don't take literally,' the Abbot said.

The Purlisa closed his eyes. 'Which Jamides is too *modern* to take literally.' He opened his eyes again. 'But we won't worry too much what Jamides thinks, will we, Queen Blue?' While Blue was searching for a diplomatic response, he went on. 'The creature began to squeeze the boundaries of Midgard, causing earthquakes and tidal waves and hurricanes and the like, and eventually it became obvious that if something wasn't done the whole of Midgard would be destroyed. All life would be wiped out.' He shivered. 'Dreadful thought. So the Emperor appointed a series of heroes to tackle the problem. The serpent ate most of them, but one discovered the only effective weapon against it was a hammer – swords or projectiles or anything of that sort simply wouldn't work. So he used his war hammer and the serpent shrank to manageable proportions. It ceased to give trouble and things settled down in Midgard for several thousand years.'

'Where exactly is Midgard, Purlisa?' Blue asked.

'It's our present reality,' the Purlisa said. 'The whole of the Faerie Realm and the Analogue World – all of it. It takes in Hael as well, I believe. It's all the dimensions of reality we can experience.'

'Oh,' Blue said.

'Now the Purlisa thinks the trouble will be starting up again.' The Abbot smiled.

'I *know* it will be starting up again,' the Purlisa said soberly. 'Your friend Brimstone –'

'No friend of mine,' Blue murmured.

'– has called up the Serpent. Called it into our reality: into Midgard, that is. I saw it clearly in my vision. This will start the cycle again. The beast can only grow and grow. Unless we find a hero to stop it, our reality will eventually be destroyed.'

There was a long moment's silence. Eventually Blue said hesitantly, 'But, Purlisa, surely the story of the Midgard Serpent is a myth?'

'Of course it is!' the Abbot snorted.

'*Perhaps* it is,' the Purlisa told her calmly, 'but my vision shows that Mr Brimstone called up a serpent of some sort before he went insane.' He blinked benignly. 'And the earthquakes have already started.'

Blue glanced at the Abbot, who nodded reluctantly, then said, 'But, of course, Buthner has always had earthquakes from time to time.'

'So far,' the Purlisa said briskly, 'the quakes have been confined to the deep desert. But they will get worse until a hero slays the serpent.' He smiled with great warmth at Blue. 'Which is where you come in.'

Blue stared at him without speaking. She liked the Purlisa hugely, but that didn't mean she necessarily believed him. The Midgard story *did* sound like a myth – even the Abbot thought so. Perhaps Brimstone really *had* called up some sort of serpent – he'd called up enough demons before she put a stop to that nonsense, and he might well have discovered some other source of nasty creatures. Perhaps what he'd been doing caused an earthquake. But that hardly mattered. Because none of this was her affair. She wasn't the hero they needed. She wasn't even the heroine they needed. And she had other things to do. Henry could be dying somewhere while the Purlisa had her off chasing serpents. She opened her mouth to speak, but the Purlisa beat her to it.

'Your love Henry will perish if you do not do this thing,' he said.

Sixty-One

Although she would have died rather than admit it, Madame Cardui felt old. There was so much to do and, for the first time in her life, she had started to doubt her ability to do it. She was back in her office at the Palace with a full support staff now – a written order from Blue had sorted out that silly misunderstanding about her imprisonment – but even so she felt her grip on things slipping and slipping and slipping.

Part of it was the plague. There were constant reports of its spread now, and not just the panic that followed the outbreak of any major illness. These were genuine cases, striking indiscriminately at young and old. Two of her staff were plotting its spread using maps from the Situation Room beneath the Palace and the grip the disease now had throughout the Empire was worrying. Or to face facts, frightening. It was crossing borders too, as plagues did, into neighbouring countries. Which meant it was only a matter of time before those borders began to close, with a devastating affect on trade.

Worse still, there were more and more deaths being reported. Most worrying of all, many of them were now occurring among the young, who in theory should have had a large reserve of their future to draw upon. The plague seemed to be growing more virulent. Or possibly – and this was something she dreaded to contemplate – it meant that no one, young or old, had very much future left. It was possible the entire Realm was facing a disaster of unparalleled magnitude.

Dear Gods, she wished Alan were still here. He would have known what to do. If there was anything still left to do ...

It felt as though her Intelligence network were crumbling too. Perhaps an exaggeration, but it really did not seem to be functioning as efficiently as it once had. She appeared to have lost Chalkhill, for example. A dreadful man and quite possibly a double agent, but even as a double agent he could be useful. Clearly there was something going on with the Brotherhood, and her instinct told her there might even be a connection with the plague. Was it possible the imbeciles were experimenting with germ warfare? She found the idea hard to accept, but Lord Hairstreak was using the Brotherhood as a power base now and she would put nothing past him.

When the knock came to her door, she assumed it was a secretary and murmured, 'Come in', then looked up to find Nymph standing over her. 'My deeah, what a pleasant surprise. I thought you were still in the Analogue World with Pyrgus. How is the poor –?' She caught Nymph's expression and stopped. 'What's wrong?'

Nymph said, 'Pyrgus has caught an Analogue disease.'

Sixty-Two

Henry thought his hands were turning blue.

He stared at them, frowning. They weren't *actually* blue, not cobalt or azure or navy or anything like that, but they definitely had a bluish *tinge*. At first he'd thought it was his imagination and then he'd thought it was a trick of the light, but now he was certain something physical was happening. Maybe the desert did that to you. There might be something in the sand, or something in the spectrum of the sun, the way a desert sun at home would give you a deep tan.

The interesting thing was Henry was toughening up and drying out, a bit like an old boot. (An old *blue* boot.) Neither his arm nor leg hurt much any more. His thirst was a constant low-key background he could generally ignore and he needed far less of the liquid Lorquin produced from time to time. He could also keep going for longer before he had to stop and rest. He was even developing that peculiar loping gait Lorquin had. It was a half-conscious imitation, but the new way of walking ate up the miles with minimum effort.

Henry was less successful in his attempts to find his way around. Lorquin made valiant efforts to teach him. The secret was, apparently, to study the angle of the sun along with patterns the wind made in the sand. Henry could follow the bit about the sun easily enough – it moved across the sky much the same way it did at home – but try as he might, he couldn't see the patterns Lorquin saw in the sand. And the deep desert was as featureless of landmarks as it had always been.

For some reason Henry had assumed Lorquin's people would be fairly close to the place where Lorquin killed his draugr. And maybe they had been when Lorquin set out on his quest. But they were nomads and they were certainly not close by now. After two days of walking, there was no sign of them. But then he still couldn't see anything when Lorquin announced they'd arrived.

Henry looked around. He'd half expected a rock face with caves, or inhabited ruins, or a community of crude tents. But all around him was a plain of flat, featureless sand. Even the rolling dunes had disappeared.

'Welcome to my village,' Lorquin said, grinning proudly.

Henry looked around again. Was Lorquin's village invisible? Somehow it didn't make sense. Why cast a spell over an entire community? And if you did, how would people find each other? No, it wasn't invisibility. But there wasn't any village round here either. After a minute, feeling foolish, Henry said, 'Where?'

He started violently as something *whooshed* up out of the sand. Then something else and something else and something else. In an eye blink he was surrounded by a ring of blue-skinned, naked people. Some of the men carried spears. One sported fearsome – and very colourful – tattoos. They glared malevolently at Henry.

Henry took a step backwards, his heart suddenly thumping. But Lorquin hurled himself forward to embrace a glowering, ugly, beetle-browed individual with what looked suspiciously like filed teeth. 'I did it, Dad!' he shouted. 'I killed the draugr!'

The words galvanised the gathering. In seconds people were leaping and whooping in a lively dance. Several of the men came forward to thump Lorquin on the back and Henry noticed one of the younger girls grinning at him. A plump woman with kind eyes and a broad smile pushed through the crowd to hug him fondly: Henry imagined this had to be Lorquin's mother and fancied he even saw a family resemblance. One unusually tall man (a tribal chief?) called out, 'Tonight we feast!' The announcement was greeted by a loud communal cheer; then Lorquin was being pushed from one to another, fondly shaken, kissed, grinned at, congratulated.

Then suddenly it stopped. In the absolute silence, they turned slowly and stared at Henry.

Henry took another step backwards, smiled nervously and said, 'Ah –' He stopped smiling, licked his lips and wondered if there was the slightest possibility he could outrun these fearsome people in the desert. Somehow, he didn't rate his chances.

Then Lorquin had his father by the hand and was dragging him across. 'This is my Companion,' he announced.

And with that the atmosphere changed again, dramatically. Suddenly Henry was closely surrounded. People were smiling, people were touching him, tugging curiously at his clothing, people were talking to him in such a jumble of voices that he could understand none of it. He was aware of a collective body odour, not at all unpleasant, but spicy and strong. The word *Companion* bounced across the hum of noise like a ball. It was clear the whole tribe took their customs as seriously as Lorquin.

The tall man shouldered his way through the throng, said something to Henry that he couldn't catch, then abruptly stood still and stretched to his fullest height, slowly rotating his head in a bizarre movement that took it round further than Henry would ever have believed possible. 'Vaettirs coming,' he said shortly, although there was nothing in sight for as far as the eye could see. He wound back his incredible neck and glanced in Lorquin's direction. 'They pursued you long.'

What happened next was so swift Henry scarcely had time to follow it. The members of Lorquin's tribe took one another's hands, but in a very specific sequence that reminded Henry a little of a Mexican Wave. Lorquin was last in line, but lunged forward to grab Henry's hand. There was a sensation of falling, or, more accurately, sinking, as if he was in quicksand. To his horror, he realised that was *exactly* what was happening – the entire tribe was sinking into the sand and him with them. He started to call out, but the sand was up to his shoulders now, then his neck, his chin, his mouth ... He was drowning in sand!

Henry started to struggle violently, but Lorquin had an iron grip on his hand. Seconds later, the quicksand engulfed him.

Sixty-Three

He was aware of a haze of dusty orange light. It wasn't bright, but it was bright enough to see the others and, as his eyes adjusted, things became a little clearer. They were moving like a shoal of fish, swimming. But not through water: he was sure of that. He could breathe, for one thing, and breathe easily. Yet the swimming thing was exactly what he was doing. He could go up or down just by kicking with both feet. He could move forward by sweeping with his arms. Lorquin was close by. The boy had let go of Henry's hand, but was signalling him to follow.

The tribe were stretched into an elongated V formation, like a massive flight of geese, with the tall man at their head. They plunged forward and downward, heads first, in an easy motion, for all the world like a school of dolphins. But where were they swimming? All Henry could think of was sinking into sand, but this clearly wasn't sand: you couldn't swim through sand. You couldn't even swim in quicksand – all you did there was drown. Yet he'd sunk into sand and there was no water in the desert to make quicksand and they were definitely swimming (and breathing!) and ...

And it was actually a nice sensation. Henry did something he very seldom did and lightened up. Still swimming, he rolled over on his back and tilted his head so he could still see Lorquin and the tribe. The orange light was brighter high above him and he thought he could just about make out the position of a diffuse sun. They were swimming underneath the sand. They had to be. Nothing else made sense, even though that didn't make sense either. It was like being underwater, except they were under sand. He was swimming and breathing and floating and it was really, really lovely.

A curious chirping sound reached him – that was like a dolphin too – and as he twisted his head he realised it was coming from Lorquin, who was signalling him to catch up. Henry pushed powerfully with his legs and was rewarded by an exhilarating spurt of speed. This was utterly delicious! Once he'd managed to grow wings and fly when he translated to the Faerie Realm, but even that had been nothing like this. Sand swimming was warm and comforting and wonderful.

He kept wondering how it was happening. Lorquin and his people looked like faeries – primitive faeries admittedly, but not some sort of creepy different race. And even if they were some sort of creepy different race that had evolved the trick of swimming in sand, that hardly explained how Henry could now swim in sand as well. All that was needed was Lorquin to take his hand and drag him under and now he was doing it!

There was a city ahead.

Henry blinked. (How could you blink under *sand?*) He could see towers and spires and walls and turrets rising up out of the seabed – not the seabed: he wasn't under water, but he couldn't think what else to call it. He could see segments of paved roadway. It was a little gloomy up ahead, but he could definitely see it. Unless this was some sort of mirage, some gigantic illusion, there was a city out there … and they were heading directly for it.

He kicked strongly until he caught up with the others and swam beside Lorquin. '*What's that up ahead?*' he tried to ask, but for some reason the words came out as a series of dolphin chirps.

Lorquin turned his head to smile at him and emitted another series of chirps in response, but Henry could make nothing of them. He rolled, then swam upwards a little to get a better view. The city was resolving itself more clearly and now he could see it was largely ruins, like some vast underwater Atlantis swallowed by a prehistoric tidal wave. Henry wanted to shout with excitement, but kept his mouth tight shut and listened to the pounding of his heart instead.

Up ahead, the leaders of the tribe reached a flat stretch of crumbling pavement and abruptly dropped down. Now, suddenly, they moved towards the towering buildings at a walk, no longer swimming. Henry had a moment of panic as he caught up – what was happening here? – but then, without warning, popped through some sort of invisible membrane and floated, light as thistledown to reach the pavement himself.

He took a few hesitant steps after the others and experienced the curious sensation of increasing weight. But the weirdest thing was he'd felt this way before. As a kid in the bath, he sometimes let the water drain away without getting out. As he lay there and the water disappeared, his body – no longer buoyed up – grew heavier and heavier until it reached its normal weight. It was exactly like that now, except this time he was standing up.

Lorquin appeared beside him, cheerful as ever. 'We're home,' he said without a single dolphin chirp. 'We live here.' He smiled hugely up at Henry. 'You can live here too,' he said. 'Because you are my Companion.'

Sixty-four

Madame Cardui had never been to the Analogue World before and it took her less than half an hour to decide she didn't like it.

The worst of it was the utterly *hideous* clothing she was forced to wear. No sense of style, or cut, or colour *whatsoever*. And naturally no woven spells. So everything just hung on one's body with all the panache of splattered porridge.

'What are those?' she asked coldly when Nymph produced a particularly repulsive garment.

'Trousers,' Nymph said briefly.

The girl was worried about Pyrgus. They were *both* worried about Pyrgus. But all the same ... 'Men's garments?' Madame Cardui asked her. 'You expect me to indulge in *cross-dressing?*'

Nymph shook her head. 'No, no, Madame Cardui. These are not men's garments. These are part of a woman's suit. Trousers and a jacket. Muted colours, darker shades. These sort of clothes are very popular in the Analogue World.' She hesitated, then added, 'Particularly for the older woman.'

Madame Cardui glared at her. 'Then I shall *certainly* not wear them.'

She settled eventually on a heavily frilled blouse,

open at the neck and worn with an ankle-length gypsy skirt and open sandals. As an afterthought she added a silk scarf for extra colour. It was a far cry from what she was used to, but at least it showed a little *flair*. Nymph looked at her uncertainly. 'No arguments,' said Madame Cardui coldly. One had to keep up standards, even in the Analogue World.

Translation, as it turned out, was rather fun. She would have liked to use one of Alan's portable transporters – just as a small remembrance – but he had made so very few of them before he died and all had eventually begun to exhibit that unfortunate fault which turned people inside out. So she stepped with Nymph into the cold blue flames of the official Palace portal. Which produced a sensation similar to stepping off a cliff, something which, curiously, she found enjoyable.

But *enjoyable* was not an adjective one would readily use to describe the Analogue World, she discovered. For their stay in this ridiculous dimension, Pyrgus and Nymph had rented a small country estate suited, if only just, to the status of a Faerie Prince and his consort. But the place, it transpired, was built on granite with such a high quartz content that portal technology would not work in the immediate vicinity. The young people took the inconvenience in their stride, of course, and Nymph had arranged transportation from the actual (and thankfully well-concealed) portal outlet.

Madame Cardui stared at the carriage, aghast. 'What is that?'

'It's called a motor car,' Nymph said.

'Why is it such a peculiar shape?'

'They make them that way,' Nymph said vaguely. She walked across to open the door.

Madame Cardui peered inside suspiciously. 'I thought they used horses to draw their carriages?'

Nymph shook her head. 'That was a long time ago.'

Madame Cardui straightened up, frowning. 'So they use spell technology now?'

Nymph shook her head again. She smiled slightly. 'Most humans don't even *believe* in magic any more – you know the problems Henry's had with it.'

'So how does it work?' Madame Cardui asked. 'I assume it *does* work?'

'There is a mechanical engine,' Nymph said. 'Concealed in that bulge on the front.'

'Good grief – is it safe?'

'Not very,' Nymph admitted, 'but we haven't far to go.' She climbed into the extraordinary contraption and signed for Madame Cardui to join her.

'Where is our driver?' Madame Cardui asked as she did so.

'I shall drive,' Nymph said.

'*You*, deeah?'

'Pyrgus taught me,' Nymph said, smiling proudly. 'He's quite good at it.' She leaned forward and unlocked something in one wall of the carriage. The entire structure shook and growled like a demented cat.

'Does it always make that noise?' asked Madame Cardui.

Far to go or not, the journey was frankly sordid. The carriage didn't fly, wouldn't even hover, so that it jerked and rattled and hummed and growled on primitive wheels (wheels!) along trackways that were filled – positively *filled* – with similar repulsive vehicles. Everything was smell and confusion and noise and poor Nymphalis had to steer the thing herself. Not even an elemental to lighten the load.

Matters improved somewhat as they neared Pyrgus and Nymph's Analogue home, mainly because it was some distance from any major centre of population and consequently there were far fewer – what was it Nymph called them? – *motor cars* about. But that did not make the Analogue World any more appealing. The sky was the wrong shade of blue, where it showed blue at all. The clouds were generally of an irritatingly different shape to Realm clouds. Even sunshine wasn't right. It had a curious whiteness about it, not at all as pleasant as the rich gold of faerie sunshine.

Eventually Nymph manoeuvred their carriage off the public trackways altogether and through a set of tall, imposing gates. Madame Cardui shivered. 'Those aren't iron, are they?' she asked.

'Yes, they are,' Nymph said.

'But, my deeah, don't you realise how dangerous iron can be?' It occurred to her that Pyrgus's mysterious 'Analogue illness' might easily have started from a brush with iron. The metal was quite lethal to a faerie.

'They use a lot of it here,' Nymph said offhandedly. 'It doesn't seem to have quite so strong an effect as it does at home.' She caught Madame Cardui's expression and added quickly, 'We take great care, of course. There is very little iron in the house itself.'

Very little? The child said *Very little?* In any sensible faerie household there would be none at all. For Madame Cardui, even the fashionable protected iron, with its vaunted safety guarantees, held no appeal.

The house, on the whole, was less disappointing. It was small for a prince, but looked mature and the architecture was actually quite interesting. She recalled having read somewhere that there was a slight gravitational difference between the Analogue and Faerie Worlds: not enough to be noticeable, but enough to affect building materials under stress, hence architectural styles. It wasn't the only difference she noticed.

'Where are the servants?' she asked Nymph sharply as the ghastly vehicle pulled up at the front of the house. They should have been lined up at the doorway, ready to greet their mistress. She did so hope Nymph was not letting standards slip.

'We don't have any,' Nymph said as she locked whatever it was in the carriage she had unlocked and removed the key.

Madame Cardui blinked. 'Don't be ridiculous – of course you have servants.'

'We have a cook, because I'm not much good at that and Pyrgus doesn't know how to find his way to the kitchen. And there's a nurse looking after him while I'm away. But we don't have servants the way you mean. They're actually quite difficult to find here, even when you offer gold.'

Madame Cardui climbed out of the carriage shaking her head. She could see she would have to do something about the way Pyrgus and Nymph were living if they were forced to stay in the Analogue World very much longer. Pyrgus was a man, of course, so one expected him to be clueless. Nymph should have known better, but she was a Forest Faerie and that was a wholly different culture. She shouldered her reticule of healing spells. When she removed his present illness, she would make time to organise their household properly. Even with a crisis at home, there were some things that had to take priority. Besides which, it wouldn't take long.

The nurse proved far too familiar when addressing her betters, but at least she seemed genuinely concerned about Pyrgus's condition, even to the point of insisting that he required to be treated urgently by an Analogue doctor.

'I *am* a doctor,' Madame Cardui told her grandly. Which was, of course, true since her healing spells were likely to be far more effective than any Analogue leech-craft.

The woman had the effrontery to glance at Madame Cardui's sandals, but backed off under an icy stare, leaving them free at last to proceed unhindered to poor Pyrgus's bedroom.

But as they stepped through the doorway, Madame Cardui went chill. One look at the figure in the bed told her everything she needed to know. She dropped the ret-icule of useless spells. 'This isn't an Analogue illness,' she said quietly. 'It's temporal fever.'

Nymph stared at her in disbelief. 'You can't have temporal fever in the Analogue World,' she said.

'That's what we all thought,' Madame Cardui said soberly. 'But clearly we were wrong.'

Sixty-five

'I don't see any mountains,' Blue said.

'They'll appear in a moment,' the Abbot told her.

'It's an optical illusion,' put in the Purlisa. He smiled benignly. 'Look,' he added, 'there they are now.'

Blue turned to follow his gaze. The mountains stood out stark and blue against the near horizon. 'The serpent is there?' she asked. 'In a cavern in those mountains?'

The Purlisa nodded. 'Such was my vision.'

'And Henry is there too, held by the serpent?' She wasn't sure she believed any of this, but the Purlisa *had* been able to describe Henry on the basis of his vision and the description was completely accurate. Besides, she had no other clue to Henry's whereabouts.

From the corner of her eye she saw the Abbot give the Purlisa what looked like a warning glance. But the Purlisa only nodded and said, 'Yes.'

They were standing at the head of the small party of monks who had escorted them this far. A wiry pack animal of a breed Blue did not recognise carried minimal supplies, including her designated weapon. Blue said, 'What happens now?'

The Purlisa looked at her but said nothing.

Blue said, 'Will you help me?'

The Purlisa still said nothing. Beside him, the Abbot looked away, embarrassed.

Blue turned to stare into the mountains. 'I go up there alone?'

'Yes.' The Purlisa stretched out a hand to pat the pack animal. 'You can take the charno. He will carry your weapon.'

'Won't you need him?' Blue asked. 'For your supplies?'

'The supplies will remain with you,' said the Purlisa. 'As monks, we are used to deprivation.'

'The journey back is not long,' the Abbot added. He still looked embarrassed.

'How can I be sure of finding the right cave?' Blue asked.

'It is your destiny,' the Purlisa told her simply. He handed her the reins of the charno.

After a long moment, Blue turned and led the beast away. The monks stood silent, watching, until she disappeared into the foothills.

Sixty-Six

The charno was an odd-looking creature, with enormous feet and long drooping ears, that squatted on two powerful hind legs like a giant hare. They were high in the foothills before Blue realised it could talk.

'You know they've conned you,' it said suddenly.

Blue blinked.

'The Abbot and that midget,' said the charno. 'Conned you.' It had a rough, scraping voice, the sort some men developed through drinking too much spirits of grain.

'I didn't know you could talk,' Blue said foolishly.

'Don't have much to say usually,' the charno told her.

'What do you mean, conned me?' Blue asked.

'Got their own agenda. Your boyfriend's not up there yet.'

Blue stared at the creature. The strange thing was she believed it, at least about the monks' agenda. There'd been too many peculiar little glances between the Abbot and the Purlisa. But she wasn't sure they were actually lying to her. Especially not the Purlisa, who was probably the sweetest man she'd ever met. After a moment she said, 'Do you have a name?'

'Charno,' said the charno.

'I meant a personal name.'

'You can call me Charno with a capital "C",' said the

charno. 'That's how we do things,' he added without specifying who he meant by *we*.

'How do you know Henry's not up there, Charno?' Blue asked.

The charno tapped the side of his nose with a forepaw. 'Got my sources,' he said. He turned a toothy head to look pointedly up the mountain. Blue followed the direction of his gaze and discovered he was looking at a cave mouth. ''Sides,' he added. 'I eavesdrop.'

'Why do the Abbot and the Purlisa want me to go up there?'

'Abbot doesn't. It comes down to the mad midget.' He reached up with one huge hind foot to scratch behind his ear.

'You don't think there's a serpent up there?'

'*Something* up there,' said the charno. 'Serpent. Dragon. Oompatherium. Dunno. Just know it hasn't started munching on your boy, 'cause he's not there yet.'

'*Yet?*' echoed Blue.

'He's not there.'

'You said *yet.*'

'No I didn't,' said the charno quickly.

'Yes, you did – twice.'

'Didn't mean to. He's not there. Henry. Not there.' He looked away furtively.

'You're not telling me the truth,' Blue said.

'Yes, I am.'

'Then why won't you meet my eye?'

'I'm an inferior species,' said the charno.

Blue snorted, a sound that reminded her of the Abbot. 'Look here, Charno,' she said firmly, 'we can do without this nonsense. The Abbot and the Purlisa aren't the only ones with an agenda, are they?'

The charno stared down at the claws of his huge feet. 'No,' he admitted sheepishly.

'You don't want to go up there, do you?'

'Would you want to go up to a cavern full of man-eating serpent? Well, *you* would, but *I* wouldn't. I don't have a boyfriend up there.' It was the longest speech the charno had yet made, probably showing the measure of his upset.

But Blue pounced on his last sentence. 'So Henry *is* up there?'

'No,' said the charno. 'No. I told the truth about that.'

'But he *will* be here?'

'Might,' said the charno. He stared innocently up into the sunwashed blue of the sky.

Blue reached out to take his reins. 'Come on,' she said. 'We're going up.' For a moment she thought he might resist, like a stubborn donkey, but he climbed to his feet and plodded obediently after her.

'Hope you won't regret this,' he said.

Sixty-Seven

There was a rocky apron outside the cave mouth. Blue stopped when they reached it. 'You don't have to come in,' she said.

'Humph,' said the charno cynically.

'What *humph?*' Blue asked crossly. 'Why *humph?*'

'You'll need the hammer.'

Blue looked at him blankly, then remembered. 'Oh, the *war* hammer! Yes, I will.' The Purlisa had insisted a hammer was the only effective weapon against the Midgard Serpent and the Abbot had produced an antique used in ancient battles. It was an odd thing to have in a monastery and another reason why she was suspicious about their whole story.

'Can't carry that yourself,' the charno said.

'Of course I can,' Blue told him.

'Tried, have you?'

In point of fact she hadn't. The Abbot, or his monks, or *somebody* had loaded up the charno. She'd hardly done more than glimpse the hammer. It looked quite large, but she assumed if she was meant to use it against some monster, they wouldn't give her something too heavy to carry.

It occurred to her suddenly how mad this whole thing was. If there really was a serpent in the mountain, she was about to face it like a mythic warrior, armed with an ancient weapon supplied by men she'd only met a day before. But she wasn't a mythic warrior, wasn't any sort of warrior at all. She was only a princess – she still thought of herself as a princess, even now they'd made her Queen – and in the myths it was the princess who was rescued, not the other way around.

She realised two things then. The first was that she didn't entirely believe the Purlisa's story about the serpent, however much she liked the little man. The second was that she would do anything for Henry, anything at all. She would fight a serpent for him if there really was a serpent. She would cross a desert for him. She would follow any clue, however slight, in the hope of finding him. That had to be love, hadn't it?

'No, I haven't,' she said, answering the charno's question.

The charno reached round and flipped open the catch on his backpack. He drew out a bulky bundle, undid the linen wrappings and revealed the war hammer the Abbot had supplied. It was a substantial weapon with an ornately carved oak shaft and the sort of battering that comes with ancient battles. The charno handed it across to her.

Blue took the weapon and immediately dropped it to the ground. The thing weighed a *ton!* Although the charno handled it as if it were a feather, it was literally too heavy for her to lift.

'See?' the charno said.

There was a simmering anger in Blue that had nothing at all to do with the charno, but she took it out on him just the same. 'What's the point of that?' she demanded. 'What's the point of giving me a weapon I can't use? Are they trying to *kill* me?'

It was a rhetorical question but the charno said soberly, 'Told you they were conning you.'

That brought her up short. For the first time it occurred to her that what Charno said might actually be true. Not in some light-hearted and amusing way, but literally, seriously, in a way that might be harmful to her. She liked the Abbot, liked the Purlisa, so her whole instinct was to trust them. But wasn't that the very essence of the problem? You *had* to be likeable if you wanted to fool people. Nobody was going to trust some shifty-eyed scoundrel. Had the Purlisa and his Abbot conspired to send her to her death?

But *why?*

'But why?' Blue asked the question aloud.

'Search me,' said the charno, shrugging.

Frowning, Blue said, 'But they must have known I'd discover the weapon was useless to me.'

'Weren't meant to find out until you were inside the cave.'

Blue looked at him. 'When it was too late?'

The charno nodded. 'Yes.'

'You would have carried the hammer and handed it to me when I was facing the serpent?'

'Yes.'

'Why didn't you?'

'I'm not that loyal,' said the charno. 'Serpents eat charnos.'

It made complete sense, except that it didn't make any sense at all. Why would the Abbot and the Purlisa want her dead? They'd met her only a day before. She'd stumbled on their monastery by accident. 'You think there really is a serpent?'

'Probably,' the charno said.

They stood looking at each other on the rocky apron,

Blue still dressed like a young man, the charno's soulful brown eyes on a level with her own. Behind them loomed the entrance to the cavern, ominous and dark.

The trouble was she didn't really trust the charno either.

The trouble was, for all the lies, Henry might still be in there.

Sixty-Eight

There were subtleties about his situation Henry didn't understand.

They started with the ruined city. It was clear Lorquin's people hadn't built it. There was nothing about it in the tribe's most ancient legends, with the sole exception of the legend telling how they found it. Henry heard it from Brenthis, the tribe's main storyteller.

Long ago, Brenthis said, at a time when the world was lush and well watered, the Luchti were foodstuff for the savage race of Buth. They were held in pens or allowed to roam across great fenced estates, but each year in spring, two-thirds of their young were slaughtered and stored to feed the Buth.

One day a Luchti woman named Euphrosyne discovered a marvellous ark that allowed her to speak directly to Charaxes. *Like the Ark of the Covenant in the Old Testament*, Henry thought when Brenthis reached this part of the story. And Charaxes sounded just as bloodthirsty as Jehovah because he visited a Great Disaster on the Buth, which destroyed them entirely. This freed the Luchti, but dried the land so that it turned to desert and the Luchti became wanderers in the desert, always and ever in search of food and water. *And that sounded suspiciously like the Exodus of the Children of Israel from Egypt*, Henry thought, frowning. It was spooky the way some things in the Faerie Realm reflected the history of his own world. But Brenthis was still talking and Henry dragged his attention back so he wouldn't miss anything.

Thanks to the marvellous ark, Brenthis was saying, Charaxes journeyed with the Luchti and when they reached a desert flatland that seemed to hold no hope of life, they learned a secret practice of the mind that permitted them to alter certain aspects of reality. It was a difficult discipline that took them long months to perfect, but when they did so the entire tribe sank beneath the desert sands to discover the ruins of a mighty city, the like of which had never been seen by anyone before. And there, in the ruins of the city, they had lived ever since, though they roamed the desert wilderness on quests as Lorquin had done and to celebrate their release from slavery.

It sounded to Henry like the sort of legend that was a misunderstanding of actual events. Perhaps Lorquin's people really had been held captive in the distant past. Perhaps their captors, the Buth, had been defeated in war or fallen afoul of some natural disaster. But who had built the city? And how was it maintained in this impossible bubble beneath the sand? How was it – even now, in ruins – supplied with light and air and copious supplies of water? Most mysterious of all, how had the Luchti found the means to reach it? Whatever mental discipline they used was far beyond Henry. When he wanted to travel to the surface, he had to be accompanied by Lorquin or some other obliging member of the tribe.

But the city was only the start. He still could not

understand how the Luchti survived. From everything he'd seen, there simply was not enough water, not enough food, not enough shelter to sustain them. Difficult enough for Lorquin and himself (and impossible without Lorquin's special skills) but the Luchti, he discovered, was an extensive tribe. How did the desert support them? When he asked the question of Brenthis, the storyteller only shrugged and remarked, 'Are we not as skilful as the vaettirs?' Which was true enough in that the vaettirs and their draugr obviously survived as well, but not very helpful as an explanation.

Henry got no explanations for several other matters that concerned him either. The Luchti didn't know why their skin was blue, beyond saying it was the 'will of Charaxes'. (Henry's own skin didn't seem to be changing any more than it had when he first noticed a bluish tinge.) They didn't know anything about the Analogue World, or Queen Blue and her Empire in the Faerie Realm. They didn't know the name of their own country (it was just 'The Wasteland'). They didn't know how Henry had come to be in the desert or, far more importantly, how he might get back.

What they *did* know was that the tribe was overdue a celebration.

Lorquin was full of it. 'It's really *my* celebration, En Ri,' he said. 'Because they couldn't hold it until I slew the draugr. But it's not *just* about me. It sets the tribe's song-lines for the next year and it gives thanks to Charaxes and everybody gets to eat a lot and dance and I might find a wife and –'

'*Wife!*' Henry exclaimed. 'Lorquin, you're only ten years old!'

'I know,' said Lorquin happily. 'And Ino will consult

the bones and Euphrosyne will speak with Charaxes and there'll be drumming and everyone will drink much *melor.*'

Henry frowned. *Euphrosyne?* Ino was the squat man with tattoos and seemed to be some sort of witch doctor, but Euphrosyne was the woman who had found Charaxes' mysterious ark at the very dawn of tribal history. 'How old is Euphrosyne?' he asked curiously.

'Twenty years and seven months,' said Lorquin promptly.

'She's not the same Euphrosyne who found the ark, is she?'

Lorquin favoured him with a strange look. 'If you were not my Companion, En Ri, I might think you were a little simple. Euphrosyne is the daughter of the daughter of the daughter of the daughter of the –'

'I get it!' Henry told him hurriedly. There was clearly some sort of priestly line going from the original Euphrosyne, passed from daughter to daughter in the service of Charaxes. He wondered if they'd preserved the actual ark. It would be interesting to see.

'– of the daughter of the daughter of the daughter of the daughter of the daughter of the daughter of the daughter of the daughter of the daughter of the daughter of the daughter of the daughter of the daughter ...'

Henry crept away and left him to it.

Sixty-Nine

It started with a single drummer.

Henry watched as the man entered the city's enormous central plaza. His drum was a tapered wooden tube, open at one end, covered in what might be goatskin at the other and brightly decorated with tiny painted skulls that could only have come from some small rodent.

The man walked vaguely across the cracked paving, staring up at the ruined buildings for all the world like a tourist who had stumbled on a new attraction. Then, somewhere to one side of the square, he squatted with the drum between his knees, stroked the goatskin and began to play a single tap ... tap ... tap with no discernable rhythm. The drum had not much resonance: either that or the under-sand environment absorbed much of its sound.

'Do we go down yet?' Henry asked softly. They were standing by a window in what remained of the second floor of a squat building. Blue faces were at the windows of many buildings around them.

'No,' Loquin said without elaboration. His eyes were very bright.

A second drummer appeared from the shadow of an alley. He moved with greater focus, walking directly to the centre of the plaza, ignoring his environment. He too squatted down and began to play, but this time there *was* a rhythm: both drums together sounded like a massive heartbeat, and now there was the resonance that had been lacking before. Henry fancied he heard a collective sigh from the watching tribe.

There was no change for long moments on end: *thud-boom ... thud-boom ... thud-boom ... thud-boom ...* The sound was mildly hypnotic.

Two more drummers entered the square, their heads turned upwards. They moved in time with their drumbeats, but with a curious gait, taking two steps forward, one step back. They reached the original drummers and squatted down beside them. The drumbeats were now rolling across the plaza without pause.

Henry, who'd once been hypnotised by Mr Fogarty, was sinking into a torpor as the stately rhythm seized him. But he jerked upright, heart pounding, as a massive shout erupted. Eight more drummers poured into the plaza, leaping and dancing. Their bodies were streaked with elaborate designs in bright white paint that turned them into fiercely prancing human zebras. After a single circuit of the square, they joined the original four and all twelve fell into a new, sharper, faster rhythm. The sound rolled out across the ruined city like an endless peal of thunder.

Lorquin was visibly excited now, shifting from one foot to the other.

'Now?' Henry asked. He knew the celebrations would take place in the plaza and everything so far was a preliminary.

'Not yet,' Lorquin said a little breathlessly. 'Soon.'

Women of the tribe began to dance into the square.

Their bodies were painted too, but not at all like the drummers. Elaborate whorls of green and red, sun-yellow and a glowing orange, contrasted with their deep blue skins to turn them into plumaged birds. Henry had never seen anything like it before and for some reason the sight made his heart leap with pleasure.

The women paraded the square in time to the powerful drumbeats, strutting like peacocks, turning and twisting. Every one was smiling. Several looked positively delirious with joy.

'Now,' Lorquin said.

For some reason it caught Henry by surprise. 'What?' he asked, frowning.

Lorquin gave him the sort of fond look that a father might give an idiot child and said patiently, 'Now we men go down.'

It was weird how that word *we* acted like a small hook into Henry's heart. *We men.* Lorquin, this child with him, this child who had rescued Henry in the desert, was a man now because he'd slain his draugr. But Henry was a man as well, accepted by the tribe as a Companion, his bravery unquestioned, his maturity unquestioned. All his life, Henry had grown up in a house that was dominated by women. Even in the early days his father hardly counted against the certainties of his mother and the whining manipulations of his sister. When his father left, Henry found himself with three women to contend with after Anaïs moved in, and most of the time he felt under siege. But now he was one of the men, almost part of the tribe. Now he had companionship and acceptance. *We men.* Even though the words came from a child, Henry liked them.

'Now?' he asked, suddenly smiling.

Lorquin smiled back up at him. 'Yes, now.'

They emerged from the ground floor to join a stream of tribesmen headed for the square. Henry fell into the rhythm at once, a staccato shuffle punctuated by resounding *grunts* timed to the distant drumbeats. Like Lorquin, the men were naked – although the white paint on their bodies made them look clothed. Henry had removed his shirt (desert temperatures were as hot as a tropical beach and here, beneath the sands, there was no possibility of sunburn), but couldn't quite bring himself to go the distance with his trousers. He'd declined Lorquin's offer to decorate his skin – 'I will *illustrate* you, En Ri,' Lorquin told him cheerfully – yet for all that he still felt a part of the whole celebration, probably because the tribesmen accepted him so readily.

The communal dance moved at a stately pace, the massive snake of male bodies intertwining gracefully with the women's movements. Sometimes they were packed so closely together that their bodies actually brushed one another. Henry should have found it hideously embarrassing, but somehow didn't … even when several of the younger, prettier girls smiled at him. For the first time in his life, he felt a part of something greater than himself.

The dance became wilder and the tribe began to chant in time with the basic rhythm. Although the chant was in a language Henry didn't understand, he had picked up the words within minutes. Soon he was chanting with the best of them. The combination of the drumming, the rhythmic movement and the chanting made him increasingly light-headed, but he found he didn't care. When someone passed him a gourd of yellow liquid, he drank it down without a thought.

Seconds later, the top of his head exploded. The feeling was absolutely wonderful. He was energised, powerful, intoxicated. He was as strong as any man here. He was old; he was young; he was wise. He was in love with Blue.

Lorquin materialised briefly by his side. 'Melor!' he called above the chanting and pointed at the empty gourd.

Henry nodded back, grinning hugely.

It became a bit of a blur after that. Henry recalled dancing faster and faster, chanting louder and louder. At some point he lost his trousers and didn't care. His head, his whole horizon, was filled with the drumming and the chant.

Then he found he was seated, squatting on the ground watching while Ino the tattooed shaman muttered and shook and swayed and shouted in the centre of the plaza. Henry couldn't remember whether Ino had taken anything before his performance began, but he certainly looked drugged now. The encircling tribesmen, Henry among them, swayed in time to his movements and cheered when he hurled a handful of bleached bones onto the paving. A young boy, younger even than Lorquin, rushed forward to examine them where they fell, then fearlessly trotted across to whisper in Ino's ear. The shaman shuddered and convulsed and shouted aloud.

'The song-lines are set,' grinned a man squatting next to Henry. He seemed pleased with the development, but Henry himself had not the slightest idea what was going on.

Ino fell down sometime after that and had to be carried away. No one seemed concerned.

The drums fell silent and a new chant broke out, soft, slow and melodious. After a moment Henry realised only the men were singing and joined in. The bass vibration of the plainsong overcame him so that he closed his eyes and swam through darkness on a raft of sound.

The men's song ebbed and flowed for an eternity; then suddenly it stopped and there was total, utter silence. Henry opened his eyes again and looked around benignly. There seemed to be a sense of expectation reflected in the surrounding faces. The men began to sing again, softer this time, like the background hum of insects on a summer's day. Then came the women's voices, swelling pure and clear across the dry air. Henry felt tears spring to his eyes as they plunged and swooped like birds, carrying a melody so plaintive that it seized the heart and carried it away.

The women's song continued for a long, long time and while he could pick out no more than a few words here and there, to Henry it seemed they were singing an ancient history of the tribe, telling of its tribulations at the time of their captivity, telling of the freedom granted by Charaxes, telling of the sorrows and the joys, holding a burden of emotion that was almost too heavy to bear.

Then, one by one, the voices fell away until only a single lone woman remained singing. Henry craned to see who she was and eventually located her, a plump girl scarcely older than himself, whose eyes were closed tight and her head flung back as she carried the remainder of the song.

The girl continued singing while four men shuffled into the plaza, carrying two long poles from which a smallish wooden box was slung on leather thongs. Henry's heart jumped. Was this the ark of Euphrosyne? He leaned forward to get a better look, but others around him were doing the same and blocked his line of sight. As the men lowered the box reverently to the ground, he could see that it definitely looked old, perhaps even old enough to be the original ark. But beyond that, it was difficult to make out much detail.

The light was failing now and the thing itself was quite a distance from him, on top of which, the men who had carried it were fussing round it, removing the leather thongs and placing it just so in what he supposed must be its ritual position. From what he could see, the wooden surface of the box seemed to have metal inlays, possibly silver and gold, although they could just as easily be steel and brass.

The singing stopped. For Henry it was as if the entire tribe held its collective breath. The four men fanned out, taking their poles with them. To his surprise they had managed to construct a frame table and the ark now stood at chest height on top of it.

Another pause, then a scrambling movement to his right as the tribespeople parted to allow a woman through. Unlike the others, there was no paint on her body. Instead she wore a shimmering golden robe that dropped from shoulder to ankle and might actually have been cut from silk. The effect was astounding – she was the first of the Luchti Henry had yet seen who wore anything at all – and hugely enhanced by the silver mask that hid her face. She walked, head high, towards the ark.

Beside Henry, a man murmured, 'Euphrosyne ...' He pronounced the name the way a Greek might: *You-frosssin-ee.* At once his neighbour echoed the word; then it was taken up into a quiet chant: 'Euphrosyne ... Euphrosyne ... Euphrosyne ...'

As the woman walked to the ark, the pole-carriers moved to escort her like proud bodyguards or priests.

She reached the frame table and fell on her knees, arms stretched upwards in a gesture of supplication. 'Charaxes!' she called. 'Charaxes!' She had a light, clear voice. For some reason Henry recalled Lorquin telling him this Euphrosyne was only twenty years old.

The crowd took up the call. 'Charaxes! Charaxes! Charaxes!'

The ark began to glow.

Henry blinked. A reaction from the ark was the last thing he expected. This was obviously a religious moment for the Luchti, but Henry, who was Church of England, had never come across glowing arks before. The cynical thought passed through his mind that it might be something engineered by Euphrosyne or her priests. Then he remembered these were the Luchti, who roamed the desert naked. They hardly had the technology for glowing arks.

Heedless of the glow, Euphrosyne leaned her head against the side of the ark as if listening. 'Charaxes speaks to her,' murmured the man beside Henry. There was a matter-of-fact tone to his voice as if this was more or less routine for the occasion. But then the masked woman stood up and slowly turned her head as if searching the faces of the crowd and at once there was a murmur of surprise.

The movement stopped. It was difficult to be certain with the mask, but Euphrosyne seemed to be looking at someone close by Henry. She began to walk across the plaza. In a moment of growing nervousness, Henry thought perhaps she might be walking towards *him*.

He swallowed. She was standing directly in front of him. 'Charaxes wants to speak to you,' she said.

Seventy

The walk across the plaza was the longest Henry could remember taking in his entire life. He could feel every eye upon him. He could sense the tension in the tribe. The very fibres of his being told him this was bad news. What was he supposed to do? How was he supposed to talk to a god?

God used to speak to people fairly often, according to the Bible, but Henry was painfully aware the only ones who heard him nowadays were lunatics. But even that wasn't relevant in this situation. Charaxes wasn't the God you prayed to every Sunday, then ignored for the rest of the week like any other sane Anglican. Charaxes was the god of the Luchti and they believed in him implicitly. Charaxes led them out of bondage. Charaxes guided them to this hidden city. Heaven alone knew what other things he'd done that Henry hadn't heard about. How were the Luchti going to take it when they found out Henry couldn't hear him? Unless …

An earlier suspicion resurfaced. Maybe Euphrosyne and her helpers faked it. Henry seemed to remember reading somewhere that priests in Ancient Greece – or was it Ancient Egypt? – had secret speaking tubes built into statues of their gods. When the faithful came to worship, the Head Priest spoke down the tube and the congregation thought the god was talking. Speaking tubes were probably a bit sophisticated for the Luchti, but maybe Euphrosyne was a ventriloquist.

Henry decided that if the ark did talk to him, he'd play along. What did it matter if Euphrosyne was fooling her people? It probably brought a bit of comfort into their harsh lives. And if the ark didn't talk, maybe he could pretend it did. Maybe he could claim it gave him a secret message. Something nice to cheer up the tribe. You're God's favourites so he's looking out for you, sort of thing. It was kind of dishonest, but now he'd thought of it, it was probably the least he could do. They'd taken him in as one of their own and Lorquin had saved his life. He owed the Luchti big-time.

Euphrosyne reached the ark and stopped so abruptly Henry almost walked into her bottom. (Was there a penalty for walking into the bottom of a priestess of Charaxes?) Close up he noticed that the ark inlays really were precious – silver and gold, without a doubt. He'd seen no sign at all that the Luchti worked metal, but the ark looked so ancient it might well have been made by an early civilisation, possibly even the one that built the city.

Euphrosyne undid a catch, opened the lid, then stepped back a pace. Henry could see a short metallic rod protruding from the ark. She turned back towards him and, to his complete surprise, removed her silver mask. Underneath, she had a pleasant face – not particularly pretty, but fresh and cheerful. She smiled broadly at him. 'Charaxes speaks now,' she said conversationally.

Without the mask she looked so much less daunting that Henry immediately forgot his earlier plans. 'What do I do?' he asked. It suddenly occurred to him she might be a medium who'd go into trance and speak for the god. If so, that would make things easier.

'Walk to the ark and say, "I am here," ' Euphrosyne told him. 'Charaxes cannot see, but he will hear you.'

For some reason it never occurred to Henry to do anything other than what he was told. He took three steps forward, licked his lips and said softly, 'I am here.'

'What the hell do you think you're playing at?' Charaxes demanded clearly from the ark. Henry took a step back, his blood chill, his heart thumping. That wasn't the voice of a god.

It was the voice of Mr Fogarty.

Seventy-One

There was an emergency team waiting as Madame Cardui and Nymph stepped out of the Palace portal. Two of its members moved into the flames at once and re-emerged seconds later carrying the prostrate Pyrgus on a stretcher. 'Place him in stasis immediately,' Madame Cardui ordered.

'One moment,' said Chief Wizard Surgeon Healer Danaus pompously. He was dressed, as always, in the formal robes of his profession. The stretcher-bearers stopped.

'What is it?' Madame Cardui snapped. She disliked Danaus. He was one of the old guard at the Palace, hugely experienced and very good indeed at his job. But he was officious and arrogant and had a grossly inflated idea of his own importance.

'The placement of a living Prince of the Realm in stasis requires an executive order from the ruling sovereign,' Danaus said.

Madame Cardui glared at him. 'The ruling sovereign isn't here.'

'Precisely.'

The body on the stretcher was no longer that of a young man, not even the maturing adult who had sought refuge in the Analogue World. Pyrgus looked positively shrunken now, wrinkled and old, as if the illness that had seized him was accelerating.

'This is an emergency,' said Madame Cardui.

Chief Wizard Healer Danaus favoured her with a patronising smile. 'I'm afraid there is no provision in the legislation for emergencies.' He adjusted his robes. 'Perhaps –' He stopped abruptly, eyes wide.

Nymph was by his side now, her dagger pressed into his throat. 'I am the wife of Prince Pyrgus,' she said icily. 'Perhaps it would be sufficient if I signed the executive order?'

Danaus swallowed visibly. 'Yes,' he said, his voice scarcely more than a squeak. 'Perhaps it would.'

Stasis magic was normally used for preserving corpses, so Pyrgus was taken directly to the mortuary. Madame Cardui shivered, and not simply because of the cold. She had no personal fear of death – strange how it faded as one grew older – and she accepted its inevitability among the old. But Pyrgus, for all his elderly appearance, was not old. Although he would never have thanked her for saying so, he had been scarcely more than a boy when the time fever struck. To see him now, wizened, shrunken, clearly close to death, was an abomination.

Although her dagger had disappeared now, Nymph stood close to Chief Wizard Healer Danaus. But he seemed to need no further encouragement and his team worked with silent efficiency. Nonetheless, Nymph watched each move closely. Pyrgus had already been left in his coma too long. She was not prepared to take the slightest chance of any further delay.

There was an exclusion cabinet already set up, looking for all the world like a transparent coffin. But it had to be prepared and activated before it was any use to Pyrgus. A nurse began to apply the spell coatings using a broad brush. While she worked with cool efficiency, Nymph felt a rising tide of frustration. She was far more angry with Danaus than she cared to show. The man had been warned of Pyrgus's condition. He should have had everything ready instead of cavilling about legal niceties.

The coatings were tricky since different spells were required on different surfaces, but they were finished eventually.

'Why aren't they putting him inside?' Nymph demanded, as the nurse was replaced by a different member of the team.

'We require the catalyst,' Danaus said, watching her warily. He risked adding, 'This is difficult work.'

It probably was. Nymph noted it was being carried out by a Faerie of the Night. There were more Nighters working in the Palace since Blue became Queen. It was official policy now, but Nymph still felt vaguely uneasy. She watched as the man laid an adhesive strip along the bottom of the cabinet. He attached a small jewel to one end and what looked like a metallic fuse to the other. Nothing he did seemed particularly difficult to Nymph, but she supposed there was not much tolerance in the placements. Certainly the Nighter seemed to work with as much caution as speed. He glanced at Danaus and nodded as he finished.

Danaus nodded back. 'Trigger,' he said quietly.

The Nighter clicked his fingers and a small spark jumped from his thumb to the end of the fuse. There was a spluttering sound and a sudden smell of burning as the fuse ignited. The adhesive tape vanished in a silent flash and the tiny jewel began to pulse and glow. Seconds later it too exploded silently in a burst of greenish light.

Danaus walked over to inspect the cabinet. He sniffed several of its surfaces and bent over to examine the interior closely. After long moments he straightened up. 'Put His Highness inside,' he said.

Nymph said quickly, 'Chief Wizard Healer, is it true there is a risk with this procedure?'

Danaus glanced at her without affection. 'Yes. Stasis is normally used to preserve dead bodies or inanimate objects. There is a negligible risk when it is applied to living systems.'

'Negligible?'

'Statistically measurable, but small.' He hesitated, then added, 'Certainly your husband would be in far greater peril if we did not place him in stasis now. Were I smitten with the fever, it is what I would want for myself. The process of the disease must be stopped until we can find a cure.'

'Good,' Nymph said. 'Proceed.' She made a silent decision to kill Chief Wizard Surgeon Healer Danaus if any harm befell Pyrgus.

If he sensed her thought, Danaus didn't show it. He nodded to his team and seconds later Pyrgus was sealed inside the cabinet. He looked disturbingly like a corpse now, although Nymph could see the gentle rise and fall of his breathing. But even that would stop when the cabinet was activated. Everything would stop. Pyrgus, who was being eaten by Time, would halt in Time.

Danaus took a tiny six-inch wand from a pocket of his robe and snapped it over the cabinet at the level of Pyrgus's throat. The ark hummed for a brief second, then was silent. Pyrgus's breathing stopped. 'It's done,' Danaus said.

Perhaps it was the sheer *stillness* of Pyrgus that Nymph found upsetting. His face began to blur, as if tears were clouding her eyes, yet strangely she did not cry – she never cried. There was a knot of nausea in her stomach that almost certainly came from worry. She turned away and felt herself sway.

'Nymph deeah?' Madame Cardui said.

There were too many people in the room. They appeared and disappeared and busied themselves in hordes that ebbed and swelled like some strange tide. There was something wrong with the light, for it flickered incessantly.

'Nymph?' Madame Cardui said again.

She needed to get back to the fresh air, away from the death smells. They would take Pyrgus away, now they had placed him in stasis. They would carry the cabinet to his Palace quarters and post guards to ensure he was not disturbed. They would continue their search for a cure. There was nothing more she could do here.

'Nymph, what's the matter?' Madame Cardui asked in sudden alarm.

Nymph took a step forward and the world spun around her.

'Nymph!' It was close to a shout now.

Then came the plummy voice of Chief Wizard Healer Danaus, confident and firm. 'Stand back, Madame Cardui,' he said. 'She has temporal fever.'

Seventy-two

Blue came to a decision. 'I'm going in,' she said.

It occurred to her that she'd been caught up in a myth. She'd cast herself (or perhaps the Purlisa had subtly cast her) as a heroic figure off to slay the monster. Or else, she realised, as a tragic figure about to be captured by the monster. Until now, she'd never thought of looking beyond the two great mythic roles: conquering hero or captive princess. But the fact was she didn't have to accept either of these roles. There was a third way. She could creep into the cavern, avoid the serpent if there really was a serpent and find out whether Henry was inside. If he wasn't, she could then creep out again. If he was, she'd try to figure out a way to rescue him, preferably one that *didn't* involve her slaying a great monster.

'I'll come with you,' said the charno.

'No need,' Blue said. The charno might be working on the orders of the Abbot for all she knew. But it didn't matter. Now she'd stopped thinking the way they wanted her to think, she was back in control.

'Who'll carry the hammer?'

The hammer was a joke. The only weapon that could kill the Midgard Serpent according to the Purlisa and it was too heavy for her to carry. So why had they bothered to send it? They must have known it was something she could never use.

'The hammer doesn't matter,' Blue said.

She expected an argument, but the charno said nothing, simply watched her with his great brown eyes. Despite her suspicions, she felt sorry for him. Even if he was a creature of the Abbot and Purlisa, he was only doing his job.

'You can go home now,' she said. 'I'll be all right on my own.'

'I'll wait,' said the charno. 'I can carry you back afterwards. You and Henry.'

She had a sudden ridiculous picture of herself clinging to the back of this giant hare as it plodded through the wasteland. She couldn't even begin to imagine how it would carry Henry as well. The charno was a pack animal, pure and simple, totally unsuited to carrying a passenger. Unless – despite everything she had to suppress a smile – he put them both in his backpack.

Blue shrugged. 'As you wish.' She turned and walked with great deliberation towards the entrance of the cavern.

'Wait!'

She sighed and turned again. 'What is it now?' she asked the charno.

'That wasn't me,' the charno said.

Blue started violently as something moved behind the charno. The man was so dusty, battered, tattered and thin that for a moment she failed to recognise him. There was dried blood on his face. 'Chalkhill?' Blue gasped. What on earth was Chalkhill doing here? She narrowed her eyes. Was it really Chalkhill?

Chalkhill took a step forward, then sat down abruptly

on the ground. 'Sorry,' he murmured. Then, more loudly, 'Forgive me, Your Majesty.'

Blue stared, completely at a loss. Chalkhill was an old enemy – he'd once tried to kill her and his involvement in various plots against the Realm was well known – but she'd heard nothing of him for more than a year. Now here he was in the Buthner wilderness, halfway up the Mountains of Madness, beside the entrance to a cavern that supposedly contained the Midgard Serpent. This could not be a coincidence. But for the life of her she could not imagine what it meant.

It was the charno who made the next move. 'Water?' he asked, handing Chalkhill a flask from his backpack.

Chalkhill drank greedily and the water seemed to revive him. He struggled to his feet. 'Excuse my appearance,' he said, still with difficulty, as if his appearance made any difference about anything. 'But you must not go in there.'

Blue found her voice, if only just. 'Really?' she said coldly. She half turned back towards the cavern entrance.

'You don't know what's in there!' Chalkhill shouted in something close to panic.

The last time she faced Chalkhill directly, she'd had a company of Palace commandoes at her back. She doubted she would need them now. Chalkhill looked as weak as a kitten. In truth he looked half dead. She opened her mouth to reply, then shut it again. Brimstone in the cage at the monastery! Chalkhill and Brimstone, the two old partners! They'd been working together again. They had to be. And now Brimstone was mad.

'The Midgard Serpent?' Blue asked innocently, staring directly at Chalkhill.

Chalkhill's mouth dropped open. 'How did you know?'

This was getting her nowhere. Or perhaps it was getting her somewhere, but she just didn't know how. What did it matter if Chalkhill and Brimstone were up to their old tricks? What did it matter whether or not she could trust the Purlisa? What did it even matter if they were all telling the truth and there really was some sort of monster in there? The only thing that mattered was Henry. She made another move towards the entrance.

'Please …' Chalkhill said.

Something in his voice stopped her short. She looked at him again. 'Why don't you want me to go in there?'

'You'll be killed,' Chalkhill whispered.

'Why would you care?' Blue asked him coldly.

'I'm working for Madame Cardui,' said Chalkhill.

It was so utterly outlandish that it might actually be true. Blue felt her own jaw drop and quickly closed her mouth. Chalkhill was tricky enough without letting him see he'd surprised her. She needed time to think. Madame Cardui had never mentioned Chalkhill, but that was completely in character. As the Realm's Spymaster she engaged in all sorts of activities she told no one about. Not even her Queen. Sometimes, Blue had long noted, *especially* not her Queen. And Chalkhill had a background in espionage. He'd spied for Lord Hairstreak. Dammit, he was Lord Hairstreak's Spymaster in the bad old days when her uncle was a real threat to the Realm. So it *could* be that Chalkhill was now working for Madame Cardui. He wouldn't be the first of Hairstreak's agents she'd turned for her own advantage. The question was, in what capacity?

'She asked you to look out for me?' Blue ventured, frowning. It was by way of a testing question. If Chalkhill *was* lying – and Blue very much suspected he might be –

then he would seize the suggestion, unaware that until just days ago, Madame Cardui had accompanied Blue personally and only left her due to a wholly unexpected development. In such circumstances, Madame Cynthia would never have allocated an agent to follow Blue.

But Chalkhill shook his head. 'She asked me to spy on Silas Brimstone.'

That made sense, some sort of sense at least. As an old partner, Chalkhill would be a logical choice to spy on Brimstone. So Chalkhill might be telling the truth. Time to push him. 'Was it Brimstone who called up the serpent in this cave?'

'Yes.'

Which was what the Purlisa claimed. 'That's what the Purlisa said,' Blue murmured, echoing her thought.

'Who?' asked Chalkhill.

The question sounded genuine, which meant he didn't know the Purlisa. Or the Abbot presumably. Blue said, 'Why?'

'Why what?'

'Why did Brimstone call up the serpent?'

'I don't know,' Chalkhill said. 'But if you go in there, you're dead. I only just managed to escape.'

He was lying about something. Blue was sure of it. But what? 'You were in the cavern?'

'When he called it up? Yes. It was the most frightening thing I've ever seen. I wouldn't go in there without an army backing me and even then I'd think twice.' He looked at her pleadingly, as if willing her to stay out of the cavern.

Blue said, 'Is Henry in there?'

Chalkhill blinked. 'Henry?' He shook his head.

'No ...' She could almost hear him thinking, *Who's Henry?* as if Henry was the last thing on his mind.

This time he sounded genuine, but she was far from sure. All the same, if Henry wasn't in the cave, there was no need for her to face the serpent. (If there was a serpent.) There was no need for her to go in there at all.

Which was what Chalkhill wanted.

How could you trust Chalkhill? The man was a toad and always had been. Why would he want her to stay out of the cave? The idea that he was concerned about her safety was nonsense, even if he was working for Madame Cardui.

Blue decided to stop speculating and concentrate on simple facts.

Fact one: she had no idea whether Henry was in the cave or not.

Fact two: the Purlisa and his Abbot both wanted her to go into the cave.

Fact three: Chalkhill clearly didn't.

She looked at the charno, but couldn't think of any facts about him, except he had big feet.

Blue turned on her heel. 'I'm going in,' she said a second time.

Seventy-Three

Henry felt as if Euphrosyne had ceased to exist, as if the Luchti had ceased to exist, as if the entire city had ceased to exist.

'But you're dead,' Henry croaked, his voice scarcely above a whisper.

'Yes, I know,' said Mr Fogarty impatiently.

'What happened?' Henry asked.

'Old age happened,' Mr Fogarty told him. 'My time ran out, I suppose. I'm not sure – death's not as clear-cut as you'd think.'

'No,' Henry said. 'No, I didn't mean that.' He was having trouble believing what was going on. But the voice was definitely the voice of Mr Fogarty. And it was talking to him, talking properly, not like some old recording. He couldn't see how Euphrosyne could have faked that. Or anybody else. He took a long, shuddering breath. 'I mean, where are you?'

'Good question. Not sitting on a cloud playing a harp, that's for sure.'

After a minute, Henry realised that was the only answer he was going to get and said, 'No, I mean –' He stopped himself. He knew he was falling into one of his famous waffles and that was really, really stupid. If he was talking to Mr Fogarty, if he was talking to somebody who had *died* and was *still* dead and was somehow talking back, then he was in a position to find out stuff, important stuff, nobody in the whole world knew about. It was incredible, but it was happening. He started again, his voice firmer this time. 'Can you remember exactly what happened when … when it happened? When you –' he coughed discreetly '– passed on.'

'Of course I can,' said Mr Fogarty. 'I'm dead, not senile.'

'Will you tell me?'

'Look, Henry, there are other things I need to talk to you about right n—'

For once in his life, Henry found the courage to interrupt him. 'Please,' he said. 'This is really important.' On inspiration he added, 'It might, you know, help us sort of … communicate properly. Better. Or something.'

It sounded fairly feeble, but it seemed to touch a chord. Mr Fogarty said, 'Okay. We have time. It was like this: I woke up in the bed –'

'So you didn't actually have fever? You weren't in a coma or anything?'

'No, I was awake.'

'And no fever?'

'Look here,' said Mr Fogarty, 'if you're going to keep interrupting me –'

'Sorry. Sorry. No, please, go on.'

Mr Fogarty sighed. 'I woke up in the bed and everything was fine for a couple of minutes, but then I had the odd sensation of being under water. I –'

'This wasn't a relapse, was it?'

'No, nothing to do with the fever. Nothing like the fever. Why do you keep asking about the bloody fever? I –'

'Are you sure?'

'Oh, for Christ's sake, Henry!'

'Sorry. Sorry. Go on. I won't – I won't say –'

'It was more of a sinking feeling. I was weak, but that was no surprise. You ever get the fever you'll know it weakens you. But this was different. It felt as if my body was shrivelling. I've never had that sensation before. Then my eyesight got blurred: that's when it felt like being under water.' To Henry's surprise he hesitated, then said, 'Sorry I snapped at you. It's only natural you're curious. You can ask questions if you like.'

Henry blinked. Death seemed to have mellowed Mr Fogarty a bit, but probably best not to say so. He opened his mouth to ask a question, then discovered he didn't have one. So all he said was, 'Thank you. Yes, thank you. Yes, I will.'

Mr Fogarty said, 'Everything started to go numb. Can't say I liked that much, but to be honest with you I didn't realise I was dying. But then I got cold and the room started to fade away. I couldn't hear the noises outside any more. That's when I knew I was in trouble, but – know something? – I didn't really care. Some reason, nothing seemed to matter. After that, I couldn't be bothered to breathe any more and I felt my heart stop.'

'Wow!' Henry exclaimed.

'Didn't matter,' said Mr Fogarty and Henry could almost hear him shrug. 'Strange that. You spend your whole life trying to keep going, and in the end it doesn't matter.' He paused thoughtfully for a moment, then went on. 'Odd thing was, I was still there. Couldn't see the room and I know I wasn't thinking straight, but I was still me. Surrounded by a sort of ... luminous darkness,

I suppose you'd call it. All a bit drifty-dreamy. Then I passed out.'

He said it with such finality that Henry said tactlessly, 'You were dead.'

'Interesting thing was I didn't stay dead,' Mr Fogarty told him.

'You didn't?'

'No. I was only out for a few seconds, felt like. Then I was in the dark, like I was half asleep with my eyes shut. Then it all started to lighten up and I was back in my hospital room at the Palace.'

Henry had stopped following this. 'So you weren't really dead?'

'Oh, I was really dead all right, except I didn't know it. Felt better than I had in years. All the arthritis gone, eyesight sharper, lot more energy. There were healers coming in and out – you know how the buggers hate to leave you alone – but when I tried to tell them I was better they ignored me. Took me a while to figure out what was going on, but when I walked through a wall, the penny dropped. I was a ghost. Funny thing was, I never noticed the old body on the bed before then. But there it was, eyes closed, pious expression, gone-to-meet-my-Maker look and far too pale to be healthy. I was really dead all right.'

'So that's what you are now?' Henry asked. 'A ghost?' He wondered how Mr Fogarty's ghost had found its way here, got itself into a Luchti ark. He wondered how Mr Fogarty was able to talk now when he couldn't talk to the healers in the bedroom.

'Not exactly,' Mr Fogarty said. 'This is hard to explain: I'm not sure you'll get it until you've been through it yourself. The thing is ... know how you go to sleep every night and dream?'

'Yes ...' Henry said uncertainly.

'After you're dead, you dream while you're awake.'

Mr Fogarty was right: Henry didn't get it. 'You mean you went to sleep?'

'Listen to what I just told you,' Mr Fogarty said with more than a hint of his old irritation. 'You *don't* go to sleep. But you dream while you're awake. I even had a visit from Beleth, thought *That's it – I should never have robbed those banks.*' He gave a short, sharp laugh.

'Beleth?' Henry asked. 'The Demon King? You mean there's, like, a Hell?'

'You know there's a Hell,' Mr Fogarty said impatiently. 'You were the one got Pyrgus out of it. But you don't go there after you die: that's just something they make up to scare you.'

'But you just said Beleth ...'

Mr Fogarty sighed. 'I just said Beleth came to visit. Made sense. After all, he was dead too after Blue slit his throat. But it wasn't Beleth. I was *dreaming*. I *dreamed* Beleth turned up. The trouble is, it's very hard to tell when you're dreaming and when you're not. Dreams feel real and reality feels peculiar. Took me a long time to figure out what was going on. But then Jesus arrived to take me to heaven and I thought *Hold on, this isn't right, not after everything you've done.* So I figured I had to be dreaming. After that I watched what was happening more carefully and got to where I could tell when I was dreaming and when I wasn't. At least most of the time. Sometimes I'm not sure – like now.'

'You're not dreaming now,' Henry said at once.

'No, I don't think I am.'

Henry suddenly became aware of a hand on his elbow. He glanced up to find himself looking into the sober face of Euphrosyne. 'There is not much time left, En Ri,' she said.

'She's right,' Mr Fogarty said. 'That device you're using is really interesting – hugely advanced psychotronics: God knows how these people got hold of it – but it runs on some sort of pulse battery I haven't quite figured out yet. I think it may be linked to the position of the sun. Anyway, the point is we won't be communicating much longer and there are things I have to tell you.'

'Yes, okay,' Henry said. For no reason at all, he found himself wondering why the Luchti thought Mr Fogarty was the god Charaxes. And what they'd done for a god before Mr Fogarty died. Come to think of it, that didn't make sense. The first Euphrosyne was talking to Charaxes long before Mr Fogarty was even born.

'Okay, Henry, pin back your ears,' said Mr Fogarty briskly. 'And if we get cut off, have them work the gizmo again the minute it comes back on – okay?'

'Yes, okay,' Henry said again. Now he was starting to feel nervous, but this time he knew the reason. When Mr Fogarty used that tone, it always meant trouble – usually for Henry.

Mr Fogarty said, 'When you're dead, you can see into the future.'

'Like when you had time fever?' Henry asked brightly.

For some reason the question irritated Mr Fogarty. 'No, not like the time fever. Now I get to see what you should do – what you *have* to do – to make things turn out right. Boy, what would I have given for that when I was a kid? Almost worth dying for, except for the catch.'

'What's the catch?' Henry asked curiously.

'Catch is when you're dead you can't do anything about your own future any more. I know what I should have done, but I didn't, and now I can't, it's too late, so what's the point of that? You'd think they'd organise things better over here.'

Henry wondered who *they* were. He wondered where *over here* was. There were a lot of questions he wanted to ask, but he was worried about the business of the battery running down. It was probably his imagination, but he kept thinking Mr Fogarty's voice was fading and he didn't want it to go altogether before Mr Fogarty finished telling him what he wanted to tell him. 'Yes,' Henry murmured, nodding agreement that you'd think they would organise things better over there.

Mr Fogarty said, 'But I know what *you* should do to make things turn out right, Henry. I know what you *have* to do. I know *exactly* what you have to do …'

It wasn't his imagination. The voice was definitely fading. Henry swung round to Euphrosyne. 'Can't you turn the volume up or something?'

Euphrosyne shook her head. 'Charaxes will leave soon.'

That was just his luck! That was just his bloody luck! He swung back to the ark. 'What do I have to do?' he shouted. 'What do I have to do to make things come out all right?'

The voice from the ark was fading fast, but Henry could still hear the words quite clearly.

'You have to rescue Blue,' said Mr Fogarty.

Seventy-four

'Is she in isolation?' asked Madame Cardui.

Chief Wizard Healer Danaus said a little tiredly, 'Standard procedure in these cases now, but to be frank with you, I doubt it's really needed. We've found no evidence whatsoever that the fever is contagious.'

'She didn't pick it up from Pyrgus?'

'Prince Pyrgus should never have got it in the first place. When the epidemic began we put in place strict procedures for all the royals,' Danaus said. 'None of them should have picked up an infection.'

Assuming Pyrgus did what he was told, Madame Cardui thought. *He was never very good at that.*

But Danaus was going on: 'Besides, he was in the Analogue World. According to everything we know, it is utterly impossible for the fever to manifest there.'

'Yet it did,' murmured Madame Cardui.

'Yet clearly it did,' Danaus agreed.

After a moment, Madame Cardui asked, 'What treatment are you giving her?'

'Nymphalis? At the moment none.' He hesitated, then said, 'Well, that's not true – palliative treatment. She's comfortable, there are nurses round the clock, we use spells to keep her temperature within tolerable limits. But when it comes to anything that will make a real difference to the disease –' he shrugged '– we don't *have* anything that will make a real difference to the disease.'

'But you're still working on a cure?'

'Of course. Would you like to see?'

The offer took her by surprise, but it was welcome nonetheless. 'Yes,' she said. 'Yes, Chief Wizard Healer, yes I would.'

They were already in the medical wing of the Palace. Now they walked together through the long white corridors that led to the research unit. Danaus stopped her before a large observation window. 'Best you go no further, Madame Cardui.' He gave a very small, wry smile. 'In case I am mistaken about the contagion.'

The window was spell coated to give them an overhead view of an entire ward with both alchemical and ritual laboratories set side by side at one end. To scrutinise any bedroom or the activities of the laboratories themselves, all one had to do was concentrate. But even without specific concentration, the place was obviously a hive of activity.

'We have two types of patient here,' Danaus said in a lecturing-to-students voice. 'Nobility, Palace staff and now our first royal in residence, Prince Pyrgus, in stasis –'

'Royals-in-residence,' Madame Cardui corrected him mildly. 'Plural. Now you are looking after Nymphalis.'

'Ah, yes, a *forest* royal is she not?' His tone told what he thought of Forest Faeries. He turned back to the window. 'As I was saying – the first type of patients are those who are here for care. Then we have the hoi polloi who are here for experimentation.'

Madame Cardui smiled slightly to herself. 'A little cynical, perhaps, Chief Wizard Healer?'

'Not in the least,' said Danaus easily. 'They are a great deal better off in my unit than they would be dying in the streets. And since we only attempt treatments we believe have a chance of succeeding, there is even the possibility they might be cured before the very highest in the land.'

'But the treatments are dangerous? Some of them at least?'

'The situation is grave. Some of the spells are extreme. Would you rather we tried them out on our royal family first?'

'No,' said Madame Cardui honestly. In fact, Danaus was doing exactly what she would have done in his position, what any realist would do. She suddenly noticed Nymph lying in one of the beds and concentrated to bring her room into clearer focus. The girl looked asleep, but there were subtle signs that she was actually still in a fever coma. Her face was still a long way from the grey aging Pyrgus was now showing, but it already seemed to exhibit a disturbing maturity in place of her fresh-faced youth.

Madame Cardui turned to look at the Chief Wizard Healer. He was a big man, tall, overweight, with soft, fleshy features. For the first time she realised how tired he looked. His face was drawn, his complexion was pale and his eyes were suffering from far too little sleep. She still disliked the man, but decided now she had been far too hard on him. He was, after all, carrying the weight of a crisis, ultimately responsible for the lives of all those in his care, incessantly pressured to find a cure for a terrifying and hitherto unknown disease. What's more, while he had been careful to halt Madame Cardui in this observation chamber, she knew that he spent all of his days now, and most of his nights, down there in the wards. The man might be a pompous ass, but he did not lack courage. Nor did he spare himself in doing his job.

She said, 'Why did you not have Nymphalis placed in stasis?' But it was purely a question, not a challenge.

Danaus clearly accepted it as such. 'She's young. This is her first bout of the fever. At this stage, she may lose a few days of her future, but hopefully nothing significant. As I said before, there is a small risk involved in stasis. With Prince Pyrgus we really had no option, but Nymphalis is a different case. Besides –' He stopped.

'Besides what?' asked Madame Cardui.

'I was going to say we are hopeful that when we find a cure, we can reverse the premature aging. But frankly I have no idea at all whether that's true. Most of the time we just try to keep up a brave front.'

It was something she'd had to do herself in past crises and she sympathised. 'What progress have you made with a cure?' she asked.

Danaus sighed. 'Very little, if I'm honest. The main problem is the fever shows none of the characteristics of any conventional infection. In many ways, it doesn't behave like a disease at all. Approaches that have delivered good results in the past simply don't seem relevant here.' He squared his shoulders slightly. 'But we try. And we will continue trying.' He glanced back towards the observation window and added, 'Obviously if the fever progresses in Nymphalis as it has done in Prince Pyrgus we will place her in stasis long before her situation becomes critical.'

'Thank you,' Madame Cardui murmured. Her mind returned to an earlier point and she said, 'Chief Wizard Healer, you mentioned that in your opinion the disease is not contagious …?'

Danaus looked more tired than ever. 'Confidentially, Madame Cardui, we have tried to pass the infection from one patient to another in a controlled experimental group. We did not succeed. Even mixing blood from a diseased patient with blood from a healthy one will not do it. Frankly, we have no idea at all how the disease spreads.'

'But it *is* spreading?' Madame Cardui said. She realised suddenly that with her various concerns, she had not been taking as careful note of the epidemic as she should have.

'Oh yes,' Danaus said grimly. 'More than a thousand new cases reported every day now.'

Madame Cardui went chill. 'More than a *thousand?*'

'Worse than that,' Danaus said. 'Latest analysis suggests we may be into a geometrical progression. The number of reported cases have doubled every few weeks. The figures have to be rechecked, of course, but if the trend continues, it may be only a matter of weeks before the entire Realm is infected.'

'Weeks?' Madame Cardui exploded. 'Why did you not tell me this sooner?'

Danaus gave a small, fatalistic shrug. 'What could you do to prevent it? Really, what can any of us do?'

She stared at him and forced herself to relax. He was right, of course. Everyone was doing everything they could. To tell her of every development in the progress of the plague would simply add to her worries without making the slightest difference to anything. Suddenly she felt very, very tired. In less troubled times she would have headed for her quarters, locked the door and slept. As it was ...

'Thank you, Danaus,' she said quietly. 'I shall leave you to your work and try to get on with mine.'

But as she swept off down the corridor, exhaustion overcame her.

Seventy-five

Blue waited until she was inside the cave before she swallowed the first catsite crystal. Catsite was toxic. One or two crystals wouldn't kill you, but the effect was cumulative and once the build-up reached a critical point, death followed quickly, with no advance warning. But what option had she? If she was to search these caverns without alerting the serpent, she could hardly stomp about waving a flaming torch or levitate a glowglobe. Not that she'd smuggled any glowglobes into this godsforsaken country. Or levitation spells, for that matter.

Catsite had no magical charge, but its base structure was alchemical so that the crystal tingled in her throat and stomach. Deceptively, the sensation was rather pleasant. For a moment, nothing more happened; then the chemical seized her nervous system and her surroundings sprang suddenly into stark relief. The colour tones were peculiar – everything had a greenish tinge – but that apart, she could now see in the dark.

The cave entrance sloped downwards, narrowing almost at once to a passageway that quickly curved out of sight. Disturbingly, there was a scattering of bones on the floor, as if an animal had recently eaten something here ... although exactly what she had no way of knowing. She listened, fervently wishing the alchemists had found a way of giving her better hearing. There was no sound that she could detect, so she moved forward cautiously down the slope.

The passageway continued to descend after it curved, but as she followed it, the right-hand wall fell away so that she was looking down into a broad underground gallery that acted as a terminus for further passageways. The slope on which she was standing clung to the open wall like a mountain road, but meandered eventually into the gallery itself. To her left was another opening, whether to a cave or a further passageway she had no way of telling; besides which, it was too high for her to reach without a difficult climb. She decided on the gallery and followed the slope cautiously downwards.

By the time she reached the bottom, it was obvious this was no simple cavern. There were passageways branching everywhere and while some of them might be dead ends, she had a strong suspicion she was entering a warren. If so, the prime danger was not some mythic serpent – which she was still not sure actually existed – but the possibility of getting lost.

Blue slipped the backpack from her shoulders and opened it on the floor. She'd never learned to pack tidily, so she had to rummage, but she found what she was looking for eventually. She took out a smallish cylinder, pointed at one end like a stubby pencil, and pressed the base to activate it. The cylinder hummed briefly. Experimentally, Blue took three steps forward, then glanced behind her. Nothing. She blinked her eyes twice in quick succession. Now she could see a luminous filament that trailed through the air from the device in her hand to the exact point where she had switched it on. Another blink and the filament disappeared. Perfect. She dropped the activated cylinder into her pocket. Now wherever she went she left a trail. When she wanted to return, she had only to follow it. Best of all, the trail was visible to no one except her.

She returned to the backpack and rummaged again. While she was getting herself organised, she might as well sort out something else. She was still cross about the hammer – ridiculous to give her equipment she couldn't use – but she frankly didn't believe there was a creature on the planet that could only be killed by one weapon. Her hand closed on the handle of the Halek knife and she drew it lovingly from the backpack. Pyrgus would kill her if he ever found out she'd borrowed it. The blade had been his pride and joy for years. Blue held it up just inches from her face, so close she could feel the aura of the trapped energies tingling on her skin. There was nothing this could not kill, whatever the Purlisa said about the serpent.

Blue stuck the blade in her belt for easy access and slung the pack across her back again. Now, where to go? Looking around, she counted eighteen passageways leading from the gallery. After a moment's indecision, it occurred to her that since she had not the slightest idea where any of them led, one was as good as any other. She walked at once into the nearest.

It proved narrower than she anticipated and rubble on the floor made it hard going, but the passage opened out eventually so that she could move more quickly. After a time she spotted a light up ahead: not simply her cat-site vision, but an actual glow. She slowed cautiously, fearful that she might not be the only explorer down here, but as she got closer, she discovered the glow was coming from some sort of fungus clinging to one wall.

A little further on, the passageway simply ended in a blank wall.

Blue retraced her steps without the need of her luminous filament and selected another passageway in the gallery. Although this one descended quite sharply, it was wider, clearer and altogether easier going. But the passage forked several times so she was forced to make arbitrary decisions and would have been helplessly lost without her filament. All the same, she made good progress for several hundred yards before she realised something was following her.

Blue froze.

The sounds were faint, but definite, an intermittent shuffle punctuated by soft clicks. She had the impression of a large animal attempting to move silently, but not succeeding very well. Was this the Midgard Serpent? It didn't sound like a serpent, which would surely have produced a slithering noise. The problem was, it didn't sound much like anything else either.

She pushed down a small surge of panic and forced herself to think. She was deep underground in a strange country. The gods alone knew what might be living in these passages. Bear was one possibility. Lion was another – wingless haniels sometimes made their homes in mountains. Yet somehow she didn't think it was either of these, or any natural beast. Her stretched imagination presented her with altogether different horrors: foundlings, crandibles or wisps, perhaps – she hesitated to think it, but thought it just the same – perhaps even an undead.

Suddenly she couldn't get the idea out of her head. Undeads were rare. Since they couldn't reproduce, they teetered as a breed on the edge of extinction. Yet somehow they always managed to rebuild their ranks from the bodies of their victims. Was something stalking her? Had she become prey for a vampire or a grint?

The sounds came again, closer this time. Whatever was trailing her might be trying to keep quiet, but stealth was clearly not its natural mode. Which meant it had little fear of attack. Logically it was likely to be something very, very dangerous.

Some *Thing* very, very dangerous, her mind corrected her.

Blue drew the Halek blade from her belt and slid into a narrow crevice in the wall of the passageway. Her plan had formed itself. She would hide here until the creature stalking her passed by, then emerge and stab it with her lethal knife. She was taking an enormous risk. If the thing glanced in and saw her, she was trapped – and with scarcely enough room to wield the blade. If the thing really did turn out to be undead, she was far from certain even the energies of a Halek knife would destroy it. Furthermore, she was well aware, as everyone was well aware, that if a Halek knife shattered, its lethal power turned against the person holding it, killing them instantly.

But this was another situation like the catsite – what else could she do? If she ran, her footfalls would alert her pursuer at once and she had no guarantee that this passage was not another dead end.

She held her breath and waited.

Whatever was pursuing stopped and snuffled, as if sniffing the air. Blue closed her eyes briefly. If it caught her scent, she was finished. But then it was moving again, no faster than before. Abruptly it occurred to her that the curious clicking noise might be the sound of claws on the stone floor. If so, the thing had a deliberate tread. It certainly didn't seem to be rushing in for the kill, at least not yet. Perhaps it hadn't detected her. Perhaps …

It was so close now she could hear its breathing. Then suddenly there was a large bulk passing her hiding place. Moving on pure instinct, Blue stepped out of the crevice, raised her blade and …

'Don't,' said the charno.

The flooding of relief was so extreme that Blue simply stood there shaking and panting as she tried to catch her breath. Eventually she said angrily, 'What the *hael* do you think you're doing?'

'Following you,' the charno said.

'Why?' Blue demanded. 'Why? I said you didn't have to. I can't use the stupid hammer. Midgard Serpents eat charnos; you said so yourself. So why … did you have … to frighten the life …'

'Thought you might like the company,' the charno said.

'The Purlisa put you up to this, didn't he?' Blue said on sudden insight. 'The Purlisa and the Abbot?'

The charno nodded. 'Yes.'

'They wanted you to make sure I came in here!'

'Yes.'

'Then why did you try to persuade me not to?' Blue demanded.

'Reverse psychology,' the charno said.

For a moment she thought she'd misheard. Then she said, 'What do you mean?'

The charno shrugged. 'The Purlisa said you were perverse.'

This time she was sure she'd misheard. '*What?*'

The charno gave a patient sigh. 'One of those people

who always do the opposite of what they're told. He was worried you might decide your Henry person wasn't down here.'

'And he told you to make sure I came in anyway?'

'Yes.'

'By telling me not to?'

'Yes.'

Blue's eyes were like saucers, part from surprise and part from fury, much of which came from the realisation that the Purlisa was absolutely right – she *did* have a perverse streak. 'And *is* Henry down here?'

The charno shook his head. 'No.'

'What about the serpent thing?'

'Oh, yes,' said the charno.

'And I'm supposed to fight it?'

The charno shook his head again. 'No, you're supposed to be captured by it.'

'Well you and your precious Purlisa can forget that, for a start!' Blue snapped. 'The only reason I'm standing here is that I thought I might have a chance to rescue Henry. If you've all lied to me about Henry, then there is absolutely nothing in the Faerie Realm that would make me stay down here a minute longer.' She blinked her eyes twice to reveal the luminous filament. 'I'm going back to the surface.'

To her absolute astonishment, the charno transformed itself into a grinning clown. 'I'm afraid it's much too late for that.'

Seventy-Six

'Get him back!' shouted Henry in sudden panic. All very well to say he had to rescue Blue, but from what? And when? Was she in trouble right this minute, or was this something Mr Fogarty saw in the future? Was she ill? Had she picked up the time fever thing? And, most important of all, where was she? He needed to know more! But the stupid ark only sat there, silent and inert.

Euphrosyne smiled and nodded. 'Soon, En Ri,' she said.

Henry felt like shaking her, but didn't. Instead he said firmly, 'No – now!'

'It is not possible now,' Euphrosyne said calmly. She was still smiling, but there was an absolute finality in her voice that stopped him dead.

Henry felt his panic deflate like a punctured balloon. Euphrosyne would help him if she could. Every one of the Luchti would help if they could: they might be primitive but they were about the nicest people he'd ever met in his life. But he wasn't going to get anywhere by shouting at them. He needed to know what he was doing, needed to ask intelligent questions, needed to *show* them how they could help. He had to stop feeling so much out of his depth. He needed *information*. Most of all, he needed information about Mr Fogarty and how, incredibly, he was able to talk to these people as their god after he was dead.

'Euphrosyne,' Henry said. 'That was Charaxes I just talked to, wasn't it?'

Euphrosyne nodded enthusiastically. 'Yes.'

'And your people have talked to Charaxes for centuries, haven't you?'

She nodded again. 'Yes.'

Out of the corner of his eye he noticed other members of the tribe were approaching, Lorquin among them. Even at a distance, he could tell they were happy. However confused he was now, he seemed to have muddled through the business of their ceremony. To Euphrosyne he said, 'How was Charaxes able to talk to you centuries ago?' Mr Fogarty wasn't dead centuries ago. Mr Fogarty wasn't even *born* centuries ago. So how did Mr Fogarty get to be the god of the Luchti?

Euphrosyne said happily, 'With the ark.'

'Yes, I know with the ark, but Charaxes wasn't *there* centuries ago.'

She looked at him blankly. 'Charaxes is always there, otherwise how could we be here? How could *you* be here, En Ri?'

'You mean Charaxes created the world?' Mr Fogarty as a creator god was more than he could cope with. There was something badly wrong here. He wasn't understanding what was going on.

'Oh no,' Euphrosyne said. She looked almost shocked. 'The world was created many billions of years ago in the Great Explosion that caused the universe. Charaxes had nothing to do with it. They were not born yet.'

They? There was more than one Charaxes? It had

never occurred to him that the word might be plural. 'Euphrosyne,' Henry said, 'who are the Charaxes?'

'Our ancestors,' said Euphrosyne promptly. 'Was that not your illustrious ancestor you just talked to, En Ri?'

Well, it wasn't, but a lot of things were clearer now. The ark wasn't some religious object like the Ark of the Covenant designed so the Luchti could talk to God. It was a device that helped you get in touch with dead relatives. Mr Fogarty wasn't a relative, but he was certainly dead and he was a lot closer to Henry than either of the grandfathers Henry had never even known. He gave a relieved sigh. Now he understood, he might be able to get things moving.

'Is there any way,' he asked, 'any way at all that I can get in touch with my Charaxes again? Like, now, I mean?'

'I can help you, En Ri,' said a strangled voice behind him.

Seventy-Seven

Henry turned to discover the voice belonged to Ino. The tattooed shaman looked awful. His eyes were still glazed and his legs were so rubbery that he had to be supported on either side by burly tribesmen. There were angry scratches on his torso as if he'd been attacked by a cat – heaven alone knew how he'd got those. The blue of his skin had taken on a greenish tinge, a particularly bilious combination that made him look like a standing corpse. But he grinned cheerfully at Henry. 'I can call up your Charaxes,' he said.

Henry glanced from Ino to Euphrosyne and back again. 'Are you all right?' he asked.

'I set the song-lines,' Ino slurred almost inaudibly. His legs gave way again so he sank down in the grip of his companions.

Lorquin pushed himself to the front of the group now surrounding Henry. 'Setting the song-lines is very difficult,' he explained. 'Only a clever man like Ino could manage it. Now he wishes to help you, En Ri. He knows you want to speak again to your Charaxes.'

'Yes, but is he all right?' Henry hissed. He drew Lorquin to one side and said quietly, 'How can I ask him to help me – he looks ghastly.'

'He always looks like that,' Lorquin said. 'It's the tattoos.'

'It's not the tattoos,' Henry insisted. 'He looks as if he's about to fall down.'

'He always looks like that too,' Lorquin said, 'after setting the song-lines. But if you do not allow him to help you, how will you speak with your Charaxes before next year?'

'Next *year?*' Henry exploded. He lowered his voice hurriedly. 'Euphrosyne said we could use the ark again soon.'

'Next year will come sooner than you think,' Lorquin assured him philosophically. 'But if you wish to speak with your Charaxes before then, you must use Ino. It is not so clear as the ark, but better than no speech at all.'

'But Ino is *ill!*' Henry exclaimed. 'He can hardly stand up. I mean, it's nice of him and all that, but I can't ask –'

'You are not asking, En Ri,' Lorquin said firmly. 'He offers you a gift. Ino is a man as you and I are men, En Ri. You must permit him to act as men must act in friendship. You must trust him to judge his own strength.'

Henry stared at the child, wondering how somebody so young had managed to become so wise. He looked at Ino, who was swaying a bit, but now contrived to stand unaided. 'Yes, all right,' he said. Then quickly, 'Thank you, Ino. Thank you very much.'

Despite Lorquin's reassurances, it wasn't easy, and it wasn't all up to Ino either. The entire tribe formed themselves into a circle again; three of the drummers pushed to the front and began to beat out a steady, complex rhythm. The sounds had an immediate affect on Ino, whose eyes rolled back in his head so only the whites were showing. Then he began to shuffle forwards and backwards in short, random movements. After a while he started to drool, then convulse. Henry watched him nervously. The shaman looked much like a B-movie zombie.

Henry's nervousness increased when he tore his eyes away from Ino to glance around the assembled tribe. Many – face it, Henry, *most* – of them had rolled-back eyes now and were swaying in time with the rhythm as if they'd fallen into trance. Even Lorquin looked slack-jawed and dazed.

Several of the women began to dance again, but it was a wild, discordant dance that sometimes led to their colliding with one another. Several of the men burst into loud, erratic shouts. The whole scene had the feel of something that was gradually getting out of control and Henry didn't like it. What he liked even less was the fact that the weird drum rhythm was getting to him as well. His eyes felt heavy and his mind kept getting soggy so that he had to jerk his attention savagely to stop himself falling asleep.

But then the drumming stopped. At once there was a shrill ululation from the women and Ino flung himself violently on the ground to begin spinning like a break-dancer. His eyes were glazed and dead, every limb spas-tic. Then he started to bang his head on the flagstones. To Henry's horror, it made a crunching sound.

'I say –' Henry put in nervously.

Ino responded to Henry's voice as if he'd been stung. From flat on the ground he made an impossible leap high in the air to land in a squatting position. He gave a gut-wrenching scream.

'Charaxes!' chanted the tribe at once. 'Charaxes! Charaxes! Charaxes!'

From his squatting position, Ino glared up at Henry like an angry dog. The resemblance was so striking that for a moment Henry thought he might actually attack; then his eyes closed, his face went entirely passive and his lips began to move. The tribe stopped its chant at once.

Henry pushed aside his fear and squatted beside Ino. The shaman's mumbling sounded like a two-way conversation heard through a thick door, but Henry could not make out a single word. 'What?' Henry asked. 'What are you saying?'

Then Lorquin was by Henry's side. 'Don't speak, En Ri,' he said quietly. 'Ino talks with your Charaxes.'

Henry waited. Ino turned to him abruptly. 'I see him,' he said.

'See who?' Henry asked foolishly.

'I see your Charaxes. He wishes you to say why you did not do as he instructed you.'

Henry looked at the shaman blankly.

The shaman stared into his eyes, blinked twice and said, 'He has taken my filament.' The voice he used was a woman's voice and Henry recognised it at once.

Henry went cold. 'Blue …?' he whispered. His stomach knotted. Was Blue already dead?

'I can't find my way back,' Ino said.

'Blue? Blue, where are you?'

'In the dark,' said Ino clearly. The voice was sounding more like Blue each second.

'What filament?' Henry asked. 'Who has taken it?'

'The clown,' Blue said. 'He took it.'

It was making no sense at all. But the voice was Blue's voice: he was certain of that. Somehow he was talking to Blue through the mouth of the Luchti shaman. 'What clown?' Then, more urgently, 'Where are you, Blue?'

'The serpent will get me,' Blue said. She sounded dreamy, as if she was half asleep.

This was getting worse and worse. Henry felt like taking Ino and shaking him, except that one look at Ino's face was enough to show the shaman was no longer there. His eyes, which had looked blind before, now seemed fathomless and empty. He had sunk down from his squatting position so that now he was seated on the ground, every muscle relaxed like a rag doll. With a massive effort Henry forced himself to be calm. 'You're being attacked by a serpent?' If she was being attacked by a serpent, there was nothing he could do, nothing at all. Even if miraculously she was only half a mile away, he could not get to her in time to save her.

'Soon,' Blue said in her dreamy voice. 'The Trickster took my filament.'

Since clowns and serpents and filaments made no sense, Henry concentrated on the one thing that might. 'Where are you, Blue? You have to tell me where you are.'

'In the dark,' Blue repeated; to Henry's horror her voice seemed to be fading.

'In the dark *where?*' he asked desperately. 'Are you in the Palace? Are you in the city? Blue, where *are* you?'

Blue said something, but so faintly now that Henry couldn't catch it.

In a mounting panic he reached out to grip Ino's arm. 'Where are you, Blue?' he shouted. 'Please, darling, tell me where you are!'

'She's in the Mountains of Madness,' Ino said crossly in Mr Fogarty's voice. 'And don't call me "darling".'

Seventy-Eight

'Do you have a diagnosis?' Madame Cardui asked, buttoning her blouse.

Chief Wizard Healer Danaus, who had carried out the examination with his back turned, said quietly, 'I'm afraid you test positive.'

'I have the time plague?'

'In its early stages, yes.'

They were in the Chief Wizard's private consulting rooms. There was a guard on the door and military grade privacy spells were in place. With Queen Blue no longer in the Palace, her Gatekeeper dead and Pyrgus in stasis, Madame Cardui was painfully aware the state of her own health had political implications. She said quietly, 'What do you suggest?'

'Immediate stasis,' Danaus said bluntly.

'Impossible,' said Madame Cardui. She finished adjusting her clothing and added, 'You may turn round now.'

Danaus turned his large bulk slowly. He had a sober, strained expression on his face. 'Impossible ...?' he echoed tiredly.

Madame Cardui said briskly, 'Until Her Majesty returns, I am needed in the Palace.'

Danaus shook his head. 'No one is indispensable.'

Madame Cardui sighed. 'I'm afraid I am, Chief Wizard

Healer. At least until Queen Blue returns, and possibly beyond then. It is simply impossible for me to go into immediate stasis.'

'Impossible or not, it is necessary.' They stood looking at each other in silence; then, to her astonishment and not a little shock, he reached out to take her hand. 'Cynthia,' he said quietly, 'Prince Pyrgus is a young man – hardly more than a child. You have seen how the fever has ravaged him. Gatekeeper Fogarty was a mature man when he caught the fever. You saw how quickly it killed him.' He looked deep into her eyes. 'Forgive me, Cynthia, but you are older even than Gatekeeper Fogarty. You may not feel it, you do not look it, but that's the simple fact of it: I have your medical records.'

Madame Cardui extricated her hand gently and turned her head away. 'Yes,' she said, 'that's true. Alan never knew how many years there were between us – the difference between faerie and human physiology, of course – and I felt no great need to tell him.' She looked back at Danaus, her eyes suddenly fierce. 'But it's not the age that counts, is it? As I understand this plague, what is really important is the amount of future one has left remaining. Is this not so, Chief Wizard Healer? An eighty-year-old faerie with a hundred years remaining is surely better off than an eighty-year-old human who might be lucky to have ten?'

'You are not an eighty-year-old faerie,' Danaus said gently. 'You do not have a hundred years remaining.'

'No,' Madame Cardui agreed, 'but you take my point.'

'I understand the point you are making, but there is something else that must be taken into consideration. Our research shows that the disease progresses more quickly when contracted late in life.'

That was something else he hadn't mentioned before. She blinked, but managed to keep the irritation from her voice. 'You're saying that the disease uses up the remaining future of an adult at a faster rate than it uses up the future of a child?'

'That is exactly what I am saying. The plague is at its most virulent when it first strikes. Had you contracted this disease fifty years ago, it might take months, perhaps even years, to burn up the future you now have remaining. But since you have only just become ill, the time left to you will be short.' He hesitated, then added, 'Perhaps very short.' He looked at her soberly. 'Your only hope – your *only* hope – is immediate stasis. That at least will keep you alive indefinitely, even if it does not permit you to function.'

'You did not recommend stasis in the case of Princess Nymphalis.'

'Your case is entirely different – I've just explained that in great detail.'

She knew she was being an irritating old woman. She also knew he had her best interests at heart. The trouble was Chief Wizard Healer Danaus exactly lived up to his title. He was a healer first, foremost, always and nothing more. His grasp of politics was confined to lobbying for an increase in his department's budget. He saw the time fever solely as a disease to be battled, a plague to be stopped. He had no realisation of its wider implications. He would not see, for example, how it weakened the Realm, left it open to revolution from within or attack from without. He would not see the importance of strong leadership at a time like this. Comma functioned perfectly well as a holding operation, but he did not have the experience to handle an emergency. Danaus could not realise how precarious a position they were all in with their Queen absent. (And Madame Cardui blamed herself for that little eventuality. She should never have allowed Blue to leave the Palace. But she had been so concerned with Alan's visions that her judgement had been clouded – she admitted that now, at least to herself.)

Madame Cardui took a deep breath. 'Your diagnosis of my condition is based on early warning signs, is it not?'

'There is no doubt in my mind,' said Danaus grimly. 'You have the fever. To try to convince yourself otherwise would be a grave mistake.'

Madame Cardui shook her head. 'I understand I have the disease, but the fever has not actually manifested yet.'

'It could do so literally at any minute.'

'But until it does, my future is not in peril?'

'Technically no. But –'

'Chief Wizard Healer,' Madame Cardui said with a note of finality in her voice, 'there can be no question of placing me in stasis now. I have far too much to do. I would suggest you put a stasis chamber on standby. When the fever manifests, you have my permission to place me in it immediately.'

'That assumes I, or some other healer, will be with you when the fever manifests,' Danaus said.

Madame Cardui said nothing.

Danaus said, 'Madame Cardui, I cannot stress strongly enough the risk involved in what you are asking me to do. At your age, the fever could burn up your available future within an hour or so at most, probably less and possibly a great deal less. If the fever strikes while you are asleep tonight, you will be dead by morning. If the fever strikes while you are alone, you could be dead before anyone arrives to help. Even if the fever strikes while you are surrounded by people and I am miraculously standing by your side, you might be dead before we got you to the stasis chamber.'

'That's a risk I'll have to take,' said Madame Cardui.

Seventy-Nine

Damn, damn, damn, damn, *damn* – the catsite was wearing off! Blue couldn't believe it. Of all the foul luck. That creature, that clown, that disguised charno person had snatched her filament and disappeared, leaving her to find her way out of the maze of passages unaided. She might have managed it too – she had a good sense of direction and a fine visual memory – but without the catsite in her system she was blind. Already her eyesight was fading. Where once she could see for yards along the rocky corridor, now only a few steps ahead were visible. Beyond that everything faded into a thickening fog.

Dare she take more catsite?

Fortunately the creature had left her backpack. She rummaged in it now, found the catsite and felt her heart sink. The remaining crystals had clumped together and were in the process of fusing. Catsite did that sometimes if you failed to separate out the crystal structures in advance, which – dammit – she hadn't. She could break off a portion – she could still do that – but not a small portion. All the fused crystals were far larger than the originals. What it meant was she would have to take a massive second dose ... or no dose at all.

Blue forced herself to stay calm. There was a good

side and a bad side. The good side was that a massive dose of catsite would last a very long time, probably far longer than she'd need to explore these passages, rescue Henry if he was here, and make her escape. The bad side was a massive dose of catsite would almost certainly kill her.

After a long moment she decided to see how far she could get with the remains of the catsite in her system. No sense risking any more until she absolutely had to. After all, she could still see, if poorly, and she had no way of knowing how long it would be before the catsite cleared her system completely. Enough of it might hang around to let her do what she needed to do.

An hour later, Blue knew it wasn't enough. She was on her knees in a narrow passageway, near blind now, inching forward more by touch than sight and very much aware she was completely lost. For a moment she experienced a massive sense of desolation. Did it matter if she took more catsite? Even with full vision again she would still be lost. When the creature stole her filament, he took away all hope of orientation. How could she hope to find Henry? How could she hope to rescue him? And if, miraculously, she did, how could they hope to find their way out?

The moment passed and something of her old self-confidence reasserted itself. She was no worse off now than she'd expected to be. If she risked another dose of catsite, there was every chance of doing what she'd set out to do.

She was reaching for the crystals when she saw a pinpoint of light ahead.

It was too good to be true. If there really was a light, it had to be another patch of the luminous fungus she'd seen earlier. But there was no greenish hue. The light was clean and clear, like sunlight. She began to crawl cautiously towards it. Minutes later she knew for certain this was no fungus patch. Minutes more and she was able to stand upright, able to move forward without reliance on the fading catsite. She began to run. She knew she should exercise more caution, but the light was a beacon now; her heart was pumping. This might even be a breakthrough to the surface, a way out, a means of starting again.

Blue ran from the passageway into a vast subterranean cavern. It was well lit, but not from any surface sun – the light was pouring from an opening into a second, smaller chamber. It was too bright to be sunlight, although where it came from she had no idea. There was a heady smell of magic in the air. She could have sworn it was the potent stench of summoning.

She stopped, confused. The floor of the cavern looked a little like an angry ocean, a grey turbulence with flecks of green and blue and white. She could make no sense at all of what she was seeing; then something moved and the scene resolved itself abruptly. The cavern was filled with the blue-green coils of a massive serpent, a creature so huge it could never have been the product of the natural world. The head that slowly turned to gaze at her was larger than a peasant's cottage. Seated between the serpent's tree-trunk horns was the clown who'd tracked her earlier. A small loop of filament dangled from his fingers.

He smiled at her brightly. 'What kept you?' he asked.

Eighty

'Who are you?' Blue screamed. She felt suddenly furiously angry. With the Abbot and the Purlisa who had sent her here. With their charno, who had transformed into this clown (or this clown who had disguised himself as a charno – she wasn't sure which). With Madame Cardui for transporting Henry. With Mr Fogarty for dying just when she most needed his advice. With Pyrgus for getting ill. Most of all with herself for somehow walking into this incredible, bewildering, nonsensical, stupid, stupid, stupid, stupid situation. Then, because it was all she really cared about, she shouted, 'Where is Henry?'

'Ah, Henry,' said the clown. 'The hero of our tale.' He looked around ostentatiously. 'Henry?' he called. 'Where are you, Henry?' Then, 'Henry, Henry, Henry' as if calling to a cat. He turned back to Blue and smiled again. 'No one of that name here.'

Blue opened her mouth, then closed it again. The clown hadn't said, *Who's Henry?* or *Who do you mean?* Instead he'd done his stupid clown act, playing games with her as if he knew exactly who Henry was. This had to be a set-up. The clown had been sent by the Purlisa, disguised as a charno, to … to … to what? Lure her into the cavern? She'd already agreed to go into the cavern. Make sure she did? The reverse psychology business? But why a disguised charno? Or a disguised clown? And why send her into the cavern in the first place if Henry wasn't here? The more she thought, the more confused she became. What was going on here?

It occurred to her suddenly that in her confusion, she was missing out on the biggest, most obvious puzzle of the lot. The clown was sitting on the head of the most massive reptile she'd ever seen in her life. Was this the Midgard Serpent the Purlisa had talked about? Had he been telling the truth about that at least? But if it *was* the Midgard Serpent – or even if it wasn't – why didn't it attack the clown?

'*Serpents eat charnos.*' The remark made by the charno echoed in her memory. But the charno had still followed her into the cave, then turned into a clown and stolen her only means of leaving and ...

She stopped the train of thought. Maybe it wasn't like that at all. She'd briefly seen a charno in the passageway before it turned itself into this clown, but maybe that wasn't the *same* charno who'd accompanied her from the monastery. She wasn't sure she could tell one charno from another in bright sunlight, let alone in the depths of a gloomy cave. Suppose *her* charno was still outside, waiting patiently. Suppose this clown thing had taken the shape of a charno – a simple illusion spell would do it – just to confuse her?

Then why turn back to a clown the minute she stepped out? And if the clown wasn't sent by the Abbot or the Purlisa, who was the clown? And whoever the clown was, how did he manage to sit on the head of the world's largest serpent without being eaten like a charno?

It was all too much for Blue. Too many questions,

not enough answers. But there was an answer to the only question that mattered. Henry wasn't here.

'I'm going,' Blue said shortly and turned to leave the cavern.

The serpent twitched and a segment of its enormous tail closed off her exit.

Blue swung round again. The serpent was staring at her with vast, glittering eyes. The clown hadn't moved. His legs dangled down on either side of its nose.

'Do you control this thing?' Blue demanded. 'Tell it to let me out!'

Back into the passages, Blue, with the catsite worn off and no filament to guide you? her mind whispered. She pushed the thoughts aside. First things first.

'Control?' asked the clown, affecting a look of astonishment. 'He's an adolescent, bless him. Nobody controls an adolescent.' He shook his head sadly. 'Stays out all hours. Keeps bad company. Gets innocent girl serpents pregnant.' He pursed his lips, opened his eyes wide. 'Won't do a *thing* I tell him.'

Blue pulled the Halek blade from her belt, turned and in a single movement plunged it into the serpent's tail.

The energy discharge was massive. It poured from the knife like a lightning bolt, twisting and crackling. An overwhelming smell of ozone filled the air. The clown jerked suddenly and looked down as if something had bitten his bottom, then slid from his perch on the serpent's head and leaped nimbly onto the floor. 'That *tickled!*' he exclaimed.

Blue withdrew the knife. The crystal blade was intact, but dull and lifeless as if every ounce of energy it had contained was now discharged. The serpent watched her curiously. It had not moved so much as a single coil.

Blue dropped the useless Halek knife and ran. She could not leave the cavern the way she entered, but there might be other exits. Maybe the light was sunlight after all, pouring through the roof of a side-chamber. She ran towards it.

Without haste, the serpent coiled itself around her and held her fast.

Eighty-One

'This isn't right,' said Henry.

'What isn't right, En Ri?' asked Lorquin.

They had been trotting together for hours across the desert sands, baked by a relentless sun that somehow wasn't having anything like the effect on Henry that it used to. His adventures with Lorquin and sojourn with the Luchti seemed to have toughened him up a lot.

'You coming with me,' Henry said. 'This could be really dangerous.'

Lorquin said, 'En Ri, you were my Companion when I became a man. It is fitting that I am your Companion now.' He gave one of his sudden, broad smiles. 'Besides, how would you find your way without me?'

That was true enough. Although Henry had picked up several tricks from the Luchti, finding his way in the desert was not one of them. Try as he might, he still could not see the patterns Lorquin saw. 'All the same,' he said, 'I want you to stay out of the way if there's any trouble. You just show me how to get to the mountains and then ...' He trailed off. He'd been about to say, *And then you can go back to your people*. But several things occurred to him at once. The first was that he didn't *want* Lorquin to go back to his people. He'd come to love the kid (the *man*, Lorquin would say fiercely) and he didn't want him simply to disappear. Lorquin was like the little brother Henry never had. That was part of the reality of his situation now. Another part was the fact that if he was going to rescue Blue (from what?) he might need all the help he could get, even from a youngster. Henry was no hero. He avoided fights whenever he could. He'd do anything in the world for Blue, but he knew his limitations. And assuming they did manage to get Blue out of whatever pickle she'd got herself into, there was the question of getting home again. They might need Lorquin's help there too. '... then just keep out of the way,' he ended lamely.

'I shall behave as a Companion is supposed to behave,' said Lorquin piously.

They trotted in silence for another hour; then Lorquin said suddenly, 'We have reached our destination, En Ri.'

Henry looked around him. The sandy desert had given way to rocky wasteland, but otherwise he could see nothing of note. 'I thought we were going to the mountains,' he said.

'We have reached the mountains,' Lorquin said.

And indeed they had. The mountains loomed ahead, solid, threatening and gloomy. Henry blinked. He had no idea how he could have approached an entire mountain range without noticing. It just went to show how distracted he'd become. He stopped, staring up at the more distant peaks and suddenly realised how ill prepared he was for this whole adventure. All very well for Mr Fogarty to tell him he had to rescue Blue in the Mountains of Madness. But from what, in the Mountains of Madness. And *where* in the Mountains of Madness? They could spend the next month searching and never find her.

He realised he'd spoken the last thought aloud when Lorquin said, 'Perhaps I can track her, En Ri.'

Henry didn't quite see how, but he had long since stopped underestimating Lorquin's abilities. Nonetheless he said cautiously, 'You don't even know what she looks like.'

'Of course not, En Ri,' Lorquin said. 'But the mountains are haunted, so very few people come here. I can pick up the most recent trails. If we follow each, one will likely lead to your Blue.' He looked carefully at Henry's expression and added, 'It will be quicker than searching all the mountains.'

'Yes,' Henry said doubtfully. Anything would be quicker than searching the entire mountain range, but that was about all you could say for Lorquin's plan. The trouble was, he didn't have a better one. 'Yes,' he repeated more firmly. 'Yes, good idea, Lorquin. Thank you.'

In fact it took far less time than he imagined. They rested first for half an hour; then Lorquin led him to a place in the foothills overhung by two huge boulders. 'We start here,' he said.

Henry looked around. 'Why?' he asked curiously.

'We approached the mountains from the deep desert,' Lorquin said. 'I believe your friend may have approached from the great city or the dwelling of the holy men. In either case, she would have used this pass. It is the easiest road into the mountains.'

Henry stared at him. The boy was nothing short of incredible. Give him a suit and an office in London and he'd be running the city in a month. After a moment, he said, 'So what do we do now?'

'Rest, En Ri, and gather your strength for your great ordeal ahead. I will tell you when I find her trail.'

When not *if*, Henry noted. He placed his back against one of the boulders, sank down into a comfortable squat and watched. Lorquin circled the site twice, his eyes on the ground, then trotted through the pass. As he disappeared from sight he called back, 'I shall return for you, En Ri, when I find what we seek.'

Only minutes passed before he did return.

'You haven't found something already?' Henry asked, pushing himself to his feet. This was incredible, even for Lorquin.

'Several people have passed this way recently,' Lorquin said. 'Regrettably, I cannot say for certain if one of them is your friend.'

'So we don't know which way to go?'

'Oh, yes,' Lorquin said. 'All went to the same place.'

'They did?' Henry frowned suddenly. Had Blue travelled with an entourage? Or was it a more sinister picture? 'I don't suppose you know how many there were?'

'First many came here in a caravan,' Lorquin said, 'but most would not risk the mountain path, so two went ahead alone with a heavy cart. I do not think either of these was your friend because they were both men, although they may have taken her in their cart. Later another came with a charno –'

'What's a charno?' Henry asked. He also wondered how Lorquin knew he was trailing two men. Why not two women, or two boys? Maybe they left footprints and he judged the size of their feet.

'It is an animal trained to carry the possessions of people who do not know it is better to travel without possessions,' Lorquin said. 'The person with the charno was a woman, so it may be your friend.'

'You can tell all this from the trails?' Henry said.

'If you wish, I can teach you, En Ri.'

'Not just now,' Henry said. He felt a growing surge of excitement. 'If Blue really is up there, we may not have much time to lose.'

'That is wise,' Lorquin said gravely. He glanced back the way he came. 'There is something very dangerous in these mountains.'

Eighty-two

Madame Cardui stared at the pathetic creature, utterly appalled. 'You allowed your Queen to enter mountain caverns guarded by the *Midgard Serpent?*'

Chalkhill looked at his feet and mumbled.

'Speak up, you wobbling cretin!' Madame Cardui snapped.

Chalkhill jumped. 'Yes,' he said more loudly.

'And when she entered these mountains, you simply ... ran away?'

'I came here to tell you, Madame Spymaster,' Chalkhill protested. 'I came as quickly as I could. I even hired a flyer at my own expense, a highly dangerous flyer in a poor state of repair so that I risked life and li –'

'Oh, shut up, Chalkhill,' Madame Cardui told him tiredly. 'I suppose one can expect nothing from a pig but a grunt.' She shifted her position on the suspensor cloud so she could glare at him more fiercely. 'How did the Midgard Serpent find itself *in* these caverns, Mr Chalkhill? How did the Midgard Serpent happen to enter our reality at all?'

'Called up,' muttered Chalkhill. He wondered how she made him feel so ridiculously guilty when *none of this was his fault!*

'Called up, Mr Chalkhill? Who could possibly be *stupid* enough to call up the Midgard Serpent?'

'Brimstone,' Chalkhill said without meeting her eyes.

Madame Cardui smiled bleakly. 'Your old partner,' she hissed.

'Yes, well, you can't hold that against me.'

'Can't I?' asked Madame Cardui. 'If Queen Blue has been harmed in any way, you'd be surprised what I could hold against you, Mr Chalkhill. So you'd better tell me what else you know.'

Chalkhill licked his lips, wondering how far he should go with the old witch. The situation was grave, very grave, and might easily get worse. But in every crisis there were always men who played clever and refreshed their status, men who kept their nerve and came out on the winning side. The trouble was, it was difficult to decide on the winning side just now. The imbecile girl Queen was probably dead by now, which would normally swing the balance far in favour of Lord Hairstreak, despite his diminished fortunes. But Hairstreak was heavily dependant on Brimstone in this enterprise – solely dependant on Brimstone in fact – and Brimstone was mad. He'd been fairly mad to call up the Midgard Serpent in the first place but – Chalkhill swallowed – that rotten stroke of luck in meeting up with a cloud dancer had finished him completely. Where did that leave Lord Hairstreak now?

Chalkhill came to a decision. Wherever the balance of power lay, certain things remained constant. One was that information was valuable. The other was that timing was everything. The trick now would be to tell her Raddled Witchship enough to keep her satisfied, while keeping enough back as a bargaining chip for later. When it was clearer who would eventually come out on top.

He composed his features into an expression of sublime innocence and delivered a concise report.

Eighty-three

'Lorquin, you know you said there was something very dangerous in these mountains?' Henry asked

Lorquin was gazing keenly to one side, as if focussed on something in the middle distance, but he still said, 'Yes?'

'How did you know?' Henry asked. 'I mean, did you see it?'

'I sensed it,' Lorquin said, as if sensing danger was the most natural thing in the world. He tore his eyes away from whatever he'd been looking at in order to look at Henry. 'Why do you ask, En Ri?'

'I wondered if that might be it,' Henry told him.

Because Lorquin was in the lead while they were following invisible tracks, they had left the main path behind. This was not, Lorquin explained, because those they were following had done the same, but rather because they had not. Lorquin was worried Blue might have been taken captive, so he'd advised Henry to circle, thus avoiding meeting up with Blue's captors unawares. As a result, they were now on a narrow plateau looking down on a rocky apron that fronted a dark cave mouth. On the apron stood one of the scariest creatures Henry had ever seen.

The thing looked vaguely like a kangaroo, but far

larger, with muscular arms and shoulders and quite enormous clawed flat feet. It had a long head with prominent horselike teeth and giant hare's ears laid flat so they almost reached down to its neck. Strangest of all, it was carrying a substantial canvas pack strapped to its back. It was standing like a guardian by the cave mouth.

Lorquin looked down. 'No, that's not it,' he said.

They were downwind of the creature and speaking quietly so there was no chance of its hearing. After a moment, Henry said, 'Are you sure?'

'That is a charno, En Ri,' Lorquin said. 'I spoke to you of it before.'

Henry looked at him for a moment, trying to remember, then smiled suddenly. 'You mean a *pack* animal!?' The charno was an unlikely looking pack animal, even though it did have a pack, but it was there by the cavern and the pack was large, which could mean only one thing. 'Do you think it's been carrying supplies for …?' Well, for whoever they were following. Blue's captors, if she was captive, or Blue herself if she wasn't. All or any of whom, presumably, were now inside the cave.

'Let us find out,' said Lorquin. Before Henry could stop him, he was headed down the slope.

'Hey, wait a minute!' Henry shouted without thinking.

Below them, the charno looked up with large brown eyes.

Eighty-four

She was still alive. She was still uninjured. Actually she was almost comfortable: the serpent held her gently and the coils of its giant body had a warm, muscular feel, not at all the cold, slimy sensation she'd expected. But she couldn't move. Her arms were trapped by her sides. The serpent's grip was firm and utterly unyielding. She had no chance of escape.

Unless she could talk her way out.

From her vantage point in the coils of the serpent, Blue looked down at the clown. 'You're not my charno, are you?'

'Of course not,' said the clown. He bowed, elaborately. 'I am a simple entertainer, as you can see.'

There's nothing simple about you, Blue thought, with feeling. What she needed now, more than anything else, was information. She needed to find an edge, otherwise she was stuck here, lost to Henry and the Realm, with ... with what? A suspicion was beginning to form in her mind, but until she found out exactly what was happening here, she could never take control. *A step at a time,* she thought. *A step at a time.* Aloud she said, 'I mean, you weren't the charno who came with me from the monastery. You just took the shape of a charno when you were following me in the caves.'

The clown clapped his hands in mocking applause. 'Well done,' he said. 'And well done for realising you must find out what is happening here. Most people never reach that stage and then I have to kill them.'

Blue noted the threat, but ignored it. Her suspicion was strengthening. She'd had one brush with the Old Gods already. This clown creature looked nothing like the monstrous Yidam (who'd liked her, remember, so all might not be lost), but he had something of the same feel. She looked him up and down. 'That isn't your real form either, is it?'

He applauded again. 'Indeed not. This appearance is just symbolic of my nature.'

For some reason it felt important to see what lay behind the façade. 'Will you show me what you really look like?' she asked without much hope.

To her astonishment he changed at once, transforming into a strikingly handsome young man. 'Of course,' he said. He turned round slowly, like a preening peacock. His looks were amazing, but there was something more than that – an aura about him that was almost tangible … and hugely, physically, attractive. As he completed the turn, he looked directly into her eyes and grinned. 'Do you fancy me?' he asked.

Blue felt the breath catch in her throat and a sudden tightness grip her chest. She would die rather than admit it, but the truth was she *did* fancy him – a lot. He was the most beautiful man she'd ever seen, dark-haired, dark-eyed and that grin was so mischievous, so … dangerous. He was a man you'd have to reform, but until you did … ah, what a wild ride it would be!

She tore her eyes away and at once there was a different image in her mind. Henry. Henry wasn't handsome – not that handsome anyway, hardly handsome at all really. And Henry didn't have that irresistible hint of danger hanging round him. But Henry, for all he irritated her at times, was brave and kind and sensitive and caring and she'd loved him for years. Now she was no longer looking at this godling from the Old Time, his emotional impact waned quickly. Ignoring his question, Blue searched her memory for something the Purlisa had said, then asked one of her own. 'You're Loki, aren't you?'

For an instant he looked genuinely surprised, even taken aback. Then he rallied to give another of his extravagant bows. 'At your service, Lady. How did you know my name?'

Blue said, 'You're famous.' It came out without hesitation, driven by an instinct that he'd be flattered.

One look at his face confirmed the instinct was correct. He smiled at her and it was no longer the mischievous grin, but a broad, open smile of pleasure. 'Well,' he said, 'nice to know some of us are still remembered.'

She drew breath to lay on a little more judicious flattery, some lie about how greatly he was revered throughout the Realm, then stopped. *Don't overdo it,* a voice warned in her head. He might look young and attractive, but he was not at all what he seemed. And the Old Gods were dangerous, all of them. So far she'd been lucky in her dealings with the two she'd met, but it would be madness to push her luck. Besides, she wasn't just dealing with Loki. She was held captive by the Midgard Serpent.

The serpent could wait. She had to concentrate on Loki. *And stop looking at him like that,* she told herself crossly. *Think of Henry, if it helps.* She forced a conversational tone into her voice. 'How do you do it?'

she asked. 'Change from charno to clown to beautif—
to what you are now. Is it illusion magic?'

Loki shook his head. 'I'm a shape-shifter. It's a talent
I've had from birth.'

'Do all the Old Gods have it?'

'Just me.' He tilted his head to one side and half
turned it as if listening, but made no further comment.

Get down to it, Blue's instinct told her. As casually as
she could manage, she said, 'Why don't you have your
creature put me down and we can talk about what it is
you want of me?'

With no particular expression, Loki said, 'He's not
my creature – he's my son.'

Blue could have kicked herself. She'd *known* the beast
was his son. The Purlisa had mentioned it in his exposi-
tion of the myth. The trouble was the myth was so
incredible. Almost impossible to get your head around
the reality when you met up with it. In an attempt to
recover, she asked quickly, 'What's his name?'

At least it seemed Loki had failed to take offence, for he
answered calmly enough. 'His name is Jormungand.'
He swung his eyes slowly over the vast, incredible bulk
of the Midgard Serpent and added, almost with a hint of
awe, 'And you tried to kill him.'

This is not going well, Blue thought. She coughed
slightly. 'Yes, I'm sorry about that. Very sorry, really.'
Then something occurred to her and she said quickly,
'Somebody told me only hammers could harm him.'

'Yes, they do say that, don't they?' Loki nodded.

His expression was unreadable. When it became clear
he was not going to say anything more, Blue forced a
smile and said cheerily, 'Well, my little knife doesn't
seem to have harmed him.'

'Perhaps luckily,' Loki remarked enigmatically.

It was like the underground passageways – some of them were dead ends. Loki hadn't told his astonishing son to release her and the serpent hadn't done it of its own accord. There was no chance, as she'd hoped, of her scuttling away like a mouse, hiding or escaping. But then she wasn't sure she wanted to escape, not yet. 'Is Henry here?' she asked. It did not for an instant cross her mind that Loki might not know who Henry was.

'Not yet,' Loki said.

Not ... yet?

For the first time it occurred to Blue she might be dreaming. This whole encounter had a dreamlike quality about it. Mythic figures ... overwhelming dangers that somehow failed to harm her ... the idea that Henry was not here but possibly soon would be ... Was she actually asleep in her chamber in the Purple Palace?

If she was, the realisation didn't help her waken. Besides, for all its strangeness, this didn't *feel* like a dream.

Although she desperately wanted to ask more about Henry, some instinct told her she might be looking in the wrong direction. If she was to get out of this mess, she needed to know what she was dealing with. She took a deep breath and asked the critical question. 'Why have you come to this reality?'

She knew, positively knew, she was on the right track. There was a change in the atmosphere of the cavern. Loki's head swung round to stare at her intently. Even the great serpent shifted slightly, loosening its coils – although not enough for her to wriggle free.

Loki looked away from her again. 'My little boy came because he was called,' he said casually.

'By Brimstone?'

'Silas – yes. Such a dangerous thing to do, don't you think? But Silas paid the price.'

Blue said cautiously, 'So it wasn't a cloud dancer?'

Loki smiled. 'Oh, it was a cloud dancer, all right. Poetic justice, I imagine.'

She wanted to ask a lot more about that as well, but she had a feeling he was trying to divert her. 'And why are you here?' she asked.

'I was called too,' Loki said, but without the edge this time.

'Brimstone called you both?'

'Oh no, just Jormungand.'

Blue glared at him suspiciously. 'Then who called you?'

Loki smiled smugly. 'That peculiar little creature the Purlisa.'

The Purlisa? Why would the Purlisa call up one of the Old Gods – particularly this Old God – when he was so concerned about the Midgard Serpent? Surely one entity from that dimension was enough? Except, of course, she no longer knew what to believe about the Purlisa.

'To make sure all goes well for you and Henry,' Loki said as if he'd read her thoughts.

Eighty-five

Lord Hairstreak was furious. And helpless, which made things worse. He glowered with impotent rage as the guards marched him from the ferry to the Purple Palace. He'd already suffered the indignity of a body search. Now he was escorted like a common criminal. On whose orders? he wondered. The guards had been more than a little vague about that. They were Palace Guards all right, which meant they were theoretically responsible to his niece, Queen Blue. But Blue was away from the Palace at the moment – he knew that for sure. Unless she'd just returned, of course. The possibility struck him as interesting, but why have him arrested? There was no way she could have got wind of his plans.

Not that he'd been formally arrested. He might have lost his political influence and most of his money, but he was still a Lord, still of the Blood Royal (albeit on the wrong side of the blanket), which meant he had been 'invited' to accompany the Guards. When he declined, they insisted, politely but firmly. Later, when he was searched, he knew even the veneer of courtesy had been abandoned.

The irony was that the Guard Captain was one of his own men – or rather what used to be one of his own men – a Faerie of the Night. Blue had instigated an ecumenical policy soon after her coronation: demons, Faeries of the Night ... all were welcome to Palace service. It was supposed to help draw all sides together in a spirit of harmony and cooperation. Adolescent naivety, if ever he saw it, but the irritating thing was it seemed to have worked. There was a time when he could have counted on a Faerie of the Night to do his bidding absolutely. Now he couldn't even get this one to give him a little information.

He made one more try. 'Captain, what exactly is this all about?'

'Couldn't say, sir,' said the Captain.

The dark bulk of the Purple Palace, long blackened by time, was looming over them now, and he noticed they were skirting the main entrance in favour of a lesser door, another indication that this was no formal invitation from his niece. But it was none of the usual business entrances either, not the way of the diplomats, not the way of the merchants, not the way of the petitioners. If his memory of Palace geography served him, they seemed to be taking him towards the cellars. Who had quarters in the cellars? No one, so far as he was aware.

In a moment they were inside and, sure enough, they were leading him downwards, through a series of descending corridors and stairways. The going grew gloomy as they entered the older quarter of the Palace, what had once been the original keep, and as they turned a brick-lined corner, Hairstreak suddenly realised he was not being taken to the cellars at all, but to the ancient dungeons.

The sheer insult almost took his breath away. Clearly someone had not only ordered his arrest, but his imprisonment. And not in State Quarters, but in some dank cell where he would rot for the remainder of his days while the world and its wiles revolved without him. It was so outrageous he could scarcely believe it. Nothing like this could have happened in the old days. The very suggestion would have sparked a rebellion throughout the Realm. But those days, it seemed, were gone. His old enemies could act with impunity now – or at least so they believed. The question was, *which* old enemy?

The Guard Captain opened a door and pushed him, none too gently, into a well-lit room. At once he had his answer. 'Ah, Madame Cardui,' Hairstreak murmured. 'How kind of you to invite me.'

The old witch was reclining on a suspensor cloud. Someone had mentioned she seemed to be using suspensors a lot these days, a possible indication that her bones were growing brittle. But brittle or not, it never did to underestimate her. She was wearing something long and flowing, with woven hypno-spells suggesting grace and beauty. She seemed very much at ease, which was a bad sign. The chamber was unfurnished except for the bank of glowglobes that gave it light and a heavy maroon velvet curtain that cut off a portion of its area near the back.

'How kind of you to come,' said Madame Cardui. She gestured to the guards, who withdrew at once, closing the door behind them. 'I would ask you to sit down, Lord Hairstreak, but I seem to have neglected to provide a chair.'

'No matter,' Hairstreak said. 'I imagine our business will not take long.'

'That's a matter of opinion,' Madame Cardui told him. She gave him a hard stare. 'Or cooperation.'

'It's all cooperation these days,' said Hairstreak easily.

'I was just thinking that on the way here.' What he was thinking now was that, in an emergency, he might get away with killing her. The body search, while humiliating, had missed the stiletto implanted in his upper thigh. He could reach the weapon through a side pocket, drive its tip behind her ear and let the poison coating do the rest. With luck, the guards might imagine she was sleeping until he managed to get clear, and the poison, of course, was undetectable. It would be nice to have Cardui out of the way. But possibly not just yet. For the moment he needed to know why she'd had him brought here and what she wanted.

'I'm delighted to hear it,' Madame Cardui said. 'In that case our business certainly will not take long.'

He waited. She had her hideous translucent cat with her, unhygienically curled up on the same cloud: the scabby creature must be nearly as old as she was and still refused to die. It glared at him malevolently, but at least it was too slow to act as her bodyguard now. Presumably she kept it out of habit or from some misplaced sense of gratitude. A great mistake. When something outlived its usefulness, you got rid of it.

'Lord Hairstreak,' Madame Cardui said gently, 'why did you decide to start the time plague?'

So that was it. He'd wondered how long it would take her to become suspicious. To test how much she knew, he adopted his most bewildered expression and frowned. 'The plague, Madame Cardui? I don't understand ...'

'Of course you do,' said Madame Cardui sharply. 'This is no natural disease – we both know that. My Chief Wizard Healer confirmed it earlier today. It does not spread in the normal way, it does not react to any conventional treatment and it attacks its victims with an unprecedented ferocity. This is not a disease, Lord Hairstreak. It is a weapon. And I believe you are the one who is wielding it.'

Not bad, Hairstreak thought. Considerably less than the whole truth, but logical and pointing roughly in the right direction. Age hadn't blurred her focus yet. But she was certainly less careful with her words than she used to be. *I believe you are the one who is wielding it.* Belief was not knowledge. If she had proof she'd have said *I know you are the one ...*

So this was a fishing trip.

He spread his hands. 'Madame Cardui, I appreciate that you and I have never been the best of friends, but where is the logic in your position? Time fever is an unconventional disease, I grant you that, but are you suggesting I somehow ... *manufactured* it? And if I did, to what end? You use the term *weapon*. The plague has attacked Faeries of the Night and Faeries of the Light without distinction. What sort of weapon is that?'

'A subtle one,' said Madame Cardui. 'This is not a direct attack on the Faeries of the Light; it is something designed to undermine the very foundations of the Empire, to create a crisis that will prepare the State for revolution – a bloody revolution led by you, Lord Hairstreak, in an attempt to regain the power you have lost.'

Rather a nice idea, Hairstreak thought. But considerably less efficient than the plan he really had in play. Clearly she had no idea about that as yet. So all that remained was for him to extricate himself from this little meeting and get back to more important matters. 'An interesting notion, Madame, but one without the slightest foundation. Now, if you'll excuse me, I must –'

He stopped. He had been about to turn on his heel and leave – she could not hold him without proof positive and he knew now she had no proof at all. But when he tried to move, nothing happened. He felt perfectly normal, yet his entire body was paralysed.

'Lord Hairstreak,' Madame Cardui sighed, 'I don't have time for this. None of us has time for this. The plague is increasing exponentially. Let me be frank with you. I have no idea about the details of your plan. I do not know how you started the plague. I do not know how to stop it. That's why you're here. Normally I would wait patiently for my agents to find out, but I no longer have that luxury. I need to know at once. And you will tell me.'

There was no scent of a cone, no indication of a magical field, so it had to be one of the newly developed techniques of mind magic. Who'd have thought Cardui could have mastered the disciplines at her age? He could possibly fight his way free, if he could muster sufficient concentration, but it might be easier to use the element of surprise. So best pick his time. Pretend he was unaware of the paralysis as yet, distract her, lull her into a feeling of false security, then jerk free. Once he'd broken the spell, it would take her minutes to lay it on him again. More than enough time to use his stiletto.

He smiled easily and shook his head. 'I cannot tell you what I do not know. I assure you, Madame Cardui –'

She made a small hand gesture. The curtain at the end of the room swung back and Hairstreak felt his blood run cold. He was looking at an Aladdin mind machine. The chair was prepared, restraints at the ready. The helmet was already flashing green. The viewscreen was blank, but would not remain that way for long. Worst of all, he could see the dangling lead with its metallic card.

'I told you we had run out of time,' said Madame Cardui.

His paralysis broke, but not her power over him. He felt his right leg rise awkwardly then push outwards to set one foot flatly on the floor. He teetered, regained his balance, then felt his left leg follow suit. Jerkily he began to walk towards the Aladdin, manipulated like a puppet on strings.

'You can't do this!' Hairstreak screamed. The device was normally used on Trinians – the metal card slid into their skull slots – where it was a relatively harmless way to recover memories. But for a Faerie of the Night, or a Faerie of the Light for that matter, it drained the entire mind, leaving the victim in a vegetative state. Inserting the card was notoriously tricky too. The metal was phase-shifted for ease of insertion and the brain had no pain receptors, but even a slight misplacement resulted in disaster. He had to break her hold on him and break it fast.

'I'm afraid I can,' Madame Cardui told him soberly. 'When the future of the Empire is at stake.'

His legs jerked again and he took another staggering step forward. Once she placed him in the chair he was finished. The restraints would hold him automatically and from that point on she was freed to work the machine itself. His plan, his real plan, was near the surface of his memories. She would have everything on screen and recorded within minutes – half an hour at most. Not that it mattered. By then he'd be a vegetable or a lunatic, beyond caring.

Hairstreak lashed out at the mento-magical controls

that held him. The weakness in the system was that it relied entirely on the mental discipline of the person using it. Surely an old hag like Cardui would be no match for a man like him.

But the old hag forced him to take another step forward, then another. Her control actually seemed to be strengthening. He was only feet from the chair now.

He stopped trying to fight the magic and concentrated instead on taking back control of his own body, forcing it to go elsewhere. The manoeuvre must have caught her by surprise, for he spun round so he was no longer facing the Aladdin and even managed a faltering step in the other direction. But then she had him again and he was headed back towards the chair. Should he tell her everything? Abandoning his plan was almost unthinkable at this stage, but at least it was better than ending up a mindless husk.

Hairstreak stopped. Would she believe him, even if he made a full confession? What he'd done seemed impossible, even to him. And it could not be undone, not now, with Brimstone gods-knew-where and Chalkhill useless as ever. There was a dull thud behind him. She would never believe he was powerless to halt the process now, not without confirmation from her cursed machine. Which left him back where he'd started.

He realised suddenly that he had stopped moving. He was no longer lurching towards the Aladdin chair. He moved one arm experimentally and discovered it was back in his control.

Hairstreak spun round. Madame Cardui was lying huddled on the floor.

His mind raced. With luck she might have broken her neck. But her eyes were open and she was still breathing.

What had happened here? The suspensor cloud was still in place, although no longer floating. Presumably it had cushioned her fall. But what caused the fall? Her eyes were glazed and beads of sweat had broken out on her forehead. She was no longer in control of the cloud or, more importantly, of him.

It didn't matter. She was helpless. Hairstreak reached for his stiletto.

Eighty-Six

'What kept you?' demanded the charno.

'You can talk!' Henry said breathlessly. Despite his surprise, he found it comforting. Somehow a creature that could talk seemed a bit less likely to attack him.

'Think so,' said the charno. 'Are you going to answer my question?'

'You mean you were expecting us?' Henry asked. He found himself wondering if life could get any stranger. He was in fairyland, halfway up a mountain with a little blue boy, talking to a giant hare.

'Not him,' said the charno, nodding towards Lorquin. 'Just you.'

'Why?' Henry asked, bewildered. 'Why were you expecting me?' Or how? How could this creature be expecting him?

'Purlisa told me to keep an eye out.'

Henry stared at it. After a moment, he said, 'Who's Purlisa?'

'Holy man,' said Lorquin. 'He lives with the monks in the monastery.'

What monastery? Henry thought. But that could wait. He'd opened his mouth to ask something more relevant, without quite knowing what it would be, when the charno said, 'Blue's inside.'

'Ah,' Lorquin said.

For some reason it hit Henry like a thunderbolt. Although they'd been following what Lorquin believed to be Blue's tracks, the confirmation brought a stark reality. Blue was inside and in need of rescue. He felt sudden, overpowering fear mixed with an almost over-whelming excitement. Above it all was a sensation he'd never experienced before. It was as if he'd become the focus of the universe. His entire life had coalesced into a single point.

Without a word he turned and began to walk towards the cave.

'Serpent in there,' said the charno.

Henry stopped. 'Sorry?'

'She's in there with the Midgard Serpent,' said the charno.

Henry stared. After a moment he asked, 'What's the Midgard Serpent?'

'Big snake,' said the charno. He glanced briefly at the sky and added, '*Very* big snake.'

Lorquin shook his head. 'If the charno speaks the truth, we face one of the Old Ones.'

Henry didn't like the sound of that. 'How do you know this stuff?' he asked almost angrily.

Lorquin shrugged. 'The stories of my tribe.' A sheep-ish look crept across his face. 'Not a snake but a sea serpent. I listened well.'

Not a snake but a sea serpent said the boy who'd never seen the sea. Blue was in there with one of the Old Ones in the shape of a ... big ... monster ... *thing* ... sort of Old One god serpent snake, which was insane except he realised suddenly it didn't matter. Whatever it was, it didn't matter. However scared he was, it didn't matter. He had to get Blue out. He loved her, that's what mattered. He turned again.

The charno sniffed. 'You tackling it without a weapon?'

Henry stopped dead. For the first time since they'd set off from the deep desert, he realised he was unarmed. It was incredible, but until this very moment the thought of weapons had never occurred to him. He had been thrown by Mr Fogarty's communication, then utterly focused on Blue and the fact she needed rescue. How stupid could you get? What did he think he was going to do – steam in and fight the serpent with his bare hands?

Lorquin said, 'I have our weapons, En Ri.'

Henry looked at the boy and was swallowed by a wave of pure and utter love. Of *course* Lorquin had their weapons! Lorquin was the child-man who survived the desert, killed the draugr, saw the trails, saved Henry's life and thought of things like that. Lorquin was his Companion in this bizarre ordeal, just as Henry had been Lorquin's Companion the day he became a man. 'Lorquin has my weapon,' Henry told the charno proudly.

Lorquin pulled two short flint blades from his pouch and solemnly handed one to Henry. It was only inches long. Henry stared at it. 'This is my weapon?' he said softly, as much a question as a statement.

'The blade I used to gain my manhood,' Lorquin said. He smiled fondly.

'Won't work,' said the charno.

Lorquin's eyes narrowed as he turned. Henry caught his arm quickly. 'No, it's all right, Lorquin,' he hissed. Then, to the charno, 'He killed a draugr with this knife.' He looked down at the blade, feeling considerable sympathy for the charno. Henry couldn't help feeling Lorquin had got lucky – very lucky. The blade looked as if it would give problems killing a rabbit. But he had enough on his plate without a hassle between Lorquin and the charno.

The charno said, 'Hammer's the only thing that will hurt the Midgard Serpent.'

There was something about the flat certainty in the creature's voice that stopped Henry dead. 'You mean a war hammer?'

'Something like that.'

Henry looked at Lorquin. 'We don't have a war hammer, do we?'

Lorquin shook his head.

The charno said, 'I have.'

There was an uncomfortable silence. Was he waiting for an offer? After a long moment, Henry said, 'Do you think we might borrow it?'

For an answer, the charno reached into his backpack and withdrew an ancient hammer. He handed it to Lorquin, who happened to be standing closest. There was a loud clang as Lorquin dropped it on the rock. 'It is too heavy for me, En Ri,' Lorquin said.

Henry stepped forward and tried to lift the hammer. By using both hands and holding his breath, he managed to move it an inch or two. He let it drop again. 'Strewth, that's heavy!' he exclaimed. He looked at the charno accusingly.

The charno shrugged. 'Special metal,' he explained.

Henry looked at the weapon. He could probably carry it if the charno helped him get it on his shoulder, but there was no chance at all that he could actually use it in a fight. The thing was far too heavy. 'This is no good to me,' he said reluctantly. 'I'll have to stick to Lorquin's knife.'

'Serpent will kill you,' said the charno with no particular inflection.

Henry turned towards the cave mouth. 'That's a chance I'll have to take,' he said.

Eighty-Seven

Chief Wizard Healer Danaus could not believe it. He simply could not believe it. It went against all the laws of magic, all the laws of nature. And it was an unmitigated disaster. Unmitigated.

He could hardly wait to tell Madame Cardui.

He rehearsed his announcement as he bustled along the Palace corridors.

'*A spell failure, Chief Wizard Healer?*' she would ask.

'*Spell failures are rare, Madame Cardui.*'

'*But not impossible?*'

'*Not impossible, as you say. However, in this instance, we have checked for spell failure.*'

It wasn't spell failure. That was the incredible thing. Spell failure was the first possibility he thought of. Spell failure was the first thing he had checked, then checked personally, then checked again and rechecked. It wasn't spell failure.

'*Then what is it, Danaus?*' asked Madame Cardui inside his head.

The trouble was, he had not the slightest idea. Nothing in his years of experience gave him a single clue. Stasis was reliable magic, tried and tested. The first stasis cabinet had been designed and constructed over seven hundred years ago, if memory served. There had been design improvements since then, of course, but the basic principle remained the same. And it was a fundamental principle, a basic law. Stasis *couldn't* stop working. Except now it had.

He realised he was growing breathless and forced himself to slow down a little. He would really have to lose a little weight. But in the meantime, what on earth *possessed* Madame Cardui to set up an office in the old dungeons? So far from anywhere – especially the infirmary – in her condition. And if she didn't care about herself, you'd imagine in a national emergency, she'd want to be close to the nerve centre, but no …

A servant girl emerged from an entrance and got in his way. Danaus brushed her aside impatiently without further slowing his pace. His mind was still on what he had to tell Madame Cardui. She would want details. She always wanted details. How had he discovered the problem? How had it manifested? When? Where? Who had noticed? What had drawn it to their attention?

The answers were simple enough, as it happened, and fortunately he'd been there to witness everything personally. He checked off the sequence of events. The nurse noticed the deterioration in Nymphalis's condition and called him at once. He examined Nymphalis, confirmed the nurse's observation (but why the *acceleration* of the disease?) and ordered her immediate removal to stasis.

And he had supervised the setting up of the stasis cabinet himself, placed beside the one that housed Prince Pyrgus – a humane touch that, he thought. Heaven alone knew what had prompted him to wait and watch after Nymphalis was placed inside. Some healer's instinct, he expected, since there was absolutely no need and he had other urgent matters to attend to. But he had stayed and watched and that was when he noticed Nymphalis continued to deteriorate *after she had been placed in stasis!* Impossible. No one needed to tell him it was impossible, yet he saw it with his own eyes.

After that he'd checked on Pyrgus too. The problem wasn't quite as obvious there, since Pyrgus had already aged so much and further changes were far slower. But a careful comparison with his medical records showed his deterioration was continuing. Which meant only one thing. Stasis, their *only* reliable treatment for temporal fever, was no longer working.

He was negotiating stairways now, some of them so narrow they posed real difficulties for someone of his bulk – the original keep seemed to have been built by dwarves, and skinny dwarves at that. When he delivered the news to Madame Cardui, he planned to complain – and complain bitterly – about her choice of office. What was the point of it? he wondered. What was the point of making a difficult situation just that little bit worse?

He met up with guards at the end of the corridor, but fortunately they recognised him and let him pass. All the same, he wondered. It did seem strange that Madame Cardui would post guards at the approach to her office. Or perhaps it didn't. If the truth be told, Madame Cardui had always been a little ... paranoid. Such conditions tended to get worse with age.

He reached the door and pushed it open without knocking. When on an urgent mission it was always as well to emphasise the urgency right from the outset, otherwise people wasted time on inconsequentialities. Burst in, state the problem, make an impact, that was the way to ...

Madame Cardui was lying on the floor. A black-garbed figure was kneeling over her. It turned as Danaus entered and for just the barest instant he did not realise who it was. Then, 'Lord Hairstreak – what has happened?'

Hairstreak pushed something into the folds of his jacket. 'Your appearance is timely, Chief Wizard Healer,' he said sharply. 'Madame Cardui has collapsed.'

Danaus knelt quickly beside him. 'What exactly happened, Your Lordship?'

'We were discussing matters of state. The Spymaster was reclining on a suspensor cloud when she … lost consciousness. The cloud collapsed, but broke her fall – it's dissipated now.'

'When did this happen?' Danaus asked. He reached out to place a hand on her forehead.

'Just now. Moments ago – less than a minute, I think. I was about to raise the alarm when you arrived. Is she dead?'

Danaus shook his head. Her breathing was shallow, her colour bad, but she was definitely alive. For the moment.

'I was not sure what to do,' Hairstreak said.

'There was nothing you could do, Your Lordship,' Danaus told him. 'Madame Cardui is in the grip of temporal fever.'

And a stasis chamber would no longer halt its ravages.

Eighty-Eight

'Well,' said Loki cheerfully, 'can't stand here all day gossiping. I have to get this place prepared.'

He had subtly altered his appearance again: no longer the darkly attractive young man and not quite the clown, but something between the two that was far more disturbing than either. Still wrapped in the serpent's coils, Blue turned her head away and tried to think. *To make sure all goes well for you and Henry.* What did he mean by that? What did he know of Henry? What was he *really* doing here? She swallowed. 'This thing is hurting me,' she said.

Loki looked up at her and grinned. 'No, he's not. Gentle as a lamb, my boy. You just want him to put you down so you can escape.'

'I give you my word I won't,' Blue said. It was half true. She desperately needed to find out about Henry.

'Of course you will,' Loki said. 'I certainly would in your situation. But never fear. I'll have my Jorm set you down in a moment.' He smiled fondly at the massive serpent. 'That's what I call him, you know. My Jorm. So much more friendly than Jormungand, don't you think? His mother picked that name because of its size. She likes big names on account of being a giant herself.'

This was driving her out of her mind. Straightforward villains she could deal with – she'd been doing that all her life – but this absurd creature was so frustrating she would cheerfully have strangled him had her arms been free. But the serpent itself tolerated him and he even seemed to have control over it. The question was, how did she get control over him? How to trick the Trickster?

Loki said, 'Just let me make sure you keep your word ...'

The cavern was immense with many exit passageways leading out of it. Loki gestured. One by one the passageways sealed themselves like sphincters, then smoothed into blank cave walls. Blue watched, astonished. There was no smell of magic, no fizzle of a spell cone: it simply happened. Escape route after escape route was cut off until only two were left – the archway into the cavern that contained the blazing light and a narrow passage a little to her right. But even as she watched, an iron grille slid down to seal the archway. Blue shuddered. The metal was lethal to faeries.

Loki glanced at the one remaining open passage. 'For poor, dear Henry,' he said, smiling.

Blue snapped. 'What do you know about Henry?' she demanded. 'What are you doing here? Tell this brute to put me *down!*'

'Put her down, Jorm,' Loki said obediently.

To Blue's surprise, the serpent released her at once. She slid down its body to the floor while the creature itself uncoiled and relaxed. She half imagined she could hear it grunt. 'Thank you,' Blue said tightly. She brushed at her clothing to give herself something to do and time to think. Out of the corner of her eye she could see the Halek knife where she dropped it. The blade was clear again and had begun to sparkle. The weapon had recharged itself.

'Well now,' said Loki, 'time to get this place prepared. Dusting, cleaning, rearranging the ornaments – a Trickster's work is never done!' He stretched both arms towards the ceiling of the cavern and released a curious howling sigh. The contours of the cavern began to change.

'What are you doing?' Blue asked in sudden alarm. She was a little stiff from being held, but she calculated she could reach the knife in three, four steps. This time she wouldn't try to use it on the serpent.

'Creating a worthy setting,' Loki said benignly. 'Wouldn't want Henry to be disappointed when he gets here.'

He kept talking about Henry. The knife could wait. No more beating about the bush. Blue said, 'Henry is coming here?'

'Yes.'

'Why?'

Loki smiled charmingly. 'To rescue you.' He turned his back to her. 'Now, don't disturb me for a moment – miracles require concentration.' He spread his arms in an inverted V, hunched his shoulders and bowed his head. There was a curious, grating rumble as the rock of the cavern floor began to rearrange itself. In a moment, a granite platform appeared, which extruded a natural pillar about eight feet tall.

The massive serpent had withdrawn its coils. Loki was immobile, his attention firmly focused elsewhere. She was perhaps three quick paces from the knife. She could grab it and plunge the blade into his back before he realised what was happening.

She hesitated. The blade had not worked on the serpent. Would it fail on Loki too? If it did, her attempt on his life would achieve nothing and anger him. Would it perhaps be best to wait, to look for a better opportunity? A part of her was aware her inner dialogue was no more than a rationalisation. What was really staying her hand was something far more powerful than fear of failure. What was staying her hand was curiosity.

Heavy chains and manacles had appeared on the pillar. With a report like a thunderclap, a massive crack appeared in the cavern floor and lava oozed to form a sluggish, glowing stream that circled the entire platform.

Loki glanced over his shoulder. 'Impressive, would you not say?'

Blue said nothing. What was he *doing*? This was an entity with godlike powers and she had not the slightest idea why he was using them.

'Need to do something about the lighting,' Loki murmured. 'Not nearly dramatic enough.' He tipped his head backwards, directing his gaze towards the roof. A heavy curtain swung across the archway with the metal grille, cutting off the blaze of light and plunging the cavern into a deep gloom reddened by the glow of the lava stream.

'Niiiice!' breathed Loki. He made another gesture with his hands.

Blue felt the result before she actually heard it, a deep, subsonic vibration that gripped her bones, then swelled into a dull background organ note, packed with suspense and threat. The whole scene was beginning to turn into some ghastly stage production where good taste was sacrificed for the sake of melodrama.

'Now, Jormungand, my dear, you must look your part!'

There were no gestures from Loki this time, but Blue heard a curious slithering noise behind her and swung round just in time to see the massive serpent shrinking rapidly and changing form. For an instant her eyes could not take in what was happening – it seemed as if space itself distorted – then she was looking at a magnificent silver-grey scaled dragon. The creature was far smaller than the serpent, but still huge. It tilted back its head and breathed a plume of flame. Heat rolled over her like a wave.

'Ah, magnificent!' said Loki. He watched fondly as the dragon stomped across the cavern floor to take its place before the platform. It curled its great barbed tail and breathed another smoky plume. Loki turned. 'Now you, my dear.'

Blue had a moment of panic. There was something in his eyes she did not like. 'Just a min –'

He reached out his right hand, which extended then extruded a single razor-sharp claw. Before she could move, the claw was at her throat. 'You need to look the part as well,' he said and slashed downwards.

Blue jerked back, but there was no blood, no injury. The claw had not touched her body at all, but her blouse was in shreds. She gripped the remnants quickly to cover herself. At once she was on the platform, manacled to the granite pillar. Below her squatted the dragon. It turned to gaze at her with lizard eyes. Beyond it stood Loki, hands on hips as he surveyed his handiwork with tilted head. 'Perfect!' he exclaimed. 'The ideal damsel in distress.' He smiled at her. 'Now all we need to do is wait for Henry.'

Eighty-Nine

It occurred to Henry this was all a bit of a mess. The trouble was he hadn't planned anything – just took off looking for Blue without considering what sort of trouble she might be in (and he still didn't know) or, more importantly, what he might need to get her out of it. The question of weapons was sort of obvious now it had been pointed out to him, but he hadn't thought of it at all. Which meant he was stuck with a miserable flint blade and a hammer he'd left outside the cave because he couldn't even lift it.

But it didn't stop with weapons. He didn't have ropes or picks for climbing, he didn't have food beyond what Lorquin might be carrying in his pouch, and the last thing he'd thought of bringing with him was a light.

He'd really lucked out when he met the charno.

In the gloom of the cavern, Henry unwrapped the torch the charno had given him. It was a peculiar device of a type he'd never seen before, but there was a leaflet with written instructions wrapped around the shaft and its heading, *Perpetual Flame,* was reassuring. Unless that was just a trade name and the torch wouldn't really last forever. He hated the thought of getting stuck in the caves with no light at all.

Apart from the heading, the instructions were in tiny

writing, so he had to carry the leaflet back to the cave mouth in order to read it. The charno, still outside, stared at him curiously. Thankfully, there was no sign of Lorquin. Henry nodded and smiled weakly at the charno, then turned back to his leaflet. It was decorated with a drawing of the torch in use by a tall robed woman who reminded him of the Statue of Liberty. Irritatingly, most of the copy droned on about how wonderful the torch was without actually mentioning how to use it. The *Perpetual* business *was* a trade name, as it turned out, but at least the manufacturers claimed it would last 'several years' in normal use, which sounded unlikely, but not so unlikely as 'perpetual'.

He wondered what normal use was as he turned the leaflet over and finally found a buried paragraph headed *Instructions for Use*. The paragraph read:

LIGHTS AUTOMATICALLY IN DARKNESS.

Henry stared at the words, thinking that couldn't be right. The damn thing had been in total darkness in the charno's backpack, for example. Did that mean it was lit in there? Of course it didn't! It would have set the backpack on fire. Unless the drawing of the flaming torch was just a symbol and the torch didn't burn with a flame, but just generated light the way an electric torch would at home. But even that didn't make much sense because it would mean the thing was quietly running down every time you stowed it away in a box, or every night wherever it was, come to that. Hardly last several years under those conditions, would it?

He skimmed quickly through the rest of the leaflet, but there were no further instructions. He smiled weakly at the charno again and carried the torch back into the cave, where he held it aloft like the Statue of Liberty, but it still didn't light. Maybe he should ask the charno how it worked. But he didn't really want to do that: it would make him look stupid. *Lights automatically in darkness.* The thing was, it wasn't totally dark in the cave. Gloomy, yes, but not totally dark since he was still only a few yards away from the entrance.

There was a passageway leading downwards at the back of the cave.

Henry didn't really fancy walking into it without a light – there could be spiders or scorpions or bears in there – but if the torch wouldn't light except in total darkness ...

He stepped into the passageway and stopped. Then he held the torch high and waited. Nothing happened. He waited some more. Still nothing happened. Trust him to end up with an automatic torch that didn't work. Then, as his eyes adjusted, he realised the tunnel wasn't totally dark at all: it had only seemed that way when he first stepped into it. There was still light filtering in from the cave mouth. Actually, there was even enough light for him to see by. He could tell, for example, that the passageway ran downwards, then disappeared around a corner. He could also see what seemed to be some bones strewn across the floor.

Henry licked his lips. Maybe if he went deeper in, it would be dark enough.

Taking care not to kick the bones, he moved on. After a few hesitant paces, he turned the corner and fumbled his way a little further along. It was definitely getting darker here. In fact, he would have judged it to be absolutely, utterly, completely dark. He raised the torch again and waved it wildly. Still nothing happened.

He waited for his eyes to adjust again, but they didn't. The darkness pressed in on him like a velvet shroud. Should he go on? Henry had a vivid imagination and it presented him with a sudden, frightening picture. He was standing in the dark on the edge of a precipice. One more step and he would fall to his death. Fall to his death in the *total darkness,* bloody useless torch! Henry thought of Blue and took another step forward. He didn't fall to his death, but he did realise he couldn't go on like this much longer. There was no way he was going to find Blue underground in total darkness.

He reached out to feel the walls of his passage and discovered one of them had disappeared. The wall on the right was no longer there, or at least no longer within easy reach, which meant that the passage had widened, or opened into another cave (or fallen away into a precipice, his imagination told him) or otherwise changed the nature of his situation, almost certainly for the worse.

Henry froze and forced himself to think logically. Forget precipices and bears. While he knew he was in a passage, could feel he was in a passage, he could turn and feel his way back to the surface. But if the passage opened out into a cave and Henry stepped into that cave in pitch darkness and tried to explore that cave, *he might not be able to find his way back*. There might be other passages. He might get confused. Dammit, he *would* get confused – he knew what he was like. He would be lost in the darkness, unable to find his way out, forever.

Not much good to Blue then.

The sensible thing, the *only* sensible thing, was to retrace his steps while he still could. This wasn't abandoning Blue, not at all, wasn't even *thinking* of abandoning Blue. This was common sense. He would turn, retrace his steps, find his way back out of the cave *and ask the charno for another torch!* The charno was bound to have one. It had all sorts of rubbish in that backpack. It had just given him a duff torch, that was all. It had to have a backup. And if it didn't, maybe it would have a match, so he could light *this* torch and forget about the whole automatic bit. Retrace his steps, that was the thing.

In a moment of utter madness, Henry took one more step forward.

The torch in his hand flared fiercely, sending up a wave of heat that singed his hair. There were two faces only inches from his own, one looking down on him, the other looking up.

'Yipes!' Henry shrieked and jerked backwards. His heel caught on something and he fell, dropping the torch. It rolled across the rocky floor for a few feet, then stopped, but still burned brightly. In the flickering light he could see he had left his passageway and was lying on a broad ledge that overlooked another cavern. There were two *things* staring down at him. In utter panic, he tried to scramble away, scattering pebbles underneath his heels. Then he realised what the *things* were.

'What are you doing here?' shouted Henry furiously.

'I am your Companion, En Ri,' Lorquin said.

The charno, towering over him, nodded and said, 'That's right. He is your Companion.'

Henry scrambled to his feet. He'd skinned one elbow and his bottom hurt. 'I told you to go home!' he hissed at Lorquin. 'I thought you *had* gone home. This is dangerous. This is very dangerous.'

'That is why I must stay with you,' Lorquin said.

He wanted to strangle the kid. He wanted to hug the kid. What did you do with somebody like Lorquin? He simply didn't recognise the normal rules. In his frustration, Henry rounded on the charno. 'What are you doing here? I thought you would wait outside.'

The charno shrugged. 'Somebody has to carry your supplies.'

Henry knew when he was beaten. He picked up the torch. 'Okay,' he said, 'what now?'

They looked at him expectantly.

'You're the leader,' Lorquin said.

Ninety

Henry led from the middle, carrying his torch. The charno plodded after him, surprisingly quietly for a beast of its size, although the clicking of its claws on the rock floor was a bit of a distraction. Lorquin went ahead of them both, sniffing the air in an irritating manner.

'What are you doing that for?' Henry asked eventually.

'Smelling the trail, En Ri,' Lorquin explained.

Henry frowned. 'You never did that before.' Lorquin had taken him all over the desert, but it was all eyesight work: he had followed subtle signs.

'It is not possible in the open,' Lorquin said. 'The wind carries off the scent, the sun burns it up. But inside is different. Scent lingers.'

Henry stopped. This was an interesting development and might be an important one. 'What can you tell?'

Lorquin gave a small but eloquent shrug. 'Several people have passed this way before. Two men together, but that was some time ago. And with them something strange I have not smelled before. Then –'

'What sort of something strange?' Henry interrupted. 'An animal?'

'Perhaps,' Lorquin said. 'I'm not sure.'

'Go on,' Henry urged. 'What else?'

'Yes, what else?' said the charno, leaning over Henry's shoulder.

'More recently a woman; a young woman. She –'

Blue! It had to be Blue! How many more young women would you get wandering down here? 'Why didn't you tell me before?' Henry exploded.

'You asked me of other things, En Ri,' Lorquin said mildly.

'I want you to follow the woman's scent,' Henry said firmly in his leadership capacity. 'That's the one I want you to follow. You can forget about the others.'

'That was the one I have been following,' Lorquin said. 'I thought it might be Blue, the woman you seek.'

'Did she meet up with the others?' the charno asked. Which was a very sensible question and Henry wished he'd thought of asking it.

Lorquin shook his head. 'The trails are overlaid. If they met together, I have not found the place yet.'

'Keep going,' Henry told him.

Several minutes later, Henry said suddenly, 'We're going back the way we came.'

'As did she,' Lorquin said. 'I can follow the scent only where it takes me.'

'Yes, of course,' Henry muttered.

'He can follow the scent only where it takes him,' echoed the charno.

'Shut up,' said Henry. The truth of it was he was feeling hugely uncomfortable. He wasn't cut out for this. Lorquin, for all he was so young, was better equipped as a hero than Henry. He could follow trails, survive in the desert, find food when it was needed, kill draugrs ... Even the charno would make a better hero than Henry. At least it could lift the hammer. But Henry was the one who was supposed to rescue Blue. And from what? He really had no idea what he was getting into. The Midgard Serpent business sounded like nonsense. Some sort of tribal superstition. How could Blue have gotten herself involved with a giant snake? Except that everybody else seemed to take the idea seriously. An idea occurred to him and he said quickly, 'Lorquin, I don't suppose you can smell this Midgard thing?'

'The whole place reeks of it,' said Lorquin. He gave Henry a curious little smile. 'But we have not found the way to reach it yet.'

They set off again and, to Henry's intense irritation, the charno began to hum a little tune.

The scent trail led them to several dead ends where they were forced to backtrack. 'She could go no further,' Lorquin explained. But one blank passage proved different from the others. 'She went through here,' Lorquin said, frowning.

'She can't have – it's a dead end,' Henry said unnecessarily.

'Nonetheless, she went through here,' Lorquin said again. He moved forward to examine the rock face.

Henry moved forward with him. 'You mean there's been a rock fall or something?' It didn't look like a rock fall.

'There was no rock fall,' Lorquin confirmed. 'Yet she is in a cavern beyond this passage and she reached it through here.'

'How do you know –?' Henry began, then stopped himself. It didn't matter. If Lorquin said that's where Blue was, Henry believed it. He ran one hand over the cold surface of the rock. 'How do we reach her?' he asked instead.

'We have to find another way,' said Lorquin calmly and made off back down the passage.

It took him the better part of an hour, during which they searched through tunnels, passages, galleries, caves and caverns. Eventually he took several steps into a high-roofed, open passageway, then stopped and announced, 'This will take us to the cavern where they hold the girl.' He looked at Henry expectantly.

Lorquin expected him to tell them what to do and Henry didn't know. His heart was beating too fast and though it was cold here underground, beads of sweat had broken on his forehead. He licked his lips with a tongue that had suddenly gone dry. 'What happens if this passage is closed off at the end like the others?' he asked hoarsely.

'It isn't,' Lorquin said. 'The scents are too strong.'

'Scents?' Henry asked. 'There are more than one?'

For the first time since they met, Lorquin looked fleetingly impatient. 'The serpent and the girl you seek and –' He hesitated.

'And ...?' Henry echoed.

Lorquin frowned. 'There is one other and something beyond, but they are strange smells. One keeps changing.'

'Changing?' Henry echoed, a little wildly.

'If you don't hurry up, the serpent will have eaten her,' the charno remarked dourly.

Dour or not, the creature was right. Henry was fiddling about, acting the maggot, wasting time when Blue was probably in mortal danger. Pyrgus would have been better at this. *Anybody* would have been better at this. But there wasn't anybody. This one was all down to Henry. An odd thought occurred to him: he was about to meet his draugr.

Without another word, he pushed past Lorquin and trotted down the passage, torch held high.

Ninety-One

Somebody was playing an organ. It was stupid, but he could hear it, a sort of creepy, deep sonorous background note that rolled up the passageway towards him and chilled his blood. It put a sort of *Phantom of the Opera* picture in his head: a mad-looking masked man in evening dress pounding on a keyboard while he laughed insanely. Not that there was any laughter, or real music come to that, but the sound did it to you, made you see pictures in your head, made you feel very much afraid. He wanted to stop. He wanted to go back. He wanted to run and keep running until he emerged into the sunlight.

Henry pushed through his fear and kept going.

There was a light up ahead, a greenish, reddish glow that had the same feel as the organ note. It made you think of things that crawled through crypts or creatures from space that burst out of John Hurt's chest when you least expected it. The light and the organ note intertwined with each other to increase his fear, but he ignored it and kept on going.

Henry stepped out of the passage into a cavern illuminated by the creepy greenish, reddish glow. The organ-note sound swelled to a crescendo.

There was a dragon in the cavern.

The creature was as tall as a double-decker bus, but considerably longer, snout to tail. It was silver in colour with overlapping armoured scales. It looked like every dragon he'd seen in the picture books of his childhood, but without the cutesy quality the artists always managed to introduce. There was nothing cutesy about this monster, nothing at all. It was rippling muscle and reptile smells and savage teeth, vast jaws and cold, bleak eyes. The great head turned towards him, snorting smoke, and breathed a tiny plume of flame. It was far and away the most terrifying thing he had seen in his life. It was mind-numbingly, petrifyingly fearsome.

For a long moment Henry stood immobile, aware he should be running for his life but utterly unable to move a muscle. Then his eyes drifted of their own accord and he saw Blue.

She was chained to a pillar of stone on a raised platform just behind the dragon. Her blouse was ripped to shreds and there was a look of panic in her eyes.

'Henry, go back!' Blue shrieked. 'Run! Please run!'

Henry gaped at her. There was a narrow river of lava running round the platform, sending up shimmering waves of heat. There were beads of sweat on her forehead and the uppermost swell of her breasts. She twisted her body violently, jerking at her chains. 'Henry, get out of here! It will *kill* you!'

He suspected she was right. One of his hands had tightened involuntarily around the flint blade Lorquin had given him, but even if he'd been carrying a bazooka, he knew he was no match for the dragon. The creature was a biological killing machine, a mass of sinew, muscle, bone and blood with a hide beyond penetration. In a moment it would race across the cave floor and engulf him in a single bite.

The scene was like a fantasy magazine cover. A *lurid* magazine cover. The colouring was lurid: a leprous green illumination intermingled with the red glow from the lava. The silver dragon was lurid – it actually breathed fire, for cripe's sake! But most of all, Blue was lurid. Her clothing was ripped to give tantalising glimpses of her body. She was chained, abused, frightened, sweaty. She was heart-stoppingly beautiful and she was *sexy*. Everything inside the cavern looked ... contrived.

Henry became suddenly aware there was someone by his side and glanced down to find Lorquin had joined him. The boy was staring at the dragon with a look of awed delight. 'Kill it, En Ri,' he hissed in a whisper. 'I will back you up.'

And there it was, the moment where his entire life coalesced, the point of ultimate decision. Run or kill. Flee or fight. Save himself or save his love. Except that he could never save his love, not from that thing. There was no way he could kill it, no way he could even injure it.

But Lorquin thought he could.

'Stay here!' Henry snapped at Lorquin savagely, then ran towards the dragon.

Ninety-two

She saw him the moment he stepped into the cavern. He looked ragged and thin and deeply tanned, rangy, toughened up beyond anything she remembered. But he was alive! That was the great thing, the wonderful thing, the marvellous thing. Wherever he'd been, whatever had happened to him, Henry was alive!

The dragon swung its head to look at him.

Even at this distance she could see the fear in Henry's eyes, but there was determination too, so that perhaps the fear wasn't really fear but only wariness. She prayed it was fear, because if he was afraid he would run away and that meant he would save himself. She desperately wanted him to save himself. If he stayed, the dragon would tear him limb from limb. She couldn't bear to find that Henry was alive, then lose him to a dragon before ... before she had time ...

Before she had time to hold him.

Blue jerked violently at her chains. She'd no idea how she got here, chained to a pillar. Loki had done it, but she couldn't remember how. One instant she'd been talking to him, the next she was on the platform, manacled, like some sacrificial offering to the monster. It had to be Loki's magic, but it was a type of magic she had never seen before.

And Loki had disappeared.

She hadn't seen him go. When Henry arrived he was simply ... no longer there. She didn't know what Loki wanted either, why he'd done what he did. It was as if he'd set up this situation, then walked away, leaving things to play out as they pleased. None of it made sense, but the danger was real.

'Henry go back!' Blue shrieked. 'Run! Please run!' She twisted her body violently, jerking at the chains, and thought she felt one of the pillar attachments shift slightly. Whatever magic he was using, Loki hadn't done a very good job. If she struggled hard enough, she might be able to get free. But she wasn't free yet and Henry was still staring at her gormlessly. 'Henry, get out of here! It will *kill* you!'

A small blue-skinned boy emerged from the shadows to stand by Henry's side. Blue had no idea who he was or where he had come from. She had never seen blue skin before, but she vaguely recalled the Arcond mentioning that there were races of that colour in the deep desert of Buthner. She wondered what the child was doing with Henry. Strangely enough, he didn't seem at all frightened, even though he was looking at the dragon.

Something else loomed behind them both and for an instant Blue wondered what new monster Loki had conjured up. Then she recognised the charno. It must have followed Henry into the caverns, Henry and the strange blue boy.

Unless, a voice whispered in her mind, *that's Loki up to his shape-shifting tricks again. He fooled you into thinking he was the charno before.* Blue jerked her chains again. Loki or the real charno – it didn't matter.

All that mattered was getting Henry out of here, getting him to safety. The boy's lips moved as he said something to Henry that Blue couldn't hear. Blue opened her mouth to shout again. Henry called, 'Stay here!' and, to her horror, ran towards the dragon.

The dragon roared.

Ninety-Three

The dragon roared and lunged towards him. Henry dodged to one side and brandished the flint blade Lorquin had given him. He had no hope of killing the beast with such a weapon, but he thought he might distract it long enough to give Blue a chance to break free. He might even be able to frighten it a little, the way wasps frightened people by stinging them when they came too close to the nest. Lorquin's flint knife might sting the dragon, make it think twice about attacking.

He dodged under the dragon's head and stabbed at its front leg. Lorquin's knife struck a scale and snapped off in Henry's hand.

From the corner of his eye, Henry saw a flash of blue as Lorquin ran into the cavern. Henry's heart sank. Was there no way to make the boy do what he was told? He was only a child, whatever he thought about himself, but he seemed prepared to tackle anything. *Anything!* Anything for his Companion ... Henry felt a lump in his throat. He doubted he could live with himself if anything happened to Lorquin. But then again, he might not have to. Short of a miracle, they would all be dead in minutes: Lorquin, Blue, Henry himself.

He threw away the useless piece of knife and dodged again as the dragon struck out with a viciously clawed front foot. The brute was enormous, stronger and more powerful than any wild animal he'd ever seen in his own world, but like many huge beasts, it was slow. No, not slow: thinking of it as slow might be a fatal mistake. But it was awkward in certain of its movements. Clearly it was not used to fighting tiny, darting enemies like himself. Maybe that was something he could turn to his advantage.

The claws missed and the dragon's momentum carried it right over Henry, its silver-grey bulk looming above him like a passing jumbo jet. Next moment he was out from under and watching the dragon charge at something he could not see. Then he heard a familiar voice and realised Lorquin was taunting the beast, diverting it.

Henry felt a pang of guilt, but there was nothing he could do to help the boy. Better to accept his courage and try to take advantage of his action. Perhaps while the dragon's attention was elsewhere, Henry could reach Blue and get her free. He spun round, ran for the platform, then pulled up short at the lava stream.

It flowed around the platform like a moat. It wasn't particularly wide. He could probably have jumped it if there were a space for him to land on the other side. But there was no space, just the steep side of the stone platform, and the platform itself was just a little too high to be reached in a running leap. Blue could jump down and clear the lava stream, but Henry could never jump *up*.

'Blue!' he called helplessly.

She was jerking at her chains like a mad thing and now, close up, he could see their fittings to the pillar seemed to be working loose. Small puffs of dust rose every time she pulled. There was a sound behind him and the whole floor beneath his feet vibrated. Blue stopped struggling, turned, then pointed. Henry spun round to find the dragon bearing down on him again like some monstrous express train.

For a heartbeat he assumed Blue was pointing at the beast; then he saw the Halek knife. The crystal blade was lying only yards away from him, its surface swimming with trapped energies.

Henry had never used a Halek knife before, but Pyrgus had told him all about them. They were specially made, in limited editions, by Haleklind wizards who guaranteed them to kill anything, anything at all. You stabbed with the knife and if the blade didn't shatter, the energies flowed into whatever it was you'd stabbed, killing it instantly. You couldn't graze with a Halek knife, couldn't wound. You could only kill. Anything.

You could kill a dragon!

Henry swooped on the Halek knife as the monster thundered towards him. There was only one problem with these knives: if the blade shattered, the energies poured back into the person using it, killing *him*. Pyrgus talked about that all the time. But Henry didn't care. The knife could kill the dragon. He could kill the dragon and save Blue.

Instead of running or dodging, Henry stood his ground.

The dragon was almost on top of him.

Ninety-four

'Henry!' Blue screamed. He was standing like an idiot with that stupid Halek knife glinting in his hand. The dragon was almost on top of him and he was just standing there, waiting.

Blue realised abruptly what was happening. Henry thought the Halek knife could kill the dragon. Pyrgus was always going on about Halek knives and how amazing they were – he had a real thing about them. For certain he'd talked to Henry about them at some time and now Henry had one in his hand. He couldn't know the knife was worthless against this creature. He hadn't been there when she'd tried to use it herself.

A horrible suspicion occurred to her. The dragon's scales were as hard as flint. She'd been lucky when she'd tried to use the knife on it before, while it was an unarmoured serpent: the blade hadn't shattered then. But that sort of luck never held and if the knife shattered now, Henry was dead for sure. Her mind laid out a picture of the dragon feeding from his body.

'Henry!' Blue screamed again. She jerked against her chains with manic violence and the fittings suddenly gave way.

Blue found herself off balance, teetering on the edge of the platform, staring down at the lava river below.

The chains ran through the loops of her manacles with a high metallic sound; then she was free, still fighting for her balance, still staring down into the lava. Her arms flailed in a desperate attempt to save herself; then she knew it was too late, knew she must fall.

Blue bent her knees and pushed off with all her strength from the very edge of the platform. Her leap carried her across the lava river, if only just, and she landed in a squatting position on the far side. Her whole body jarred and she thought she might have twisted her ankle, but there was no time to worry about that now. Ahead of her, the dragon was almost on top of Henry, who was standing, feet firmly planted, facing the beast like a warrior king.

'Henry!' Blue shouted a third time and sprinted towards him.

Ninety-five

From behind, Henry thought he heard someone call his name, but there was no time to look round, no time for anything except the monster thundering towards him. He raised the Halek knife.

The real trick would be to get out of the way when the dragon fell. The weight of the beast could crush him like a gnat if it came down on top of him. From everything Pyrgus said about Halek knives, death would be instantaneous, but the dragon's momentum would carry it forward. So Henry couldn't be in front of it when death occurred. He needed to step aside, needed to stab and kill and let the dying body thunder past. Then he needed to jump back so the reptile corpse didn't roll on top of him.

A movement at the corner of his eye distracted him momentarily. He risked a glance and discovered that, incredibly, the charno was plodding resignedly across the cavern floor. It was the strangest beast he'd ever known. What did it think it was doing? But no time for that now. The dragon, still charging, had lowered its head and Henry suddenly realised the massive flaw in his plan. If the monster breathed fire now, he would be a charred potato chip in seconds. No weapon, not even the mighty Halek knife, could save him.

But the dragon didn't breathe fire. Instead the massive jaws opened to engulf him. Henry stared directly into the creature's mouth, ringed with huge serrated teeth, a tiny flame flickering perpetually at the back of its throat. He waited until he could smell the stench of methane breath, until the floor beneath his feet was shaking from the onrush of the charging beast, then stepped gracefully to one side and raised the Halek knife.

'Henry!' Blue was at his side, gripping his wrist, jerking his arm, knocking him off balance so that his knife thrust missed the dragon completely and he fell – they both fell – in a heap as the creature rushed past.

'What are you *doing?*' Henry demanded as he fought to extricate himself from her grasp.

'Halek won't work,' Blue gasped as they were climbing to their feet.

'Hammer's the only thing will work,' the charno said and dropped the huge war hammer at their feet.

'I can't *lift* the bloody hammer!' Henry screamed at it.

There was a roar that shook his bones, a horrid scrambling of talons on stone. He swung round to find the dragon had turned, ready for another charge.

'The Halek knife's no good against it!' Blue shouted in his ear.

They were together now. At least they would die together. Along with the charno, probably. From somewhere to his left he caught a flash of blue. Lorquin was trying to join in the action. Lorquin would die too. All of them, all dead.

The dragon pawed the floor like a bull.

'Why don't you use the hammer?' Henry yelled at the

charno. The charno had carried the weapon here and seemed able to wave it around like a feather.

'Don't be stupid,' said the charno.

This was such a mess! Such a God-awful, lethal, Henry style of mess, like his whole miserable life. Mother and father in the process of divorce ... no idea where he was going or what he should be doing ... the girl he loved about to die because he couldn't save her ...

'I can't even lift the hammer,' Henry said to Blue plaintively.

'I know,' Blue said. 'I couldn't lift it either.'

The dragon charged.

Blue said, 'Maybe we could lift it *together*.'

Lorquin ran at the dragon from the side, wielding exactly the same sort of crude flint blade as the one Henry had already broken.

Blue and Henry swooped on the war hammer lying on the floor. Their hands reached out together, gripped the shaft together. They lifted the war hammer easily, swung it above their heads. Lorquin jumped astride the dragon's tail and stabbed down with his blade, which shattered against the armoured scales exactly as Henry's had done. The dragon didn't even seem to notice. It was only yards away now. Its head darted forward, neck stretched. Its mouth gaped like a fiery cavern. Blue and Henry swung the hammer.

The weapon connected with the dragon's snout and exploded in a shower of sparks. There was the most curious ripping sound Henry had ever heard. The platform and the lava stream both vanished. Light poured through an archway into the cavern. The dragon transformed for an instant into a gigantic serpent that seemed miraculously to fill the world, then disappeared. Lorquin, who'd been riding on the tail, fell to the ground, but bounded up at once, grinning broadly.

'You did it, En Ri!' he called excitedly. 'You slew the dragon!'

'I think we sent it home,' said Blue.

Ninety-Six

Henry couldn't keep his hands off her. He hugged her, kissed her cheek, kissed her nose, hugged her again. He slipped off his jacket and wrapped it round her to cover up the torn blouse. Then his emotions overcame him and he hugged her a third time. Blue didn't seem to mind. 'Nice to see you too,' she murmured with a little smile.

Henry did an odd thing. With his arm around her waist, he led her over to the small blue boy and made a formal introduction: 'Lorquin, this is Prin— this is Queen Blue of the Faerie Realm. Blue, this is Lorquin.' He hesitated for a heartbeat before adding, 'My Companion.'

The boy looked pleased, and bowed. Sensing something important was going on here, Blue bowed back.

Henry glanced towards the platform and the pillar. 'How did it happen? The dragon and everything?'

'Long story,' Blue said. 'I was looking for you.'

'I was looking for *you!*' Henry grinned happily. He felt like an idiot, but a happy idiot. It was a long time since he'd felt so happy. He hugged her again.

Blue said, 'You'll squish me, Henry.' But she was smiling and it didn't seem like an invitation to stop, so Henry kissed her. She closed her eyes and kissed him back.

'We faced a *dragon!*' he murmured when they stopped. Blue's smile broadened.

'We all need to go home,' the charno said. It gave a long, slow blink of its huge brown eyes and added, 'If you two have finished smooching.'

'Can you find our way out?' Henry asked Lorquin.

'He may not have to,' Blue said, glancing towards the archway. 'That looks like sunlight.'

'Oh, yes,' said Henry, wondering vaguely why he hadn't thought of that. He felt high, as if his feet were floating inches off the ground. He slid his arm from around her waist and ran across the cavern to find out the source of the light. He stepped through the archway and stopped. He backed away a pace and stopped. His jaw dropped.

'Good God!' Henry whispered.

Blue joined him within seconds, then Lorquin. All three stood in the archway staring into the light.

After a long moment, Blue said hoarsely, 'What is it, Henry?'

'It's an angel,' Henry said.

Ninety-Seven

Henry felt like an iron filing in the presence of a magnet. He was frightened, but he took a small step forward. The others must have felt the same, for they moved blankly alongside him. The creature in the cage was like nothing he'd ever seen before. It had the shape of a man, but far taller – nearly eight feet – so that it stooped to fit into the cage. It was muscled like a human torso, but there any resemblance ended.

The angel shone. Every square inch of its skin fluoresced the way things did under ultraviolet light. But beyond that, it glowed like some gigantic lamp, emitting a dense white light that hurt the eyes if you looked at it too long. But even that was not the strangest thing. The strangest thing was its wings.

Henry had seen angel wings before, lots of them. His books were full of them when he studied History of Art and he'd even seen them carved in marble that time his mother dragged the family on a cultural tour of Britain's cathedrals. But those wings were nothing like these. The artists and sculptors had all visualised great white feathered birdy things, as if angels had the shoulder muscles to fly like an eagle. The wings Henry was looking at now were nothing like that. They weren't feathered and they weren't even white. In fact, in a peculiar way, they didn't seem to be there at all.

Henry blinked. The angel's wings stretched out behind him in shimmering fans of radiant energy that sparkled violet and writhed like the aurora borealis. They were probably the most beautiful things he had ever seen in his life. He'd never been a particularly religious boy, but there was something about those wings that made him want to fall down on his knees and worship.

Blue took another step forward with Lorquin at her side and Henry's urge to worship suddenly evaporated. 'Careful!' he hissed in the sort of whisper you always felt you had to use inside a church. Then, when they took no notice, he said sharply and more loudly, 'Don't get too close!' His stomach had knotted. For some reason he was convinced the angel was every bit as dangerous as the dragon.

Blue ignored him as usual. She had a curiously vacant smile on her face and her eyes were wide. Lorquin looked even more peculiar. His face was ecstatic, but his eyes were utterly blank. Together they took another step forward so that now they were no more than a few feet from the cage.

The angel moved its position and the sweep of energy from those weird wings flowed outward to envelop Blue and Lorquin.

'Blue!' Henry shouted in sudden alarm.

Blue changed. Henry watched it happen. In an eye blink she was a mature woman, her hair streaked with grey, the first clear signs of furrows on her brow. Then just as suddenly she was old – not old the way Pyrgus was old when Henry saw him on Mr Fogarty's lawn, but *really* old, like Mr Fogarty himself or Madame Cardui. She still stood upright and there was the familiar hint of arrogance in the tilt of her head, but otherwise she was hardly recognisable.

'Blue!' Henry screamed again.

The change in Lorquin was, if anything, even more spectacular. He looked across at Henry and gave his bright, familiar smile. But it was a smile on the face of a man now, handsome, tall and broad and proud. It was the smile of a hero who had fought hard and seen much.

Then the wings swept back and folded and suddenly Blue was Blue again and Lorquin was a boy.

Henry heard his own voice shout, 'Don't go near the cage!'

Blue said quietly, 'We must release him – he's in pain.'

Of course the angel was in pain. He'd been confined in this cage – in this *reality* – unable to stand upright for *weeks*. But worse was the magic Brimstone had used to confine him: it burned the angel's body like hot irons. Henry knew all this, but he didn't know how he knew.

The angel turned its head and looked deep into his eyes.

'We must release him,' Blue said again.

The angel was *talking* to Henry, but talking without words. It was the strangest sensation, intimate and warm, like being with somebody and discovering you were in love. No wonder these creatures had been worshipped. Knowledge flowed from the angel's mind into Henry's own. No wonder they had been called Messengers.

Blue made to move forward again, but this time Henry was too quick for her. He darted forward and grabbed her arm. 'If you go any closer, it will kill you,' he said soberly.

Blue looked at him blankly, then looked at the angel. 'He wouldn't harm me,' she said, a little dreamily.

'He doesn't want to,' Henry told her. 'But he shouldn't *be* in this reality. He distorts it, changes the flow of time. It's worse when he moves those wings – they send currents out across the whole Realm – but if you get too close, it doesn't matter whether he's moving or not. Just being *near* him will kill you.'

The dreamy look vanished from Blue's face. 'How are we going to free him?' she asked.

'*We're* not going to free him,' Henry said. '*I* am.'

Blue caught on at once. 'It won't affect you because you're from the Analogue World? This isn't your reality, so you can get close to him without it killing you?'

Henry took a deep breath. 'I think so.' He hoped to heaven Blue would leave it at that, not ask any more questions.

'Are you sure?' Blue asked.

Henry let go of her arm. 'Only one way to find out,' he said. And walked towards the cage.

Ninety-Eight

Chief Wizard Healer Danaus frowned. He was looking down on the frozen body of the Forest Princess Nymphalis, locked in stasis beside the body of her husband, Prince Pyrgus. Both showed the age ravages of temporal fever, Pyrgus more than Nymph so far – since stasis ceased to hold the fever, he had turned into an old, old man – but Nymph certainly. From a young woman she had transformed into a mature woman, a middle-aged woman really, and he had been vaguely considering increasing the intensity of the stasis field. Not that he believed it would do any good – you were either in stasis or you weren't – but he disliked the feeling of helplessness that came when there was absolutely nothing one could do. Thus he stood staring at Nymphalis and ... and she looked a little younger.

Which was impossible, of course. The temporal fever was a one-way trip. Even when stasis still stabilised it, *nothing* reversed the effect. So possibly he was imagining it. Wishful thinking sometimes had an influence on observation, even *trained* observation. All the same, he couldn't rid himself of the feeling she seemed younger. Her skin tone looked better. He could have sworn there were fewer, if only just a *little* fewer, wrinkles.

On impulse, Danaus stepped across to the stasis

cabinet that held Pyrgus. The shock was so great that he actually gasped aloud. Pyrgus too looked younger, a *lot* younger. There was no possibility of a mistake. The effects of the fever were reversing.

For once Danaus forgot his dignity and ran down to the wards. But even before he reached them, the commotion told him something dramatic was happening. As he burst into the corridor nurses were scampering in all directions, healers were hurrying to and fro, but most astonishing, most amazing, most bewildering of all was the fact that patients were on their feet as well, patients who just that morning on his rounds had been lying in deep comas.

Danaus grabbed the arm of a blue-coated healer as he hurried past. 'What's going on?' he demanded.

'Spontaneous remissions,' the healer told him shortly.

It was the sort of stupid thing they'd all been trained to say when they had no idea what was actually happening. 'I can see that,' Danaus snapped. 'What's caused them?'

The healer shook his head. 'Don't know, sir.' Then, annoyingly, he smiled. 'But it's great news, is it not, sir?'

Great news but bewildering. By the time Danaus had made a few cursory examinations to convince himself the effect was genuine, reports were pouring in from outside of "spontaneous remissions" throughout the capital city. He had not the slightest doubt that similar news from the surrounding country would be arriving soon.

With so many patients suddenly recovering, the administration burden was heavy and it was late afternoon before he suddenly remembered Nymph and Pyrgus were still in stasis. And hot on the heels of that realisation came another: Madame Cardui was in stasis too.

He'd had her placed there as a matter of course for a woman her age even though all the evidence was it would no longer hold back her disease. What else could he do? Stasis might have staved off her inevitable death for a few more hours. Or she might be dead already.

Or possibly she'd undergone a spontaneous remission like all the rest.

He was on his way to find out when someone told him Queen Blue had returned to the Purple Palace.

Ninety-Nine

It was raining, of course. Since he'd inherited Burgundy's old Keep, Lord Hairstreak had found it more economical to leave the weather spells in place than have them neutralised. So the Keep remained exactly as it had been when Hamearis was alive: a Gothic nightmare clinging to a cliff edge, buffeted by breakers and lashed by heavy rain and howling winds.

No matter. It suited his mood.

Hairstreak climbed out onto the battlements, wrapping his cloak around him. From this vantage point, he could see the approach road and the angry sea. There were no ouklos, no carriages of any sort. There were no boats, no flyers overhead. No one visited now. If they had, there were no servants to greet them.

The chill insinuated itself inside his cloak, but he ignored it. Where, he wondered, had it all gone wrong? It seemed such a very short time ago since the whole world and its potential had stretched endlessly before him. His sister married to the Purple Emperor. His followers solidly behind him. It had seemed only a matter of time – and a short time at that – before the Faeries of the Night took control of the Realm, with himself at their head.

How different things looked now. His brother-in-law,

Apatura Iris, the old Purple Emperor, dead, resurrected and dead again. His daughter on the throne. Hairstreak's old demon ally, Beleth, dead as well and Blue now Queen of Hael. All the old alliances and arrangements in tatters. The Lighters more firmly in control than they'd been for centuries. How had it all gone so horribly wrong?

His hands reached out to grip the stonework of the battlements. Where, he wondered, had his money gone? Oh, it was simplistic to say that with Beleth dead his major source of income disappeared as well. But where were his properties, his reserves, his massive lines of credit?

The plain fact was that maintaining a political presence was ruinously expensive. The bribes alone were crippling, and if one did not keep up appearances, no one took you seriously. So in a frighteningly short space of time, his reserves had shrunk, his properties sold off or repossessed, his lines of credit dried up. And with them went his so-called friends, although that was no surprise. He'd never been under illusions about any of them. Ultimately, he'd relied on no one but himself.

He still thought his last scheme had been a good one. Lighters ... Nighters ... men of means always wanted servants and always would: the cheaper the better, which was why demon service was so appealing. One payment and you had a slave for life. He could never understand why the arrangement had never really caught on with the Lighters – they were quick enough to abandon their religion in other areas when it suited them. But the new scheme was even better! How could anybody object to angels?

Where did it all go wrong?

He stepped closer to the edge and felt the wind pluck at him like giant fingers. He felt, as he had felt so often in the past, a little angry, a little resentful, greatly disappointed, but most of all confused and weary to the bone.

How had it all gone wrong?

Lord Hairstreak stepped from the battlements and launched himself towards the cliffs below. As he fell, the wind spread his cloak so that he looked for all the world like a giant bat.

One hundred

The conclave took place in the Throne Room, an interesting choice since it meant Blue was prepared to accept that word of any decisions made would quickly leak through the Palace and from there, more quickly still, into a waiting world.

Madame Cardui looked from face to face. Of them all, Blue actually looked a little older, a young woman now, rather than a girl, calm enough by all appearances, but perhaps a little worn by her experiences. Beside her sat Henry. Except for the tan and a little weight loss, his appearance was much as it always had been, but his manner was different. He seemed far more at ease with himself, more confident, more – what was that Analogue expression? – laid back. He still didn't say a great deal, but his eyes moved a lot and you had the impression they missed very little.

Comma seemed watchful too, but at the same time pleasantly relaxed. He'd carried out his duties with dignity and surrendered the throne without fuss when his sister returned. Among the others, Nymph looked as Nymph had always looked: serene, confident and beautiful. All traces of the temporal fever were gone and it was as if she'd never been ill a day in her life. Pyrgus actually looked younger, as if his disease had gone into reverse but then hadn't stopped where it started. Madame Cardui gave him the barest ghost of a smile. All that was probably her imagination, of course, but really he sat there like a boy again ... and like his father as a boy. Strange how the years went around, even without the aid of temporal fever.

Although normally not included in a meeting of this type, Danaus was present as well. He looked as he always looked: tall, overweight, overbearing, full of his own importance, trustworthy and competent. His work on the fever had earned him his place here now: he deserved to be told directly what it had all been about.

The one notable absentee, Madame Cardui noted with a wave of almost inexpressible sorrow, was Alan. His advice would be sorely missed. She wondered briefly who Blue would appoint as her new Gatekeeper. No obvious candidate sprang to mind.

The great doors of the Throne Room closed and eyes turned expectantly to Blue. It was Hairstreak, Madame Cardui thought – she was sure of that – but how or why she did not know.

'It was my uncle,' Blue said without preliminary, as if reading Madame Cardui's thoughts.

Frowning, Danaus said, 'He caused the temporal fever?'

Blue nodded. 'He was the cause, yes.'

'It was some sort of weapon, I assume, deeah?' Madame Cardui asked. 'Warfare by disease? He planned to use it to weaken your position?'

But Blue shook her head. 'He didn't plan any of it, not the fever, not warfare. No coup, or anything of that sort. The spread of the fever was a side effect of his actual plans.'

'You really are annoying, Blue,' Pyrgus said impatiently. 'Why don't you just tell us what happened without dragging it all out?'

Blue suppressed a smile and said imperiously, 'Very well. You know how much money and influence our uncle lost when I became Queen of Hael ...?'

Pyrgus said, 'You're talking about the slave trade? The way he used to make money off demon servants?'

'That's exactly what I'm talking about. He tried to recoup his fortunes by reviving the trade.'

This time it was Pyrgus who frowned. 'But he couldn't. You'd never let him use demons the way Beleth did.'

'Not demons,' Blue said. 'Angels.'

There was absolute silence in the Throne Room for almost fifteen heartbeats; then Madame Cardui said, 'You can't be serious, deeah.'

'Completely,' Blue said soberly. 'Hairstreak commissioned our old friend Brimstone to evoke and trap an angel – Brimstone was an extremely skilful diabolist, you'll recall. I don't know exactly how he did it, but he managed the commission. The idea was that once a successful method of evocation was in place and Brimstone demonstrated he could hold an angel captive, Hairstreak would start capturing angels on a commercial scale, then hire them out as servants – essentially slaves. Angels are extremely powerful, as you know – far more so than demons. The potential for such an enterprise ...' She shrugged. 'Well, among the unscrupulous, it's gigantic.'

'A moment, Your Majesty,' Danaus put in formally. 'What has this to do with temporal fever?'

'It was the direct cause, Chief Wizard Healer,' Blue said. 'As you know, Haven is a great deal further from the Faerie Realm than Hael. Brimstone's brutal capture of even a single angel placed an enormous strain on the fabric of our reality. Very soon people began to experience this as time slippage – what we called temporal fever and thought of as a disease. But it wasn't a disease, not really. It was the way our reality was being distorted.'

Danaus looked appalled. 'Why on earth didn't this Brimstone person release the angel when he discovered what was happening? Why didn't Lord Hairstreak make him?'

'They didn't know,' Blue said. 'Neither of them. They thought temporal fever was a disease, just like the rest of us. I doubt any of us would have found out the truth if there hadn't been –' she glanced briefly at Henry '– an intervention.'

'What sort of intervention?' Pyrgus asked curiously.

'That doesn't matter,' Blue said firmly. 'What matters is that the angel has been released, our reality is returning to normal and the effects – the temporal fever, as we called it – are dying out.'

For a moment, Pyrgus looked as though he might try to push her for more information, but when he spoke again he said only, 'What do we do about Uncle Hairstreak and Brimstone?'

'Nothing,' Blue said.

Madame Cardui raised an eyebrow. 'Nothing?'

'Brimstone is insane,' Blue said bluntly. 'He will be no further trouble to us. My uncle ... well, doubtless he *will* be trouble if he gets the chance, but as things stand at the moment, he has failed abysmally to improve his position and any move we make against him might well provoke some sympathy for him among the Faeries of the Night.'

Madame Cardui watched her admiringly. The girl was learning some real political skills at last.

Blue stood up abruptly. 'There may be another important announcement later,' she said firmly, 'but for the moment I think that's all I have to tell you.'

One Hundred and One

The sound of the water was overlaid by distant street noise from the city: the rumble of carts, the occasional call from a merchant. The city came alive at night in ways it never did during the day. Henry was sitting with Blue on a bench beside the river, half hidden by a mimosa bush. They were holding hands.

'What was the important announcement you mentioned?' he asked her. 'The one you said you might make later?'

'I don't know,' Blue said. 'Why don't you tell me?'

Henry looked at her blankly and Blue looked away.

After a while, Henry said, 'It seemed staged somehow.'

He was thinking of their adventure with the dragon and Blue seemed instinctively to know this. 'It *was* staged,' she said. 'By one of the Old Gods.'

'Why?' asked Henry mildly. He looked out across the river, aware they were talking about this because he still was not quite ready to talk about what was really on his mind.

'I think to help heal our reality,' Blue said. She hesitated, then added, 'And to make sure our stories followed the proper form.'

'Whose stories?'

'Ours,' Blue said. 'Yours and mine.'

There was a wading bird in the shallows of the river.

At first Henry didn't recognise it – then the curve of the beak brought to mind a picture he'd once seen in a book on Egypt and he realised it was an ibis.

'I didn't understand that,' he said to Blue.

'A priest once told me the Old Gods believe that mortal lives are lived to act out certain stories. Sometimes they intervene to make sure the stories turn out the way they should – they way they were fated to, I suppose.'

'So we weren't really in danger from the dragon?' Henry said. 'It was just a story – like a play on stage?'

'The dragon could have killed you,' Blue said soberly. 'I don't know what it would have done to me. The stories are real: they're the patterns of the ways we lead our lives. Some of them end in tragedy. Like you being eaten by a dragon.' She smiled slightly. 'But you were brave, so it didn't happen.'

They sat in silence for a long time after that. Then Henry said, 'Blue?'

'Yes, Henry?'

'Do you remember the last time we walked here by the river?'

Blue nodded. 'Yes, I do.'

'Do you remember what you said to me?'

Blue nodded again. 'Yes, I do.'

Henry licked his lips. He was aware of the sudden pounding of his heart and hoped it wasn't noticeable to Blue. He took a deep breath. 'You asked me to marry you.'

'I was very young then,' Blue said without inflection.

He felt something deflate inside him. But he'd gone too far to stop now. Besides, what was he afraid of? He'd faced a dragon, hadn't he? He licked his lips again. 'Do you still want to?' he asked.

There was silence broken by the lapping of the water.

After a long time Blue said, 'It doesn't matter what I want, does it? Not really. You have a life in the Analogue World.'

'I don't like it very much,' said Henry. 'I don't want to be a teacher.'

'What about your parents?' Blue asked mildly. She was staring out across the water and had let go of his hand.

'Mum has Anaïs,' Henry said. 'Dad's gone – I don't even see that much of him. He's living with his girlfriend and making a whole new life for himself and he's happy. At least I think he is. At least he doesn't have Mum telling him what to do all the time.' Henry tried to reach for her hand again, but she drew it away gently. All the same, he went on earnestly. 'But that isn't the point, is it? I'm going to be gone myself soon – I mean, even if I stay in the Analogue World, I'm going to be gone soon. I'd go to university or teacher training and there's not one nearby, so I'd have to board. I'd hardly see them, either of them. Then after that, I'd have my own life as a teacher or whatever. You grow up, you leave home: that's the way it is. If I stayed here it would be just the same as if I married an Analogue girl and bought a semi-detached somewhere.'

She still wasn't looking at him, but he thought he caught the ghost of a smile on her lips. 'Not *quite* the same,' she said. 'Where would you tell them you'd gone?'

Henry blinked. 'How do you mean?'

'Fairyland?' Blue said, one eyebrow raised. She'd obviously picked up the term somewhere and knew its connotations.

'I thought I might do what Mr Fogarty did and pretend I planned to emigrate – New Zealand or Australia or somewhere. Somewhere far.' He drew a deep breath. 'I thought there might be some sort of spell cone I could use to help them accept it.'

'My,' said Blue, 'you *have* been working things out.' She gave him a quick, sidelong glance. 'What about your education?'

'I could finish that off here,' Henry said. 'It would be a lot more interesting.' He waited, staring at her. When she said nothing more, he asked, 'Well, do you?'

'Do I what?'

'Still want to marry me?'

Blue turned to look at him directly. 'Are you asking me to marry you, Henry Atherton?'

'Yes,' Henry said impatiently. 'Yes, I am.'

'Why?' Blue asked.

'Because I love you,' Henry said.

Blue looked away again. 'I can't marry a commoner.'

'What?'

'I can't marry a commoner,' Blue said again. 'I'm Queen of Faerie, Queen of Hael. I can't marry a commoner.' She turned back to him and now she was smiling broadly. 'I'll have to make you a Faeric Lord.'

Henry was staring at her in disbelief. 'You mean you *will* marry me?'

'In a heartbeat, Henry,' Blue said softly.

He kissed her after that.

One hundred and Two

There was fresh gravel on the streets and banners hung from every house. Henry couldn't believe the crowds that lined the streets. He waved through the window of the ouklo, the way the Queen did in London on a State occasion. The cheering never stopped, not for an instant, as the carriage carried him towards the great cathedral. His heart was thumping so hard he wondered if it would survive the ceremony.

The carriage sank down slowly onto the cathedral courtyard, a footman opened the door with a flourish and Henry stepped out. He'd been here once before, for Pyrgus's coronation, and the scene wasn't all that different. The cathedral itself towered above the soldiers on parade, the courtiers, the waiting crowds. It was a gigantic building, much larger than anything he'd ever seen at home, yet the architecture was a lacelike filigree that could be supported only by magic. Or perhaps divine intervention, Henry thought in passing. Now he'd seen an angel with his own two eyes, he was prepared to believe anything was possible.

Pyrgus was walking towards him, grinning broadly. He was dressed in some elaborate naval uniform that presumably went with one of his titles. He shook Henry's hand, then hugged him, patting his back furiously. 'You dog,' Pyrgus murmured. 'You old dog.'

'Is she here?' Henry whispered. There was a part of him that knew this simply wasn't happening, or if it was, it was too good to be true. He wished Lorquin was with him for moral support, but Lorquin was back with his tribe now and would have been totally bewildered by what was happening here anyway. So Henry had to face this all alone, afraid Blue wouldn't turn up, or she'd turn out to be already married, or something else would go wrong. There was no way Henry would *actually* get married, not to a Faerie Princess, not to Blue.

'Not yet,' Pyrgus whispered back. 'She mustn't come until you're in your place. The Royal Barge is moored at Cheapside, but they'll send off a signal now you're here.'

If it hadn't been for Pyrgus, Henry would never have found his way into the cathedral. As it was, he had only a confused impression of military salutes and cheering crowds and a soft pinkish snowfall he finally discovered was rose petals.

It was even worse inside. The cathedral was a confusion of colour and incense smells. There were at least a hundred Priests of Light in startling golden robes and rank upon rank of the nobility, each vying with the others in the elaborate structures of their costumes. In the centre of the cathedral floor was an enormous fire that sparked and crackled, yet somehow failed to give out too much heat.

The waiting was terrible.

Every few seconds Henry kept asking Pyrgus, 'Is she here yet?' Every few seconds Pyrgus grinned and shook his head and told him, 'No.' Henry craned his head to watch the doors until his neck ached. She wasn't coming. She'd had second thoughts. She'd run off with someone who was better looking.

'How long does it take the Royal Barge –?' Henry began. Then he heard a commotion behind him and knew she must be there. He turned and she *was* there, standing alone without servants or retinue and so beautiful he nearly cried.

The whole proceedings went by in a daze. There was a thorny branch, symbolic of God-knew-what, and a spreading tree that actually appeared to be growing inside the cathedral, and they had to walk around the fire a lot. (He'd caught a glimpse of Nymph's face in the crowd while they were doing that. She was smiling broadly, but seemed to be weeping too.)

The ceremony was conducted by Archimandrake Podalirius, an almost overpowering bearded figure with a voice that rumbled up like thunder from his boots. 'Do you pledge yourself to Henry?' he asked Blue at last. 'Do you promise the great Lords of Light that you will hold to him and love him, here, now and in worlds beyond? Do you agree, before the Realm and those who gather here, to marry him?'

And Blue, quite clearly, said, 'I do.'

Epilogue

The Portal Temple was packed with revellers, but they fell silent at once when the great portal itself flared into life.

'Is everything ready at ... you know ... the other side?' asked Henry in a whisper. This wasn't quite the most exciting part of an exciting day, but it came close. His eyes were locked on the cold blue flames.

'Yes, sir,' grinned Chief Portal Engineer Peacock.

'He's talked about this far more than he ever talked about marrying me,' Blue said, smiling broadly.

'I can attest to that,' Pyrgus confirmed. He was colourfully dressed for the occasion and smelling of some particularly odious aftershave.

Henry licked his lips. 'What do you do now?' he asked the engineer. 'Throw a switch or something?'

'I thought you might like to do that, sir.' Peacock indicated a red button.

Henry reached out, then hesitated. 'You're sure he's there? At the other end? I mean, he hasn't wandered off or anything? He wanders off a lot.'

'We've modified the portal in accordance with the principles Gatekeeper Fogarty discovered,' Peacock said. 'There's a lock on. All you have to do is press the button.'

Henry fought the lump in his throat. If there was

anything that could have made this day more perfect, it would have been to have Mr Fogarty here. But this was next best thing in a funny way. Henry pressed the button.

The blue flames flickered as Hodge stepped through, his tail curled high. He stopped and looked around the assembled wedding guests. Then he sat down, placed one leg behind his ear and began to wash his parts.

Glossary

Key:

FOL: Faerie of the Light
FON: Faerie of the Night
HMN: Human

Analogue World. Names used in the Faerie Realm to denote the mundane world of school and spots and parents who look like they might end up getting divorced.

Angel. A messenger from God.

Antiopa, Nymphalis (Nymph). Daughter of Queen Cleopatra, Princess of the Forest Faerie.

Apatura Iris. (FOL) Father of Prince Pyrgus and Queen Blue. Was Purple Emperor for more than twenty years.

Arcond. The ruler of Hass-Verbim.

Atherton, Aisling. (HMN) Henry Atherton's younger sister and pain in the ass.

Atherton, Henry. (HMN) A young teenage boy living in England's Home Counties who first made contact with the Faerie Realm when he rescued the faerie prince, Pyrgus Malvae, from a cat.

Atherton, Martha. (HMN) Headmistress of a girl's school in the south of England. Former wife of Tim Atherton, mother of Henry and Aisling.

Atherton, Tim. (HMN) Successful business executive. Husband of Martha Atherton, father of Henry and Aisling.

Bartzabel. A demon guardian.

Beleth (a.k.a. the Infernal Prince; the Prince of Darkness). Prince of Hael, an alternative dimension of reality inhabited by demons.

Blue, Queen Holly. (FOL) Younger sister of Prince Pyrgus Malvae and daughter of the late Purple Emperor Apatura Iris.

Brenthis. Tribal historian of the Luchti.

Brimstone, Silas. (FON) Elderly demonologist and former glue factory owner.

Brotherhood, The. A magical Lodge of FONs which isn't nearly as powerful as it used to be.

Buthner. One of the countries that make up the Faerie Realm.

Callophrys Avis. (FON) A member of the Brotherhood.

Cardui, Madame Cynthia (a.k.a. the Painted Lady). (FOL) An elderly eccentric whose extensive contacts have made her one of Queen Blue's most valued agents.

Catsite. A toxic crystal that, taken in small doses, enables you to see in the dark.

Chalkhill, Jasper. (FON) Business partner of Silas Brimstone and, secretly, former head of Lord Hairstreak's intelligence service.

Charaxes. Luchti ancestors.

Charno. An intelligent and (somewhat) articulate pack animal that looks like a giant hare.

Cheapside. An area of the FOL capital.

Coffee. A bitter drink that leaves humans wired and gives faeries a psychedelic experience.

Comma, Prince. (FOL/FON) Half-brother of Prince Pyrgus and Queen Blue. (Same father, different mothers.)

Cripple's Gate. An entrance to the FOL capital.

Danaus. Chief Wizard Surgeon Healer of the Faerie Realm.

Demon. Form frequently taken by the shape-shifting alien species inhabiting the Hael Realm when in contact with faeries or humans.

Doppleganger. A freeze-dried replica that can replace a person in a location while the real person escapes. Much used by spies and adventurers.

Draugr. The vaettirs' mother.

D'Urville. (FON) A confused butler who looks after the headquarters of the secret Brotherhood.

En Ri. How the Luchti pronounce 'Henry'.

Euphrosyne. The discoverer of the Ark in Luchti mythology.

Faerie of the Light (Lighter). One of the two main faerie types, culturally averse to the use of demons in any circumstances and usually members of the Church of Light.

Faerie of the Night (Nighter). One of the two main faerie types, physically distinguished from Faeries of the Light by light-sensitive catlike eyes. Made use of demonic servants.

Faerie Realm. A parallel aspect of reality inhabited by various alien species, including Faeries of the Light and Faeries of the Night.

Faerie Standard. The *lingua franca* of the Faerie Realm.

Flyer, personal. A Realm aircraft roughly equivalent to a flying sports car.

Fogarty, Alan. (HMN) Paranoid ex-physicist and bank robber with an extraordinary talent for engineering gadgets. Fogarty was recently made Gatekeeper of House Iris in recognition of the help he gave to Prince Pyrgus, even though it was Fogarty's cat who nearly ate Prince Pyrgus in the first place.

Fogarty, Angela (a.k.a. Mrs Barenbohm). (HMN) Alan Fogarty's daughter.

Forest Faerie. The way you refer to a Feral Faerie if you don't want to give offence.

Gatekeeper. Ancient title used to describe the chief advisor of a Noble House.

Gravistat. Faerie preserving fluid that petrifies corpses.

Great Myphisto, The. Madame Cardui's late husband.

Guardian. Spell-driven security hologram.

Hael. Faerie name for Hell.

Hairstreak, Lord Black. (FON) Noble head of House Hairstreak and leader of the Faeries of the Night.

Halek knife (or blade). A rock crystal weapon which releases magical energies to kill anything it pierces. Halek knives are prone to shattering occasionally, in which event the energies will kill the person using them.

Haleklind. Homeland of the Halek wizards.

Haniel. Winged lion inhabiting forest areas of the Faerie Realm.

Hass-Verbim. One of the countries that make up the Faerie Realm. Hass-Verbim borders on Buthner.

Highgrove. An area of the FOL capital.

Hodge. Mr Fogarty's tomcat.

Horse-sniffles. A common (and not very serious) childhood illness in the Faerie Realm.

Imperial Island. The island where the Purple Palace is located.

Ino. Tribal shaman of the Luchti.

Iron Prominent. Henry's honorary title in the Faerie Realm.

Jalindra. (FOL) First victim of Temporal Fever.

Jamides. Abbot of the desert monastery in Buthner.

Jormungand. A serpent big enough to crush reality if it got a chance.

Kitterick. An Orange Trinian in the service of Madame Cardui.

Krantas. A vampire who terrorised the Realm several centuries ago.

Lamen. A magical breastplate, generally used only in ceremonies.

Lanceline. Madame Cardui's translucent cat.

Loki. One of the Old Gods of the Faerie Realm, a Trickster who also figures in Norse mythology for some reason.

Loman Bridge. The main bridge spanning the river that flows through the FOL capital.

Lorquin (Lorquinianus). A young member of Tribe Luchti and Henry's Companion.

Luchti. A desert tribe in Buthner.

Lucina, Hamearis, Duke of Burgundy. (FON) War hero and close ally of Lord Hairstreak.

Malvae, Crown Prince Pyrgus. (FOL) Brother of Queen Holly Blue. Pyrgus likes animals a lot more than politics and

at one time actually ran away from home to live as a coｍｍoner because of disagreements with his father.

Melor. A type of distilled cider much enjoyed by t Luchti people.

Midgard. A distant level of reality that embraces both th Faerie Realm and the Analogue World.

Mind-bender. A spell that influences the way you think.

Mount Pleasant. A district of the FOL capital.

Nant. An edible insect.

Nightwent. A desert bird.

Ouklo. Levitating, spell-driven carriage.

Peacock. Chief Portal Engineer of House Iris.

Portal. Interdimensional energy gateway, either naturally occurring, modified or engineered.

Prince of Darkness. Title often used to describe Beleth.

Psychotronics. An obscure branch of Earth Realm science which studies the interaction of the human mind with physical reality. The practical application of psychotronics seems indistinguishable from some forms of Faerie Realm magic.

Purlisa. An honorific term used in monastic communities to denote a person of high spiritual evolution. Equivalent to an Analogue World saint, but nicer.

Purple Emperor. Ruler of the Faerie Empire.

Severs, Charlotte (Charlie). (HMN) Henry Atherton's closest friend in the Earth Realm.

Simbala. An addictive form of liquid music sold legally in licensed outlets and illegally elsewhere.

Slith. Dangerous grey reptile inhabiting forest areas of the Faerie Realm. Sliths secrete a highly toxic acid, which they can spit across considerable distances.

Spell cone. Pocket-sized cones, no more than an inch or so in height, imbued with magical energies directed towards a specific result. The old-style cone had to be lit. The more modern version is self-igniting and is "cracked" with a fingernail. Both types discharge like fireworks.

Stasis spell. A spell that freezes something into immobility, preserving it intact for as long as the spell lasts.

Stimlus. A personal energy weapon.

Temporal fever (a.k.a. TF). A mysterious illness plaguing the Faerie Realm.

Tort-feasor. One who feases torts.

Transporter. Mr Fogarty's hand-held version of a portal, based on the thing they use in *Star Trek*.

Trinian. Non-human, non-faerie dwarven race living in the Faerie Realm. Orange Trinians are a breed that dedicates itself to service, Violet Trinians tend to be warriors, while Green Trinians specialise in biological nanotechnology and consequently can create living machines.

Tulpa. An intelligent, automatous thought-form.

Vaettir. Faerie name for the skinny, fanged, lethal tomb-dwelling thing Professor Tolkien called a barrow-wight.

Ward, Anaïs. (HMN) Henry's mother's lover.

Weiskei. The Brotherhood sentinel.

Whitewell. A district of the FOL capital.

Wildmoor Broads. A flat area of thorny shrubland north of the faerie capital much favoured by the wealthy of the Realm for their estates, since the difficulties of travelling through the area go a long way towards ensuring their privacy. The only really viable means of transport is by levitating carriage. Ground transport is attacked by prickleweed, a semi-sentient plant that will typically swarm over any vehicle and bring it to a halt in minutes. Crossing the area on foot is impossible – the prickleweed paralyses pedestrians, then rips them apart for their nutrients.

Yammeth Cretch. Heartland of the Faeries of the Night.

Yidam. One of the Old Gods who walked the Realm before the coming of the Light.